Praise for Eric Jerome Dickey

Naughty or Nice

"Hot enough to scorch fingers. Dickey is a master at writing about women and what they want and how they want it. There are three kinds of physical love in these pages: hot, red hot, and nuclear."
—*Publishers Weekly*

"A very funny and engrossing novel . . . laugh-out-loud humor."
—*Booklist*

The Other Woman

"Dickey taps the intimate emotions of a woman."
—*Entertainment Weekly*

"A fast-paced tale."
—*Essence*

"[A] sharp-edged, sizzling novel."
—*Publishers Weekly*

"The prediction here is that *The Other Woman* will show up on beaches all over the country this summer."
—*Fort Worth Star-Telegram*

"Good and gritty storytelling."
—*Kirkus Reviews*

Thieves' Paradise
NAACP Image Award Nominee

"Smartly paced . . . heart-pumping . . . electrifying . . . compelling."
—*Publishers Weekly*

"Passionate, sensual, rhythmic. If Eric's previous novels are food for the soul, *Thieves' Paradise* is the nectar and ambrosia of life."
—*The Chicago Defender*

continued . . .

Friends and Lovers

"Crackles with wit and all the rhythm of an intoxicatingly funky rap. A fun read."   —*The Cincinnati Enquirer*

"Fluid as a rap song. Dickey can stand alone among modern novelists in capturing the flavor, rhythm, and pace of African-American speak."   —*South Florida Sun-Sentinel*

"Dickey uses humor, poignancy, and a fresh, creative writing style."
—*USA Today*

"A colorful, sexy tale."   —*Marie Claire*

Milk in My Coffee

"Rich *Coffee* steams away clichés of interracial romance . . . a true-to-life, complex story of relationships."   —*USA Today*

"Heartwarming and hilarious."   —*The Cincinnati Enquirer*

"Dickey scores with characters who come to feel like old friends."
—*Essence*

Sister, Sister

"Genuine emotional depth."   —*The Boston Globe*

"Vibrant . . . marks the debut of a true talent."
—*The Atlanta Journal-Constitution*

"Bold and sassy . . . brims with humor, outrageousness, and the generosity of affection."   —*Publishers Weekly*

ALSO BY ERIC JEROME DICKEY

Genevieve
Naughty or Nice
The Other Woman
Thieves' Paradise
Between Lovers
Liar's Game
Cheaters
Milk in My Coffee
Friends and Lovers
Sister, Sister

ANTHOLOGIES

Got to Be Real
Mothers and Sons
River Crossings: Voices of the Diaspora
Griots Beneath the Baobab
Black Silk: A Collection of African American Erotica
Gumbo: A Celebration of African American Writing

Cappuccino (Movie)—*Original Story*

ERIC JEROME DICKEY

Drive Me Crazy

 New American Library

New American Library
Published by New American Library, a division of
Penguin Group (USA) Inc., 375 Hudson Street,
New York, New York 10014, USA
Penguin Group (Canada), 90 Eglinton Avenue East, Suite 700, Toronto,
Ontario M4P 2Y3, Canada (a division of Pearson Penguin Canada Inc.)
Penguin Books Ltd., 80 Strand, London WC2R 0RL, England
Penguin Ireland, 25 St. Stephen's Green, Dublin 2,
Ireland (a division of Penguin Books Ltd.)
Penguin Group (Australia), 250 Camberwell Road, Camberwell, Victoria 3124,
Australia (a division of Pearson Australia Group Pty. Ltd.)
Penguin Books India Pvt. Ltd., 11 Community Centre, Panchsheel Park,
New Delhi - 110 017, India
Penguin Group (NZ), cnr Airborne and Rosedale Roads, Albany,
Auckland 1310, New Zealand (a division of Pearson New Zealand Ltd.)
Penguin Books (South Africa) (Pty.) Ltd., 24 Sturdee Avenue,
Rosebank, Johannesburg 2196, South Africa

Penguin Books Ltd., Registered Offices:
80 Strand, London WC2R 0RL, England

Published by New American Library, a division of Penguin Group (USA) Inc.
Previously published in a Dutton edition.

First New American Library Printing, May 2005
9   10   8

Copyright © Eric Jerome Dickey, 2004
Excerpt from *Genevieve* copyright © Eric Jerome Dickey, 2005
All rights reserved

New American Library Trade Paperback ISBN: 0-451-21519-2

The Library of Congress has catalogued the hardcover edition of this title as follows:

Dickey, Eric Jerome.
Drive me crazy / by Eric Jerome Dickey.
p.   cm.
ISBN 0-525-94790-6
1. Triangles (Interpersonal relations)—Fiction.   2. Married women—Fiction.
3. Ex-convicts—Fiction.   4. Secrecy—Fiction.   I. Title.
PS3554.I319D75   2004
813'.54—dc22
2004009926

Set in Sabon
Designed by Lenny Telesca

Printed in the United States of America

For Dominique

PROVERBS 5:3–5

³For the lips of an immoral woman drip honey, and her mouth is smoother than oil:

⁴But in the end she is bitter as wormwood, sharp as a two-edged sword.

⁵Her feet go down to death; her steps lay hold of hell.

1

People called me Driver. It was my sobriquet, not my birth name.

Driver.

I'd been working for the same limousine service since I made it back on this side of The Wall. Not since the day I got out, I'd hustled here and there, but it was my first real job. After two years of living on lockdown, I found that as hard as it was living in a cage it was even rougher when you finally had freedom's sunshine on your face. I'd paid my debt, but a man with a record, no matter how legit he tries to be, will still get a hard time from the assholes holding the jobs.

Part of it was my look. I'd inherited a John Henry, railroad-worker build like my maternal granddaddy. When you were six-two and dark as an open road, you grew up knowing that America wasn't as kumbaya as it claimed to be. In some countries a man who looked like me would be a king. Where I lived I just passed for a suspect. I learned how to soften that look. I shaved my head bald and wore glasses when I could. Glasses intellectualized my appearance. Actually I needed them for reading. My world was getting blurry. When a man turns forty his body starts to change. But, to be honest, I couldn't hide what I owned. A few times I'd walked into a room and men pulled their women closer. Maybe because when some women saw me, there was a subtle shift, like somebody had struck a match down below.

Women hadn't been shit but trouble in my world.

My relationship with women was the same as my love-hate relationship with L.A. The city was expensive and pretty, decorated in palm trees and beaches, and even with smog, earthquakes, road rage, and endless traffic, a woman that beautiful was hard to leave. She heated you up in the middle of the day and with a gentle breeze she cooled you off at night.

Married women. That was another lesson I'd learned.

I say that because of the scam. Well, it was more than a simple scam. Scams involved confidence men who convinced you to *give* them their money. It took days, maybe even weeks before you realized you'd been had. And it was all done with a handshake and a smile.

What we planned was a bona fide crime.

Whether for selfish or personal reasons, we needed money, the root of all evil. I lived in Los Angeles County. The median cost of a single-family home was damn near four hundred thousand. Car registration had tripled. Gas prices were out of control. My one-bedroom apartment was in Inglewood, a city that had no rent control, and rent had shot up thirty percent, and now my rent was a little over twelve hundred a month. No matter how much I hustled, no matter how much money I made, it wasn't enough. Maybe I just wanted to make some spending money to make it through another lean year in the Bush-whacked new millennium. I could say that with Schwarzenegger as the new "governator" after California's total recall, I wanted to save up for the unknown. I could say a lot of shit. But I knew it wasn't about the state budget or an energy crisis or an economy struggling to recover.

I just wanted to impress *her*.

There was always a "her" involved.

I'm going too fast.

Let me backtrack.

* * *

I was chilling at a dilapidated pool hall in South Central, a place called Back Biters and Syndicators, named after a John Lee Hooker song. The regulars just called the joint Back Biters, an old slang term for somebody who couldn't be trusted, and it didn't matter if the hand was black or white. It was a hangout with unfinished walls, decent pool tables, and hard liquor. No snooker or baccarat, no high-end shit like that. A joint where candidates for three strikes made or lost their rent gambling on eight or nine ball, maybe shooting craps in the back.

That evening I was sitting at the bar sipping a beer with my boss, Jason Wolf, Jr. We called him by his last name, Wolf. Six-footer with a Nordic blond mane. Two years younger than me. Hair was thinning up top. Kept what was left pulled back into a smooth ponytail. Wolf was a gray-eyed silver-spoon baby who had dropped out of NYU almost as soon as he walked into the institution of higher learning. Said NYU bored him. He used to drive back in New York, but after his dad died and left him a nice piece of change, he relocated West about ten years ago and started his own thing with his windfall.

He was the only man to give me a chance on this side of The Wall.

We'd shot some eight ball, then called it quits and posted up at the small bar, beers on the counter, chilling the night away. I was reading parts of the *L.A. Times*, looking for new words to add to my vocabulary. I loved learning ten-dollar words like *abstemious* and *solipsism*, then throwing them in a conversation and watching the stupid light come on in somebody's eyes.

Wolf was stroking his goatee with two fingers while he struggled with the crossword puzzle. Both of us had on dark suits. Mine was Italian. Wolf's was more conservative, along the Brooks Brothers style. The poor always tried to look rich and the rich tried to look normal.

"Eighty-one across . . . five letters." Wolf grunted. He sounded like an old man who'd smoked since he was evicted from his momma's womb. "Driver, what the hell is baklava glue?"

"What's in it for me?"

"C'mon man. Help a brother out."

Pedro was passing by, heard Wolf call himself a brother and laughed. Pedro was the bartender, a short, clean-cut, thick Hispanic man. Looked like Enrique Iglesias with bad metabolism and a smooth salt-and-pepper goatee. Second generation in this country. He was in his forties and had married his high school sweetheart the day he got out of the army.

I said, "You hear that, Pedro?"

Pedro shrugged. "Marrying a black woman has made him black by osmosis."

We all laughed at that.

Pedro was a former aerospace worker who got downsized from his cozy sixty-thousand-dollar-a-year gig as a project engineer at Northrop almost ten years ago. He spent two years looking for a job and trying to feed his family off his 401(k) and unemployment. He retrained, then finally got on at Boeing at a serious pay cut. He was about to get downsized at Boeing, a nasty little déjà vu, but got fired before they could kick him out. Something went down. He went postal and beat the shit out of his manager and tried to choke him into an early grave. Down here, people admired Pedro for what he did. A lot of disgruntled motherfuckers wanted to do the same to both the man and the system. That was four years back, with eight months of that spent on lockdown, twice as long in anger management.

Wolf ranked on Pedro. "You're as Mexican as Taco Bell and you're breaking my balls?"

Pedro shook his head. "Here we go again. Dean Martin walks in with Sammy Davis, Jr., and the corny jokes come out."

I told Wolf, "I think he just called you Sammy Davis, Jr."

More laughter while blues man Robert B. Jones sang about a kindhearted woman.

"Driver, what's up with your people?" Wolf turned to me. "Mexicans have all the jobs that the black people used to have."

Pedro retorted, "Don't hate."

Wolf went on, "Walk on a construction site, into the kitchen at a soul food restaurant, or check out the hotel workers, hardly a black person in sight."

I shot Wolf the middle finger of love.

Pedro retorted, "It's our damn country, asshole. And for your information the original name of this land given by the *original* people was *El Pueblo de la Reina de los Angeles* but we had to shorten it because the *gringos* came over on the short yellow bus."

"Are you insulting me, Pedro? Is that a racial slur I hear?"

"Damn right. Your Brad Pitt–looking ass don't like it, hop in your Ferrari and go back to whatever part of Europe your pagan people migrated from."

"I'm Catholic. And I drive a Lamborghini."

Pedro huffed. "The cheap one."

"Cheap? You drive a Hyundai."

"The expensive one."

Outrageous laughter came from all three of us.

I said, "The original residents called this part of the country *Wenot*, Pedro. Downtown was *Yang-ya*. Next time you put a motherfucker in his place, have your facts straight."

Pedro said, "You're an asshole, Driver."

Wolf added, "A damn Encyclopedia Brown."

"You know? Walking around with his head filled with useless information."

I flipped both of them off.

We all laughed, and that felt better than chicken soup. I'd had a rough day. I'd driven a rapper to do an interview at a hip-hop radio station on Wilshire, not far from the La Brea Tar Pits. A gangsta rapper who ain't never been in a gang. He was buffed and hardcore, but rumors had been circulating about his sexual preferences. The DJ straight out asked him if he was gay. That was during morning drive time, so millions of people were listening. The rapper went off and tore up the studio. Microphones were broken, there was a big fight. Station management tried to play it down. So after a day like that, I needed some spirits and laughter.

I had to drink, had to laugh, had to get this tension off my back. A big debt hanging over my head, my own cloud and angst that let me know the devil would come to get his due.

Pedro asked Wolf, "How is the wife?"

"New one or old one?"

"New one."

"Did I tell you she flew up to Vegas with me, wanted to go to a trade show, Taser International booth. Bought a stun gun. Fifty thousand volts. Those suckers have been big since Nine-Eleven. And she got in line, let them zap her. Fifty thousand volts. She took it like she was a damn android. Got up and spent four hundred on a stun gun. Would you believe she did that?"

I shifted, hid my discomfort, and nodded. "I believe it."

"Said she wanted it for protection. She has guns all over the house. You don't buy a stun gun like that for protection. You buy that for torture."

Silence covered us all.

Wolf asked our friend, "How's the family, Pedro?"

"Just hope the grocery stores end this strike. My wife has been picketing for three months already. My daughter is in college. We have two car notes. It's killing us right now."

Pedro licked his lips, swallowed his frustration, then moved on to another customer.

Wolf asked me about baklava glue again. He was getting frustrated, I could tell. Underneath that cool demeanor he had some temper, some aggravation. The kind that trying to please the wrong woman gave a man. He had no idea who his wife really was.

I patted Wolf's shoulder, told him, "Five letters. Try h-o-n-e-y."

He thanked me.

It seemed like yesterday, but almost six months had passed since I had crept into his office, dressed in a black Italian suit, murder and another man's fortune on my mind. Almost six months to the day. I know because my mother had died late that same evening. Got the message from my brother when I was on the way to kill Wolf.

I didn't kill Wolf. Didn't have to. Wolf was already gone.

The way he spoke, I could see Wolf was the living dead. The alcohol on his breath and the dullness in his eyes told me that somebody had killed him from the inside out, had left him living in a prison of his own. One that nobody could see but him.

Women had the power to do that.

His wife, Lisa, had been a bitch in five-hundred-dollar boots. She was his second wife, both African-American. Both beautiful as sin. But Lisa. Her image lived with me. Caramel skin. Bambi-like eyes. Shoulder-length auburn hair. Happy-go-lucky smile. She had upgraded her boobs from A to C, all paid for by Wolf. Her teeth had been veneered. She had a perfect smile. A simple glance at Lisa felt like a transgression, so I didn't stare at her anymore. Even the scent of her perfume reminded me of when I was fucking her inside his home.

Wasn't for Wolf I'd either be a poster child for recidivism—back in the joint getting three hots and a cot—or sleeping on a cardboard box with America's discarded vets.

Didn't want to think about that shit right now.

He gave me a job. That was all I really wanted. Just needed to get back on my feet.

Pedro whistled, then said, "Look at that dime walking in."

My attention followed his eyes to the front door. So did Wolf's.

This dime piece was standing underneath a giant Stroh's beer sign that was hanging in the doorway. The room was dimly lit, but there was enough light to see what she had to offer. Light brown skin. Long straight hair. Nice curves. Modest frame. She moved like she had an edge about her, like she was looking for trouble. Everybody noticed her. She had more style than the secondhand-suit and FUBU crowd that populated the bar.

I asked Wolf, "Who she?"

Pedro answered, "She breezed through here a couple days ago."

Wolf went back to his crossword puzzle, more interested in his own personal mystery.

I said, "She's ripe."

Pedro nodded. "Put her hair in two ponytails and R. Kelly will be all over her."

Pedro moved on, went to sell spirits and salvation to the masses by the glass.

She moved in our direction. Some women got closer and dropped from dimes to nines to eights, kept falling like the stock market. She never lost a point. She had on a long, black leather skirt, the kind that had a split and showed off her legs. Her heels were the kind that made her legs look good and her feet feel bad. Her straight hair had deep brown highlights.

Wolf grunted. "Driver, rat's last meal. Starts with A . . . ends in NIC . . . seven letters."

My eyes were anchored to the new girl, watching her move her baklava glue around the room. She saw me admiring her. I nodded. She held onto her business face, made a motion that asked me if I wanted to challenge her on the table. I shook my head, motioned at an empty seat next to me. She shook her head, moved on, found a sister who had money to burn.

"Rat's last meal . . . starts with A . . . ends with NIC," I mumbled. "Arsenic."

Wolf scribbled in the answer, smiled like a kid who was done with his homework, and checked his watch. "I smell like two beers and fried fish from Geraldine's. Lisa's gonna pitch a bitch. Talk to you tomorrow, Driver."

"No you won't. I'm off tomorrow. Don't even think about ringing my phone."

"You ungrateful fuck. What you got planned?"

I told him that TNT was running a lot of movies I liked tomorrow, old noir movies like *Act of Violence. Last Train from Gun Hill. The Set-Up. The Big Heat. The Killers.*

Wolf said, "*The Killers.* I liked the first one with Ava Gardner. It was cold-blooded how those men marched up those stairs and killed that man without a thought."

"Yeah, they did. Without a thought. They sure did." I cleared both my mind and my throat, mumbled out my thoughts. "Lancaster and Gardner."

"He loved her. And she played him. All for the money."

I nodded.

Wolf went catatonic, like his inner voice was talking to him, telling him things, or maybe the alcohol was catching up to him. Either way, Wolf blinked out of his stupor, ran his hand over his goatee, and nodded like he understood something. His barstool screeched the floor when he stood up. Wolf took a final sip of his beer, whistled, and put his suit coat back on.

He asked, "You staying?"

A wave of tiredness rolled over me. That was my cue. I told him to hold up while I finished my beer. My sinful night was about to end, my peaceful tomorrow already planned.

He asked, "Heading to Strokers to watch Panther strip and dance the pole dance?"

Panther. A woman who had a Southern accent and schoolgirl smile like my ex-wife's.

I paused, smiled. "Nah. I've given Panther enough of my paycheck. Gonna call it a night. Maybe make a few phone calls on the way home. Stir up a midnight snack of my own."

Baklava Glue moved her hair from her exotic face, glanced my way again. A fresh dime in a room filled with old nickels, a few the size of a quarter, none that could be runner-up to Miss Barstow. A woman like that could walk into a church on Easter Sunday and ten minutes later somebody would have been shot, stabbed, or drowned in sacrifice as a show of affections.

I touched Wolf's shoulder, told him, "I'm gonna try my luck with Miss Baklava Glue."

Wolf held up and watched her for a second.

In the end he said, "She's a cure for what Viagra is trying to fix."

I winked at my employer, my friend, teased him, "Unless you want to holla at her."

"High-maintenance women like that are why I'm in the condition I'm in today. Alimony and child support on an ex-wife who decided she didn't want to be married anymore, then moved to Las Vegas just to make my visitation hell, and a now a new wife who won't stop shopping."

I asked, "That bad?"

"The wife went out for coffee at Starbucks and came back in a brand-new red Hummer."

"I saw it in the parking lot at work. Ugly-ass SUV looks like an armored car."

"And costs just as much. She's killing me. Last thing I need is to meet another pretty woman who would take advantage of my cheating heart and gum up the works."

I threw my hands up. "Told you to keep away from the high-end women."

"Not my fault. They come after me."

"Because you're rich."

Wolf set me straight, said, "Because I'm hung like a horse and they all want to ride."

Pedro laughed. He was pouring somebody a shot of scotch, listening to Wolf ramble.

Wolf flipped Pedro off and went on, "Can't help it if they love me, Driver. Just can't help it. Maybe next time I'll stick to my own kind and meet a nice Irish girl."

Pedro told him, "You're not Irish."

"I'll dye my hair red and eat Lucky Charms."

We laughed, and when the laughter died, Wolf called it a night, headed across the room. His gait should've been confident and mon-eyed, like he owned the world, but he moved like a crab, like he was cringing all the time. If you stuck a cigarette in the corner of his mouth and put a trench coat on his back, he'd look like James Dean strolling down the Boulevard of Broken Dreams.

As soon as Wolf left, Pedro gave me a knowing look, shook his head, his smile gone.

He told me, "She just called up here looking for you. She's bold. Like she don't care."

Pedro didn't say my trouble's name. We knew my sins and indiscretions.

He asked, "How does she know when you're here? I tell her you're not here and she tells me I'm lying. It's like she knows when you walk in the door. I'd be careful."

"Fifty thousand volts."

"Know what I'm saying? She's loco like a mofo."

I shrugged and pushed my chest out, waved it off like it was nothing I couldn't handle.

Pedro looked in the direction Wolf had just gone, then shook his head and walked away.

2

I took off my jacket and watched Miss Baklava Glue do her thing. She had grabbed a stick, found a hustler who wanted to test her skills, and played a few games. Twenty a game was the going rate. I was tempted to do the same. But I didn't. Just sat back and watched her. This wasn't a room filled with pros or people who had deep pockets, not like Sin City—Las Vegas. Mostly amateurs with an attitude, the kind of men and women who'd lose fifty bucks and consider it a major financial setback.

She was sexy. Different from anything I had touched before. Couldn't move my eyes away. She was aware of me. Seemed like she was watching me as much as I was watching her.

Miss Baklava Glue had a great body and a decent game. Decent bank shot. But couldn't get the cue to obey her, leaving her next shot in trouble. She made a shot, looked my way, maybe showing off. Each time I nodded her way. She got her respect by beating a few people, had a decent run for a while, but just like Gray Davis there was a sudden reversal of fortune. When it was all said and done, the hustlers had out-hustled her and she'd lost her Chicago roll. I guessed that at least two C-notes had slipped away from her.

She came toward the bar, shaking her head, looking a little angry. She didn't like losing.

We made eye contact again. Brief eye contact.

I followed her, watched those legs move in that long black leather skirt, the split showing uncharted flesh up to her thigh. Her high heels made her feet look delicate and ethereal. I loved the way heels begat shapely legs on a woman, how they elongated feminine legs. Nothing like watching a woman's sashay. It was like a fingerprint, each woman had her own way of moving. Loved to witness the calf muscles contract to slim and firm the back part of the lower leg.

She ran her hand over her hair, leaned against the counter.

I got her eye, asked, "Whassup?"

"Nothing."

"Buy you a drink?"

"I can buy my own."

I unclenched my jaw, stood firm and refused to give in that quick, squared my stance, took a breath, slow and deep. "What's a girl like you doing in a place like this?"

"Okay, you need to come stronger than that."

"Was just saying. You're silk and lace in a blue-jean world."

She licked her lips. "I can handle myself."

"Heard you've been through here before. Earlier this week."

"People do talk."

"You don't look like the type of woman who'd be hanging out on Figueroa."

She nodded. "Guess I have a fascination with danger."

"What's your name?"

"Arizona."

"Like the state?"

She gave me two thumbs up. "Somebody is good at geography."

I told her that people called me Driver.

Outclassed, I raised my palms and got ready to move on with my life. Women were like Newton's third law in reverse. When faced with a powerful force from without, like a man coming on too fast and strong, they gave the same amount of opposing force, got turned off.

She asked, "Giving up so soon?"

She posted up on a wooden barstool. I moved down a barstool, sat next to her.

I told her, "Just getting started."

She winked. "I'll let you buy me a drink."

Her voice sounded older than she looked, either from hard times or a street life, but she didn't look like she was from either world. Clear fingernails, simple diamond earrings, expensive watch. She had a mild accent, the kind that let me know she spoke another language.

Pedro came over, put down two napkins. "What can I do for Beauty and the Beast?"

I looked at her. "I think he just called you ugly."

First she laughed. Then Pedro laughed. I joined in the next chorus.

She ordered a Seven and Seven. I'd only had one beer. I asked for my friend, Jack Daniel's, on the rocks. Then she changed her order, said she'd have what I was having.

Pedro dropped our drinks, then he left so I could try my luck with this dime.

I asked, "Where'd you learn to shoot?"

She ran her palm over her hair again, did that over and over like it was some sort of a nervous tic. I smelled the sweetness of her perfume and the freshness of her shampoo.

She answered, "Wherever I could. Used to hang out at this pool hall in Sherman Oaks a couple of years ago. Before that I got my game on out in Riverside and San Berna-zero."

San Berna-zero was a nickname for San Bernardino. That was east, about an hour in no traffic. Add three hours to that drive if it's on a Friday. Add another two weeks if it's raining.

I asked, "You grow up out in the Inland Empire?"

"Maybe. Maybe not."

"You a stripper?"

"Am I a stripper?" She laughed hard. "Is that a compliment or an insult?"

"You're pretty and have the body for it. How you take that is up to you."

She shook her head and sat straight back, legs crossed at the knees, did that like the gate to her paradise was impassable.

Arizona asked, "What's a guy in an Italian suit and nice shoes doing in FUBU World?"

"Come stronger than that."

She laughed. Her nose was small, her lips full, eyebrows arched.

I said, "We all go where we feel comfortable."

"Guess Bible study was filled to the brim."

"I'm agnostic."

"Between Bible pushers and the atheists live the agnostics. So you're on the fence."

I nodded. "An independent. You?"

"Buddhist, non-practicing."

Her expression remained unreadable. She had small eyes, straight teeth, and a heart-shaped face. Her breasts looked like they hadn't been offended by time and gravity, not yet. When you were getting old, all young women start to look good. Youth was an aphrodisiac. Old women reminded you that you were old. Nobody wanted a mirror, especially in L.A.

She asked, "How old are you?"

I paused, trying to decide if I was going to lie, but didn't. "Forty. You?"

"Twenty-three."

She gave me a sideways smile, one that told me she didn't give a fuck about the chronological difference either. My answer was a smile that mirrored hers.

She said, "You could've at least said I looked like an aerobics instructor."

I shook my head. "Telling a woman she looks like an aerobics instructor is played out."

"Your whole conversation is played out."

"No, it's retro, baby. Straight throwback."

Her laugh ended with a nice smile, the kind that created crow's feet in the corners of her eyes. "Throwback. Okay, I can roll with the old school."

My sleeves were rolled up and my cuff links were off, exposing my arms up to my elbows. She motioned at my tats, asked, "What you do time for?"

I closed down for a moment. Those memories had a way of stopping me, making me think. I told her the same thing I told everybody else, that I did time for not telling. For keeping my motherfucking mouth shut. Didn't tell the truth then, didn't see any reason I should now.

Her smile broadened. Women loved bad boys. We were the men they dated and never married. The men they ran back to when they found the real world too pedestrian.

I asked, "You did some time at the free motel?"

She grinned and winked, set free a one-sided smile. She wasn't telling either.

Men loved bad girls too. For the same reasons.

We sat and sipped. She didn't cringe or frown when she sipped her Jack. She picked up the newspaper that Pedro had discarded on the counter, read over an article.

She asked, "What do you do?"

"Male exotic dancer."

She laughed again. "Man, what is up with you and this obsession with strippers?"

I told her, "I'm a driver."

"So, do you drive getaway cars, the space shuttle, go-carts, what?"

"You got jokes. I drive for Wolf Classic Limousine."

She nodded. "I bet you hear things, bet you see things."

"What kinda things?"

"Things people don't want the world to know about."

I stared at my drink, admired that warm liquid that soothed me. Started drinking after my divorce. The hue of my drink was the same as my ex-wife's complexion, golden-amber.

She pressed on, asked, "What have you seen?"

The way she was pressing me about my job should've sent up a red flag. But a man sat next to woman like her and wanted to do all he could to get her not to leave.

I shrugged. "White-collar customers get in asking me if I knew where they could score crack. Or West Hollywood bathhouses. Last month people in town for a religious convention wanted to hit the strip clubs, then came right out and asked if I knew any hookers."

Without looking impressed or disgusted, she sipped, said, "So you hook 'em up."

"Depends. I do what I can to stimulate financial growth in our depressed economy."

"So, if the pay is right you'll do a lil' somethin'-somethin' on the low-low."

Sounded like she'd moved from flirting to interviewing me. I didn't like that.

I said, "Somebody sounds a little drunk."

She shook her head, wiped her long hair back and made a face. "Not even."

"Damn. I'm wasting my money."

"Look at this." She'd turned the page on the newspaper. "Rent scam bilks fifteen families, nets nearly fifty thousand over one weekend."

Pedro was passing by. He didn't disturb us, just moved on.

I said, "Fifty thousand in a weekend? Amazing."

She smiled, gave me direct eye contact, then went back to the article.

Arizona said, "Maybe we could do some business together."

"What kind of business?"

"You hear people, Driver. Their conversations, things they don't want anybody to know about. That information you're sitting on, the right person gets it, it's worth a mint."

The years I'd lost did a number on my stomach. I faced her, took our words eye-to-eye.

I asked, "What you running?"

"Who said I was running something?"

"Don't bullshit me. Squares don't come up in a joint like this."

She smiled. "Are you a police officer?"

"Hell no."

She swayed with the bluesy music, like the alcohol was making her ramble out things she should keep to herself. "Let's just say I'm investing in a few real estate opportunities."

I stared at my drink, at that golden liquid that did some of us in. "Short or long?"

She knew what I meant. "Long con, but I'm working a short to generate cash flow."

My eyes stayed on my drink. On its color. Drifted to an old memory. Tommy Castro was singing his electric blues. Served me right to suffer. Served me right to be alone. A man like me was born to suffer. But I didn't like being alone. Couldn't stand the silence. I sipped. Tonight alcohol made me remember what being with a woman might help me forget.

She said, "Looks like you're a long way from here."

I blinked those memories away. "Look, I'm not trying to revisit the Gray Goose."

That was prison speak. A language she understood. The Gray Goose was the *wonderful* bus that drove you to the free motel, chaperoned by sheriffs with shotguns, handcuffs on your wrists, chains on your ankles and between your legs, while the man next to you either cried for his momma, or puked his brains out from the fear of getting his sphincter supersized.

"Relax." Her words remained gentle. "Just having a conversation, being hypothetical."

"Don't bullshit a bullshitter. Are *you* a police officer?"

"No."

"Working for law enforcement?"

"No. Relax. No one's trying to trap you. Guy I used to . . . date . . . learned a lot watching him scam. He used to pull thirty large just like . . ." She snapped her fingers. "He was good."

The word *was* echoed. I asked, "Where is he now?"

Her grin remained strong, but sadness erupted in her eyes. The absence of crow's feet and presence of grief told me all I needed to know. He was either in jail or dead. Or had died in jail. If he was living and had left her for another woman she would've said that with bitterness in her tone, no smile on her face. Women always dogged a man out when they were dumped.

She never answered about her friend. I didn't expect her to.

She said, "It's all about reading people. Finding out what they need."

"What do I need?"

"I don't know what you need. But I know what you want."

I should've walked away from her then. If I was a smart man, maybe a smarter man, that would've been my cue to exit stage left, get in my car, and drive home.

But I had a buzz, looked at her soft skin, skin that I had never touched or tasted, and found myself anchored by my own desires. Found myself being a man in need of a new sin.

We ended that conversation when Pedro came back to check on us. He cut me a sly stare like I was a man named Humbert trying to seduce a nymphet named Lolita.

Arizona bought the next round, ordered in perfect Spanish; her accent had turned as authentic as Pedro's. That made me look at her a different way, try to dissect her features, see if she had some Jennifer Lopez in her bloodline. I couldn't tell. America was so amalgamated, the racial lines so blurred that anybody who looked any way could be anything.

Pedro smiled and talked to her while he made our poison, kept talking in Spanish, while he glanced at her cleavage. Then he was gone.

I asked Arizona, "You're part Mexican?"

"Filipina and black. Not necessarily in that order."

"Filipinas speak Tagalog, not Spanish."

"I speak five languages. English. Spanish. Tagalog. French. Ebonics."

She was curvy but small. The Jack she'd sipped had her light-headed. It showed in her tone, in how her eyes went in and out of focus. I asked her how far she had to travel to get back home. She said she was crashing somewhere on the other side of Hollywood.

I said, "Would hate for you to get a DUI."

"I can handle my liquor."

I told her she was more than welcome to crash at my apartment. It was a lot closer.

She looked at me, knowing.

A man bought a woman a drink in a bar as an investment of things yet to come. A woman bought a man a drink to cancel those things, to keep it on the fair exchange level.

I didn't know where we stood.

She said, "Can't you recruit you a bed-warmer up in here?"

"These scallywags are all after the ballers. Black woman don't think about you until you walk into a place looking like you're rich or have a white woman. And you better not have both."

She laughed at that. She didn't agree, but she laughed.

She said, "I was supposed to go hook up with someone when I left here."

That was the game. Truth begets truth. I lowered my wall, she lowered hers. I admitted I wasn't a virgin, then she admitted she wasn't Little Red Riding Hood on her way to Granny's house. She was on her way to a scheduled booty call.

"Your body . . . your arms." She reacted like most women, stared at my arms the way men stared at loaded guns. "Like . . . muscles etched in . . . in . . . in chocolate."

"You ain't seen my muscles."

"Maybe you should show me."

"You like chocolate?"

"Love chocolate." She licked her lips like she was addicted to the taste. "Love chocolate. Love mature men. Love mature men in nice suits and nice shoes."

Our stares became tropical.

She touched my leg. "Cuff links, silk tie, shoes, suit, that tells a lot about a man. Tells me who he is or who he wants to be."

I touched her skirt, rubbed the leather over her inner thigh with two fingers. "Same goes for a woman."

We abandoned our drinks and she followed me out the front door into the bright lights and traffic in this part of the big city. Music followed her sugary walk, John Lee Hooker was back to singing, telling me that his woman left him early one morning and the blues had healed him, sang that the same blues could heal me too. Carlos Santana was cosinging with his guitar.

Outside, a brother was hustling incense and oils with names like Black Sex, Bootylicious, even had Pussy; the Afrocentric sister next to him had every knockoff perfume ever made.

Arizona said, "It's cold as hell."

"Yeah. Unseasonably cold. Weatherman said it's gonna be that way a few days."

"Been gloomy all week. Freezing out here."

Cold as hell in Southern California meant you might have to put on a T-shirt and socks with your shorts and sandals. Tonight, by L.A. standards, it was fur coat weather.

Back Biters was situated in a rundown strip mall, between Geraldine's Fish and Grits and Luther's All Nite Washerette. Outside the pool hall stood a wall of chain smokers living in nicotine clouds. A few feet away there was a line of people getting fried catfish, trout, snapper, salmon; that high-cholesterol aroma fattening the air. The Washerette was packed with apartment dwellers, reminding me I had a couple of loads to do tomorrow. At least four women were inside Platinum Beauty getting their weaves and perms hooked up at midnight. One was sleeping underneath a dryer. Music bumped from every passing car.

Arizona was moving her honey at a mellow pace, taking deep breaths like she was trying to get it together. Halfway across the uneven parking lot, I stopped her stroll, brought her to me.

She tiptoed, put her arm on my waist, let the spirits on her tongue dance with mine in slow motion. I held her face in my hands and drank her for a while, the brisk air flowing over us.

I kissed her neck, her ear, whispered, "What we gonna do?"

She slid her hand between my legs, rubbed John Henry, gave me her tongue again.

"You're a fine man with so much *duende,* you know that, Driver?"

"You have a lot of charm yourself."

"I'm serious." She moaned. "Something about you excites a woman and makes her want to do things she knows she shouldn't be doing. You have pheromones to be reckoned with."

Jermaine Dupri had Janet Jackson. Tonight I had Arizona.

Bright lights covered us when somebody sped into the lot, hit a speed bump hard enough to make some noise. I jumped, blinded. Arizona reached into her purse, grabbed something and turned defensive. Vehicles had body language and that ride moved like a death threat.

It looked like an armored car with chrome rims, but it was a Hummer. The nose-and-mouth-shaped grille looked like bared teeth. Those bright lights like angry eyes.

That vehicle bulldogged past other cars, came to a sudden stop near my ride.

The driver killed the lights, got out, moving fast.

A few people stopped and checked out the bringer of the drama, others moved on.

Five-five, but her heels made her five-eight. Caramel skin. Bambi-like eyes. Shoulder-length auburn hair underneath a scarf, Audrey Hepburn style. Low-rise jeans and a leather coat with leopard fur around the collar. My eyes went to her left hand, my way of reminding her that she wore a five-carat emerald-cut in platinum. She cranked up a harsh smile as she came toward me and Arizona, got close enough for me to see the cleavage that pimped out the curves in her upgraded boobs. Head to toe, wedding ring to thong, everything on her was paid for by Wolf.

Arizona stayed at my side. She was alert, body ready like a warrior. That let me know she had some enemies out there, the kind that could roll up on her at a moment's notice.

When the owner of the Hummer was closer, I licked my lips and said her name. "Lisa."

Lisa held up a few feet away, stared at Arizona, dissected her, then glowered at me.

"Whassup, Playa," she said, her voice small, tight, and cold.

"My name is Driver. Same name your husband calls me."

"Is that right, Playa?"

Lisa's thin nostrils flared.

I told her, "You just missed your husband. We had a couple of beers and he left. Said he was on the way home before it got too late."

Her eyes cut deep. Lisa's father used to be chief of police in Compton, then mayor of the same city until a stroke took him out of office and sent him to a convalescent home. Her old man lived in Compton but she grew up in Ladera with the Black and the Bourgeois.

Lots of people were around. Too many for anybody to act a fool without notice.

Lisa did an about-face and went back to her Hummer, sat there in the darkness.

Arizona asked, "What was that all about?"

I shrugged, told her that Lisa was my boss's wife. They were having problems.

"That grenade has a loose pin." Arizona glanced Lisa's way, then turned back to me, read my face, said, "Pretty woman. Worn around the edges, but pretty."

I diverted where she was taking the conversation, asked, "You strapped?"

She reached into her purse again, showed me her switchblade. It was the kind that you flipped open when you gave it some wrist action. She put it back inside her bag.

An engine revved, lights flashed, a horn blew. We moved away from the middle of the aisle. Lisa zoomed by us. Behind her angry eyes I saw the edges of her dark side glowing.

I swallowed the regret in my throat, asked Arizona, "You following me home?"

"Three things about me, Driver."

"Okay."

"I'm not a stripper. Two, it takes more alcohol than that to impair my good judgment."

"Uh huh."

"Third, I'm not a whore. I might look young, but I'm not easy or naive."

My lips moved up into a one-sided smile. Hers did the same.

Checkmate.

I asked, "It's still early. Barely after midnight. What time you have to get up?"

"Hustlers set their own hours, you should know that."

"That's bull. I'm a hustler."

"You're a working man. True hustlers don't have a nine-to-five. Real hustlers never *think* about getting a nine-to-five. We're too busy trying to take a nine-to-fiver's money."

She pulled out a bar napkin from her cute little purse, wrote down a phone number in red ink and handed it to me. Area code 818. Hollywood and parts of the San Fernando Valley.

She told me, "I have connections with access to flat screens. Fifty-inch. Electronics for twenty-five percent. Jewelry for twenty percent. A referral gets you a small kickback."

She sounded as smooth as a politician. I'd bet that everything she had on had fallen off a truck. Her connections made her the woman to know. I handed her my black and gold business card. It was actually one of Wolf's business cards with my cellular written in at the bottom.

She said, "Want to help stimulate economic growth in our depressed economy, hit me."

"What about stimulating other things?"

She waved the business card I had given her. "Then I'll hit you."

Her tight eyes were devilish, her skin innocent, almost angelic under the streetlights. She traced her fingers over my chest, down my shoulders, to my biceps, over my forearms, then her fingers lingered across my palm. I caught her fingers for a moment, then let her go.

She took sugary steps away, blew me a kiss. "I'm already late for my date."

"I see."

Arizona headed toward a BMW. Silver. Convertible. New. She let the top down, then looked back at me and winked, did that in a way that sent me a message, told me she wasn't bullshitting about the business. That chump change she had lost inside wouldn't be missed.

The streetlight turned red as soon as she pulled out of the lot. Arizona pointed something at the streetlight and—I don't know if it was real or my Jack Daniel's talking to me—the streetlight changed right back to green.

She vanished into the night.

I crawled into my car, shaken and stirred.

3

Ten minutes later I was fighting traffic in the strip mall that held Magic Johnson's Starbucks, Fatburger, and TGIF. It was late, everything had closed hours ago, but out of habit I rode the lot to see what kind of stragglers were still hanging out. Parking lot was empty.

Arizona had me restless, my mind in a bear hug. Could've kissed her until sunrise.

She'd driven away and left me aroused, my insides on fire. Erotic thoughts and a nonstop movie of us played in my head. Another tease. Look at me. Forty going after a twenty-something that looked like a brand-new dime. Had to get off Fantasy Island. I pulled over and whipped out my cellular. Women with complexions from cream to coal had come and gone and would be happy to come again. Thought about calling Panther, maybe swing by Strokers, donate a few bucks to her college fund. But that movie starring Arizona played in my head again.

The alcohol in my blood told me to take my ass home and call it a night.

My spot was down on La Cienega between Centinela and the 405, a beige stucco building sitting on the edges of Inglewood,

Westchester, and Los Angeles, right in the middle of at least two miles of apartment buildings, none that could pass for the Taj Mahal. California was twelve percent black; this had to be the epicenter of Los Angeles's contribution to those demographics.

I lucked up and found street parking within a quarter mile of my place, an apartment-dweller's equivalent of winning the lottery. As soon as I got out of my car, that familiar red Hummer whipped up next to me. If I hadn't been thinking about Arizona all the way home I would've looked in my rearview and saw that my boss's wife was stalking me.

Lisa let the passenger-side window down, sang out her sarcasm, "Playa, Playa, Playa."

The way she said that irked me like fingernails across a chalkboard.

My heart sped up and I gritted my teeth, wondered how psycho she was going to get.

"Somebody sad because his PYT didn't come home with him? What, you didn't offer her enough money? She looked young. You should've given her some Now & Laters."

I ignored her, strutted away, climbed the stairs and went straight to the bathroom so I could pay my water bill. Lisa was banging at my door before I was done handling my business.

From my side of the door I said, "Go home to your husband, Lisa."

"We have a fifteen large situation that needs to be rectified one way or another."

I snapped out my aggravation. "Sue me."

Her tone matched mine. "I want my money."

"Or what? What are you gonna do?"

"Or I tell Wolf about us."

I laughed, calling her bluff. Wolf had her locked in with an airtight prenuptial agreement, the kind that gave her nothing if the marriage ended. He'd learned a hard lesson from his first marriage. Man met broke woman. Treated her like a queen. Shit didn't work out. Woman walked away with half of his shit, stereo included. Even a deaf woman would take the stereo just to piss a man off. Lisa was scorned when I met her. That was why it was so easy for us to fall into bed a few days after we met down on Crenshaw at Yum Yum doughnuts.

Fast-forward three months. Three hot and steamy months.

She wanted her husband dead. I needed to better my situation, get some financial relief.

And I wanted her to be my woman. Wanted her more than anything in the world.

I went to do the job, but Wolf didn't get killed. Couldn't do it. All bets were off. That was why she ran back home and crawled in his bed when her killing plan fell through. Between that prenuptial and his insurance policies, Wolf was worth more to her dead than alive.

I told her, "Ain't no us, Lisa. Your wedding ring should tell you that."

"When I was sucking your dick my wedding ring wasn't a problem."

"Lisa—"

"When you took my money my fucking ring wasn't a problem."

"Lisa—"

"I'm not going to allow you to keep ignoring me."

I thumped my head against the door a few times, then walked away. It was quiet for a minute. I thought she had bounced. Then she started banging on my front door nonstop.

"Open the door before I make a scene."

I yanked the door open, ready to shake some sense into her ass. She was in the hallway, the overhead light flickering, making her alternate from being a silhouette to an enraged woman holding a Glock in her hand. The business end of that death maker pointed at the ground. She used to be a cop back in the Rafael Perez days, so I knew she knew how to use it in a bad way.

She lowered her voice. "That was stupid. Nobody knows I'm here."

My eyes were on her gun. My breathing became nonexistent. She had my attention.

She smirked.

I licked my lips. Thought about trying to take her gun and whooping her ass with it.

"You tricked me out of my money, played me good. Right, Playa?"

"Call me Playa again and I'll grab you around your pretty little neck."

"Think twice about that. This .40 is loaded with hollows that would liquefy your heart on impact. I'd be on the 405 before your body hit the ground."

"What, I'm supposed to be scared?"

Like a fool I took a hard step toward her. The light flickered from life to death.

She raised her gun and acted like she was going to fire a warning shot at my groin. Cops carried the model 22. They used to carry a smaller model, the 9mm, but they took the step up to the Glock .40 because they were emptying their clips and folks were still coming at 'em.

I walked away. Took my coat off, eased it on the sofa, then went to the kitchen and got me a canned 7-Up. Lisa put her gun and purse on the kitchen table, then went into the bathroom.

I yelled, "Why don't you make yourself at home."

"Fuck you."

"Take that carnal invite up with Wolf."

She came back out and stared at me, said nothing for a moment, gave me dramatic silence. "Guess you forgot who helped you when your phone was cut off. The cell phone you have now, guess you forgot I bought that for you."

"I didn't forget."

"When your Crown Vic was broken down and you needed it fixed so you could take your mother to the hospital. When you were in a financial bind I was there for you, Driver."

"What you wanted in return . . . it was too much."

"It's easy for you to feel that way now. I'm the one out of fifteen large. You double-crossed me. Six months have gone by. Six months. You're putting me in a bad position. I either have to do nothing or do something. If I do something, you're not going to like it."

She went back in the bathroom, closed the door. I heard her urinating.

She had me nervous in a dozen ways. I looked around at my space, tossed things in the garbage, moved a stack of books and crossword puzzles to the side, tried to stay away from her.

The toilet flushed.

Lisa came into the living room. I went back to the bathroom. Couldn't stand being in the same room with her. I rubbed my hand over my chin, felt my stubble, hints of gray speckling my chin. I threw tap water on my face, damned my reflection for fucking with her.

My phone rang. I ran out to grab my phone before Lisa tried to answer it.

Lisa wasn't in the living room.

I picked up the cordless. The caller-ID read JASON WOLF, JR.

My heartbeat sped up.

I clicked the green button; words crawled up my throat. "Thought you'd be 'sleep."

"We have a problem."

"What kind of problem do we have, Wolf?"

I hadn't heard the front door open or close. Went to the window. Nobody outside.

Wolf repeated himself, "We have a big problem."

Then I saw Lisa's coat resting on the sofa. Her scarf and jeans were there too.

I said, "I'm listening."

I looked down at the carpet. A black bra and thong made a trail to my bedroom door.

Wolf said, "We have an account coming in from this publishing company in New York. Margaret Richburg was scheduled—"

"Okay."

The scent of her high-end toilet water told me that she was on the other side of that door.

Wolf went on, "But his publicist left an urgent message. The jerk doesn't want anybody white driving him around the city. Especially a Jewish woman. Man, I tell you, your cousins have a long way to go before they realize what Martin Luther King, Jr., was preaching about."

"Uh huh."

"Racist people, man I hate all of them bastards, don't matter what color."

I eased the bedroom door open.

Wolf went on, "So I'm going to need you to pick him up tomorrow afternoon."

"Sure, Wolf. No problem."

"I'll phone you in the morning with the specifics."

Lisa had turned off the bedroom light.

The window had been opened. Moonlight fell across the room.

She was standing on top of my bed. Naked.

Wolf said, "Driver . . . group of islands . . . starts with an A. Eleven letters. Ends in GO."

I licked my lips, seconds passed before I told him, "Archipelago."

"How do you know this off-the-wall shit?"

"Guess I'm just . . . just . . . a sponge . . . remember shit other people . . . forget." I faded.

Lisa had pretty facial features—a modest and beautiful nose, cheeks that made her look younger than forty, almond-shaped eyes—but something about them didn't go together, never photographed well. Her cheeks and nose looked bloated in pictures. But she owned the perfect body. Her pride and joy. Small waist. Ass had a nice hook. Tits were plump, had no sag. Only a trained eye could tell that she'd had them done and had spent a pretty penny on the upgrades.

Words caught in my throat, my mind ablaze. I said, "Wolf, where's the wife?"

"She hopped in her truck and went out to Albertson's as soon as I got in."

"Remember Pedro just told you that Albertson's is on strike. Vons too."

He grunted. "Guess she's crossing the picket line."

Lisa was on my bed doing a fuck-me dance. She made her ass shake, moved what she had like it was a twelve-cylinder Rolls.

I asked, "Why didn't you go with her?"

"Call came in about the New York client. Wifey was in a hurry. I'm tired anyway."

My mind was so messed up by Lisa's naked body being in my face and Wolf's loyal voice in my ear. It was like we were all here in this claustrophobic room at the same time.

He asked, "How'd you make out with the young girl at Back Biters?"

"The young . . . oh . . . I . . . I . . . got her number."

"She was a pretty woman."

I stared between Lisa's thighs, remembered her sweetness. "Yeah."

There was a heavy pause.

"Just like my wife. She left here wearing those Jimmy Choo shoes and a cashmere Burberry scarf. Thousand-dollar shoes and a thousand-dollar scarf to go spend five dollars on turkey sausage at midnight. And she put on perfume before she walked out the door. New perfume." He took a breath. "I love that woman, Driver. Love her and she drives me crazy."

"I know, Wolf. She knows it too."

We hung up.

The moment I put my phone down her cellular rang. Lisa stopped dancing. Her shoulders tightened and her expression changed, like she realized she was naked.

I told her, "Answer it. You're so bad, answer it and tell Wolf where you are."

We stood in a world muted by our own betrayals.

Her cellular rang four times then stopped.

She said, "I don't love him, Driver."

"But you in the same bed with him every night."

"Can hardly stand for him to touch me."

Guilt and jealousy were rising inside me like a crest of fire.

She whispered, "I know you're not going to pass this up, are you Driver?"

I licked my lips, swallowed hard.

I repeated my thoughts out loud. "Wolf gave me a job, Lisa. I'm not gonna fuck it up."

"He didn't give you anything I can't take away with a phone call."

"And you didn't give me nothing I couldn't buy for a hundred dollars."

She had come at me hard and I had gone back at her using that same prison tone. Hated what I had said, but that stopped her cold. Handicapped her attitude. Her eyes wanted to water.

I softened my attitude, rubbed the bridge of my nose. "Let it go, Lisa."

"Let it go? Who do you think I am?" She snapped. "Am I just supposed to forget the fifteen thousand you owe me just because you punked out and had a moral attack?"

"You know what happened; you know where the money went."

"Excuse me for not getting all teary-eyed, but I want my damn money."

"Give me some time."

"Three days from now, six months will have gone by. Your time is up."

"You take payments?"

"I gave you half in good faith. You reneged, and you've given me nothing in good faith. I'm serious about my money. Either I do nothing or I do something. I want my money the same way I handed it to you. All twenties. In a McDonald's bag. You will get it to me in three days."

"Three days? You know what I make. Best I can do is maybe five hundred a month."

She repeated that she wanted her fifteen large. "I know people,

Playa. Some very bad people, the kind who have earned tattoo tears. I know two men who will come after you and do some very nasty things to you for half of what you owe me. They're bad like Jesse James, and the kind of dirty work they do, they'll make you wish you had stayed in jail."

"You threatening me?"

"Just handling my business."

We tumbled into a stare down. I should've killed her right then, stuffed her body in her Hummer, left that bulky gas-guzzler in some dark and urine-stained alley down in South Central.

She shook her head, sneered. "You're forty. You have what, three suits?"

"Four. Bought another one."

"No property. Renting. Living a Spartan lifestyle."

"Nothing wrong with traveling light."

"I offered you a chance to come up. Handed you fifteen large. You spat in my face."

I said, "Let's be real, Lisa. It wouldn't've worked."

"Bullshit."

I reminded her of other failures, said, "Scott Peterson."

"Peterson was an idiot. We could've flown the Cessna cross country and been in Florida playing golf with O.J. by now."

Silence revisited us.

She frowned at my belongings. "I offered you a brand-new world. We could've retired young, become snowbirds, closing up the home in Hancock Park each winter and heading to a tropical island. I gave you my heart and you spat in my face. You deceived me."

I didn't argue.

She shook her head. "You have the nerve to come to work every day. To *my* business. To torture me with your presence. You know how that makes me feel?"

I didn't answer.

She looked away from me, stared at nothing. "You're my *sancho*, Driver."

"What does that mean?"

"It's Spanish. Means we have unfinished business." She sucked her lip in, folded her arms, looked sad and vulnerable. "You're my *sancho*, and I'm your *jeva*. Just your *jeva*."

I didn't know what *jeva* meant. The way she curled her lip told me it was vulgar.

She was off the bed, feet away from me, still naked, her eyes filled with anger, but her body telling me she wanted me to do other things to her that would make that anger go away.

I looked at her anger and beauty, shook my head, softened my tone, said, "Go home."

"Tell me you don't love me, Driver. You used to tell me you loved me."

She eased her breasts on me. Resurrected an old lust. Memories came back strong.

Love you, Driver. Those words echoed in my head. Couldn't remember the number of times she held onto me and moaned that like she was losing her mind. *So much I love you.*

I repeated what I said before, told her to get dressed and go home.

She whispered, "Sure you want me to leave?"

I put my hand up to her face, held her in a gentle way, heard her sigh, felt her weakening and melting under my touch. Her tongue eased out of her mouth, reached for mine.

She said, "Love you, Driver. Love you so much it hurts."

I thought about putting my mouth on hers, kissing her the same way I had kissed Arizona. Maybe I could close my eyes and pretend she was Arizona. Do all the things to Lisa that I had planned to do to the exotic sin that had teased me back at Back Biters.

I put my mouth close to her ear, whispered, "Go home, Lisa."

I stepped away from her. It wasn't easy. She was emotional, needed me to blanket myself around her, give her what I'd taken away, but I couldn't do that for her, not anymore.

She said, "The tight-eyed bitch you were all over at Back Biters, she was pretty."

I ran my hand over my head, rubbed my aggravation, gave her jealousy no response.

She went into the living room, put her clothes back on. I stood by my bedroom window. What I hated the most was that despite all of the hard talk, I had a diamond-hard erection.

When she dressed she folded her arms, looked away. "Walk me out."

I shook my head. "You have a gun. Walk yourself."

Her arrogant disposition had been softened by her true emotions. "Please?"

I grabbed my suit coat. She went to my fridge and helped herself to a 7-Up. She didn't open it. She never drank 7-Up straight from the can. She said there were too many germs on the lip of that metal, no matter how good you wiped it down. Lisa led the way and we headed back out into the night. I passed her, was walking fast, trying not to get too close to her, trying to get her out of my life as soon as I could. The faster I moved the more she dragged her feet.

She tied her scarf on her head and laughed. "You're Wolf's bitch. He pays you enough for rent and eats, keeps you under his thumb. You think he gives a shit about you? If you were in prison he'd get the top bunk. Be a man, or did you lose your manhood in prison?"

My lips tightened, jaw clenched. I faced her. "Fuck you."

"Your sorry ass. Content living in a damn one-bedroom apartment, across the street from Piss Alley and Hoodrat Row. You ain't shit. Fucking Uncle Tom-ass loser swindling convict."

I grabbed her arm. She jerked away, kept talking down to me. I grabbed her arm again, growled for her to shut up. She tried to pull away, but that was like a housefly trying to tow a freight train. She scratched my arm. Kept scratching. I ended up pushing her away from me. Pushed her glitz and glamour hard and she stumbled into a parked car. She got her balance.

"See, this is the real you, Driver. A suit can't hide the real you."

Traffic was passing. People were in the windows. I raised my palms and stepped away from her. "Walk yourself. And hell no, I don't love your crazy ass. Never did."

I'd made it about ten steps when there was a *whoosh* followed by pain in the back of my head, on the right side, behind my ear. The sharp and sudden agony sent me down on one knee. Defenses kicked in. I stumbled to my feet swinging at everything and hitting nothing but cold air. Thought I had been shot. Or hit by a brick. Then I saw a 7-Up can rolling away from me, dented from impact. I held onto my ear like I was trying to muffle the pain. Eyes watered. Couldn't hear for a moment. And my balance was off. I pulled my hand away from my head and saw a deep redness staining my fingers.

Heard some dude in a passing car yell, "Damn! She fucked him up!"

I rampaged after Lisa like a raging bull. My balance was still off. For a moment I had double vision. I saw two Lisas running away from me instead of just one. Both of them got in her Hummer, slammed the door hard, locked it, four breasts rising and falling with every breath.

"I hate you," Lisa kept screaming. "I fucking hate you."

We stood there, engulfed in anger, separated by glass like wild animals at the zoo, breathing like dragons, frowning and cursing each other down while cars zoomed by. Both sides of La Cienega were nothing but rows crammed with overpriced apartments, a thousand windows and twice as many eyes facing the streets. But this was L.A. Nobody gave a shit.

"Yeah, open the door, Miss Badass. I'll show you who hates who."

She pointed her Glock at me, her scowl exponentiated by rejection and betrayal.

My chest stuck out like my flesh was covered in Tenifer, the same indestructible material that coated her burner. I didn't back down. Anger brought out the stupidity in most men.

She tried to run over my feet, then backed up and tried to sideswipe me. I threw a hook, tried to knock off her side-view mirror. Damn thing folded in, was collapsible. She revved up her gas-guzzler and bullied me out into the street. A thousand headlights sped toward me going seventy miles an hour. I jumped out of the way, horns blared and I took to the curb.

Lisa bogarted her way into traffic, accelerated, screeched away.

My heart pounded. Fear was in my chest begging me to let it out.

Sweat rolled down my face, stung my eyes. Head was glazed with a thin sheen of piss-tivity and perspiration.

I yanked my suit coat off, but it was too late to keep it from being soiled with my blood. My suit pants were ruined, a hole in the fabric from when I had gone down hard on my knee.

I headed back home, cursing, limping, trembling.

4

Blood drained down my back as I sped up Genesee. Not the Genesee in Hollywood, but the narrow street that had been carved and curved into the urban hills in Baldwin Vista, the homes resting high over La Cienega and Rodeo. I rode Genesee until it changed to Carmone.

My head throbbed with every heartbeat, pain level a six moving toward seven.

The house I was looking for might've been sitting on the largest lot in the area. Up here, with real estate priced out of control, the better part of a million dollars bought you a thirty-five-hundred-square-foot crib and a two-car garage. But that's what you paid for three bedrooms and three baths in this part of town. L.A. was an expensive and greedy bitch. Years ago houses up this way weren't worth half of that. Fuck stocks. Property was the best investment in the West.

Blood was running down my neck. I needed medical help, but I didn't have insurance. The only person that I knew who had some bootleg medical skills was waiting for me.

I found the house that I was looking for. The wrought-iron gates opened up before I could blow my horn. He must've been alerted when my headlights flashed across the bay windows. The plantation shutters were open and I saw his lean silhouette. He looked like a prisoner.

I parked next to a convertible sports car, a BMW Z4. Rufus was at the front door before I made it up the stairs. He was a tall man with a broad nose, white skin, and gray eyes. Contact lenses made his red eyes look gray. His thick locks hung down to the middle of his back, honey blond with red streaks here and there. Colorless goatee. At least four silver earrings in each ear. I'd seen the eyebrow ring before. The nose ring and the one in his lip were new to me.

Always trying to draw attention to himself.

He had on faded jeans and a light-blue T-shirt with the picture of the new ULTIMATE SPIDER-MAN dead center. A novel was in his left hand. Comic or novel, I couldn't remember a time when I hadn't seen him with some kind of a book in his hand.

He frowned and shook his head. "Lights didn't come on."

"What?"

"Motion sensor's not working. Lights didn't come on."

I didn't care. "Rufus, need you to look at a cut behind my ear."

Rufus was fidgety, too nervous for me to play it off. Whenever he saw me his eyes turned into dull stones, then misted up with bad memories. My eyes became harder, darker.

Sirens. Drug-sniffing dogs. Handcuffs. The memory of being driven away by the police. Talking to Momma on the phone from behind bars. Writing my ex-wife and praying to hear from her. The fights. Being in The Hole. All of that came back in a rush for me too.

Luggage was by the front door. Four suitcases.

I asked, "Going on vacation or something?"

"Made reservations. Was going to San Francisco for a few days." He moved his stray locks away from his face. Anger peppered his tone. "Flight left without us on it."

"Another one of your friends . . . what, another funeral?"

"Not this time."

"What's up?"

"Domestic issues. Relationship more down than up. Want the details?"

I shook my head.

He said, "Didn't think so."

"Rufus, I'm bleeding to death."

I followed Rufus from the foyer into the living room. Off-white marble floors led us to burgundy leather furniture and cream-colored carpet. The carpet was top of the line and so was the padding. Made me want to take my shoes off and run around the place barefoot.

Sensual paintings with expensive framing and exotic sculptures decorated the place.

I motioned at a couple of pieces on the wall, said, "The art is bangin'."

"Those three are all David Lawrence. All of them are originals."

My body was tight with anger. "Never heard of 'im."

"He died, actually killed himself over a woman. That's her in the pictures."

I wiped sweat from my nose, glanced at the art. "The woman he killed himself over?"

"Yeah. He painted her naked. Some freaky shit to paint your wife naked over and over."

I looked over her dark skin, sexy eyes. "She's bangin'."

"More like banging her head against a wall. Heard she went crazy. Straight Bellevue."

I shrugged, wiped away more sweat, wished he would stop chitchatting and hurry up.

"The prices on his works have quadrupled, shot through the roof. Great investment."

"Rufus, I'm bleeding to death over here."

He tossed his novel on the leather coffee table. Rufus turned on several lights with a remote. He came back and looked at my wound. "This is ugly. What happened this time?"

"Bar fight."

"Awful, awful, awful. Who whooped your ass?"

"Ain't nobody whooped nothing." I winced with the pain. "I need stitches?"

"Let me clean it up and I can tell you better. Don't bleed on anything."

Rufus hurried away from me. His hips had more sway than a Vegas showgirl.

I snapped, "Rufus."

He straightened his back, firmed his shoulders, and did his best to walk like a man should. A contrived impersonation of masculinity took him up the spiral staircase.

He called back. "This is a surprise. Haven't heard from you in a minute."

"Been . . . been busy since Momma's funeral."

I looked out the bay windows, saw the lights all over the city.

Two minutes passed with my head throbbing while I took in the marble floors, abstract art, and soft music that came out of the speakers in the ceiling. The kitchen was high-tech, stainless steel Viking refrigerator and reddish marble counters. Not a speck of dirt or a thing out of place.

Outside the window I had an unobstructed view of downtown L.A., mid-Wilshire, traffic on the 10 freeway, Century City, parts of Beverly Hills. It was like being in a castle staring down at the poor folks in the Bottoms. Up here there was no huddling of the common man.

I clasped my hands. Wished this million-dollar world were my life. I missed my chance.

I called out, "What's this book you reading?"

"*Dawning of Ignorance*. That writer is getting a million dollars to write a book."

"Good for him."

"I have all of his books on the table."

"Does it look like I give a shit?"

"A million dollars."

I snapped, "Dammit, I'm bleeding to death, Rufus."

"Just don't bleed to death on the furniture. Pasquale would have a cow."

Rufus came down the staircase, medical kit in hand, a bigger box in the other. He handed me the bigger box. Inside was a painted statue of the Green Goblin, not a toy, but the kind for adult collectors. It cost at least two C-notes. I knew because I'd had my eye on it for a while.

I asked, "What's this?"

"Happy belated birthday."

"You serious?"

"Four months late. Better late than never. I wanted to get you the Wolverine stat—"

"No, this is cool. Damn. Thanks. This is tight."

He smiled. "You're going to have to get the Spider-Man half on your own."

"Rufus . . ."

"I know. You're bleeding to death."

He told me to follow him. I held on to my gift as we moved past a library. There was a built-in floor-to-ceiling bookcase.

I asked, "How many books do you have?"

"Close to four thousand. We're a regular public library."

"Can't believe you've read that many damn books."

"Yep. The ones I really like I've read at least twice. And I remember almost every word. Oh, last year, did I tell you I went to my therapist? He said that he thinks I have hypermnesia."

"A few hundred times, Rufus. You told me a few hundred times."

"Sounds like amnesia, but it's the opposite."

"I know what it means."

"It's my superpower."

"Guess you're ready to join the Avengers."

"I remember most everything in the books I read. Most, not all. Hypermnesia. There's a word for you, just in case. Means that I have an abnormally vivid or complete memory or recall of the past. I can see everything that happened to me growing up. I remember everything."

Thousands of books decorated their library, all either hardcover or leather-bound. And he'd read some of those novels at least twice. That almost got an envious smile out of me.

Then we passed the media room—a space the size of my apartment that had six televisions anchored to the walls, most tuned into different sports channels—and moved into the kitchen. One of the televisions was on some tabloid show. Eric Benet, Kobe, and Bill Clinton were being made poster children and highlighted on a segment called "Why Men Cheat."

I put my Green Goblin on the floor and posted up at a barstool at the kitchen counter. Rufus put on a pair of thin rubber gloves like doctors wore. He did that more for my protection than his own. He opened a bottle of peroxide and started cleaning my wound.

He didn't mention the tear in my suit pants or the blood on my shirt and suit coat.

He said, "I'm doing better. Thanks for asking."

I ignored his sarcasm. "Good."

"They have some experimental drugs down in Mexico."

I made an uncomfortable sound, then said, "Uh huh."

"With the cocktails, the new advances in research, doctors think I might outlive you."

"Cocktails?"

"They call 'em cocktails. It's about fifteen meds mixed up. Like a cocktail."

"You got insurance?"

He nodded. "Cremation. No funeral."

"Quit tripping."

"Not tripping. I've buried a lot of my friends. Not as many lately, but I've sang at so many funerals. Been to so many."

"We all have."

"You haven't seen what I've seen. We saw gunshots and knife wounds when we grew up. But the people I know . . . my friends deteriorated inside-out, looked they had been exposed to plutonium. Tried to blame it on Mother Africa. That shit came from some nuclear experiment."

"Rufus."

"What?"

"Don't like thinking about that kinda shit. You're my brother, you know."

"So cremate me. Just e-mail the people on my buddy list and tell them I've crossed over to receive my glory. Ridiculous how a funeral and a casket cost twenty thousand."

"That's how they get you. You go in all emotional and while you're crying over your dead momma they stick a vacuum cleaner in your wallet."

"You know? And if you add in how much money people pay to come see you get put in the ground . . . I don't want to leave people in the same situation Momma left us in."

I nodded. "Daddy too. He didn't leave us nothing but a stack of bills."

"That cancer ate him up."

Momma used to say Reverend Daddy's sins were eating him alive from the inside. Cancer turned his hulking frame into an ashen shell. His will to live was gone long before he made it back to the dirt. No matter how I felt about him, wasn't easy watching my old man die. Momma used to pray, ask Him why she was being tested. At times I think she thought about killing herself. Sometimes I think she thought it was her fault. People always looked for somebody to blame. She hated my old man. Not because of the lies in the pulpit or the women he had bedded, but because he was dying, and his deterioration was a financial burden on us all. The closer my old man was to death, the less my momma called out to God. And the irony of it all was the closer my old man was to death, the more he called out to God.

Rufus asked, "What about you?"

"Anything happens to me, don't claim the body. Let them bury me in a pine box."

"You can be so morbid."

I told him, "You think I'm joking?"

"Twenty thousand to put somebody in the ground."

"Rufus, focus on my head wound."

Rufus didn't think I'd need stitches, but getting stitches would help it look better when it healed. I didn't care. With all the scars I'd earned, I didn't care about one more. He had some kind of special Band-Aids; they were narrow and were used to close up wounds like mine.

When he was done he said, "Time for a game of bones?"

With the pain in my head and the alcohol in my bloodstream, that was the last thing I felt like doing. But I looked at my Green Goblin statue, smiled, yawned, and said, "Sure."

"One quick game. I know it's late. Let's go out back. Warmers are on."

We went through the sliding glass door and I copped a seat over by the pool. Rufus went inside and came back with a box of dominoes in one hand, a bottle of Jack Daniel's in the other. He poured me a shot of JD. I didn't want it, but I didn't turn it down. Maybe because at the bottom of every bottle of JD lived the truth. I wasn't born in a house with real morals so I hadn't been brought up to be a man with many self-disciplined habits. Plus I knew Rufus. Refusing a drink would hurt his feelings. We sat back and played bones like we did when we were kids.

Elbows on the glass patio table, sitting underneath warmers, I steepled my hands, looked across the board and asked, "How's your money looking?"

He leaned back, pulled his lips in. "I know I owe you my part from Momma's funeral . . ."

"In a bad situation. Could use some financial help right now."

"All of my money goes toward my medication. Unbelievable how much medicine costs. The shit should be free. We can go to Mars, but healthcare? And between battling Epstein-Barr over the years, and now this damn sciatic nerve flaring up, I'm taking more meds than any one person should. Seems like I take horse pills all day long."

He vented about the system. I sighed and shut my eyes for a couple of seconds.

He tugged at one his locks, said, "Maybe I could ax Pasquale—"

I made a rugged hand motion. "It's *ask*, not *ax*. Ask. Ask."

"*Ax. Ax.*"

"Half a degree in nursing, plus all these books you read, and you still can't say ask?"

"Well color me imperfect. Don't get irritated 'cause I can't say it like that."

I shook my head. "Say *ass kicked.* Like you wanna get your *ass kicked.*"

"Huh?"

"Just say *ass kicked.*"

"Ass kicked."

"Now say *ass k—*. Leave off the *icked.*"

"*Ass—k. Assk. Assk.*"

"Better. You're getting there."

He laughed and kept repeating. "Assk. Assk."

A sensor beeped four times. Rufus jumped.

I stood up, Lisa's threat flickered through my mind. "Somebody breaking in?"

"Four beeps. That means the front gate's opening. Pasquale's home."

Rufus shifted, looked uncomfortable, both pissed off and ashamed. Without a word, I grabbed my coat, put my keys in my hand. He followed me toward the front door.

He said, "Your pant leg is torn. Blood-soaked collar. Your suit is jacked. Totaled."

"Was waiting for you to say something."

"You know me."

"Like I know myself."

"You know what they used to say. I'm you with all the fucked-up genes. Your doppelganger. You inherited all the good stuff from Momma and Daddy. You have the broad shoulders, the square jaw, the prominent cheekbones. I got what was left over."

"Shut up, Rufus."

"Asthma. Allergies. If I had been like you, Momma and Daddy would've accepted—"

"Don't start with that motherfucking bullshit."

"It's true." He laughed like he had accepted his truth, like there was no pain inside him. "I'm the before picture and you're the after. I'm Bruce Banner and you are the Incredible Hulk."

The closer we got to the front door, the more Rufus's shoulders softened, his strut easing back toward being the stroll of a Vegas showgirl. Each step he took broke my heart.

His soft hands and manicured nails never would've lasted on the other side of The Wall. I'd hate to think of the things they would've done to a fragile and easygoing man like him, how they would've passed him around, sold him for the price of a cigarette.

He was my brother, we shared DNA, I loved him, but I wasn't and never would be cool with the kind of man he was. I didn't understand and wasn't wired for that kind of understanding. I never talked about him to the people I knew. We hardly talked. When we did we avoided any big issues. We lived no more than five minutes away from each other, but we lived in different worlds. At least we did in my mind. He knew how I felt about his lifestyle. He knew because when he came out of the closet, I tried to kick his ass back inside.

Reverend Daddy had done the same thing, in his own way.

"Shoot him, Rufus."

That was Reverend Daddy. Hearing that voice inside my head made me stop moving.

"Be a man and shoot the bastard."

Then it all came to me in a flash. I saw him in my mind, like he was right before the cancer. Skin the hue of maple syrup. Veins in his thick arms looked like ropes. Moustache credit-card thin. Smelled like Dial soap mixed with sprinkles of Hai Karate. I opened and closed my fists, remembered the pain. I was in an alley standing next to Reverend Daddy, hands hurting from beating a man down. The man in question was around thirty. Six-two. Two-hundred. Hard talk, soft body. His name was Ulysses. Light-skinned. Hair in braids. He'd called Rufus a faggot in front of some of Reverend Daddy's congregation. Had done that two months before. Long enough for retribution to be served cold. Reverend Daddy's style.

"Shoot the motherfucker, Rufus."

Ulysses had been beat down. Reverend Daddy had told me to do that, to tenderize that foolish man the old-school way. His eye was swollen the size of a grapefruit. Jaw broken like Ali's after that fight with Joe Frazier. Nose twisted, broken. He'd peed his pants. Was begging. Pleading with Reverend Daddy to let him live. Apologizing for slandering his youngest son.

I was fourteen. Rufus, twelve. Rufus was just as tall as our old man. I was taller.

Rufus held the .38, the barrel shaking, each rugged breath telling how terrified he was. Scared to not shoot that man in the head because he'd have to deal with Reverend Daddy.

Ulysses found his God, prayed over and over, his pants drenched at the crotch.

Then my little brother changed. Looked confident.

Rufus pulled the trigger.

It clicked.

Rufus grunted and pulled the trigger over and over and over, frustrated.

The gun was empty.

Reverend Daddy put his hand on Rufus's shoulder, got him to stop pulling the trigger, looked him dead in his eyes, almost smiled. That was as close to a smile as he ever gave Rufus.

We walked away. Ulysses's moans and prayers faded with our every step.

After that Reverend Daddy cranked up his Buick, let Rufus ride up front that time, and took us to a place he knew about over on Central Avenue. Miss Thelma's place. Reverend Daddy picked out the prettiest yellow girl he could find. Had that redbone take Rufus upstairs.

I sat down in the living room, hands aching.

Reverend Daddy put his hands on me. "You did good today. Real good."

I'd beat down Ulysses the way Marvin Hagler had destroyed Tommy Hearns. My demonic right hand hit him so hard I thought he'd vaporize. Watched that man buckle and go down like a beach umbrella in the wind. Under my daddy's eyes, I was brutal.

A pretty girl came back and left a glass of lemonade at my side. She winked at me. Reverend Daddy was taking in a glass of Jack, watching television and not watching it at the same time. He leaned my way, seasoned my lemonade with the spirits, then went back to the television. Pretty girls sashayed back and forth, smiling my way, the answer to that smile costing more than I could afford.

We waited for my brother to be transformed into Reverend Daddy's image of acceptance.

Reverend Daddy said, "Son, I'm just doing what your momma asked me to do."

I nodded.

He said, "Hate unites people. It's almost like we need somebody to hate in order to pull together. When we stop hating, we all seem lost, like we have no direction."

"I don't hate my brother."

"Wasn't talking about your brother. Just going over my sermon."

"Sure."

"But your brother . . . this thing . . . this devil inside him . . . he ain't like us. Most people are sheep. They do what they are led to do. He has been led in the wrong direction. We have to look over him. Get him back on the right path."

His speech faded. I went back to watching and not watching the television.

Rufus didn't say much when he came back down. The pretty girl he had done his thirty minutes of therapy with, she closed her red robe and pushed her lips up into a whore's smile.

Reverend Daddy stood, gave her the same regard as he did all women, his fedora in one hand, empty glass of whiskey glued in the other. He asked, "How he do this time?"

"Better than the last time."

"What that mean?"

"He did good, Reverend."

"He like it?"

"Yessir. He made me call Jesus so much I thought—"

"Don't blaspheme, child. Remember who you talking to. I'm His representative."

"Yessir. I apologize."

They talked like Rufus was resting in a cot on the moon.

My eyes went to my brother. He saw how I was worried about him. It was always unspoken between us. Never knew how to say what I felt, hardly knew right from wrong. Just followed my old man's wishes like the rest of his sheep, without questioning.

Reverend Daddy took out his wallet and handed the redbone girl a folded twenty.

He asked her, "You here next Saturday?"

"Yessir, Reverend."

"I'll bring him back 'round the same time."

"Yessir."

"You tell anybody he come in here and do thangs with you?"

"Yessir."

"Who you told?"

"Everybody I see."

"Good. Make sure you come to church one time."

"Yessir."

"Tell everybody you see, young and old."

After that Reverend Daddy took us up to Thrifty Drug Store, bought us ice cream.

By the time Rufus and me made it to the foyer, the front door opened. Pasquale stepped inside. A walnut-colored man with dark hair that curled like ocean waves. He was average height with a chiseled body dressed in FUBU and Timberland. All Hollywood muscles, the kind made for television and would never last two minutes in a street fight. He was an actor on one of those Negro Night sitcoms, played a heterosexual teacher that all the pretty women wanted.

I nodded. "What's up, Pascal?"

"Pasquale," he corrected.

I gave him a rugged smile, then a brief nod. There was no love for me in his eyes, that same reflection in mine. He spoke out of the left side of his mouth. He thought that made him look cool and tough. I'd seen tough. He wasn't it. It just made him look like he'd had a stroke.

He cleared his throat, checked me out, saw my ripped pant leg, might've seen the blood staining my shirt and suit coat, then twisted his lips and told me, "Good evening."

His eyes went to Rufus, returned to my hard stare, then back to Rufus. The energy was off, like he was waiting to see how Rufus was going to greet him. Rufus was waiting to see what Pasquale was going to do. My brother stood between us, shifting back and forth, pulling at his locks, then toying with his earrings, eyes glazed over, his soul sinking in quicksand.

Alexithymia. That fifty-dollar crossword-puzzle word popped into my aching head. Maybe because Rufus kept moving, as restless as a shark, like he had to keep swimming in his thoughts so he wouldn't have to stop and acknowledge everything that felt wrong in his world.

Rufus said, "We missed our flight."

Pasquale shrugged a gangsta shrug. "Changed my mind."

"Changed your mind?"

"Changed my mind."

Rufus's jaw clenched, made a popping sound, his gray eyes misted up.

A bright light flashed across the bay window. Somebody in an Expedition was turning around in the driveway, their high beams clicking low to high and back to low. I saw the egotistical rims. Spinners. Those cost ten thousand each. It headed back down the hill.

Shoulders square, Pasquale moved his gangster stroll across the marble foyer to the lush carpet, took to the spiral staircase without looking back, took the stairs two at a time.

Rufus walked me outside, his arms folded. I told Rufus part of the truth about my injury. Told little brother that it was because of a loan I'd gotten from Lisa that I needed to repay.

I said, "She called me an Uncle Tom."

"No she didn't. She called you Uncle Tom and she's riding the pink dick?"

"Bet."

Rufus shook his head. "You should've beat her ass. Remember how you beat down that security guard at Boy's Market? That's how you should've slapped some sense into her ass."

We both laughed a raucous laugh at that memory.

After Reverend Daddy died, if we did have food stamps, that ghetto money could be used to barter for other things the same way people bartered with cigarettes behind The Wall. So when we got to Boy's Market, Momma taught us how to steal. She'd sewn pockets in the linings of our jackets. The trick was to work quick and not put anything too heavy in your jacket lining. The weight would be a dead giveaway. Rufus got caught when he was sixteen. I was eighteen. Security followed Rufus out, grabbed his jacket, and a pack of frozen chicken wings fell to the ground. I was behind them, so he didn't see me walking in his shadow. Cat was bigger, older too. Had gray hair in both his Curl and the bottom of his goatee. But I always protected my brother the best I could. No matter what the cost. There were two blows. I hit that security guard in the middle of his face. He hit the ground. His bloodied and broken nose told me that the fight was over. I knew right from wrong. But, right or wrong, you didn't grab a man in the ghetto without expecting a fight.

Rufus laughed and slapped his legs with his palms. "Lord, I can still remember how he looked up at us and screamed. *Run. Make it look like I'm chasing you. Nigga, I don't wanna lose my fuckin' job. I got three kids. This all I got. Pick up the chicken and run, nigga, run.*"

I couldn't help but laugh. "You grabbed that chicken and ran like the wind."

"If I'd run home *without* that bird, Momma would've beat me until Gabriel blew his horn. After Reverend Daddy, Momma picked up right where he left off. She'd hit you and you'd just stand there and look at her. I'd look at you and think, Lord, please don't let that nigga hit Momma. She'll kill us all."

Our laughter gradually died. Thought about the days when I'd shoot craps to come up on some cash, break into somebody's home, hook up with an older woman who had a fetish for young dick. Sometimes I just got a job. We let the misty memories of our past go. Then I closed my eyes, had another one of those moments I had from time to time. A sort of philosophical moment where I wondered if the life and things around me were just a product of my own mind.

Rufus said, "Yessir. Reverend Daddy taught us how to lie and Momma taught us how to steal."

"That they did."

I touched the wound behind my ear. Blood and pain told me this life was real.

I opened my eyes, told my brother, "I need quick cash to get her off my back."

"When did she start tripping?"

"When I quit dicking her down."

"Duh. Why didn't you just keep on fucking her? All she wanted was some attention and some dick. Hell, she's frustrated with pinky and wants the chocolate thunder."

We laughed like two men in a locker room. His was deep and true, mine uneasy.

The anger in Lisa's eyes; still saw it. I told Rufus that she had pointed her Glock at me.

That changed his disposition.

He said, "She's a horrible human being. The fruit doesn't fall far from the tree. She looks like her mother, but she's a nutcase just like her father. That Jekyll and Hyde would smile at the people at noon then destroy his enemies at midnight. He ran Compton the same way she's coming at you. People cheered when he had a stroke. That stroke saved a lot of people's lives."

"Could you make it sound a little worse, Rufus? Could you do that for me?"

A cool breeze rustled through the palm trees.

He folded his arms and rocked. "Should I ask how much you owe her?"

"Don't ask. And change your damn posture."

He straightened up before he asked, "Do I need to call somebody?"

"I'm cool. She's bluffing."

"You should sneak in her house and piss in her Listerine."

"*Rufus,* c'mon man. That's nasty."

"Or put some depilatory in her perm. Remember when I did that to Peter? He had curly hair and used a mild perm to make the curls a little wavier. I bought extra-strength perm and mixed it together with Nair and put it on his head, rubbed it all through his damn hair. When he said it was starting to burn, I told him, 'Well, you only have a few more minutes.' "

My expression shut his laughter down.

He said, "You should look up Ray Ray. Now that's one crazy-ass nigga. He'll fuck a heifer like Lisa up for a value meal at McDonald's and you won't even have to supersize."

I thought on it and shook my head. "A man handles his own problems, Rufus."

"Oh, please. If that was the case Bush would've gone to Baghdad his damn self."

"Whatever."

"If you can't find Ray Ray, what about Andre?"

"Rufus, I'm not calling in the cavalry because of a damn woman."

"Newsflash. A bitch with a gun ain't no woman. That bitch has balls."

We both sat there, rubbing hand over hand, same thing Reverend Daddy used to do.

For a moment, I wished I had done whatever it took to keep the peace. For a moment. I thought about Wolf, how good he had been to me, like another brother, and I shook my head. I wasn't a saint. I'd bedded a few married women, would experience another married woman and send her home wearing my scent without a second thought, but not if she was the wife of a friend.

We all had our lines in the sand, even if those lines didn't run deep.

"Rufus, can you borrow . . . get a cash advance from . . . from . . . a charge card?"

Rufus sucked his lips. "I'm broke and my credit is so fucked up right now it ain't funny. Insurance doesn't cover all of my expenses. I'm on disability because of Epstein-Barr. Hell, I was about to call you and ask you for another loan."

His ailments were old news. I let out a sigh. Epstein-Barr was also known as Chronic Fatigue Syndrome, the yuppie disease that made him feel like he had the flu off and on.

He said, "Hell, maybe I should write a book like *Dawning of Ignorance* and see if I can get a million dollars."

I motioned at the house. "What about Mr. Hollywood?"

Rufus shook his head and said, "Things are pretty bad between us right now."

I didn't press what was up. Didn't want to know.

"We have some issues." He nodded. "Pasquale had to get a second to get a lot of work done around here, outside of that he's tight with his money, unless it's going to benefit him."

"How bad are things with you and your . . . him? Nothing physical. No fighting or no bullshit like that."

"Nothing like that."

"I'll kick that motherfucker's ass if—"

"Nothing like that. He's a pacifist. Nothing going on I can't handle."

I went back to silence. That was all I wanted to know.

"Pasquale's done enough for me," Rufus said, then looked down at his hands. Big hands, uncallused, nails trimmed to perfection. "Too much. I need to come up with money myself. Plus he's put so much money into decorating this house. Redid the kitchen, all four bathrooms."

I nodded. He wouldn't loan Rufus money to bury my momma. So

I knew he wasn't going to loan a dime to help keep me alive. My life wasn't his responsibility anyway.

"So axing . . ." He paused. "*Ass-k . . . assk . . . asssking* . . . him wouldn't do any good."

I smiled a brief smile. He did too. For a moment we were two little boys.

His voice cracked, "That should've been me in Memphis."

"Shut up, Rufus."

He folded his arms and pulled his lips in, those dull eyes misting up.

I got inside my car, started my engine, put my brother's million-dollar lifestyle in my rearview, took to the narrow street and headed down the hill to mingle with the hoi polloi.

I'd left without telling my brother good-bye. Or I loved him. We always parted like that. Abruptly and with tension, like we were running away from any real emotions that festered inside us. Habits we picked up from our parents. Only we understood our dysfunctionality.

I gripped the steering wheel, the cool night air chilling my skin. I'd almost told Rufus that Lisa had paid me fifteen thousand to kill her husband. But Momma had died and left us in a bind. I had used that money to bury Momma. Didn't seem like I had a choice at the time.

Just like I didn't have a choice when those drug-sniffing police dogs started barking.

No. Rufus wouldn't've survived on the other side of The Wall.

Like I did when frustration bloomed and spread inside me, I told myself that I'd made some fucked-up choices in my life, but saving Rufus and burying Momma were the good ones.

A man had to do right by his momma. And blood was thicker than water.

My cellular phone beeped. It was hooked up to the car charger. I had at least one message. Hoped it was Lisa, but the call was from Arizona. She had hit me about an hour ago.

"Too bad you didn't answer. Plans changed. My friend won't be in town until tomorrow. Was hoping you'd have paged me. I like that. You're different." Her voice was honey. "Love chocolate. Love mature men. Love mature men in nice suits and nice shoes."

She paused, made a few sounds, all soft and sensual, arousing and disturbing as hell.

"Your kisses . . . haven't had kisses in a long time. Forgot what that was like. You were corny, but for some reason I was feeling you. Been a while since I was this attracted to a man."

Her silky moans echoed. Water splashed. Echoes. Water. She was in the bathtub.

"You got my pussy so wet. Was imagining when I was rubbing your dick. Would be nice to let you slide inside me. You could hold my ass. Put your mouth on my neck. I could suck your tongue. Ride you nice and slow. Then you could fuck me good and hard."

Delicate sounds became deep breathing, harder panting, and orgasmic swallowing.

"God. I just . . . I just . . . I came." Water splashed again. "Came . . . so . . . hard."

I imagined her damp face, her wet breasts rising and falling with her erotic breathing.

"Yeah, think I had too much to drink. Good thing you didn't answer."

She ended her pleasure call.

My night had been horrible. She was the last thing I needed right now. The last thing.

But I needed to escape the pain and the memories. Needed a good-feeling reality.

I dug in my suit pocket and found the napkin she'd given me, dialed her digits. It didn't ring, just beeped three times. A pager. I punched in my number. Waited for her to call back.

Ten minutes later I was back on my side of town, hunting for a parking space.

My cellular didn't ring. My head didn't stop throbbing.

Shaken and stirred, I listened to Arizona's message again. Then again. Again.

That was why I didn't notice I had been followed.

5

The 7-Up gave them away. The same 7-Up can Lisa had branded me with, that dented can warned me. I'd parked, gotten out of my car, started heading to my apartment.

Then somebody stealthing up behind me kicked that 7-Up. It whined across the concrete.

I swung around. Two men were closing in, a lion and a jackal. Both had intent and stone faces, coming at me the way men came at you on the yard and treated you to a shank down.

What was surreal became real.

My defenses went up, body came alive.

They stopped just beyond striking distance, still close enough to be point blank.

I asked, "There a problem?"

They just stood there, soundless, like they were waiting on the wind to change direction.

Four eyes stared down two, the tension between us muting out the sound of street traffic, sirens, and music coming from one of the apartments across the way on Hoodrat Row.

I repeated, "There a problem?"

The square-head brother to my left, the lion, he was the one who answered me. "We'll know in three days."

He had a head bigger than O.J.'s. His nose had been broken at least once, was smooshed and took up too much of his face. He had baby teeth. Like everything around his teeth had been supersized and didn't send the Tooth Fairy an update. He was a big guy, a six-footer. Loose jeans. Lakers jacket. Built like he played defense for the Raiders. He weighed about two-ten, give or take a Big Mac with cheese, steroids on the side.

The other one, the jackal, kept his narrow face and slanted eyes on me. Cold as hell out here and all he sported was a wife beater. He was a pock-faced, thin man. Markings up his neck to his throat. If his skin was a ride at an amusement park it would be called Tattoo-land. My first guess was Tehachapi, maybe Wayside. Either way, both of them had studied at Penitentiary State. The question was whether they earned their bachelors, masters, Ph.D., or dropped out.

My hands became sledgehammers.

Lisa said she had two men to do her dirty work. I felt alert, my buzz gone. I didn't notice how much the temperature had dropped anymore.

A million cars roared by and not a soul on the broken and slanted sidewalks but us.

I tried to guess which one was going to rush me first, or maybe look for the weak link, rush that motherfucker before he could charge at me, take out one and hope for the best.

Another car pulled up and parked a few feet down on La Cienega. It was a young man, his girlfriend, and their five-year-old son, all neighbors who lived in the next building.

The lion and jackal regarded the car, its passengers, then they both took steps back.

The brother said, "Fifteen large. Three days."

I stood tall, bared my teeth. I stepped toward them. Neither moved or batted an eye. Fear didn't paralyze me; it motivated me toward a violent conclusion, usually in my favor.

My neighbors unloaded, went into their building. That's how long we stood there.

I said, "Why wait? Bring it on."

The lion looked at the jackal. "He's an arrogant fuck."

"Yeah, he's an arrogant fuck."

"He won't be in three days."

"Not at all."

The lion took a step back. He kicked the 7-Up can toward me again, letting me know he had kicked it on purpose the first time. He turned around and headed in the other direction. The jackal took a few steps backward, then followed. They headed down La Cienega toward a black Expedition. Same one I'd just seen stalking outside Rufus's place. I ran to get back inside my car and catch them before they left this concrete jungle. By the time I fumbled my keys out of my pockets and got my car started, they had vanished into the night. I went down La Cienega with as much speed as I could handle, but about a mile away the street split. Either they had zoomed to the left and got on the 405 South, or stayed right and went deeper into Inglewood.

I stopped chasing that vapor trail and drove back home, found another space. Sat there holding the steering wheel with the car engine throbbing in my hands, thinking deadly thoughts.

I wanted to hunt them down, but it was better to kill a master than hurt a slave.

My cellular rang. Lisa's cellular number showed up. Her bully-boys had called her.

I answered with a snap, told her, "You have my attention."

"Do I? And how did I finally get your attention?"

I battled with my breathing, fought to hold on to the last edge of my calm the way a drowning man held onto a rope. I rocked, my damp hands still struggling to dry each other.

My brain was working overtime, looking for something to say to fix this. I remembered what Rufus had told me to do. Wolf was my friend, but if that would get his wife off my back, I'd do what I had to do. I never should've started up with her. She'd become my bête noire.

She said, "My husband is waiting for me to come to bed and be his wife."

I wiped the stress sweat away from my eyes, said, "Lisa—"

"You're a big guy. A rock-hard body. Rough around the edges. A bona fide certified playa. Laying the pipe all over the city. Get my money from your women, Playa."

"I'll drive to Hancock Park." My tone was raw. "All three of us can have a sit-down."

"Come this way, I'll activate an acceleration clause in your three-day grace period."

"Meaning?"

"Start driving toward Hancock Park, you'll be dead before you make it to Wilshire."

She hung up.

6

Sunrise tapped on my shoulders three hours later. Hours had gone by like minutes.

My tension headache didn't let me sleep much. But I dozed long enough to get rid of the edge and keep from feeling postal. I woke up to the smell of Tunisian oils, gurgling grits, and turkey sausage. Rollerblades and snow skis were on the wall by the front door. Peach and red walls with erotic art by Kimberly Chavers, another artist I'd never heard of. Lots of pillows and scented candles. I wasn't at my apartment. I'd grabbed a few things and left Inglewood last night. Headed south of LAX and squatted at a colorful studio apartment in Manhattan Beach.

"For real, Momma? The IRS went to Buckhead and jacked all of Peabo's stuff? Everything in the man's house? How much he owe in back taxes? *A million dollars.* Dag."

She had been up all night. She didn't get off work until somewhere between one and two-thirty and was as nocturnal as Dracula. Daylight wasn't her friend.

"Momma, you have to go online and sign the petition. Uh uh. Then send it to everybody you can. Yes, ma'am. Got a pen? Okay, it's Helpmarcus.com. Uh huh. It is absurd. I mean, they found something to make him guilty. Well, that's what those women do. Have consensual sex then when their daddies find out start hollering rape. No, ma'am, times ain't changed, not at all, not for us. I wrote him a letter and let him know that there are people out here who care."

They went on for a while, talking about a young brother who was getting railroaded in that good old Southern injustice system. I only got crumbs of the conversation.

I pulled the covers from my eyes, saw a stack of crumpled one-dollar bills on her dresser, six-inch stilettos tossed on the floor next to black leather thigh-high boots, then caught her moving around over by the small stove, first scratching one of her breasts, then stirring the grits, her cellular phone up to her face, trying to talk low and failing, irritating me. She had on thick white socks, black T-shirt, and red boy shorts.

"Momma, you get the shoes I sent you? They fit? Good. You wore a pair to church already? You're worse than me. Cooking breakfast. Yes, ma'am. Love you too, Momma."

She didn't look anything like she did when she worked. Minus the G-string, scanty bustier, and vivid makeup she wore at her night job, she was plain and simple, body withstanding, because she was a cornbread, fish, and collard greens kinda woman.

Her hair was long and colored deep brown with highlights, tied back in a ponytail. The rest of her was all a gift from above, maybe below, depending on your relationship with her.

Words that described her arranged themselves inside my aching head, phrases I never used because they sounded corny as hell, shit like *hauntingly equine* and *beauty so enchanted*.

She hung up her phone. "Driver, you sleep?"

I yawned and sat up, pain, anger, and dehydration clinging to me like a tick.

I played it all off, put on a smile and said, "Was in the middle of omphaloskepsis."

"Omfa-what-the-hell?" She laughed. "You and them big words. What the heck is that?"

"Fourteen-letter word." I reached for my cellular phone. "Form of meditating I do in my drawers with my eyes closed."

"You and your faux-cabulary."

"Always using ten-dollar words and ain't got but two in my pocket."

She laughed. So did I. She had an easygoing way about her that lightened my soul.

"Didn't mean to wake you, Driver. Momma called. That woman can talk."

"It's cool." My voice was thick, gruff. "Gotta get up. Gotta get to work."

I called her Panther. Her sobriquet. Doubt if that was her birth name. She was born near Atlanta, had a small waist and the fullness of a Southern gal, and still owned edges of an accent.

I struggled with a yawn, sat up, and punched the number one on my speed-dial. My cellular dialed Rufus's home phone number. Pasquale answered on the third ring, sounding sleepy. I'd called twice through the night and nobody had answered.

I asked, "May I speak to Rufus?"

"He's sleeping. Who's this?"

He was fucking with me, he knew my voice. "His brother."

"He's asleep."

"Wake 'im up."

"Call back at a decent hour."

"Look, Nigga. Man, stop playing. Tell him his brother called."

"Good morning to you too."

"Tell him I called."

"How's about some respect?"

"How's about telling my brother to holla at me?"

I hung up feeling both irritated and relieved. Nothing crazy had happened overnight. Lisa had hurt me, scared me, left me tripping. She'd bluffed me hard last night.

Panther was watching me, her eyes telling me she didn't know what to think, do, or say. Just like I'd done with Rufus, I'd shown up at her door looking like a wounded warrior.

I created another smile, let that become my mask, faced Panther, tendered my tone, asked, "When did you move from Hawthorne and 119th down to this spot?"

She paused, got tight around her mouth. "Gave that apartment up after Christmas."

"Cool studio. Nice area."

"Yeah. Love having the beach right outside my door."

I made my way to her bathroom, cozy space, more candles, lipsticks and mascaras, pretty little bars of soaps, sweet-smelling lotions, the accoutrements of a woman. I looked in a colorful basket she had on the counter. Scented shea butter. Exotic butter body cream. Fizzling bath grains. Everything had a label on it that said she had bought it at www.pamperingu.com.

A boom box was on the counter next to the basket, CDs by Annie Lennox and Jonny Lang at its side. So were bottles of medicine. I hit play on the CD player, let Jonny Lang's singing "Red Light" cover my being nosey.

You could tell a lot about somebody's problems by looking in their trash and medicine cabinets. You find out all you wanted to know about a person's diet. Their bills. Credit. Things left in the trash told a man when a woman's cycle was on and popping. Garbage cans and medicine cabinets, info people didn't want the world to know was in those two places.

Her medicines were both Nefazodone and Paroxetine, antidepressant meds used to treat panic attacks, social phobias, all kinds of anxiety. The Nefazodone was unopened. The Paroxetine was forty-milligram tablets, a prescription of ninety pills almost gone.

Her real name was on the bottles. Cynthia Smalls.

I thought about the bottles of miracle drugs my brother had in his medicine cabinet.

Jonny Lang's guitar and grizzled voice sang me back into the front room. Panther was putting the food together, singing along. She had an untrained church-singing voice, Southern and spiritual, moving. I pushed the colorful quilt and red sheets to the side and sat on her futon. She put a bowl of cheese grits, turkey sausage, home-made biscuits, and herbal tea on a tray.

I asked, "You eating?"

"Can't. My bedtime. It would settle on my thighs."

She'd cooked for me. Good woman. I added sugar to my grits, stirred it up, ate.

I said, "You've lost some weight."

"Been working out a lot."

"Running?"

"Nah. Tae Bo."

"Where?"

"Billy Blanks's sister's class."

"Heard she was tough."

"She's a damn Nazi."

"You're toned."

"Been pushing weights after class too."

"Trying to get buffed?"

"Light weights. I don't want muscles."

She sat next to me, her leg touching and warming mine while I ate.

She asked, "You gonna tell me how you busted your head?"

"Slipped, tripped, and fell."

"Rrrright. Thought we were the kind of people who kept it real with each other."

Then I changed the subject, asked, "You still kicking it with . . . ?"

She shook her head and gave me a smile that said she didn't want to talk about *him*.

I waited a moment before I asked, "How've you been?"

"It's been rough." She shrugged. "Sick and tired of being sick and tired."

"What's the problem?"

"I'm lonely. Want to stop fucking and start making love."

Even with what I'd seen in her bathroom, her heartfelt words caught me off guard. Maybe the timing was bad, the personal shit in my head wouldn't let emotions settle in a place where I could handle this conversation. I nodded, kept my attention on my grits and sausage.

She rubbed my hand. "Sorry for rambling. It's just weighing heavy on my heart."

"It's cool. Everybody gets sick and tired of being sick and tired of something."

"I get really attached to people. The wrong people for the right reasons. That's just the way I'm made." She laughed at herself. "I don't have control of my emotional barometer."

I asked, "What's going on with you?"

"Did some things I'm not too proud of. Same old."

When I was done, she took my tray away, rinsed off the dishes. I walked up behind her, kissed her on her neck. Whatever she wore tasted like sugar, made me want to lick it all off.

She yawned, looking more bored than sleepy. "We gonna do something before you go?"

"You wanna?"

"I always wanna. And I know you didn't call me because you like my cheese grits."

She smiled but I could see the truth behind her eyes. She needed to get away, lose all thoughts and sense of time. Wanted me to do for her what she couldn't do for herself. Sometimes it felt like sex was a good way to mask deeper issues. Everybody was running from something. Sex was the easiest thing to run to, cheaper than alcohol. Nothing more soothing than scratching an itch. Sooner or later all that scratching made a wound, then a scab.

In my eyes Panther was young, beautiful, powerful.

Small breasts. Full lips. Tight eyes. Skin deep brown, baby smooth. Thick and curvy.

I kissed her neck. She cooed. I sucked her skin until she was hot as a thousand suns.

She moaned. "You do that, I lose my breath and my legs part like clouds."

I touched her, licked her shoulders and spine, got her riled up on the inside. I shouldn't have, but I pulled her boy shorts down, took her slow and easy right there. Real slow. Let her lose her breath over and over, let her have knowledge of me moving across every fold and ridge.

She pushed back into me and shivered like I was scraping against her soul.

My mind was stuck at a red light. I'd lost control of my life a long time ago, when I first heard those sirens and made a hard choice that would let Rufus remain free while I became the one in shackles. Panther has had a rough time too. When I first met her and she invited me into her private world, she'd tell me about Atlanta and its bosky landscape, about Club Vision, Phipps Plaza, Café Intermezzo, and a million streets named Peachtree.

She was lovesick, lonely, and confused. I was a passenger on the same road.

She used to call me when she was on her way home. For a while I used to kick it with her, was at her apartment over in Hawthorne a few nights a week. Panther loved to cook and hated eating alone. She'd throw down black-eyed peas, corn bread, and some of the best fried chicken I ever had, or catfish and yams, a different Southern meal each time. I'd bring Jack Daniel's for me, then have a six-pack of soda, Kool-Aid, Riesling, whatever she wanted. We'd eat, cuddle up, start rubbing each other's pain away the best we could, and we'd use each other.

One woman could kill a man's soul but a different woman had the power to make him feel alive, if only until sunrise. Damn shame how sunrise highlighted those problems again.

She got me through some rough nights.

Last night was rough for me. I was glad she called me back right after I was finished dealing with the lion and the jackal. After that phone call with Lisa, I needed a safe place to rest.

Panther was in love with a married man. I'd fallen for another man's wife. The only difference was I had given up my sin and she was hoping for hers to come back.

Panther was cool, a great woman from what I could see, but she wasn't the kind I'd get serious about. I still had fantasies of some

wholesome and trustworthy woman stumbling into my world. Doubt
if Panther's Southern-fried family wanted a divorced felon in their
family pictures. Bad boys didn't make good husbands. And I doubted
if a man wanted a wife who went off to the strip mines every night.
At some point that would create some problems.

But I liked her. Liked her too much for my own good.

Panther reminded me of my ex-wife. Maybe when I walked into
the strip mines to have a drink and saw her, I felt some sort of a
needed connection to my past. Not all ghosts were bad.

Panther took me to the futon, took charge and mounted me,
closed her eyes tight, bit and sucked her bottom lip, went into a slow
ride, whispered, "Too bad sex ain't a spectator sport."

"Why you say that?"

"You're good. Like the way you . . . get up on it like you own it."

"You should've met me twenty years ago."

"When I was in preschool?"

We laughed. Laughter made me flex inside her, she tightened
around me all at once. She moved the way she danced. Isolated body
parts. Matched my rhythm. Used her hips, moved in sort of a circu-
lar motion while moving back and forth. Tightened up like she was
doing kegels.

I slapped her backside, rubbed her Sankofa tattoo, squeezed her
flesh over and over.

She said, "You are so doggone mannish."

"You know you like it."

Her pheromones made me lose control. Made me wanna act like
I was in a Lexington Steele video and do some special things to her.
Don't know why we had that kinda chemistry.

She kept talking, swaying and sounding like she'd had two shots
of my friend Jack Daniel's. "Seems like forever since the last time I
had sex. I'm tighter than new braids."

Her sounds spread around the room.

She turned over, got on her knees, ass up high, that heart-shaped
backside looking good in the morning light. I rubbed her flesh, ran
my fingers over her Sankofa tattoo, held her waist.

"Damn, Driver . . . sweet Jesus, sweet Jesus. Driver. That's. My. Spot."

Couldn't count the number of times I'd had sex to see if I could still feel. The same way people hurt themselves to see if they were alive, I fell into the arms of nurturing women. I focused on pleasure instead of pain. For some people sex was the same as self-mutilation, and serial sex could be more anesthetizing than anything. It wasn't always about lust or getting over. Some of us had to be reminded that we could still feel. Even if it was just in our loins.

"I'm . . . coming . . . again . . . Driver . . . you are so hard . . . hurts so good . . . hurts so good."

Her left leg trembled and she held on to the sheets. She was intoxicated, in a good place.

"God, you're hard . . . that's it baby . . . *ooo* yeah . . . I feel you . . . come for me . . . come for me."

Electricity moved up and down my spine.

"That's it baby, take this pussy, take this pussy."

Heaven surrounded me.

"Mmmmmmhhhh. Oooooo. Driver."

She moaned so sweet. Her hands gripped the sheets, nails dug into the covers. I held her hair, spanked her, bit her, gave her measured strokes. But most of my mind was somewhere else, doing the quick math on my life, not liking the bottom line.

"Get it baby that's it get it baby Driver mmmmmmmm damn mmmhhhh."

Sweat dripped from my flesh. I grunted over and over. If I had a heart attack on the downstroke and died this morning, I'd die with nothing to show I'd ever lived.

I showered while Panther rested underneath the colorful quilt and soft sheets.

Tiredness heavied my eyes. Lisa wouldn't leave my mind.

Fifteen thousand in the hole.

I stared at the money scattered on Panther's dresser.

She moaned. "Nice suit. You're sexy as hell."

"Thanks."

"Dag, Driver. You sex so doggone good."

"That's your wild ass."

"You're the best I've ever been with."

"Yeah, you too."

"Now I'm blushing." Her smile was so broad. "Thanks."

"You feel it, respond to touches, kisses, not a boring lover."

She laughed. "Sex is only as good as the weakest partner."

"Well, you've raised my game."

On the dresser was the smoky money from her late-night hustle. We sexed each other every now and again, but I didn't know her in a way that would allow me to form my lips to ask for a loan, not even for one of those smoky greenbacks, let alone fifteen thousand. Sex was shared, company shared, but when it came to money, that was a lot of people's line in the sand.

I asked, "Know where I can get a burner?"

A burner was a gun. Hadn't had one in years. Never thought I'd need another one.

Without questioning me she yawned and asked, "What you looking for?"

"Something easy to hide with a decent kick."

"Something to stop a man or a mule?"

My fingers went to my fresh injury. "Both."

She became silent. That made me uncomfortable.

I went on, "I know a couple people, but they can't get what I need as fast as I need it."

"Why not ask them then?"

"One's dead. The other in jail."

The other truth was that I was a felon. I didn't have the right to bear arms anymore. I'd rather let Panther get me what I need instead of having to go out and get it. Too risky. And I knew she knew people. She worked at a strip club on the edges of Gardena and South Central and she had to know people with their ears to the streets, people who could find some heat.

I added, "I would check my connections at Back Biters, but I have to work this morning and nobody's up in that joint until late in the evening. Kinda need something quick."

Time leaned against the wall while I waited for her response. Outside of cheese grits and us pleasing each other, I didn't really expect her to help me out; I was throwing a Hail Mary.

She evaluated my injury before she whispered, "I'll ask around."

Time sighed and moved, went wherever it had to go.

A while later I touched her face. "What you said, you know, about being lonely . . ."

She took my hand. "It was nothing. Saw this documentary on Rita Hayworth yesterday. Four failed marriages, kids by two men, all the men she met either controlled her for money or just wanted her pussy, never found love, died of Alzheimer's. Shit made me sad, that's all."

"Panther . . ."

She shushed me like she wanted me to stop before I said something stupid. She took my hand, kissed my fingers and my palm, told me she'd call if she could get me what I needed, then told me to have a good day. Part of me ached. We never shared tongues. Wasn't that kind of party. Tongues were saved for lovers, everything else was open season. I knew the routine. Soap, clothes, cuff links, I did inventory and made sure I had everything I'd brought with me.

Panther's soft voice followed me. "Only two kinds of trouble in the world. Love trouble. Money trouble. You don't come across as a man with love problems. I'm going with the money trouble. Be careful, Driver. I don't look good dressed in all black, not when I'm crying."

I didn't say anything. Didn't think I was supposed to.

She ended her little speech with "Don't get dead on me. You're a nice guy."

The thing about a young girl was if you talked to a young girl long enough you realized that she was a young girl. She might have a mature moment, but somewhere along the line she digressed into being concerned with shit you haven't given a fuck about in the last twenty years.

Panther hadn't done that yet.

Overnight bag in hand, dressed in a fresh black Italian suit, white shirt, rimless glasses, spit-shined shoes, I locked the door on my way out, pulled it tight and stepped into the cool air.

The morning was dull and gray, as overcast as my mind. Fog strolled the beach cities. Temperature right at fifty degrees, but would be close to seventy by noon. Pick a freeway or a surface street and traffic was already a bear with PMS. Head ached, and add to that ache my dehydration—side effects from going drink-for-drink with Miss Baklava Glue, then sipping on that JD at Rufus's place, not to mention the lion and jackal—and I was in a pretty foul mood.

Don't get dead on me.

I asked myself why I was going to work. Why I bothered working for Wolf. My job wasn't much, but right now it was all I had. If that was taken away, I'd go back to being nobody. Just another lost soul wandering the piss-stained and dilapidated boulevards. Months ago there were no Italian suits, just living hand-to-mouth, nothing but borrowing and hustling.

I took out my phone, called Lisa's cellular. Got her voice mail. Hung up. Cursed.

I didn't worry about Wolf finding out it was me calling his wife. My number didn't show up because I had it blocked, only read RESTRICTED on her caller-ID. But she knew it was me.

7

The office and cars for Wolf Classic Limousines were on Century, right outside LAX.

I parked my car in the reserved underground section Wolf had for employees. Employee parking was on P2, one level below the spots he had for sedans and town cars.

Lisa's ugly-ass Hummer was there. Wolf's Lamborghini wasn't. They slept in the same bed but never rode in together. Nobody in L.A. rode together. Barren car-pool lanes told you that this was a city filled with selfish people. Maybe just people who didn't have any friends.

I put on my work face and went in to grab the keys and paperwork on the sedan I'd been assigned. The paperwork told me that I was picking up Thomas Marcus Freeman. I grabbed a marker and made a sign, my client's last name in block-style letters. While I did that I talked to a co-worker, Sid Levine. Thin boy who always wore the same jeans with a different T-shirt. Pimply face and orange spiked hair. He was a young cat, a UCLA student who maintained the computer systems. Time to time he came in at four in the morning to man the phones until the receptionist made it in. He could get some studying in while he clocked in a few dollars.

I told Sid I'd seen the Hummer in the garage, then asked, "Where's the boss's wife?"

"She had an early pick-up." He put his C++ book to the side, pulled up the sleeves on his tattered Old Navy sweatshirt. "A Michael Jackson impersonator."

I laughed. "Heard they weren't getting too much work these days."

"Not with all the child molestation charges." Sid shrugged. "I think this cat worked as one of Michael Jackson's decoys or something."

I redirected the conversation again. "So, the boss's wife is actually working."

"Surprised me too."

Everything seemed normal. Too normal. Like Disneyland. I kept talking to make it look like my asking about Lisa was no big deal. "What's that screen on your computer?"

"Updating the GPS software. Wolf got a new car in. Making sure GPS is on point. Easy stuff, grunt work." He showed me that one of Wolf's cars was in Sherman Oaks, another heading down the 5 to San Diego. "Wolf knows where all of his property is at all times."

I nodded. Wolf's system was tight. That electronic surveillance let him know if his drivers were exceeding the speed limit or if his car was going outside of boundaries. Reminded me of men and women on house arrest. They had the same electronic leash strapped to their ankles. They stepped too far beyond the front door and Big Brother was notified.

I said, "A man has to protect his investments."

"He's expanding his fleet big time. Gonna go head-to-head with Davel."

Sid talked about stretch limos, luxury cars, SUVs, fifteen-passenger vans, cargo vans, minibuses, even a couple of additional Cessnas that Wolf was acquiring to beef up his arsenal.

Jealousy made me clench my jaw tight.

A lot of the cars were already out there, picking up and dropping off. The system showed six cars were in the lot across the way. I'd

only seen three sedans and two stretch limos when I pulled in. I
peeped toward the front to see who had pulled up since I got here.

I held my breath and waited for Lisa to come inside. Nobody
walked in.

I asked, "Where is the boss's wife driving the impersonator?"

"Mrs. Wolf rolling a limo to San Diego. She'll be gone at least
four hours."

I sipped a cup of coffee, then stuck my head inside Wolf's office,
double-checked to see if he'd just shown up. Lisa's face stared back
at me. Her image and the pictures of Wolf's kids were on his desk.
His deceased parents were in bigger photographs on the wall.

This could've been my office. Those could've been my pictures.

"Nobody would suspect you." Lisa had guaranteed me that a few
months ago. *"We don't have any connection. If you kill him, you'll
be scot-free with thirty thousand in your pockets."*

That was before the suits. Before I became a hypocrite and took
this job.

That day I was at the laundromat, clothes in the dryer, my stomach
growling, and I was trying to decide if I was going to head down to
Yum Yum Donuts to buy a chocolate twist. That was down on
Crenshaw and Rodeo nestled inside a shopworn strip mall that held
Conroy's Flowers and Hamburger Haven. It was a corner where the
homeless parked their baskets and squatted on the concrete, where
beggars hustled at the Shell station and tried to come up on some
spare change by offering to wash car windows with nasty water and
dirty newspaper.

I stepped outside of the laundromat, moved through the drizzle
and saw her.

I'd seen her kicking it outside, dressed in a black business suit,
leaning against a black town car, umbrella in hand, talking to two
members from Los Angeles's most notorious gang, the LAPD. This
was one of their resting spots, on the backside of Conroy's facing
Yum Yum.

She saw me just as I made it to the doughnut shop. We caught eyes. I recognized her.

I knew she was the daughter of the man who used to be chief of police in Compton, then mayor of the same city. A man who had a reputation that would make Suge Knight cringe. He was to Compton what Tom Bradley had been to L.A., only he had a lot of scandal.

The black-and-white pulled away, sirens blaring as they hit the strip hard and fast, screeching and swerving. Quiet as it's kept, cops were the worst drivers in L.A. Lisa hit the remote on the car she was driving, stepped over loosened asphalt, and came inside Yum Yum. I'd copped a table facing the parking lot, had a crossword puzzle and a pencil in front of me. She grabbed a chocolate twist and an orange juice. Spoke to me. I did the same. I put my crossword puzzle away and offered her a seat. She told me her name was Lisa. I already knew that.

Lisa said, "You know who you look like?"

"Somebody on the wall at the post office?"

She laughed. "Alonzo Mourning. That's why I kept looking at you."

"Quit trippin'. I don't look anything like Alonzo."

"You do to me."

She asked me what I did. Back then I was doing what I could. Installing water heaters, fixing relief valves, installing smoke detectors, landscaping, didn't matter. I didn't like living life the hard way, but I took it the way it came. Some days it was steak. Some days ground beef.

She said, "Saw you down by Slauson last week. You were going in the post office."

"Yeah. I went up there to see if I could get a job licking stamps."

She laughed. "Licking stamps. Sounds . . . interesting."

"Work is work."

"What kind of work you do?"

"Right now, anything I can find. You know how hard it is to get a legit job when you have a felony on your record. Everybody keeps looking at you like you're a criminal."

She laughed.

We talked. No rapid fire, crudely poetic, vernacular dialogue. Just talked like two people who had roots in the concrete jungle. Only I had gone to public school and she went from being a Montessori baby to a private-school child. Money was never an issue in her home, not like it was in mine. Didn't take much talking to realize she was headstrong and political, just like her parents. She flipped through a *Watts Times* and got on the subject of how deregulation had killed black radio in L.A., then about how Wal-Mart was killing the revenue at the mom-and-pop stores on the strip. All in all, it was the type of small talk people had when they were feeling each other out. She was trying to see what kind of man I was. I'd already put a hint of my past on the table. A man who wanted to work but had no real job. I saw her five-carat issue sparkling on her left hand. She leaned away, kept her body language professional, but the way she gazed at her ring, then looked at me, told me that her and hubby got along like Shaq and Kobe.

She said, "You fix things that are broken?"

"I'm a decent handyman."

She put her business card on the table. Told me to call her on her cellular.

I understood.

Seven days later she was in my bed. We'd talked a few times, then I asked her to meet me up at the Ladera Center, thought we could chill on the patio outside of Magic Johnson's Starbucks, where the community went to flirt and loiter. That was a no-go. She wanted to come to my crib, didn't want to do anything in public. She parked in the back alley, did that so her ride couldn't be seen, came into my place, kissing me, taking her clothes off, taking charge. Hunger in her eyes and the way she moved her body. My apartment wasn't too far from LAX. She could swoop this way, stay an hour or two, and get back home before she had any missing hours.

She told me, "Wanted you so bad."

"I could tell. Man, I could tell."

"Haven't had sex in at least two months."

"What's wrong?"

"Hubby's never really sexual. His ex-wife told me the same thing happened with her. They had kids and he works a lot. The funny thing is, I used to think he was unusual, but a lot of married people complain about the same thing. Same exact thing."

She rambled, guess she did that because she had some sort of sexual remorse. She justified what we'd done, told me that her husband had had an affair. I didn't ask for the details.

We sat up, ate snacks, and talked about politics. Smart woman. That excited me.

She told me, "We lost the revolution."

"When did we lose? I didn't even know we'd reached halftime."

"Game was over when the white man figured out how to make us stop fighting."

"How did he do that?"

"He gave us a few jobs. Our people got a little change in their pockets and forgot about the Middle Passage. My daddy understood that. Understood people. He used to tell me that black people weren't loyal to the black community, not on the level we should be, not on a level that makes a real difference, not like the Jewish people on the other side of town. We're loyal to whatever improves our own economic condition on a personal level, not as a culture."

"I'm not buying that."

"Well, when a black person prefers to buy a new car over a house, you tell me. Image over substance, immediate gratification over economic longevity."

Then she invited me to her pad. The house her husband had bought. Bold, even for me.

Lisa squatted in Hancock Park. Lounged in an eight-bedroom estate that was built back in the forties. The kind of place that had an enclosed tropical backyard set off with five different types of palm trees, a steam room the size of a small home, and a guesthouse larger than most three-bedroom apartments. All that and a swimming pool that was bigger than my rented nest.

Hancock Park was the real deal. Old money. Bankers. Music moguls. Real celebrities.

Lots of dirty money. Blood money. Honesty never got anybody to the top.

Her supersized crib was on Plymouth, north of Wilshire and south of 5th, on a strip of two-story Spanish- and Mediterranean-style homes that looked like mansion row. The streets were wider, the yards bigger. An area where it seemed like you could shake the palm trees and watch hundred-dollar bills float to the ground. This side of town made the affluent black people congregated in areas like Baldwin Hills and Ladera Heights look like paupers. The girl who grew up on the other side of Wilshire had done well, had come up like a motherfucker.

We talked about her husband. His name always came up. I made sure it did.

"He bounces to Vegas once, maybe twice a month." She told me that. "Flies up there for the weekend. Does the part-time daddy thing."

"Racking up the frequent-flier miles."

"He has his own plane."

"He charters?"

"No, he flies. Has a Cessna Skyhawk. Leather seats. The whole shebang."

"How much that set you back?"

"About two hundred thousand."

"Damn. Can't you get a used one? With fabric seats?"

"He keeps it parked at Hawthorne Airport."

I ran my tongue over my teeth. "He can fly you anywhere."

"I have my pilot's license too."

"That's tight. Mansion. Planes. A damn Lamborghini."

"One plane, not planes."

"Y'all are balling out of control."

She tisked. "Money doesn't buy happiness."

"Well, it's nice to be able to pick where you're gonna be miserable."

We were in her heated pool. Naked. Adam and Eve. Swimming laps under the moonlight, her husband gone to Las Vegas to see his kids. I'd parked a block away and crept down in the darkness, didn't get there until close to midnight.

She said, "I wish it was like this all the time."

"What you mean?"

"Just me and you."

"That would be cool."

"I want to divorce him."

"Why don't you?"

She clasped and unclasped her hands, told me that her husband had her in an airtight prenuptial agreement. She walked and the fairy tale ended, she'd have to give up everything except her socks and drawers. All she would be entitled to was what she came in the front door with. Wouldn't even get to keep her half of their season tickets to the Lakers. Compared to what she had now, what she brought to the table was a sack of crumbs.

I looked around at her world. Sat on the edge of her pool and looked at a tropical paradise filled with guesthouses, steam rooms, swimming pools, and maids that showed up three times a week to dust and cook and clean and pick up every crumb that was left on the floor.

We moved the party to the back of the grounds. I followed Lisa's naked sashay, water raining from her skin, and we stepped into a Jacuzzi big enough for fifteen people. Waterfalls were all I could hear. Warm water all I could feel. Lisa went underwater, took me in her mouth. I touched her hair while she made love to me, touched her hair and gazed up at the waterfalls, at the enclosed yard, then at the house, through glazed-over eyes I stared at that castle.

She came back up smiling.

I nodded. "Yeah. Would be hard to give this up."

"The only way I'd get to keep this, to keep all of this and have you . . ."

I paused. Waited for her to finish wiping water from her face and give me her words.

She said, "I keep hoping that his fucking plane will crash on the way to Vegas or back. Double indemnity would kick in and the postman wouldn't even have to ring my bell."

I didn't say anything. Her tone told me how serious she was. That shit was disturbing.

Point blank, she asked, "Ever killed anybody?"

I swallowed, took a hard breath. "Beat a few motherfuckers down."

"How bad?"

"Sent a few busters to the hospital."

"You hurt a lot of people when you were in jail?"

"Didn't fight as much on lockdown, not after that first couple of fights got me respect. That's about it."

"Never killed?"

I skipped my answer. "What about you?"

"Shot a couple of gangbangers." She said that like it was no big deal. "That was in my rookie year. One came at me with a butcher knife. The other wouldn't put down his weapon."

"That's self-defense."

"Hell yeah. I was scared as fuck. You have no idea how scared I was. It's one of our basic instincts. Self-preservation kicks in and you do what you have to do to survive."

I thought about self-preservation. Doing what I had to do to survive.

I asked, "You go out on stress?"

"Yeah. I did."

"Therapy?"

"For what? I just wanted to take some time off and chill. I went to Europe."

My eyes went to hers. There was coldness in her eyes. Like someone who had been shoved around too much, too long. She created an instant smile and that coldness turned warm.

She said, "Twenty thousand. How does that sound? Like a fair price?"

"You serious?"

"This could work. Like strangers on a train, we have no connection. No e-mails. No faxes. When you come by here, you come at
night and leave while it's still dark."

"Yeah, I'm your phantom fuck. Your backdoor lover. I don't exist."

"Not to anybody but me. Hardly a phone call between us. You
don't come on the days that the maid comes. Nobody sees you.
They're too busy nurturing their own indiscretions."

I went silent. Looked around at her paradise. Asked myself if I'd
kill to have it.

She said, "You could do a lot with twenty thousand. It would be
tax-free money, so that's the equivalent of thirty large."

"Not like I'd notify the IRS."

"What would you do if you had that much money? I'm talking
cash money."

For a man like me, twenty thousand was a million dollars.

I said, "Sit on it until hard times got softer."

Momma needed some financial relief. She had been up and down
since Reverend Daddy died. Living off public assistance. Rufus, he
wasn't doing well, wasn't really working, living off Pasquale, taking
experimental drugs. That money could help a lot with a few of his
bills.

"Could be a good start."

"Yeah. Could be."

"Or better yet, you could stack your chips. Try and buy a house."

I mumbled out my dreams. "Yeah, buy a house. Get up on some
real estate."

"Real estate is a win-win."

I nodded my agreement. Thought about getting that money and
moving east, as far as San Bernardino, where property was cheaper,
get away from every-fucking-body that had dragged me down, then
felt bad for thinking about myself, nobody but myself.

She said, "That's where the money is. Property. You're a good
handyman. Maybe buy something, do the repairs yourself, and flip
it. Do that once or twice, you'd be rolling."

"Yeah. I could buy something and flip it. Double, hell, triple my investment in a year."

"Well? Twenty thousand. How does that sound?"

"That could help me come up big time."

She smiled like she was nothing but sunshine. "I want you to come up."

"Why?"

"Because I love you, baby."

"How would you get up on that much cash without raising a red flag?"

She laughed and shook her head. I'd forgotten who I was talking to. It was all relative. When people lived in houses like these, that kind of mad money was stuck in a sock drawer.

I went back to the pool, swam a few more laps, and thought about it. Twenty large. In my world that was a lot of money. Momma and Reverend Daddy never had that much money, barely made much more than that in a good year. I'd never held that much money, not all at once. Had never seen those kind of digits standing side-by-side, not in my checking account.

Lisa had come out of the Jacuzzi, was sitting on the edge of the pool.

I got out on the opposite side, away from her, thinking about self-preservation.

She kicked water my way, asked, "You love me?"

I nodded. Too much was on the table. Wasn't time for a broke man to shake his head.

She swam to me. Kissed my neck down to my penis, took me in her mouth again, did all of that without warning. Her mouth was warm, her movements smooth. It took a moment, things were on my mind, but I rose hard and strong. Moaned with my hand in her wet hair, watched that part of me vanish into her face, then reappear, then vanish, reappear.

She moaned. "We could be like this every day."

She stroked me with her hand, smiled and watched my expression.

Skills. She had skills. When I told her that I was about to come, she took me in her mouth, made greedy sounds, swallowed all I had to give. She kept going until I was drained, became too sensitive. Had to hold her face and ask her to stop. She bathed me with her tongue before she moved away.

She rested her head in my lap, her smile wide and hot.

She said, "To be honest, I miss being with . . . with a black man. You have no idea. I need you. I need your history, your pains, I need you to give me all that and let me give you mine."

"Why the white boy?"

"Dunno. Think I was going through a phase. You know, fuck what people think. Mad at black men. Done with black men. I mean, this white guy stumbled into my world and—"

"Stumbled?"

"Before I left LAPD I caught him speeding and running a red light down Crenshaw and Adams. Wolf was polite, but came on strong. Took my badge number. Sent me flowers."

"Drove you around in his Lamborghini."

"Yup. Took me to his house in Vegas. On the way we hit that strip between Barstow and Vegas and opened that bitch up. By the time we zoomed out I-15 and passed by the Zzyzx exit sign, we were moving like a jet plane. He let me gun it all the way to Baker."

I reached over, rubbed her breast. "Bet that made your panties wet."

"Sure did. It was orgasmic. Then he took me to the track and let me run it. You haven't lived until you run a Lamborghini on a track."

"And the Cessna . . ."

"Multi-orgasmic."

"Treated you like you were Cinderella."

"Australia. Paris. I'd never been treated like that. Treated me better than my daddy. The only thing that bothered me was that he wasn't . . ." She motioned at her complexion.

I said, "You knew that going in."

"And he lied."

"The affair?"

"What he called his 'momentary lapse in faithfulness.' "

I nodded. "He fucked around."

"I think that was inevitable. All women expect that at some point. He's handsome. Rich. We all expect men to be men." Her eyes darkened, became those of a woman scorned. "What hurt me was . . . when the affair came out he slipped and confessed something else."

"What?"

She shook her head. "I don't like being fucked over. Not at all."

"What did he confess?"

"I told him that he could've gotten that bitch pregnant and he told me that there was no way for that to happen." She laughed an angry laugh, an intense laugh, the bitter kind that showed the dark side of a person's soul. "He'd had a vasectomy after his first divorce. He can't have kids. Here I am trying to get pregnant, thinking that something's wrong with me . . ."

"Damn."

"He'd been acting like he was all for us having a baby. Had me paranoid, walking around thinking my shit was fucked up."

I chuckled at the man's brilliance. "He got his nuts cut on the DL."

"I knew about his court-ordered child support, about his divorce, about his property, his cars, knew everything before the first date. No lawsuits. No bankruptcies. Clean as hell. He didn't even have a speeding ticket. I found out all I could about him, but that got by me."

"No tickets. You didn't write him up?"

She smiled.

I went on, "You knew everything *before* the first date? What's up with that?"

She ran her hand across her hair. "Nothing. Skip it."

I told her, "You ran a background check on the white boy."

"Damn right. Of course. But not everything shows up when you run background."

"Not medical."

She nodded, then shook her head. "Not medical."

I asked, "You run background on all the men you date?"

She nodded my way. "Memphis. Your wife and brother were with you. They found a hundred pounds of marijuana and fifty thousand in cash in your Explorer. Trafficking. You would've done at least six years, but you had a good attorney, jails were overcrowded, your crime was nonviolent, had a clean record, a first-time offender, got away with doing two years."

I stared at her. A very uncomfortable stare. She'd been swimming in my Kool-Aid.

She said, "It's public record. Can be pulled on the Department of Corrections Web site."

I let her words ride. The reason I'd never be allowed to vote was available to anybody with access to cyberspace. God bless the Internet. It was my record, but it wasn't the truth.

She went back to talking about her husband, voiced her own angst while I marinated in mine, said, "So, with the prenuptial that says none of this is mine, and since he can't get me pregnant, won't consider having a child anytime soon, you know how that shit makes me feel?"

I cleared my throat. "Tell me."

"Like a whore. Makes me feel like I'm here just to service him. I'm nobody's whore. What he's done . . . the lies . . . how he's bamboozled me . . . people get killed over crap like that."

"What was his excuse?"

"Oh, please. He said he could have it reversed when he was ready. When *he* was ready." Her anger had tripled. "I'm forty. I'm not twenty-five. You know what I'm saying?"

I nodded. "You're serious about . . . him having an accident."

"I'm serious, accident or otherwise."

I took a deep breath, let it out slow and easy.

Her frown deepened, made her skin wrinkle and look ten years older as she gazed around at the topography. "You don't know how hard this is."

"How hard what is?"

"I gave up my job. Quit the force to be his wife and help him run his business. Wanted to have a normal life, come correct and devote myself to him, be old-fashioned, let him lead."

I sat up. Put my feet in the warm water, moved them back and forth.

She sat up, leaned against me. "I don't like being fucked over."

Time crept by on the edge of a cool breeze. She rubbed my back, my shoulders.

I said, "I don't like being fucked over either. Don't like people playing Dick Tracy."

"Are you mad because I know about your record?"

I didn't answer, just asked, "What happens if he gets killed, accident or otherwise?"

"He's covered. Insurance pays off the house."

"His kids?"

"His kids are taken care of, but so am I."

"Then?"

"Life goes on."

"That simple, huh?"

"Then, after I dry my eyes, all I'll need is a king. A queen in a castle like this, a king will be all I need. I'll be able to afford everything. But a woman can't do everything by herself. I'll just need somebody to give me beautiful and strong babies. Somebody to be here and be Daddy."

I glanced around. You got invited into a playground like that and it was hard to unplug yourself and go back to your own reality. I'd been in prison. I'd grown up on the shopworn side of L.A. and stolen to put food on the table. This was the picture-perfect life we all wanted. You wanted them fucking palm trees, that damn pool, the Jacuzzi, the eight bedrooms. You wanted the woman. You wanted all of that shit. I'd savored another man's wine and loved its flavor.

Lisa kissed me. "Love you."

"Love you back."

She pulled me on top of her, put me inside her. I moved slow and easy. Moved like that until her back arched, an orgasm heated her spine, and she sent her soft message to the moon.

She caught her breath, held onto me, whispered, "You come?"

"Nah."

"Don't. Save it for me."

We went into the steam room. She rubbed me down with a sugar scrub, massaged me, cleansed me, then took me in her mouth again. Got me firm then mounted me. She was on fire, horny as hell, filled with desire to please. Had me whimpering, moaning, holding her ass. She came strong then went down to her knees again, took me back in her mouth, licked me like I was made of candy. I vanished. Reappeared. She wouldn't stop until I came again. Came so hard.

She swallowed my seeds, posted up her wide smile again. "Love the way you taste."

I couldn't talk. Hadn't caught my breath.

The steam was so thick we could barely see each other. She adjusted the settings, did the same with the temperature on both the side and overhead showerheads.

I said, "What you're talking about . . . killing a man . . . that shit ain't easy."

"As easy as we make it."

"I was locked up with men who thought putting somebody in the dirt was a good idea."

"Those were stupid people. I used to be a cop. Still am in my head."

"Lot of cops are on lockdown. Ask Rafael Perez."

"I know what to do, how to do it. Keep it simple."

"The simple art of murder ain't that simple."

"It can be. Christmas, he sends everybody home. Stays at the office a little while to make sure everything is cool. Then forwards all calls to a service. He gets killed in his office."

I ask, "On Christmas?"

"You're agnostic. It's just another day to you."

"But still . . . Christmas?"

"When everybody has their spirits up and guards down. Make it

look like a robbery at Christmas. Shoot him. Stab him. Drown him.
I don't care as long as it gets done."

"Shooting him would draw attention."

"Stab him O.J. style. I can show you how to do it."

It was getting hot.

She whispered, "Like you said, you're my backdoor lover. A
phantom. You'd never be a suspect. A year from now your nights
will begin with blow jobs followed by a lavish dinner."

"Is that right?"

She nudged me and gave up a short, erotic laugh. "I'll be sucking
your dick to put you to sleep then sucking it again to wake you up to
have breakfast in bed."

"You're gonna cook for a brother?"

"No. I'll order in. Me and the kitchen ain't friends like that."

"What would I have to do? What would fair exchange be?"

"Just give me babies." She sounded small, vulnerable. "Love me
like I love you."

"I can do that."

"You love me?"

I nodded. "Love you."

I wanted to have a kid too. I'd had a stepson. My ex-wife had
been a package deal. I was getting older, looking at forty in the mirror like it was an evil bastard. Hard to get a job at forty, let alone get
one with one big strike on your record. Old age was creeping up on
me. Old age and no real promises to better my situation. People
looked at a man like me and thought I didn't feel. I felt every-fucking-
thing. I just wasn't allowed to show it and still be called a man.

We left the steam room. Went into the house. Antique mirrors.
Artfully stacked books. Chinese carpets. Chandeliers. Marble every-
thing. Pictures of her and her husband standing with celebrities like
George Clooney and Magic Johnson decorated the family room.
What caught my eye were the pictures of his two kids, Brandon and
Fiona, ages five and seven. The little boy looked like Wolf with a black
man's skin. The little girl could pass, go either way.

Lisa dried her feet on the carpet, grabbed bottled water from the kitchen, then took me upstairs to one of the guest bedrooms. Never to her marriage bed. That didn't bother me. The bedroom she took me to had golden walls, vibrant pictures, and red velvet curtains. The room should've been in a museum, or in a Harlem brownstone.

She said, "Twenty-five thousand? How does that sound?"

Her rich words made me swallow the last of my debilitated morals.

I sucked on my bottom lip a while, came back and said, "How thirty sound?"

Thirty could help Momma and Rufus and still leave me in a position to get up on some property, at least a one-bedroom condo. I expected Lisa to balk, at least cock her head like the RCA Victor dog and make a Scooby-Doo sound. She didn't blink twice. Maybe because what was a lot of money to me wasn't a lot of money to her. My fortune was her chump change. Maybe because it wasn't her money she was spending anyway. And I didn't think she was serious, just angry and testing me. She had too much to lose.

She said, "In Egypt, back in the day, they used to consummate a deal with sex."

She pulled her damp hair away from her face and took me in her mouth again. Did that until I got hard again. I didn't get as hard as before. It felt good, but I didn't bust a nut.

She made a sad face. "The pump's still working, but the well is dry."

"Pretty much."

She kissed my dick like it was her prom date, pulled the covers back and we cuddled.

I yawned. "Let me rest about an hour and I'll bounce. Cool?"

She was quiet for a moment, then she asked, "Want to drive his Lamborghini?"

I chuckled. "You serious?"

"Stay the night. In the morning you can follow me down to the quarter-mile track."

I licked my lips, imagined being in that car. "What's your time on the quarter-mile?"

"Eleven." Her wide grin told me she was proud. "I have to trust myself and stop holding back on the curves. Pedal-to-the-metal on the straightaway."

"I've never driven like that, not on a track, so I'd probably come in at eighteen."

"Way too high." She yawned and laughed at me. "You can do better."

She got up and went to another part of the estate, came back with a McDonald's bag. She dumped the contents on the bed. Stacks of twenties. It was a hellified Happy Meal. I sat up with a quickness, touched it. Put my hands all over that salvation. My heart sped up.

She took the money away, put it back in the McDonald's bag, vanished into another room, then came back, money gone, her naked silhouette easing between the sheets again.

I asked, "How much was that?"

"Around fifteen large. Good faith money."

The texture from that money had my fingers tingling.

I asked, "The other half as soon as it's done?"

She nodded, her expression as dark as her intentions. I remembered looking around at all they owned and thinking I'd short-changed myself. Should've asked for forty. Maybe fifty.

We didn't say anything else.

Then she smiled. "Forgot. I bought you a present."

She hopped up and went downstairs, her feet moving pretty fast over the hardwood floor. She came back with a small bag. Clicked on a light again. The bag had a red bow on it.

Inside was a cellular phone. I didn't have one. Needed one.

I asked, "What's the occasion?"

"And I know this Asian guy downtown. He has suits for next-to-nothing. I ordered you a couple of Italian suits. Hope you don't mind. All you have to do is go pick them up."

I crawled on top of her. Kissed her. Eased deep inside another man's wife.

She moaned. "I thought the well was dry."

"The well might be dry, but the pump is still working."

"Be rough with me. Take it. Choke me . . . tighter. Oh . . . like . . . that . . . I'm . . . coming."

By nine the next morning I had breakfast in bed. Lisa had ordered from one of the restaurants on Larchmont. She ordered every meal we ate. By noon we were down in El Toro, away from L.A., the heart of Orange County. We were out on an old abandoned military airport. The landing strips had been converted into a track. All morning she let me run the hell out of that Lamborghini, the ultimate phallic machine. Drove that bitch like she was my own.

Driving a man's car. Swimming in a man's pool. Fucking a man's wife.

I started to want that kinda life. Started to believe I deserved it.

I'd been through enough bullshit in my life. I was tired. Yeah, I deserved it.

Things changed the night I went to kill Lisa's husband.

"Jingle Bells" playing on the radio. Streets lit up. People waiting for Santa.

Gun resting in the small of my back.

What did we start talking about? Midnight. Christmas Eve. A black man. A white man. Grim reaper. Victim. When it started out you saw race. America taught you that race was always there. Race was as obvious as the weather. And harder than traffic on the 405.

Wood-paneled office. Picture of him and Lisa smiling at me.

Images of his ancestors and children on his walls.

Momma, barely dead.

I walked in that office and saw a drunken man who had been destroyed from the inside out. A pint of rum was on his desk, most of that gone. He was alone, but it looked like he was waiting for somebody.

He slurred, "What can I do for you?"

I asked, "Jason Wolf?"

"Jason Wolf is dead."

"Who are you?"

"Jason Wolf, that's my father's name. I'm Jason Wolf, Jr."

He sat back when he said that, stared at all the pictures around him. He was drunk, but he was calm. Death had walked in his door and the man sat back and sipped his rum.

He said, "My family, they keep an eye on me."

I nodded. My momma had just died. No one to watch over me.

He offered, "Drink?"

I saw that amber-colored liquid and it was like he was offering me another memory. I shook my head. Thought he was doing that to fuck with me. He didn't know my past pains. He seemed so small, so damn harmless. Not like a man who needed to be in the ground.

I said, "These your people?"

Wolf told me about his people, first his grandparents, then his parents, how they admired the politically correct in this country, the ones who went against social mores and allowed black people to eat in their homes. He'd come from a land that never had a black man as a slave. I couldn't hold him accountable for what other people had done. We talked about history. About places like Philadelphia, Mississippi, about the Choctaw Nation, places where my people had come from. We talked about injustice. Civil rights being violated by the enemies of peace.

He was three sheets to the wind. Depressed. Talkative. A man with burdens.

A man had appeared in his office and he didn't care.

I had hesitated. Had stood here with a gun ready to be pulled out, and hesitated.

People talked when they didn't want to kill. Did the same when they didn't want to die.

In the end he said, "You ever need a job, come talk to me."

"Just letting you know, I have a felony."

"It's my company. I hire who I want to hire."

That sounded better than the fifteen large I had waiting for me at home.

Other things were said. A lot of it I couldn't remember.

Momma had died. Her body hadn't turned cold yet. I didn't want to deal with that.

Life was a fog. Couldn't see past the next bend in the road.

Wolf looked up at me, his eyes deep red, bloodied.

He said, "Prison, huh?"

I nodded. Right then I was going to reach for my gun, end this business transaction.

Thou shalt not commit adultery. Thou shalt not steal. Thou shalt not bear false witness against thy neighbor. Thou shalt not covet thy neighbor's wife. I'd broken most, if not all, of the last half of the rules etched in the Decalogue. Thou shalt not kill was still up for grabs.

He struggled to clear his throat, ran his hand over his hair. It was down, not in that smooth ponytail. In the voice of a dying man he said, "Tell me about your prison."

My prison.

He said that and aroused fragments of memory. Sounds went away and I heard the batons raking against the prison bars. Anger and fear and blood in every wall. The faces. Old. Young. The innocent and guilty were all guilty. Faces lined in fear. Faces lined in hate. Some adjusted to being prisoners the same way some of our ancestors had adjusted to being slaves, not out of weakness but out of self-preservation. You either adapted or you died a horrible death.

I said, "Prison is corrosive. What it doesn't corrode it swallows up."

"Love does the same thing. Did you know that?"

Other things were said, his confession to having an affair, then his analogy about a woman never forgiving a man being in the middle of his rambling conversation. Think the man needed somebody to talk to. His money couldn't buy away the burden on his shoulders.

Not long after one in the morning my cellular phone rang.

I answered without looking at the caller-ID.

No hello on her end. Lisa simply asked, "You get my Christmas present?"

I held the phone for a moment, that gun in the small of my back.

I hung up.

The beginning of the end.

I should've given Rufus the lion's share of that money, then taken the rest and done like W.E.B. Dubois and Stokely Carmichael, quit America, gone to Paris or Africa, become an expatriate.

I stood up. "Have to go. Family problems."

Then he said, "Read this poet once. Fontaine. He said every man was three men. Who people think he is. Who he thinks he is. And who he really is."

He said that like he didn't know which he was. My expression mirrored his.

He said, "Merry Christmas. Or Happy Kwanzaa. Whatever you celebrate."

I nodded.

He said, "Well, you ever need work, stop by and see me."

I made it as far as his door before I turned back to him, to those red-rimmed eyes.

He told me, "You might pay your debt to society, but your record will never be clear. That's like asking your wife to forgive you for cheating on her."

All of that rushed through my head, replayed itself in less than two blinks.

Right now Wolf's pictures stared up at me. His family. The photo of his wife did the same. Thirty large could've been mine. I could've walked away with a poor man's lottery.

I could've walked away with this entire business.

That goddamn desk could've been mine by now. That fucking house could've been where I slept at night. I might even have had a few flying lessons out at Hawthorne airport, could've been cruising like a top gun high over the Hollywood sign in a bona fide Cessna.

If Rufus hadn't called me while I was on the way and told me that

Momma had just died, if I hadn't stalked into this dimly lit office and seen a shell of a man, if I didn't have memories of an ex-wife who had abandoned me, left me feeling the way Wolf was looking . . .

Damn, Rufus. Damn the way he's screwed up my life at every turn.

Maybe I was a fool. Maybe I was a coward. Maybe I realized it was easier to kill a man in your mind that it was in real life. It ain't easy to kill a man. Maybe I was the kind of man who would rather build his castle brick-by-brick than kill for it.

I went to Wolf's desk, snatched up a pen to use today, then closed his door behind me.

Two more co-workers had shown up, both milling around before they grabbed a sedan. Margaret Richburg was one of them. She was middle-aged, a retired schoolteacher, the driving thing being her supplemental income. Portly woman with graying hair and a warm disposition. Like everybody else, she asked about my head wound. I gave vague answers and moved on.

Margaret said, "I see Wolf pulled me from picking up Thomas Marcus Freeman."

"Sorry about that."

"Oh, please. I drove that asshole last year."

"That bad?"

"Made me want to run off the road."

"What this cat Freeman do?"

"God, had me picking up women as soon as I dropped one off. Even wanted to go by a swinger's place up in the valley. Some place he'd heard about in Sherman Oaks. Houghmandy or something like that."

"You're talking about Houghmagandy."

"Figured you would know."

"Don't hate. Houghmagandy means fornication in . . . forgot the language."

"That's the place, smart-ass."

I laughed. "Swinging. I heard that. What, he a movie star or a rapper?"

"Neither. Writer."

"Songwriter? Screenplays? Bad checks? What does he write?"

"Books. He's supposed to be one hot ticket."

"I can handle him. S'pose to be a short day. Pick 'em up. Drop 'em off."

All of us chatted, then I peeped over Sid's shoulder on my way out. His screen still showed six cars resting in the lot. When I made it to the garage, there were still only five.

8

An hour later I was at LAX, terminal five, waiting next to a column at the bottom of the escalators that led to baggage claim for Delta Airlines, Smarte Carte at my side. My head ached. My mind was stuck on what I'd gone through last night. Hoped I wasn't bleeding. Hoped I didn't have to break down and go to urgent care and get sewn up. Was hoping a lot.

It was a busy day, level orange alert.

A news van from KCOP pulled up curbside. Since I doubted if Bin Laden was flying in, somebody like Beyoncé or Halle Berry had to be rolling through. With my head hurting, I didn't give a care if Jesus had come back and was being escorted by Elvis, Martin, and Malcolm.

A crowd came down the escalator. I put my sign up.

A woman on the crowded escalator caught my eye. She owned the complexion of chocolate caramel Ghirardelli and had well-defined facial features, all small and keen. Long legs, short torso, those legs hidden behind faded jeans. A long-sleeved blouse that showed some cleavage, comfortable and sexy in a conformist way. Long hair in a single braid. Coming down like an angel from heaven. Nobody noticed her. It was almost like she was invisible.

She glanced at me, caught my eyes for no longer than a heartbeat, shifted like she felt a wave of heat down below, then looked away from me.

On her marriage finger she wore a rock. Her ring sparkled like old money, ski trips in Canada, and vacations in the Hamptons. My eyes went down, took in her shoes. They were expensive, but they were boxy, the kind of kicks you wore when you wanted to be unnoticed.

She moved on by, stopped not too far away from me.

Any other day I might've made a subtle play for her. Might've handed her a business card, my cellular number circled in red. Not today. That wasn't my disposition.

About two minutes went by. A dark-skinned brother appeared. Medium build. Five-seven, five-eight at the most. He sported a thin goatee and a unibrow that reminded me of old-school crooner Al B. Sure! Three dimes and a quarter made up his entourage: two black, two white, all had carry-on luggage. He was talking to them and signing their books like he was a literary rock star. I raised my sign, THOMAS FREEMAN printed in block letters.

The dark-skinned brother nodded, then went back to his fan club.

I tore my sign in half.

The client had on Levi's, Nikes, and a white T-shirt that read TRUTH IS STRONGER THAN LIES in red lettering, and WWW.THOMAS MARCUSFREEMAN.COM right below that in black, red, and green letters. And he had a silver briefcase handcuffed to his right wrist. If he had been suited up, I would've thought he was CIA carrying top secret documents.

I met him at the bottom of the escalator, smiled and said, "Mr. Freeman?"

He raised a finger, waggled it in my face. "It's *Freeeeeee-Man*."

Asshole pronounced his last name like it was two words. Said *Freeeeeee-Man* like the Emancipation Proclamation was written for him and the rest of us were still in shackles.

My lips went up into a bullshit smile, the kind that hid thoughts. He asked, "They send a stretch limo?"

"Sedan."

"What? You gotta be joking."

The news crew came inside. The reporter was a thin high-yellow sister, the kind L.A. employed. She wasn't attractive. Thin plus high-yellow wasn't an equation for beauty. She had a book in her hand, Freeman's solemn picture on the back. I got out of the way, let them talk, overheard them telling Freeman that they were almost ready to tape. Freeman pulled out a small mirror, checked his teeth, wiped that unibrow, got ready to snag his fifteen minutes of fame.

Again, I moved out of the way, checking my watch. I had to get out of here. Had to try and come up with that earnest money. Or maybe I should just have hurried upstairs with the little cash I had and bought a one-way ticket to the farthest destination I could afford.

But a man never ran from his problems. Reverend Daddy taught us that. He used to make me and Rufus hit the heavy bag for hours. He made us do all kinds of manual labor, which was why I was decent with fixing cars and a pretty good handyman. He did that to give us a strong backbone, but I think he was harder than most because of Rufus. He figured being a slave master would make men out of both of us. Momma never stopped him from his heavy-handed disciplinary ways. She looked at her baby boy and hoped for the same thing.

I took another hard breath when the reporter addressed Freeman. "They are boycotting you at the independents here in Los Angeles, and there was an incident in St. Louis—"

"They should boycott Jayson Blair, the man who set *real* writers back a hundred years."

My cellular rang. I pulled it out. The caller-ID read OUT OF AREA. I didn't answer.

People bumped into me. Digital cameras came out of nowhere. The paparazzi started flashing. Crowds were addicted to celebrity, even if they didn't know who the celebrity was.

My cellular rang again. Same OUT OF AREA caller.

I answered by saying my name. "Driver."

A soft voice. "What happened to your head?"

I paused, held in my urge to bark and curse. "Who is this?

"Why are you agnostic?"

I paused. "Arizona?"

"You look good in your suit. Like female Viagra."

I looked around. People were coming from all directions. No Arizona. Airport noise—chatter, blowing horns, rumbling planes, car engines—came through the phone on her end.

"Well, Mr. Freeman."

"It's Freeeeeee-man."

"Let's focus on your career. Boycotts in Detroit, pretty much the same all over the country because, now that you're on the fast track, you no longer go to the black bookstores."

I turned around, searched the escalator, curbside, then looked through the crowd again.

Arizona said, "Don't break your neck. You won't see me until I need to be seen."

"You're here at LAX? What, you leaving town?"

Arizona answered with, "Frank Sinatra keeps looking at you."

"Frank?"

"That's good. That's a tell."

"Who keeps looking at me?"

"I'll be in touch."

She hung up.

"Get your facts straight. I do African-American stores across the country, the ones who have it together. And yes, I've had senseless boycotts in St. Louis . . . death threats in Detroit . . ."

"How do you respond to that?"

People started to crowd me in. Luggage ran over my shoes. People stared at me like I was in their space. Wasn't in that kind of mood right now, not for strangers to keep stepping on my toes. Was about ready to start throwing elbows and beating motherfuckers down.

I tried to move away from the media circus. Couldn't. Crowd was too unmoving. The more people stopped, the louder Freeman talked. The louder he talked, the more people stopped.

"When I go to *black* bookstores, *black* people don't show up. They are in the white-owned establishments sipping on caffe Americanos and caramel macchiatos with an extra shot of espresso. *They* sold out. How do I have the power to make African-Americans shop in African-American stores? Tell me how to redirect my people and we'll both know."

I made it to the edge of the crowd. Looked around. Wall-to-wall, no sign of Arizona.

Freeman jumped dramatic, looked deep into the camera. "I'm the new black aesthetic. My next book, *Truth Be Told*, the one I keep locked on my wrist at all times, when it drops this summer, black prose, as we know it, will change forever. I'm about to revolutionize literature."

"Speaking of *Truth Be Told*, the rumor is you received a million-dollar advance on a book no one has ever seen. That's rare, especially for an African-American."

"Especially when African-American income is up and book buying is down."

"Exactly. Do you think that puts pressure—"

"No one sees my work until I'm ready for it to be seen."

"We're almost done. I have to admit that the first book I read from you, *Pool Tables and Politics,* bordered on tedious philosophizing and navel-gazing."

Freeman grunted like he'd been mule-kicked in his gut.

She went on, "I refused to read anything from you, until *Dawning of Ignorance*. I loved it. Your writing has matured. *Dawning of Ignorance* is so much better than your previous, not dismissive, and based on the reviews on Web sites like Amazon.com you've redeemed your—"

Freeman made a pharaoh-esque gesture and just like that he was done, walked away from the camera, went to his fans, whipped out a silver pen and started signing autographs.

The camera was still on Freeman, the reporter left hanging like strange fruit.

Somebody tapped my shoulder. I jumped. Damn nerves were

shot. I turned around and expected to see Arizona, but I looked right into the face of the woman I'd seen on the escalator. She'd taken her shades off. Her eyes caught me off guard. Not the kind of eyes I expected to see on a woman with a complexion close to mine. They were deep blue, beautiful and disturbing all at once.

She had a book in her hand. Freeman's tight-lipped expression ate up the back cover.

I asked, "You trying to get your book signed?"

She shook her head. "I'm with Thomas Marcus."

"You're his manager . . . publicist?"

Her voice was professional, but still small, timid. "His fiancée."

A rock weighed down her left hand, but I never assumed. More than once I'd picked up a client, then had to wait for his mistress. Same for the women. Wasn't my job to question. All I knew was whether they squatted in South Central or the South of France, they were all players.

She pushed her lips up into a jet-lagged smile. "Come with me."

She diverted her eyes, never made eye contact, her expression uneasy. She turned around, made her way toward baggage claim. My knee ached from where I'd gone down on it last night. She hurried away from the media like a woman running away from the source of a disease. I had to struggle to keep up with her fragrance, the scents of expensive perfume and top-shelf vodka.

She handed me a sheet of paper. Their itinerary. Nobody had told me about an itinerary.

I said, "I thought he was going straight to his hotel?"

"He wants to sign stock at these bookshops."

"Well, in traffic this could take all day."

"We have time."

But I didn't.

She pointed out a large, hard-case Samsonite and two smaller suitcases. The Samsonite felt like it had a dead fat man inside and the smaller suitcases had to be loaded with bricks. Freeman and his woman had packed like they were going on a yearlong safari in the Serengeti.

I grunted and loaded the Smarte Carte, lower back aching from tossing and turning on Panther's futon. Freeman's woman led me through the crowd, me feeling a little self-conscious and still struggling with this pain behind my ear, her walk like straight-ahead jazz.

She asked, "Our car . . . ?"

"In the structure across the street. I'll bring the car curbside."

"Brilliant. That would be lovely."

Without looking my way, she shot me an indifferent hand gesture. It was the kind of dismissive hand movement that reminded me there were two kinds of people in this world: those who rode in the backseat, and those who opened the doors so people could ride in the backseat.

My cellular rang again while I was caught at the crosswalk. Pasquale's name popped up. That meant it was my crown of thorns. Hadn't talked to Rufus two days in a row in a long time.

Rufus coughed. "You're at the airport with Thomas Marcus Freeman."

He sounded lethargic, like he was down, having a bad morning health-wise. I didn't ask for any bad news. Either way he had my full attention. I asked, "How you know that?"

"He was just on the news. You were in the background. Straighten your tie."

"Damn."

"How's your head?"

"Hurting."

"I was reading *Dawning of Ignorance* last night."

"Yeah. Knew that book sounded familiar. It's not a . . . a . . ."

"Gay book?"

"One of them specialty books you read."

"Not a *specialty* book. Get me an autographed copy."

"Rufus, man, you know I don't give a damn about an autograph."

"Just a signature and a date, not personalized. That way it's worth more when he dies."

"What's this preoccupation you have with death?"

"When you can see a big clock over your head counting down, it's your reality."

I almost snapped at Rufus. He told me that seeing me on television gave him a reason to call. Little brother was worried about his big brother. The way I showed up on his doorstep with my head busted had robbed him of his sleep the same way it would've done Momma.

He asked, "How much you owe the crazy psycho sadistic bitch?"

I took a breath. "Fifteen large."

"Are you serious?"

"Got the money from her to bury Momma."

"You owe her the whole fifteen thousand?"

"She's calling in her loan."

That wasn't the truth, but it wasn't a total lie. Rufus knew about as much about my life as I did about his. Knew as much about my truth as I did his.

He coughed. "Look, I called around and found Ray Ray. He ain't in jail this week. Let me give you his number."

"This is my problem, Rufus."

"You're my brother. She was my mother too. This is my problem."

We hung up. At least I know I did.

I hustled the luggage to the black sedan. I read the names on the tags. The two that weighed the most had tags with Freeman's name. The third bag had the name FOLASADE TITILAYO COKER. Freeman's woman had a proper, African-mixed-with-English accent and a name to match. I looked at the tag because Miss Africa never introduced herself. Folasade Titilayo Coker. A smaller tag was on the bag, red with the word MANUMIT in black letters.

I bent my knees, deadlifted that overweight Samsonite, then heaved the other bags inside the trunk. The last carry-on bag zipper busted open, its goods spilling out.

A hundred little Freemans ran out and frowned at me.

Bobbleheads. The bag was weighed down by a ton of Freeman bobbleheads.

Each had a book held high in each hand. Reminded me of Charlton

Heston as Moses when he stood on the mountaintop waving the Ten Commandments at the sinners.

I shook my head and stuffed the chocolate-colored narcissists back in the bag. Had too many of the little bastards in my hand. Dropped one outside the car. Freeman's fat head bounced and rolled across the concrete. Left knee hummed when I bent to pick it up, wanted to go south. That pain, too much alcohol, and not enough sleep made me feel my age in a bad way.

Footsteps echoed in the musty garage.

I stood tall like a bear and turned around.

They were in the shadows, watching me. The lion and the jackal.

Lisa's bullyboys were twenty yards away, leaning against different cars, both smoking and chilling out like they were waiting on a bus. I made a couple of steps in their direction, my expression asking them to bring it on. The lion flicked his smoke my way, did an about-face, headed deeper into the garage. The jackal did the same, smoke pluming around his head.

They walked away fast, but not too fast. They knew I couldn't follow them, not now.

I watched them until they were completely gone, until their smoke had dissipated.

My angry lungs reminded me to breathe again.

I tossed the bobblehead to the curb, zipped the bag up, and got inside the sedan. That was when I saw a sheet of paper underneath the windshield wiper.

I grabbed it.

It was a newspaper article. Months old. About a man who was tortured and murdered, his killers never found. They'd left that under my windshield wiper like it was their business card.

My stomach turned like peroxide and baking soda was mixing up inside me.

Should've gone after those bastards. But it was two against one. Ten years ago, hell maybe even five years back, I would've said that was cool, bring it on, and would've gone King Kong on those niggas and beat both of those motherfuckers into the pavement.

This sit-down job had softened me, made me stiff over the last six months. My body told me I was forty every chance it got. I could fuck twice as strong but might not be able to fight half as long. Right now the odds were in a young man's favor.

I punched in Lisa's cellular number. This time she clicked her phone on, but she didn't say a word. I snapped her name. She hung up. I called back. It went straight to voice mail.

She had shut me out.

I called Wolf's office.

Wolf answered. "Thought you'd be on the way to Santa Monica by now."

The CEO was at his office computer, looking at the high-tech tracker on his cars. This sedan was a red blip on Wolf's computer screen. Lisa could find me with the click of a mouse.

Wolf asked, "How is this Freeman cat?"

The black Expedition appeared in my rearview, fucking with me. I ran my tongue around my mouth, kept my eyes on them. I told Wolf, "Freeman's ego might not fit in the car."

Wolf blew air.

I said, "She broke out an itinerary. Thought this was just a drop-off."

"Grit your teeth and kiss ass until the check clears. What *she* gave you the schedule?"

Right now I craved a shot of Jack. I said, "His fiancée is with him."

"Heard about her from New York. Nigerian. Her parents are diplomats. Speaks a dozen languages. Rumor is her folks are class-conscious and not too crazy about her choice in men."

"You know a lot."

"I like to know who's farting on my backseats."

The lion posted up next to me. He nodded my way, smiled like we were friends, maybe telling me we'd get to know each other better, real soon. They drove away, forty thousand dollars worth of rims going in circles. I eased back and put my eyes on their license plate.

I asked Wolf, "Nobody's available to do a handoff?"

"Everybody's out."

The Expedition vanished in traffic. My sweaty hands strangled the steering wheel.

Wolf stopped me from hanging up. "Nation next to Egypt. Five letters. Third is a B."

Doing a crossword puzzle was the last thing on my mind.

"Kenya. No, wait. Libya." I rubbed the bridge of my nose. "Wolf . . ."

"Yeah?"

"We need to talk. Man to man. You have time for a sit-down later on this evening?"

"Driver, I really need you to handle Freeman."

"This ain't . . . this ain't got nothing to do with Freeman."

That caught him off guard. "Have to deal with my kids. What's going on?"

I wanted to tell Wolf about the shit Lisa had done right then. Wanted to open my mouth and let it all spill out. Almost did. But it wasn't the kind of thing you told a man over the phone. That would be a punk move. Had to look him in his face. Maybe between now and then I'd figure out how to tell him about my part in the betrayal between brothers, in a way that would make sense to him. Somewhere deep inside me lived an ironic chuckle. Not long ago I could've killed him. Now I couldn't tell the man something as simple as I'd been fucking his wife.

I asked, "Things better with you and the wife?"

"When she came back last night, she was all over me. She wants to take off for a couple of days. I might fly her up the coast for the next three days and get some quiet time together."

That was the same thing she had done when I was supposed to take care of Wolf, gone on vacation, taken herself out of the equation, created herself an alibi on the cruise ship *Elation*.

Sounded like she was doing the same thing now. Creating her alibi.

Damocles's sword had moved from Wolf, now it hung over my head.

9

Freeman's fiancée was standing curbside, alone and demure, transparent to the crowd.

Her man was still inside, fans taking his picture like he was Muhammad Ali.

I opened the back door. His woman eased inside like a lady. Did it with class. She sat down first, then brought her legs in at the same time, kept her knees together. Femininity was an art she had mastered. She looked up at me, those two blue oceans made contact with my eyes.

I said, "I didn't catch your name."

"Sade."

"Like the singer."

"Yes."

I told her about the broken zipper and spilled bobbleheads. She didn't give a damn.

I got in. Seconds passed like minutes. Wetness trickled down my neck. I freaked, touched my skin, and it came back wet and clear. Not blood. Sweat was dampening my collar.

Hadn't noticed what was going on inside the terminal. A tall sister was hugged up with Freeman while her shorter, flirty friend took picture after picture. Then they switched up.

My breathing had evened out, but my heart hadn't moved from my throat.

My passenger hissed. "This is brilliant. Just brilliant."

Then she mumbled something rugged in a nasally language, the kind where I could see the accent marks and dots over each foreign word.

My eyes went to Freeman. The smaller woman was trying to out-flirt her girlfriend, holding Freeman tight, pressing her breasts deep into his chest, her face damn close to his.

"Driver, please, remind the *new black aesthetic* that he has a phoner."

"Phoner?"

"Just get him, please." She flipped from being timid to frustrated, her real personality must've been rising to the top. "He has fallen in love with the sound of his own voice and will go on and on as long as someone, as long as anyone listens. This tour has become ridiculous."

I hit the emergency flashers, waited for airport security to pass by.

The short woman hugged up on Freeman saw me coming, then adjusted her rimless glasses and turned away. Her hair was pulled back into a ponytail. She looked all of sixteen, but her body said she was older. Her silky white blouse and dark skirt made her curves come to life.

It was Miss Baklava Glue. Arizona. She'd decided she wanted to be seen.

The woman with her was a lot taller and a little older, had a fuller build, all curves. Her hair was in a pixie cut. She was about my age, had dimples too. I'd seen her somewhere before.

Arizona moved away from Freeman and hurried by me. I turned back to call her name and bumped into her friend. I hit her hard. She stumbled away like she'd hit a brick wall, almost twisted her ankle. I reached out and grabbed her to stop her from going down to the ground. She got her balance and moved on like nothing had happened, jogged and caught up with Arizona.

Arizona kept going, purse in one hand, jacket over her other arm.

Freeman held onto his briefcase, asked, "What's the problem, my brother?"

I told Freeman that his fiancée said he had a phoner.

He adjusted his briefcase and matched my long stride with a quick Napoleonic strut.

His eyes were on Arizona and her friend. He grunted. "She had to tag along."

The *she* that he was talking about was his woman. He'd brought sand to the beach and his face told me he regretted it down to his bones. His woman's blue eyes were watching his every move, lips tight. His African queen was ready to piss a circle around what was hers.

I let him inside the car, my eyes hunting for the lion and the jackal. They were gone. Before I made it to my door my cellular sang. I answered. It was Arizona. I didn't want the clients to hear me curse like a sailor with Tourette's syndrome, so I moved to the trunk, opened it and pretended I was adjusting the luggage, my words muffled by airport noises.

Arizona was on the island where the shuttles stopped, her back to me, at the crosswalk, waiting for the light to turn green. Her hands were on her hips, so she must've had on a headset.

I growled, "You with those motherfuckers in the Expedition?"

Her voice remained even. "What motherfuckers in what Expedition?"

I paused and rubbed my face, peeped over the back window. Freeman's woman had her legs crossed and was going over what looked like a comprehensive schedule. Freeman's hands were free. He'd taken off the handcuffs and put the briefcase either on the floor or on the seat.

Arizona glanced my way, licked her lips.

I gritted my teeth, told her to tell me what the hell was going on.

"I need your help, Driver. It's business."

"Give me more than that."

"Short con."

"The mark?"

"In your car. Page me when you can talk."

"Talk now or there won't be another conversation."

"Later."

"I hang up and don't call this number again."

"Driver—"

"Five, four, three, two—"

"I was supposed to meet him last night. Sade found our e-mails on the computer, which were pretty erotic, typical online stuff, all fantasy on his part. She made him change his flight plans, tagged along to protect her investment. Her presence has mucked up the program."

"You worked me getting this job?"

"Yes."

"Hold on. You just met me last night."

"I'm good."

"Let me guess. Freeman didn't request a black driver."

She said, "And I made sure he didn't get a stretch limo."

"Why?"

"He'd let up the privacy glass. Then you couldn't hear him talk."

I stared her down. Smart woman to be so young. That gave me a new kind of fear.

I asked, "What am I supposed to be hearing?"

"Eyes and ears, Driver. It would help if you told me where he's staying."

"If you're talking to the bastard, you should know."

"It changed. I think his publisher changed it. And he's not telling because his woman is with him."

"Hypothetically, what else you need?"

"Need to know when he's leaving the room, if she's clinging to him. His detailed plans. What's security like at the hotel. How many ways in and out. When he takes that briefcase off his arm. If he has it on when he gets back in the car. How long he will be gone."

"Uh huh."

"I can take it from there."

I leaned forward. Rubbed my neck. Pain in my knee escalating.

She said, "With your eyes and ears, this can be an easy one. Told you I needed to run a few short cons to finance a larger one, and this is one of the smaller ones. Work with me."

Traffic passed by and we stared. Her friend looked back at me, then whispered something to Arizona. Arizona nodded and her friend turned around, came back toward me.

Arizona said, "I'll make it worth your while."

"How do you know I just won't tell Freeman right now?"

"That book he has with him, his people cut him a check for a million dollars."

Airport police pulled up, ready to lock and load. The look the cop gave me made bad memories sail around inside my head. I hung up on Arizona, closed the trunk, hopped in the car.

My cellular rang again. I answered with silent aggravation. Not a word.

Arizona said, "Wait."

"For?"

"My friend has something to give you."

"Keep it."

"You'll want this."

"Look, dammit. I'm working."

"Give me twenty seconds."

I pulled over far enough away for the airport police to cut me some slack for at least a minute, hit the emergency flashers, picked up my clipboard, pretended I was doing paperwork.

Sade leaned forward, said, "I need Starbucks. Driver, get me to a Starbucks."

"Yes, ma'am."

Freeman told his woman, "Can you wait?"

"I waited for you to finish flirting with those rude bitches."

"Respect me, *Folasade*." He snapped her full first name in a *Me Tarzan, you Jane* tone. "Can't believe that you embarrassed me like that on the flight."

"I embarrassed you? That's brilliant. Don't get it twisted."

"I mean, damn. *How much vodka does it take?*"

"*As much as it takes, that's how much it takes.*"

"You need to lighten up."

"I'm stressed, Marcus."

"Handle it," he said, putting his foot down. "I signed a new three-book deal."

She said, "Three more books, Marcus?"

"Did you see the interview? They're coming to me."

Sade's breathing thickened. "When did you sign a new contract for three more books?"

"I'm going to be immortalized on the walls of Barnes & Noble with Kafka, Hemingway, Faulkner, Hughes, and Nabokov. I will be respected. I will not be ignored. They're going to have to look up from their venti white chocolate mochas and see me looking down on them."

She tightened her lips and stared out the window.

Checkmate.

He added, "And when you get to the hotel, take it easy on the mini-bar."

Her lips tightened more. "Marcus, I demand to inspect the room before they take the luggage up. The sheets were filthy at that place we stayed in D.C."

"Don't complicate things with your bullshit, Sade."

"Sheets that atrocious at a five-star hotel. Looked like bile. And there is no telling what we can't see on these sheets. People have all kinds of sex and . . . while you're out doing your thing with your ego feeders, please be useful, pick up some sheets with a high thread count—"

"Damn. That's why I tour by myself."

"And if time permits I would like to tour the city, go sightseeing."

"The book is due. I'm working, Sade. I'm not on vacation. Did you see the schedule publicity gave me? Do you know how much it costs to go to one friggin' city? Hotel. Airfare. Transportation. We have to turn a profit. Even if I had the time, you don't get to the top by going to museums and clubs. You don't achieve by staying in one spot. It's about the hustle."

"Marcus, if we married it would be bigamy."

"What are you talking about, Sade?"

"You're already married to your publishing company. To your editor. To your next book. Those are your women. Snuggle up with that book and see how warm that keeps you."

"Come here."

"Polygamy. Our marriage would be considered polygamy, not bigamy."

Then Arizona's friend was almost at my window, her hand inside her large handbag.

Lisa was on my mind. Lisa and her gun. Lisa and her lion and jackal. This woman could be part of Lisa's crew. I put my hand on the door handle, ready to jump out if I had to, if I could before a bullet screamed my name.

Pedro had said Arizona had come to Back Biters a couple nights before I met her. I was there almost every night. That was my watering hole. Saw how she had looked at me when she walked in last night. I thought I had moved into her space. She had worked her way into mine.

I whispered my warning, "If your girl tries anything—"

Arizona replied, "Relax."

"That's what they told Kennedy in Dallas."

Her friend tapped my window. Irritation painted my face. I eased the glass down. My passengers saw her. I didn't have to turn around to see the uneasiness that painted Freeman's face. The way Sade's breathing changed, I imagined her blue eyes had turned green.

She said, "I think you dropped this."

Arizona's friend tossed a wallet in my lap and walked away. I opened it and saw my ID, cash, and cards staring at me. I patted my suit pocket. She'd lifted it when she bumped me.

Arizona's smooth voice came alive in my ear. She said, "Merry Christmas."

Hostile silence settled between us. I let my window back up.

The pickpocket's sashay took her to Arizona's side. She never looked back.

Freeman and Sade had gone back into their own world. Separate worlds. She had closed her eyes. He was on his phone bragging to some interviewer about how good his work was.

I asked Arizona, "How much?"

"Meet me and we can negotiate." Her tone remained even, all business. "We'll talk."

I hung up.

Arizona and her co-grifter mixed with the crowd and crossed the street.

They vanished into the garage.

10

The sun was easing down, slipping from the sky.

Five bookstores and three protests later, I chauffeured Freeman and Sade to their seven-hundred-dollar-a-night hotel down in Santa Monica. A swank joint called Shutters, on the good end of Pico, not far from the Santa Monica pier. Freeman and Sade were greeted by European luxury and Mexican smiles. They had two wood-burning fireplaces in the lobby and a nice bar with an ocean view. It had to be a great spot to sit and enjoy spirits while you watched the sun set on both the privileged and the homeless people in this part of the world.

I'd only been in the lobby, never upstairs. In front of the hotel, where all the Spanish valet parkers were congregated, that was where I unloaded Freeman and his ton of bobbleheads.

Then came the insult.

Freeman tossed me a bobblehead as a tip. His woman walked away when he did that.

I needed to leave and handle my business, but this time of day traffic was thick and nonmoving. I could either sit in traffic and go no-where fast or catch a seat at the bar. I chose to chill out. Mild chatter, soft music, and the scent of the ocean kept me company while I rubbed my temples and tried to regroup. Body felt heavy, every step like I was rolling a boulder up a mountain. Needed to eat a decent meal. Running on too little sleep to think straight. I looked around at this colorful fantasy world. European, Jewish, and Asian crowd. All of the secondary workers were from south of the border, the largest minority, what some people called the country's new black man. A lot of celebrities hung out at this swank joint, everybody from Robert Downey, Jr., to Angela Bassett, but no shining stars were in sight today.

I ordered coffee and stared out the windows, took in the ocean and the sunset, gazed at all the people Rollerblading and jogging. Put my eyes on a couple leaning against a palm tree. First they were holding hands, then kissing soft and easy while the sun sank into the ocean.

That reminded me of how it used to be with my ex-wife. Saw her strong legs and flat stomach in my mind. Loved to run my fingers over her brown skin. Every time she passed by me and smiled I wanted to take her to the bed and fall inside her. She moaned like no other. She loved me but didn't care for Rufus. His sexuality was in conflict with her religion. And she didn't want her son, my stepson, around Rufus. Didn't want her boy *exposed*. She tried to like Rufus, but she'd been brought up in a home that was heavy-handed when it came to the Bible.

What happened in Memphis was the end of six months of marital turmoil.

Part of me thought that she'd come back for Momma's funeral. Part of me had hoped that while I sat up front next to my brother, one of the people who passed by with tears in their eyes would be the woman I had married. I should've buried more than Momma that day. But memories were the hardest thing to funeralize and put in the ground.

In her eyes I'd chosen my brother over her. In my mind I was taking care of family.

My six-page letter to her came back to me, unopened. The word

REFUSED across the front of the envelope in bold red letters, like the last drops of blood from my marriage.

I wanted a shot of JD so bad my hand was shaking, just enough to let me know I needed to calm my nerves. Just like my wandering eye, I inherited that tension shake from my old man. Right now I could see him up in the pulpit, preaching to the congregation, telling everybody to be strong, to not be oppressed by their fears, to stand tall, to stay focused on this journey.

Momma's brown skin and heavyset image came to mind. Closed my eyes and saw the orange and red in her skin. Saw her walking around talking on that Princess phone, rollers in her hair, flowered housecoat on, a glass of lemonade in her free hand. She made sure me and Rufus read at least an hour a day. Rufus would pick up a book and vanish into that world. He'd start a book and wouldn't put it down until he got to the last page. My attention span was never like that. I'd read a chapter, maybe two, and would get antsy. But I'd read a dictionary or a thesaurus all day, learning words, fascinated by how many there were, how many I didn't know.

I whispered in Reverend Daddy's gruff tone, told myself, "Stay focused."

And despite my problems and disposition, I smiled. In the pulpit Reverend Daddy quoted scripture after scripture, sounded like a haunted, dignified, resilient old-school brother speaking for the poor and downtrodden. His deeply lined face, unsteady voice brought tears and shouts. And when he sang, he was limited in range, but could get a shout out of the coldest heart.

In that deep and powerful voice he told us to stay focused. But in the next breath he'd tell us the rules of the street, would bark out, "Fear no nigga, trust no bitches."

Fear no nigga.

Trust no bitches.

I nodded.

I took out my cellular, made a few more calls. I'd been making calls all day, trying to see how much money I could round up. If

I could add three or four, maybe five large to what I had, maybe I could get a good faith payment to Lisa, get her off my back before this got any uglier.

The calls were a waste of cell phone minutes; everybody was two paychecks behind. With all the strikes, people didn't have enough cash to put a bag of M&Ms on layaway.

Fifteen large. It might as well have been a billion.

I closed my eyes, tried to think, but felt like a dead leaf tumbling in the wind. I didn't know which way to go, so I stayed where I was, hissing almost every time I inhaled, watching a room filled with moneyed people numbing themselves to their own realities.

I looked down at my suit, my shoes, my silk tie, my cuff links. When I'd been released from jail I had on two-year-old clothes, a prisoner's paycheck, and seven dollars in my pocket. No prospects for a real job. No opportunities meant no future. Times stayed hard long enough and a man became susceptible to things that offered either pleasure or promise. Lisa had given me both. It was all about self-preservation. Then Wolf had offered me a better way. Still about self-preservation. Along the way I'd made a lot of sacrifices that added up to nothing.

Everything that was wrong in my world was bum-rushing me right now.

Sade had come back downstairs, a book in her hand. Almost didn't recognize her. Her braided hair had been let down, flowed like waves over her shoulders, cascaded down her back. Saw her in the lobby warming up by the fireplace. I don't know how long she'd been there. She was beautiful but something about her made her unnoticeable. She made her way over to the bar, looked surprised when she saw me posted up. Her energy changed. She smiled.

"Cheers, Driver."

I raised my cup. "Coffee. Black. Straight. No chaser."

"Afraid I need something a little stronger. Might have to get rat-faced."

"It's your face."

Sade sat a barstool away. Did that like she didn't want to sit by people she didn't know, she didn't want to get in my space. Or didn't want me in hers. I could tell that because she rested her purse on the barstool between us, made sure it was comfortable, like it was her friend. The purse was chocolate-colored leather, looked as smooth as warm butter. Her passkey and wallet were in the side pocket facing me. Her wallet matched her purse. She was careless. Where I came from somebody would lift that wallet without a thought. But we were on the opposite end of Pico, where the land met the ocean, not where ghetto birds were a way of life.

I said, "Sheets okay?"

"Huh? Oh. Wonderful. Everything is well done. Brilliant."

"Cool."

"How long does rush hour last here?"

"Around eight, maybe ten hours."

"They should consider having a congestion charge here, like they have in London."

"What's that?"

"You pay to go into the city during peak hours. Around five pounds. It would cut down on traffic considerably. The traffic we were in today . . . simply horrible."

"First chance I get, I'll write Governor Schwarzenegger about that."

The bartender came over. A pretty Italian woman. Reddish-brown hair. Tanned skin. Freckles. Her name tag read DANIELA. Sade spoke to her in Italian, did that without a thought.

She pressed her lips together, then softly asked, *"Che martini mi consigli?"*

Daniela answered, *"Dovresti provare i miei martini al cioccolato."*

Sade paused, put a finger up to her lips in a thinking pose. *"Sono buoni?"*

"Grandiosi. Come bersi una tavoletta di cioccolata."

"Aa, il mio genere di drink."

Daniela the Bartender made a chocolate martini for Sade, then put it in front of her with a smile, like an artist who had created a masterpiece.

Sade sipped, made a sensual sound, and gave her two thumbs up. "*Perfetto.*"

Daniela's expression said she was impressed with Sade. "Your Italian is excellent."

Sade smiled with love. "*Si, il mio primo amore era un meraviglioso uomo Italiano.*"

"That is who you are here with?" Daniela motioned at Sade's ring. "Your first love?"

Sade shook her head. "*Ha sposato una meravigliosa donna Italiana.*"

"Life goes on."

Sade raised her glass. "Life goes on."

Daniela walked away, went to tend to the other empty souls filling this ocean-scented oyster-and-calamari world. Sade kept sipping her sweetened vodka and letting out soft moans. She was like a smoker who finally got to hit a cigarette. She dropped her class-conscious grin, turned those blue eyes my way, lips moving up at the edges, as if she were seeking approval.

I asked, "Where's the world-famous book writer?"

"On the phone. More interviews. I've had all the literary shibboleths I can endure."

"Tell 'im I said thanks for the bobblehead."

"He was a straight ass for doing that."

I chuckled. Was funny hearing her curse with that thick accent. I said, "It's all good."

"No it's not." She opened her purse, took out a C-note. "Allow me to tip you properly."

I waved it away, turned down her pity gift. Reverend Daddy used to tell us about when he first moved to California, a black man wasn't welcome on this side of town, wasn't welcome west of the 405 or south of the 10. A black man had to kiss ass to work in Santa Monica and Westwood, then had to be gone back to his world, the geographical prison the white man allowed, before the sun sank into the ocean. Freeman's gesture had made me feel that low. Or maybe, despite my suit and job, Freeman had just reminded me who I really was. Still, insults from my own people were the hardest to swallow. A cheap tip was worse than getting no tip. If a customer didn't tip you could always assume he didn't know any better, maybe he was in a hurry and forgot. Getting stiffed with a bobblehead was like somebody spitting in your face.

Sade said, "I didn't mean to offend."

"I'm not offended." I lied, as usual, with the ease of telling the truth. "Not at all."

"And if I did anything improper today, if I offended you today, I apologize."

"Anything like what?"

She smiled a little. "People think I come across as being curt, or having a brusque manner, or they mistake my shyness for unfriendliness, but I . . . I . . . it's my defense mechanism—"

"Ma'am, I'm just the driver. It doesn't bother me one way or the other."

I sat there nursing my liquid caffeine. Sade had some loose change in front of her, had started tossing pennies in an empty glass the way people tossed pennies in a wishing well.

My head ached. Neck was tense. Both shoulders felt tight. I wasn't in a talking mood. Right now, in the middle of pandemonium, I just wanted to enjoy L.A., stare at the ocean and palm trees, watch that beautiful city I loved before I got back out into the traffic I hated.

Sade sat next to me, shifting, restless, things on her mind. I felt bad for the way I'd cut her off. I told her, "You don't look like the type who would hang out at a bar."

"I partake of institutions of this sort in order to overcome my social ineptitudes."

"I come for the peanuts."

Her introverted expression came back. I saw that she had changed shoes. They were chocolate, pointed on the toe with a tall, thin heel, had a nice design stitched in the rich leather. Sexy shoes. The kind of kicks that were pretty enough for you to want to know their names.

I told her, "You have stranger anxiety."

That rattled her, made her blink a few times. "Am I that obvious?"

"To me. It's cool. I'm like that sometimes, have to warm up to people."

She cringed. "Those overzealous crowds that Marcus deals with, I could never do that."

"He's the man. Maybe I should try writing a book and milk that cash cow."

"I wouldn't recommend it. Writing is one of those rarefied fields, like vexillology and tea tasting, at which only a select few can actually earn a living. Most writers starve to death and die unknown. Even the most brilliant of the lot have an impossible time selling their books."

I nodded.

She made love to her drink and gazed around the room. My mind dragged me back to my problems. To Lisa. To Wolf. Had an inner struggle with my character, the kind of battle not even Jack Daniel's could fix. My mind moved from Lisa's threat. Then to Freeman's briefcase.

Eyes and ears.

I looked toward the lobby. There was a single employee guarding the entrance to the elevators, only letting people by if they showed a passkey, the same post-9/11 security many hotels had. Had to have a key to get upstairs, or be with a guest. My eyes went back to Sade. Her attention remained on her drink. She came across as a dignified and brilliant good girl.

Sade quipped, "I do not understand this symbiotic relationship between celebrities and fans, the way they feed off each other, this celebrity obsession in our fast-food culture."

I rubbed my palms on my pants; without thinking I said, "Celebrity Worship Syndrome."

Her eyes left her drink and met mine, blinking herself out of a trance. I'd interrupted a conversation she was having with her empty martini glass. She said, "Excuse me?"

"What you saw at the airport." My mouth was moving, words coming out, but my mind wasn't at this bar, not all the way. I took a hard breath. "Celebrity Worship Syndrome."

She kept her eyes on mine. "I don't understand it. Not at all. These people are borderline pathological. They fall in love with the images they have in their mind."

I asked, "You plan on seeing the city?"

"Please. I'm jet-lagged and on East Coast time. And Marcus has been going nonstop for the last thirty-six hours. Every time I think there is going to be a break in his schedule his publicist adds something else. This is maddening. I'll eat in the room, more than likely."

I sucked my lip and nodded. Now I knew they weren't leaving, not this evening.

I asked, "You guys are staying here for a couple of days?"

"Four days. I'll be here four days while Marcus does his dog-and-pony show."

"He's coming down here with you?"

"God, Mr. Black Aesthetic doesn't even know I'm not upstairs. He probably thinks I'm in the bed. Or taking a long bath. And God knows where he is or what he's doing right now."

That told me a lot more. I chuckled. "Your room is that big?"

She pulled back into herself, ran her hand over her mane, and didn't answer.

I didn't push it.

Four days. I nodded. The questions I was asking her, each one had a purpose. I looked at her angelic face and told myself I was insane, shook those criminal thoughts out of my head.

She began venting in that nasally language again, the one where I could see the accent marks and dots over every word, her vodka perfuming every breath. But her posture remained elegant, every movement silky and modest, the body language of a charm school valedictorian.

"Never picked up a book writer before." I asked, "Is it always that crazy?"

"Hah! It was insane in Jackson, Mississippi, and Birmingham. My God. Those people."

I said, "Like watching a shark and a pack of remoras."

"I'm sorry. What's a remora?"

"A suckerfish that . . . attaches itself to the underside of a larger fish and feeds off them. Remoras and sharks. Fans and celebrities. We see those relationships all the time."

"Like parasites."

"Not the same as being parasitic. Parasitic relationships are one-sided and damaging, at the least. The shark and remora relationship, I think the word for their relationship is actually commensalism. Twelve letters. I think the shark might benefit from the remoras."

I backed down. Didn't want her to think I was calling her man a shark. He was an asshole, but I'd chauffeured worse. Way worse. This didn't faze me enough to steal my mind away from Lisa and her animal farm, the lion and jackal. Part of me had been watching the doorway, expecting them to reappear. Or expecting Arizona and the pickpocket to show up, ready to grift. No one showed up. My cellular didn't ring. But I knew we'd all meet again.

The bartender brought Sade another chocolate martini, more Italian words exchanged. I heard them mention Il Fornio, an Italian restaurant that was a few blocks away, across the street from Santa Monica Pier. Sade must've been asking about other good places to eat.

Sade told Daniela, "Please charge my drinks to my suite. Folasade Coker."

Daniela nodded and moved on.

Sade gazed at her diamond ring. Without looking up she said, "Driver?"

I stopped drumming my fingers on the counter. "Yes, ma'am?"

"I understand parasites, but how do you tell the shark from the remora?"

She let out a brief laugh. I didn't. My mind kept dragging me to a darker room.

My injury throbbed. I clenched my teeth. Pain level about a three.

I took out my wallet so I could pay my tab and the folded bar napkin with Arizona's number fell from my pocket. I balled it up and tossed it on the counter. Then I changed my mind, picked it up, stuffed it in my jacket pocket.

I tucked a few bills under my empty cup, enough for the coffee plus twenty percent.

She asked, "If I need to go anywhere, if I need to see the city, will you be available?"

I was about to tell her I wouldn't be, but I handed her a black and gold business card, licked my lips, and gave her that ambiguous smile that had no meaning. "Call the main office."

She gave me an ethereal smile in return, the corner of her eyes lighting up and letting me know she was feeling mellow and sincere. "And please accept my apology for Marcus."

"A woman should never have to apologize for a man."

"I understand. He's really an honorable guy, just not good at delivering his message."

"Then there is nothing to apologize for."

"The bobblehead."

I shrugged. "I might start collecting bobbleheads."

"If there's anything I can do . . ."

"My . . . my . . . my brother reads . . . is a fan. He reads a lot of books." Mentioning Rufus always made me feel awkward. The things he had said about me having the good genes always bothered me. I was supposed to be the strong brother. He didn't know how weak I'd been. My thoughts dissipated and everything felt awkward. I cleared my throat and said, "He wanted me to get him an autographed book. Maybe I can pick up one at the mall and swing by when it's convenient for . . . your fiancé, maybe you can talk your man into signing it for my brother."

She slid me the novel she had brought down with her, the same one she carried close to her heart at the airport. Told me it was a first edition, already signed.

I thanked her. Her expression told me that my taking that book made her feel better.

She asked, "You have a wife?"

"Divorced."

"Sorry to hear that."

"No big deal."

"Kids?"

"No kids. Had a step . . . no kids." I adjusted my coat. She was getting too personal, that made me want to get away from her as fast as I could. I said, "Enjoy your stay in L.A."

"You're not driving us tomorrow?"

"You can request me if you like."

I shot a thumbs-up to the bartender and waved good-bye to Sade. Sade raised her glass my way and said, "To sharks and remoras."

I raised my hand like I had an imaginary glass, saluted her toast, then nodded and headed down the stairs. Sade got up before I had made it to the lobby. She left her drink behind and headed for the elevator. She walked head up, eyes straight, as if there were an invisible book resting on top of her head. Her shoes told a tale. Those shoes told me a lot about her mood. She hadn't changed clothes, just taken off the boxy and conservative shoes she'd had on earlier, put on a pair that pimped out her backside and showed off her ankles. She had been chilling at a bar without her fiancé wearing sexy shoes, the kind that broadcasted sensual messaging features.

There was another side to her.

Lisa had taught me that a lot of women had a dark side, some were darker than others. Sade had things on her mind, felt like she wanted to talk to someone she thought she could trust.

I stalled near the fireplace, flipping through Freeman's book but not reading a word. I absorbed some heat and watched a low-level employee play rent-a-cop and stop Sade. He asked to see her passkey. Sade looked offended, a class thing no doubt, then dug in her purse and couldn't find hers. She shrugged, went to the front desk and showed them her ID, got another one. Sade went back to the rent-a-cop and he smiled, stepped aside, let her get on the elevator.

Sade wasn't amused.

I waited until she got on the elevator then dug in my pocket. I stared at the passkey I had lifted from Sade's purse. I walked toward the elevator, passkey brandished. Security let me by without question. My eyes went to the illuminated floor indicator, tried to figure out what floor she had gone to. I'd seen people do that in the movies. Didn't know if that worked in real life.

With this passkey I could get by security unquestioned. There were almost two hundred rooms in this palace by the sea, but only twelve of them were suites. She'd said her room was so big, so phat that Freeman didn't know she was gone. That narrowed it down to twelve doors for Sade to have walked through. Twelve rooms that could hold what Arizona was trying to steal.

I'd broken into houses growing up, stolen cars, sometimes for fun, but mostly out of need. I chilled for a minute, had words with myself, told myself that I could go for it by myself.

If only I knew Freeman's room number . . .

A thousand unlawful what-ifs clouded my mind.

No. They had just handed Sade a replacement passkey and that meant they probably changed the code. But I could still use the key to walk by the low-level guard. That was a start.

I got on the elevator, rode up to the top floor, the one that held all the suites, spied out and hoped to see Sade walking toward her over-sized room, maybe catch her going in the door. Then I'd be sure what floor she was on. I did that for all five floors. After that little joyride I went back down and left the hotel, whistling like I belonged there, like I was one of them.

I handed one of the Mexican workers a tip and thanked him for letting me park illegally, then got in the sedan, tossed Freeman's miracle book in the passenger seat, and pointed my problems in the direction of Wolf Classic Limousine. That passkey was in my sweaty hand. I rubbed it all the way back to Wolf's garage. Rubbed it like it was a magic lamp.

11

Nobody was in Wolf's office. I moved by his family pictures, his immigrant parents and the biracial children from his first marriage. His wedding picture and another glam photo of Lisa stared at me. I sat in his leather chair, adjusted Lisa's picture, made her stare at the walls.

The memory of the first time I'd walked in this room hit me hard as a Tyson punch.

I shook yesterday off my shoulders, put on my glasses, got comfortable in his captain's chair, used his PC, and logged on to the Internet. Needed to do some research.

Google.com was a good spot to start. I typed in THOMAS MARCUS FREEMAN. Over a hundred sites popped up. I did the eenie-meenie-minie-mo thing, clicked on *Publishers Weekly*.

It said that Freeman was born in Quitman, Mississippi, grew up in New Jersey. Went to FAMU, joined a fraternity, lived in Florida, married and divorced, now twenty-seven, engaged, on his fifth book, *Truth Be Told*, and had just cut a deal that was worth a million dollars.

I surfed over to Amazon, read reviews. One club said *Pool Tables and Politics*, was one-dimensional. I clicked on a review for his second book; it said that *All That Glitters: A Black Man's Obsession with Material Things* was one step below a doorstop. *Preachy. Seriously flawed.* His first two books had more single-star reviews than the Hollywood Walk of Fame.

At least the brother didn't give up. My old man used to tell us to never give up.

Freeman had a third book that dropped back in the fall of '01. *truth is stronger than lies,* all small letters. Not many reviews; all agreed that it was his best, but I guess it didn't sell. Three-year gap, like he went into hibernation, then came out swinging, dropped *Dawning of Ignorance.* Another one of those long book reports disguised as a book review said it was tight.

It was written like fiction, but it brought up some serious issues that we as black people, we as a nation need to address. This will anger a lot of people, but that's what the truth does.

Tiredness hit me in waves. It was a struggle. Had to give in and yawn a few times.

I surfed around and read more on Freeman, all of it pretty much the same jibber jabber. They hated the first two; the third didn't get any attention; the fourth made him a rock star.

He wasn't Donald Trump rich, but with my account, one was just as good as the other.

A million dollars and he handed out bobbleheads as tips.

Then I went out to the Department of Corrections Web site. In prison a man lost his identity, reduced to a series of numbers. Just like Mandela would never forget 46664 was his prison number for over twenty-five years while he was in South Africa's Robben Island jail, I'd never forget the numbers that represented me for the two I was locked down. Martyr or murderer, no prisoner ever forgot. One by one, I typed in mine. Stared at the screen and waited.

"Driver?"

I jumped a bit. Left my memories. Wolf was in the doorway. Watching me.

I didn't know how long he'd been there. I'd been too deep in thought.

Without hesitation I logged off the computer and faced his six-foot frame. He stood with his shoulders square, had on a deep blue pin-striped suit, his tie as dark and shiny as his kicks, blond hair slicked back into that ponytail, stroking his goatee.

"Hey, Wolf."

"You shouldn't use the computer in my office. Use the one out front."

"The receptionist was on it playing Scrabble."

He loosened his tie. "Anyway, don't want everyone else to think this is public domain."

I stood up, moved away from his mahogany desk. He met me halfway and we shook hands. His handshake was different, stronger than usual, he held on longer than usual, did that the way a man did when he was establishing dominance and superiority, claiming his territory.

He was the boss. I was the employee.

I said, "Had stuck my head in to holler at you. Logged on for a minute."

Lisa was right outside the door, I heard her voice, talking with another co-worker, laughing like a politician. She passed by and I caught a glimpse. She was dressed in a sharp, classy black pantsuit, low and expensive heels, glasses on, hair pulled back in a metal clasp.

She came back to the door, ignored me and called her husband, "Baby?"

"Yeah, sweetheart?"

"Honey, I told Guadalupe not to cook tonight."

"Don't tell me you're cooking?"

"Of course not. I made reservations downtown at Windows. That cool?"

Wolf joked, "Nothing like a sky-high view of bumper-to-bumper traffic."

She laughed with him. That tugged at my heartstrings, tugged hard.

Lisa looked political and privileged, not like a woman who had pulled a Glock on a man last night, not like the kind of loon who threw a 7-Up can at my head, then tried to run me down.

She tilted her head in fake surprise. "Thought you were in *your* office by yourself."

I took a step back, our positions an unintentional triangle. "Lisa. Whassup?"

"Good evening." Monotone. Strictly business. "How's it going, Driver?"

"It's going. How was San Diego?"

"San Diego was San Diego. Damn. What happened to you?"

"What?"

"Looks like you fell and bumped your head."

"Looks like."

"Be careful, Driver." She turned to Wolf. "I'm going to get a 7-Up. Want one?"

Wolf answered, "Nah."

"What about you, Driver?"

My frown eased up into that ambiguous smile.

She moved by me, her sweet-scented toilet water wafting my way, tiptoed and kissed Wolf. Her slender tongue darted into his mouth and she grabbed his ass. She wiped her lipstick from his mouth then hugged him and gave him soft touches. She gave him more love signals than I could stand to watch without feeling like I had Irritable Bowel Syndrome.

Lisa waved good-bye to me, did that with two fingers, sent that message and walked away, singing her favorite song, fingers popping, ass wagging and fake breasts bouncing, never looked back, heading toward the front of the office laughing like the world was hers.

My tongue was pressed against my teeth. "Wolf, I have a situation."

"A situation. What kind?"

"Lisa."

He stood taller, lost that James Dean stance, became a bear. "Go ahead."

Looking at him eye-to-eye, man-to-man, with my guilt, it was hard. I asked, "She bring back any groceries last night?"

He paused for a moment. "Driver, stop right there."

"Look, there are some things we need to put on the table, things you need to know."

He firmed up. "Please, Driver. C'mon, man."

"Wolf, this ain't easy for me . . . but this is *serious*. Shit ain't right."

He cut me off. "After all I've done for you, let me be happy with my wife. I've been through enough bad times to last me two lifetimes. I'm happy today. Some other time for bad news. Maybe when things are going bad tell me the bad news. Not when things are good."

He faced me. He was angry. Could tell by the way he ran his hand over his ponytail.

I repeated, "She bring back any groceries last night?"

A new, unreadable emotion flooded his eyes, gray eyes born in a silver spoon world.

"Your wife left you, Driver."

That hit me hard, caught me off guard. "My wife didn't leave me."

"Man, please. She abandoned you. Left you rotting in a cell in Memphis."

I repeated, "Rotting."

"Your words, not mine."

My throat tightened, as did my hands. He was bringing up things I'd shared while we sipped on beers and JD at Back Biters. Things I talked about when the sun was gone and the memories were too much to bear, things I didn't want to be reminded of in the light of day.

Wolf said, "Remember how you told me you loved that woman from Camp Hill?"

The sound of my teeth gritting filled my head.

"Don't go there, Wolf. My ex-wife and your wife are two different women, dammit."

"You should know."

That stopped me. "Be a man, Wolf. Tell me what you're saying."

"This isn't about me. You're the one who said he had the problem, the debt." His gray eyes came to mine. "Now, your turn. Be a man. You look me in the eye. You tell me."

I held up where I was, stared at my employer. He was shaking. My livelihood was on the line. Like most people in America I hated my job but was afraid to lose it. Hold on. Maybe I didn't hate my job. Hated working underneath a cloud that might storm on me any minute.

I asked, "You okay, Wolf?"

He ran his hand over his ponytail. "When a woman falls in love, she has a brand-new walk. When she falls out, the same. When you know she's not in love with you, it hurts. When she comes back you don't care what she did when she was gone. You just want her back."

A tense moment slipped by. Thoughts colliding like pinballs. If I told Wolf the truth, this gig was over, that was a given. This was all I had. Didn't want to give it up. Not yet. He could call LAPD. The truth about the murder plot, about the money I had taken, didn't know how all of that would go. Didn't want to be on lockdown ever again. Couldn't lose my job, not before I had another payday lined up. Lisa was his wife, that undying love for her in his eyes. That love was a huge barrier, a wall that was too high to get over and impossible to go around.

But I was pissed. He'd derailed me, brought up shit I'd told him while we sat at Back Biters, JD loosening my tongue. Anger was drop-kicking both logic and sanity out the window.

"She love you, Wolf? Or does she do all she can to emasculate you?"

That unreadable emotion changed to anger in the raw. Controlled anger.

If the roles were reversed I would've come at him, cannons blazing like the start of the Civil War. But he wasn't me. He was from a world where wars were fought with attorneys.

"Did your wife love you, Driver? That's what you need to think about."

Wolf stood there, shoulders weighed down. Wolf was a strong man, but no match for the emotions that had crippled him. Love was kryptonite, made the strong handicapped.

"Honey, everything okay in here?"

Lisa had crept back down the hallway. I looked at her, Wolf did the same. I owned a frown, he smiled. Her chest rose and fell, unevenness that came from nervous breathing.

She said, "Sounded like it was getting a little loud back here. What's going on?"

I faced her. "Since we're all here, you want to talk to me about the money I owe you?"

She tilted her head, her move so simple, so perfect, so perplexed. Her disposition was as warm as a mink coat and just as soft. "What money?"

My hands were folded in front of me. Shoulders squared off, facing her.

"So, I don't owe you any money?"

Her eyes went to Wolf. Still acting perplexed. "What's your friend talking about, baby?"

I firmed my tone. "I'm talking to you, Lisa. Do I owe you any money?"

"Driver, don't ever address my wife like that. You understand?"

"Ask her what she paid me to do, Wolf."

"Watch your tone, Driver. This isn't a bar in South Central. Do you understand?"

I backed down. I didn't like the way he talked to me, but I backed down. I'd come at him the wrong way, become emotional, made another bad move. The way he stood up for his wife reminded me that real love was thicker than a few two-dollar drinks at Back Biters.

Lisa looked scared. She had real fear. I'd never seen her unnerved before.

Wolf told her to meet him in the garage, at their luxury cars. He said that like he was pulling the strings, like he was the boss. She hesitated. Her lips pushed up, her eyes dark. She turned and left, the click-clack of her heels telling us that she was heading toward the front, her steps hesitant, just as uneven as her breathing. Then her pace quickened. She was pissed.

"Get out of my office, Driver. And the Pilot pen you pilfered this morning, *put it back*."

He said that like he was the boss. Like I was simple, nothing more than a petty thief. Like knowing a few ten-dollar words might help me win a few games of Scrabble, but those words would never earn me the titles to a Lamborghini and a Cessna. Like I could memorize a dictionary front to back and would still be a man living lower than the soles of his shoes.

Like he was white and I was black.

I told him, "Add it to the fifteen thousand I owe your wife."

Again we stared. If he asked, I was gonna tell. I didn't give a fuck.

He turned his back on me and left, that James Dean swagger rushing him to the woman who wanted to commit mariticide. Wanted him dead so all he owned could be hers.

12

Carl's Jr. hamburger joint was one block east of the Hilton. I hoofed it down there and went inside, ordered two grilled chicken sandwiches, fries, lemonade, and a diet Coke. Ten minutes later Panther walked in. She had on pink and gray running shoes, tight jeans, gray Nike sweatshirt, and a baseball cap on her long hair. She didn't have on any makeup, looked like a college student on break. She had an old, worn, black backpack with her. The kind that went unnoticed. I had caught a booth and she sat across from me.

By then I was on my cellular, venting to Pedro. He was at Back Biters serving spirits.

I ranted about Lisa. Panther wasn't paying attention, her attention and eyes on the front page of an *L.A. Times* that someone had left behind. The headline said that more soldiers had been killed in Iraq, three shot and dragged from their Jeep, beaten with concrete blocks in public. Five more had been killed when their helicopter crashed north of Kabul, read that a minute ago.

Pedro told me, "You've got elephant-sized balls."

"C'mon, man."

"Fuck a man's wife every way but loose, then go work for him."

"You better than anybody knows how hard it is to get a job with a record."

"Inexcusable. Just keep away from my wife unless you want to end up in a taco."

Pedro gave me a hard time, but he understood the walk I was walking. We were descendants of people who worked the fields, cotton and oranges. We knew trying to survive at all costs pulled some men into a spiral of evil. In hard times, morals didn't put food on the table.

I told him about the lion and the jackal. Described the six-foot-tall square-head lion, his football build. And the narrow face, slanted eyes, and pocked face on the thin jackal.

He said, "Never heard of those guys. I'll ask around."

"Niggas showed up in front of my crib last night."

"*Get the fuck outta here.* She sent some bullyboys to your door?"

I asked him for a favor. Offered to break my piggy bank and pay. He said he'd see what he could do, pro bono. I reminded him that his wife worked at a grocery store and they were in the middle of a long strike. Despite his situation, he declined my offer. He told me that if he could get me what I needed it would be pro bono. I thanked him. Then we hung up.

I sat there wrestling with my fate, my own dark and cynical demons. I wondered how many people in this city wanted somebody dead. A lot of people did, but they wouldn't admit it. They wished someone wasn't alive, or not born, a coward's way of wishing somebody dead.

If I had done what I had been sent to do, I could be riding Easy Street right now.

Panther took a chicken sandwich and the Diet Coke, skipped the fries. She had taken the bread off her sandwich, put it to the side with the trash, and cut up the charbroiled chicken patty.

She lowered her head, closed her eyes, prayed over her food. I waited out of respect, watched her give praise, thanks for waking up this morning and her charbroiled special.

This table held an ex-con and a stripper, two people who didn't live in a sugarcoated and ideal world. Then I looked at Panther. We were both of *that* world, the one where every man had a price and every woman had a past. Maybe vice versa. People like us only had two kinds of luck, bad and worse. When things were going well, Fate stuck a foot out and tripped us up.

She asked, "You okay?"

I snapped out of my thoughts. "What?"

"Looked like you were in the middle of omphaloskepsis again."

That got a laugh out of me. It was small and misplaced, but it was appreciated.

She shook her head. "You and your faux-cabulary. You crack me up."

Right now I wanted to find a place I could go and get swallowed up, take my friend JD with me, but I had to make some hard choices. Soft choices had never been a part of my world.

We ate without saying much. She was shifty. Bouncing her leg. Tapping her fingers.

She asked, "When can I see you again?"

That surprised me. "You want to see me again?"

"That's what I just asked."

"Maybe tonight, if that's cool. You working tonight?"

"Not sure." She shrugged. "Depends."

"I got some things to take care of."

"Call me. Even if you can't come through, ring my phone and let me know you're okay. We don't have to do anything. Just want to make sure you're okay, Driver."

I asked, "Why?"

Worry showed in her full lips and the corner of her brown eyes. I reached across the table and held her hand. I felt more than lust, much more than that, but not enough at the same time. Fear was an inhibitor. Love handicapped a man the same way it handicapped a woman.

She shook her head, sighed at me, then took a bite of her cut-up grilled chicken.

My head was in a dark, bad place right now. Plus I'd never been good with women, not when I had to read between the lines, that place called Venus where most of their emotions lived.

She said, "I just left the shooting range. Everything works."

"What I owe you?"

"This meal is enough."

"C'mon now. How much this set you back? I want to kick you back your cash."

"Maybe you could take me to dinner and we could call it square."

We finished our ten-dollar meal and she came over to my side of the table, checked my head wound. I touched her lips and she trembled. She recovered, looked nervous, then she leaned over and kissed my lips, got up from the table and left without saying good-bye.

My lips had never touched hers before. It was nice and warm, made me want more.

I watched her cornbread and buttermilk sashay, watched her shoulders soften, watched her get in her red sports car. She turned on her headlights. First her reverse lights came on, then changed back to her parked lights. She sat there for a few minutes, idling and thinking. Her reverse lights came back on. She backed out and zipped into the madness on Century Boulevard.

My cellular rang less than a minute after she had vanished. I answered.

Panther's voice was both urgent and unsteady. "Can't you just leave town?"

"I'm not running from no motherfucker."

"Because you have a gun."

"If for no other reason."

"Driver, you ever shot anybody?"

"Why you ask?"

"Ain't as easy as it seems. Maybe you should consider your options."

"I'm not running."

"I didn't say run. Why can't you leave for a while? I have people in Alpharetta."

"Shit. I heard you talking to your momma this morning. I know they can't get that confederate flag issue resolved, sounds like they're still lynching niggas down that way too."

"Stay inside the perimeter and keep away from the white girls in Rome, Georgia, and you'll be cool."

"Panther. Look. Can't. Look . . . I . . . I have a brother. Need to stay here."

She said, "Take him if you have to."

"He's . . . my brother is . . . he's sick."

She waited a moment. "What kind of sick?"

I almost told her that Rufus's immune system had been compromised. That he was cash-strapped and the meds to keep him in a healthy state cost a grip. That his being a kept man gave me angst, but it cost a lot to keep him well, money I didn't have, at this rate never would have.

I said, "Look, he's cash poor and I have crumbs lining my pockets so I can't afford to take him and I can't disappear on him. Gotta stay nearby. We're the end of the family tree."

I licked my lips. Tapped my fingers on the table and swallowed my discomfort.

She said, "Didn't know you had siblings. Or cared about . . . about family."

We held the phone, traffic sounds coming through on her end.

Panther said, "I have a sister and a brother. I'm the oldest."

"I'm the oldest too."

"I guess we're setting good examples, huh?"

We actually laughed.

She said, "My baby sister just turned twenty and she has two children by two men who would be more than happy to set fire to the ground she walks on."

"Kinda like Rita Hayworth."

"Yeah, I think that's why that documentary made me so sad. My baby brother is with the 10th Mountain Division. Army. In Iraq. Operation Iraqi Freedom."

I held the phone, but my eyes went to the newspaper she had left behind. She'd been reading about all the young men getting killed over the country's Bush-shit.

She whispered, "Hard to sleep at night with all that madness going on over there."

The anxiety medicine I'd seen in her bathroom was on my mind too. I didn't hold that against her. Rufus had shit like Videx, Ziagen, Viramune, and Crixivan in his cabinets. I'd seen them. Looked them up on the Internet. That medicine cost a grip and a half. Only the rich could afford to stay alive. In this country a man with no insurance died a slow and horrible death.

I asked Panther, "You crying?"

"Only two kinds of people in L.A. People who were born here and people who came here to be stars. The first kind doesn't know how to leave. The second kind leaves with their tails between their legs. It might take them a while to give up, but they leave."

I said, "I'm the first kind. L.A. is all I know."

"And I'm the second. L.A. ain't all that. You should leave this bitch."

"I know. She ain't much, but she's my bitch."

"Ever tried to leave?"

"Tried once. When I was married. Was gonna go live in Alabama."

"What happened?"

"Long story. Came right back as soon as I got out of jail."

She paused. "Just be careful, okay?"

"Panther—"

"Had two dreams about you. In the first dream, we were making love. I mean we were all in it. It was incredible. Not fast. Nobody was in a hurry. Was so sad when I woke up. It was the bomb. Was moaning in my sleep. In the second dream, we were talking. About us. Conversation going in a promising direction. You told me that you knew that I loved you."

Silence.

"I love you, Driver."

She hung up.

I sat there, leg bouncing, holding that phone, staring at nothing, and thinking. I grabbed the newspaper, found the crossword puzzle. "*Paradise Lost* character." Four letters. *ADAM.* "Sleazy speak-easy." Four letters. *DIVE.* I focused, did most of it. That helped me calm down.

I grabbed the backpack Panther had left behind, took it with me, its weight telling me that she'd picked up more than I needed. To be honest, I didn't know what I needed, but I had it.

I passed by a trash can and paused. Thought about tossing the hardware.

I'd been to jail, I'd done shady shit all my life, and I wasn't trying to do that shit no more.

That black-and-white image of Burt Lancaster flashed in my head. That scene in *The Killers* played in my mind, frame by frame. How he lay in that bed and waited for those men to come gun him down. He didn't do a damn thing. Just waited.

I gripped the backpack and moved on.

13

Within twenty minutes I was by my crib, hunting for a parking space. Traffic on La Cienega was brutal, like a drag strip, fools whipping from lane to lane, doing at least seventy in a residential zone. There wasn't a parking space so I took to the alley, left my car there. Was only gonna be here a hot minute.

I was halfway up the stairs before I knew something wasn't right. If I had any kind of Spider sense it was sounding like a fire alarm. I made another step before I stopped. My door was partway open. I dug in the backpack. Pulled out the first gun my hand touched, a .357.

It was dark. Cold.

Listened.

Heartbeat thumping. Could barely hear over the drum inside my chest.

Listened.

Heard nothing but my own anger wrestling with fear.

Took a few breaths.

Smelled.

That scent was strong, familiar. From days gone by. I knew what it was but it was hard to place at the same time. Used to smell it all over the house when we were growing up, that odor that let us know the house had been disinfected, sanitized, and deodorized.

Bleach.

I'd never forget that stench. Momma used to steal that industrial bleach from the second-rate motels she cleaned up, bring it home and wash our white clothes in the bathtub from time to time, and when she did the house held the stench of bleach all night. We'd sleep with the windows open to keep our eyes from burning. I smelled bleach and I imagined Momma in the bathroom, on her knees, washing Reverend Daddy's shirts and scrubbing the sheets in the tub.

It was strong, those fumes thickening and poisoning the night air.

Bleach irritated my eyes the second I used my foot to bump my door wider.

Darker in my place than it was outside. Quiet as death on Sunday morning.

Somebody had broken into my apartment. Didn't know if they were still here.

I smelled smoke. Thick cigarette smoke lingered like smog over San Bernardino.

I let Mr. .357 peep in ahead of me. Finger on trigger, I followed his lead.

I hit the light switch closer to the front door.

2

Two. I knew what that meant. The number of days I had left.

That message was spray painted on every wall I could see. Bright red and deep blacks. Large numbers, small letters, all the same message. Two styles. Only two styles. They worked as a team, each tripping out with their own can of paint, acting like kids on a playground.

That graffiti job wasn't all they'd done while I was at work. They had taken their time, had a little fuck-up-my-place party, left cans of beer and cigarette butts everywhere I could see.

That was the mild damage. The room had been destroyed.

My Green Goblin statue was in a hundred pieces, had been stomped into the floor.

Sofa slashed, gutted, and its insides thrown all around the room like confetti in Macy's Thanksgiving Day Parade. Television had been kicked over, busted, dead where it lay. Socks, drawers, most of my clothes were all over the joint, everything I saw had been cut to pieces.

Kitchen.

2

Everything from chicken to syrup to oatmeal to flour was all over the cabinets and floor.

Windows were closed. Bleach was strong.

I didn't see anybody hiding, but I didn't put the gun away. Coughed, followed that thickening stench and turned on every light I could find.

Bathroom.

2

That's where that stench was the strongest. It was mixing with another foul smell, one twice as rank. This second stink was heavier, not moving, waiting patiently like death.

Stopped moving. Listened.

Heard water running. Like a peaceful river.

Every slow step wetter than the one before.

Looked down.

Carpet damp, soggy, every step like sloshing through a Berber marsh.

Pushed the bathroom door wide open, the business end of my friend leading the way.

Humidity painted my face.

Heat from the hot water rushed out into the cool air.

I hit the light switch, brought that terror to life with a sixty-watt bulb.

Damn.

2

I put the gun down, took my coat off, rolled up my pant legs, cursed like I had Tourette's.

Bathtub was overflowing. Had to rush and turn the steaming water off.

My Italian suits, ties, and shirts, all my gear down to the rest of my socks and drawers were swimming in the bathtub, drowning in the clear water as it turned black and red and gray.

Three empty bleach bottles rested on top of my clothes. Three gallons total.

One gallon for each suit I owned.

My first mind was to pull the suits out, try to save them, but the way the bleach had stolen all the color told me that they were a done deal. Bleach had been poured on first, used to marinate my clothes, then the water had been turned on. I turned the water off, coughed while I opened a window, slipped on the wet linoleum, got my balance, leaned against the door, then slapped the wall over and over with the palm of my hand. If I owned the place I would've knocked holes in every wall, would've torn this building down brick by brick.

The other rank smell came from the toilet. They had shitted in my toilet.

I rushed out the bathroom. Couldn't breathe. Had to find enough air so I could scream.

I cursed all kinds of curses, kicked everything that was already broken.

Wanted to put Lisa facedown, stomp her head until her teeth were gone.

If I hadn't screamed I would've heard my car alarm going off sooner.

People didn't respond to car alarms. Took me a minute to recognize it was mine.

I hurried back downstairs, pants still rolled up, guns in backpack, and took to the alley.

My car was screaming like it had been stabbed in the heart.

I eased up on my ride, made sure nobody had done that to draw me out into danger. Walked the alley, peeped in nooks and crannies, then came back and hit the remote.

The back window had been broken out. A red brick rested on the backseat.

I looked down at the asphalt, saw where tires had burned rubber leaving my world.

Tire prints were as unique as footprints. Those came from big tires. An Expedition.

My cellular rang. I answered without saying a word, just listened. She did the same.

She whispered, *"What did you say to my husband?"*

It was Lisa, her voice so bitter.

I growled, "What your boys did . . . that's pretty fucked up."

"What the fuck did you say to my husband?"

I matched her tone, said, "Call your bullyboys off before somebody gets hurt real bad."

"You don't understand how this works, do you? You're not in charge. *I am.*"

Silence.

"This is the beginning of your end, Driver. I'm not even warmed up yet. Would be a damn shame if every time you pulled out on the streets one of my friends from LAPD found a reason to give you a ticket. Lose your license and I can have Wolf fire your ass with cause and you'd lose your chance at getting a job anywhere a bus doesn't roll. Maybe they could find a ton of drugs in your apartment. Or hidden in your car. With your record—how many more years do you think you'd lose? You're forty. Let's see, that would be your second strike, so, let me think, you'd be at least sixty when you got out. You better stock up on Viagra while you can, Playa."

I swallowed my rage.

I whispered, "Don't fuck with me like that."

"A real man always pays his debts and keeps his word. You've done neither."

My teeth gritted.

I snapped, "Don't believe you did a B&E and destroyed my apartment . . . and my suits . . ."

"Consider that penalties and interest."

More silence while I beat her ass over and over in my mind, my teeth gritting.

"Driver, only two ways out of this."

"I'm listening."

"Get my money."

"Option number two?"

"Do what I paid you to do."

Silence.

"Bet you're wishing you had returned my calls. I begged your ass to call and talk to me. How many times did you ignore me? Bet you're wishing you did now, huh? Can't believe you had the nerve to get a job, to come to my business and work damn near every day. To stand in my face, torture me with your presence. You know how that makes me feel?"

"Lisa—"

"Instead of being an Uncle Tom and drinking beer with my husband, yeah, bet you wished you hadn't ignored me, rejected me like that. Or talked to me like I was somebody and not just some bitch off the street. When you first started seeing me nothing was a problem."

I held the phone away from my right ear. She bounced back and forth from being business to emotional, didn't give me room to squeeze in a gnat-sized word, so I let her rant until the batteries ran down. Wait for the Energizer Bunny to lose energy, that was all I could do.

"Told you, I haven't fucked with you yet. You have no idea. I've been nice. That punk move you pulled, whatever you said to my husband at work, that changes things. That punk move should cost at least a one-day penalty. But I'm a woman of my word. Unlike you I do what I promise. To tell the truth, as mad as I am, I'm debating if I should activate an acceleration clause, have that balloon payment due by this time tomorrow."

In my mind, again, I felt her kicking, struggling to break free, heard her neck breaking.

I counted to five, had to do that so I didn't say the wrong thing. "Look, you know I can't pull down fifteen large just like that, but what if I could hustle you some good faith money?"

Seconds went by like hours. She responded, "Hustle up half and we can talk."

I'd stomped out to La Cienega, wanted to get into the light, never knew who was still lurking in the darkness, was in front of my building, hand in backpack, head throbbing again.

I heard Wolf's voice in the background. He was coming up the stairs to his wife.

I couldn't hear what Wolf asked, but she went into June Cleaver mode, sweet as sugar, and replied, "Not sure who the Lakers are playing tonight, sweetie. You want to eat at Staples Center instead of dinner at Windows? Fine if you do. Just let me know how I should dress."

He said something else.

She laughed like a schoolgirl. "If I wore nothing, we'd never make it out the house."

She hung up.

The same vision played over and over in my mind, my own TNT movie. Saw Lisa, my big hands around her little neck, her feet inches off the floor, kicking, watching life seep from her breath by breath, her refusing to die, me refusing let her live another day, hour, second.

Didn't trust her. I turned right, hurried my car down the alleyway and stopped in the McDonald's lot on La Tijera, parked in the back, away from all the families in search of Happy Meals. I searched my ride top to bottom, checking to see if her bullyboys had left a package of dope in my ride. Nothing. The echo of drug-sniffing dogs rang in my ears and I damn near tore that car apart. Drove back down La Cienega, found a spot on the streets, underneath a light. Sat there, sweating, gripping the steering wheel. They could've doped up my apartment. Hurried back upstairs, backpack bouncing against my leg. Flushed the toilet and opened all the windows. Lisa had me see-ing flashing red and blue lights, had my mind back in the Adjust-ment Center.

I spied out the windows, made sure LAPD wasn't screeching to a halt in front of my building, hurried and searched high and low, looked in every cabinet, closet, inside the toilet.

Another surprise.

In my bedroom closet they had left a set of clothes untouched.

One black suit. One shirt. One tie.

It was a message. Everything they did was a message from Lisa.

Work clothes.

She wanted me to come to work looking spic and span.

No.

Burial clothes.

She had left me burial clothes.

Sirens screamed by my apartment. Those noises got to me. Tensed me.

Again I rushed from wall to wall, searched high and low again, hunted for contraband.

Couldn't find a damn thing.

Shit.

She had me tripping.

Didn't find any drugs her bullyboys might have stashed.

Just the clothes they had left behind.

I stared at that suit.

That message rang loud.

My cellular rang again, jumped. This time it was Rufus. I an-swered, gruff and tight.

He asked, "You get me a signed book?"

I hung up.

14

It took two hours to make a twenty-mile drive. L.A. had over five million vehicles and all of them were going north on the 405, blocking my way from asphalt jungle to asphalt jungle.

Bleach. That stench rose from the bottom of my shoes, singed my nostrils.

I took the Ventura Boulevard exit and headed toward Studio City. Passed by Billy Blanks's gym, crossed Woodman like the instructions said, then cut a left up Ventura Canyon. It was a land of high-end apartment dwellers. Just like on my side of town, the streets were worn, crime was high, and parking sucked up here too. I guess we had equality on some levels.

I took out my cellular and called Arizona. She picked up on the third ring.

She answered with a question: "Where are you?"

"Coming down Ventura Canyon. Just crossed Moorpark."

"Park at the first place you find."

"You coming out?"

"You can come in. I'm getting out the shower. Have to throw on some clothes."

A conniving woman had gotten me in trouble. Now I had to see another scandalous woman to see if I could get out of this quicksand.

I found a spot underneath a large evergreen tree. I left the interior lights off and unzipped the backpack. Panther had given me two burners: a .357 and a .380. The .380 was smaller, easy to hide. There were bullets, a shoulder holster, and a leg strap in the bag too. Panther had gone all out, straight gangsta. Made me wonder about her, what kind of woman she really was. I thought about using the leg holster. If I sat down my pant leg could rise up and the leg holster would show what I was trying to hide. Same for the shoulder holster if I opened my jacket.

I kept it simple and went old school, did like Reverend Daddy used to do when he went out on a special visit, just put the .380 in the small of my back.

Arizona was resting in Sherman Oaks at the Premiere, a small city of luxury apartments right off Woodman. Close enough to Hollywood and far enough away from the urban areas to create the illusion of pseudo culture and safety. Black people dotted the demographics.

Surrounded by streetlights, miles of high-end apartments, and the silhouette of palm trees, I felt anger and impatience start up some hardcore Chicago Steppin' inside my gut.

I heard a door opening farther up the hallway, followed by the echo of sandals flip-flopping at a comfortable pace. Another door opened and Arizona showed up at the wrought-iron gate. That was the birth of another tense moment.

She had thrown on that same silky white blouse and dark skirt I'd seen her in earlier. Her fresh and sweet smell came to me. With no makeup on she looked younger, but her body yodeled that she was a grown-ass woman. Her expression was impenetrable, professional.

The gate let out a high-pitched squeal and slapped the stucco wall when she pushed it open. I took the steps one at a time. Without any greeting we made our way down the hallway.

I growled, "That bull you did at the airport, I don't like people messing with me."

"Sensitive. I like that in a man."

I stopped walking.

She came to a gradual halt, faced me, unaffected by my size or temperament.

She asked, "So, who do you serve?"

"What?"

"Well, Mr. Agnostic, everybody serves somebody. Man, woman, Gold's Gym . . . everyone has a master. Who do you serve?"

I didn't answer. Wasn't in the mood for a survey.

She started back walking, went back to moving her sugar like it was so sweet. I reined in my temper, followed her lazy tempo. She was messing with my head, trying to control the pace of the meeting. Good salespeople were taught to manipulate the customer.

Halfway down the long corridor she slowed down, pushed open a brown apartment door. Classical music and the scent of cloves met us. The music was playing low. I followed her into the unknown, the weight in the small of my back told me we could handle it. Lamps in the front room were on low. Everything beyond the bedroom door was a shadow. Nobody was in the small kitchen or living room, didn't hear anybody talking. She locked the door behind me.

She asked, "Something to drink?"

I licked my lips. "Any JD?"

"Don't think there's much more than water here."

She didn't know what was in the cabinets. That told me that this wasn't her nest.

"Water's nasty." I shook my head. "Fish have sex in it."

Then I stood next to the barstool at the kitchen counter. Dirty dishes were in the sink. Linoleum floor needed to be visited by a mop, soap, and water. Headshots were on the counter. The face of the woman I'd seen with Arizona at LAX smiled up at me. A stack of movie scripts, magazines with casting calls, all of that stuff was piled up on the kitchen table.

I motioned at the glossy vain images and said, "The pickpocket."

"My girl got you good."

"She got lucky."

"That's a Pee-Wee Herman excuse."

Arizona vanished for a moment, went into the bedroom. My eyes checked out the rest of the room. Stacks of books were on the glass coffee table. Freeman's *Dawning of Ignorance* was on top, a red bookmark halfway through. Freeman's other books were on that table too. Heard her in the bedroom opening drawers in the dark. Then another. Searching for something. She came back holding a plastic container, a rectangular Tupperware thing for picnic sandwiches.

Inside were at least twenty wallets.

Arizona said, "Freeman drew a nice crowd. My girl had a good day today."

"LAX?"

"Yup. She can bump and lift with two fingers."

I didn't touch her pirate's treasure. Didn't want my fingerprints on the plastic or the merchandise. I asked, "What you do with the credit cards and IDs?"

"Fenced 'em as soon as we left the airport."

"That's why you had to jet away from LAX."

"Couldn't let them go cold."

A folded play announcement slept on the counter. *The Graduate.* She saw me staring at it, then moved it out of the way, opened a drawer filled with junk, dropped it inside.

I deepened my tone. "Let's get to the business."

My tone was rough. Arizona didn't flinch. I didn't move.

She gave me a pleasant expression. "I like that about you. So direct."

She reached into her black purse and pulled out a red box of cigarettes. She lit one up. I expected a stench, but it had a nice aroma. Took me a moment to make out the scent of cloves. Underneath her cool façade, she was pissed off that I hadn't given in as fast as she wanted me to.

She did the gamming, told me she wanted to get the briefcase Freeman had shackled to his wrist. Steal it. Hold it for ransom. I listened. No more than two minutes went by.

I said, "I mean, if it's a damn book and . . . what, how do you ransom . . . ?"

Before she could answer I stood up. I walked to Arizona, moved with intention.

I whispered, "Take your clothes off."

She looked in my non-blinking eyes, stared deep, and smiled.

She took off her blouse. My eyes went over her honey brown skin, took in her breasts. She dropped her skirt. She wore no panties. Stood in front of me unashamed and bare.

I said, "Turn around."

She raised her arms over her head, stood on her tiptoes and did a slow three-sixty. A colorful scorpion was on her back, a henna, not a real tattoo. She had soft and sturdy legs, straight with a little bow in them, strong calves, not much in the hips department, a modest ass that would spring to life when she wore heels. Her body was tanned like she'd just got back from someplace tropical. Her breasts were firm, the left one pierced, a small golden hoop on the nipple, both nipples erect. She didn't have any body hair, not even over her pussy. That part of her was as bald as my head. Decent proportionality. Everything about her went together like Dolce & Gabbana.

She whispered, "I'm not wired. Relax. No entrapment. I'm legit."

I motioned toward the darkness resting in the other room. "What's back there?"

"Bedroom."

I crept toward the bedroom door, hit the light switch.

The bed was made up, but a ton of clothes were on the covers. Everything was new and still in plastic. The bathroom was on the other side of the bedroom. I went to the bathroom, pushed the door open, looked inside. The room was humid, mirror damp in the corners. Scented soaps and potpourri were in a basket. Wigs were on a stand. One was in dreadlocks, another a pageboy cut, one long and brunette, one a short red mane with blond highlights. A wicker bowl filled with makeup and lipsticks was on the counter. Tools of the thieving trade.

She called out, "Make sure you look under the bed."

"After I check the shower."

I went back to the bedroom, then stopped by the bed and read a few of the labels. Versace. Yves St. Laurent. Armani. Prada. Herrera. Narciso Rodriguez. Zac Posen.

The merchandise was hot enough to burn down half the valley. She was a legit thief.

I went back into the front room, my expression hard. Nothing I'd seen had distracted me.

Arizona was still naked.

She asked, "Satisfied? Or do you need to do a cavity search?"

"Looks like some things fell off a truck."

"Trucks are *sooo* throwback. It's all about cyberspace. It's a new day, all about fake IDs and credit cards, all about hijacking the Internet from the comfort of your own home."

She eased her skirt over her frame, then put her blouse back on. She left buttons undone, more cleavage this time. I guess she figured I'd seen all she had to offer, so it was no big deal.

She asked, "Now where was I before your paranoia kicked in?"

"Having a little book club meeting."

"We hold it hostage."

"It's a book, not the Lindbergh baby."

"The laptop it's on is priceless. To him if nobody else. What's on it is worth a cool million. No different than stealing a company's master documents. We get his intellectual property, he'll freak out."

We moved back into silence, her seven-figure words the bench we were resting on. If she was talking about diamonds or government secrets I would know where she was coming from. It was a stupid book. I didn't understand where she was going with this, so I listened.

I asked, "You fence it . . . what?"

"We steal it, then go right back to him with a ransom demand."

"I'm not feeling this."

"What's the problem? Too simple or too complicated?"

"It's not like doing a bump and lift to get credit cards."

She drew her smoke, the popping and crackling sounding like

music. Arizona frowned and blew the fumes away, then studied me. Her sweet-smelling smoke clouded the room.

Arizona nodded like she had figured something out. She asked, "Gambling debt?"

"Why you ask that?"

"Last night your head wasn't busted. And yesterday it didn't seem like you could be persuaded to help me out with this job."

My head wound sang a brief song of pain. I studied her the way she studied me.

She said, "And you don't have the same disposition you had at Back Biters last night."

"Likewise. Same goes for that cute little message you left on my machine."

"Oh, I'm the same." She winked. "You're tense."

"I'm tired. I'm the one with the day job."

"Last night you were easygoing."

"JD gets me in that frame of mind."

"Horny and easygoing, I might add."

"Your point?"

"You just saw me naked. No reaction. I won't take it personal."

She headed toward the kitchen. Her oversized slippers flip-flopped against her feet. She went to the sink and ran water over the tip of her smoke, then tossed it in the trash.

She asked, "That fresh gash in your head, something to do with Hummer Girl?"

"What, you trying to get the Sherlock Holmes award?"

"Hummer Girl hopped out of her ride like she was a vigilante, marched up on you and frowned at me like she wanted to stab me in the throat with a steak knife."

"Told you the bitch was looking for her husband."

"Nigga, please." Arizona didn't back down. "My first guess was her husband found you and beat your ass, but you don't have the kind of damage from a hand-to-hand. Spin the roulette wheel. I'm dropping my stack of chips on black and betting it all on the bitch in the Hummer."

The edges of my lips moved up again, then moved right back down, then back up, riding my irritation like a roller coaster, trying to settle on a mood. They stopped moving midway.

She asked, "Am I wrong?"

My expression remained cold and impenetrable.

She gave me a half smile, thickened her tone, asked, "So, do we do business together?"

"If I'm compensated to my satisfaction, we might be able to do something."

"Because you have a debt to pay."

I answered with a stiff look that told her to mind her own business.

She talked on, "What if you're not, as you say, compensated to your satisfaction?"

"I walk. You go your way, I go mine."

"And we're free to run this without your interference?"

"If it goes down on my watch I want a cut."

"Blackmail."

I shook my head. "Business."

"Sure you want to go out like that?"

"That a threat?"

Her eye contact was strong. "Like you said, business."

"If you want this ship to sail, tell me who threw my name in the hat."

She shook her head in a gentle way, that long hair doing a soft dance. "Can't."

"Why?"

"Let's just call it a confidentiality agreement. I'll protect my contact the same way I'll protect you, the same way I protect all of my employees. If something goes wrong they can't drag you down. And you can't drag them down. Don't take it personal. Business."

She was reading me; the blueprints to my troubles were etched on the surface of my eyes.

Arizona asked, "How deep of trouble are you in? How much you owe?"

I took a pen out of my pocket, the same pen I had borrowed from

Wolf's office this morning. Heard his voice telling me to put the pen back. He had been specific, said *Pilot* pen.

I hesitated and read the brand. It was Pilot.

That stopped me, had me sitting like a statue for a moment.

There was a snitch in the office. Somebody was watching my every move. Even knew when I borrowed a pen from Wolf's desk, down to the brand.

I pulled out a business card and wrote 50 on the back of it, then handed that number to Arizona. She read and whistled, leaned back and served me that ambiguous smile again.

She blew air. "You'd best keep playing the lottery."

"Tell me something, stop yanking my chain and talk to me."

She smiled, waited a good ten seconds before she spoke again. "My idea was somewhere between fifty and seventy-five for the job, a reasonable amount that could get us a quick turnaround, but even that depends on what information I can get about his banking accounts."

"Banking accounts. You can get that information?"

She didn't answer, just kept talking. "It's good to know how much cash the mark has access to, how liquid he is, that way we have the upper hand and the mark can't bullshit us."

I said, "If he's a money-smart man, he won't have that much cash on hand."

"True. If he's money smart. Most people aren't."

"What would my cut be?"

She told me, "I get fifty percent."

"Fifty?"

"My operation. The lion's share is mine."

"I see."

"The rest is an even split."

"How many people?"

"When it's time to disclose that . . ."

"I see. Back to the banking information."

She steepled her hands, sat back. "If I can get that information, and his accounts reflect that kind of a balance, we'll be in a better position when it's time for negotiations."

I said, "That's a lot of dead presidents to ask for and not expect him to call in the police."

"That's a lot of cash to ask for without the possibility of hurting somebody."

I nodded my understanding. "That's why you want me on your team."

"Part of the reason. But we need an inside man, in case something goes wrong, in case plans change. Eyes and ears. But with those muscles and fists you have, you look like you could put a serious hurting on somebody. Sometimes that kind of labor is a requirement. Most of the time it's not, but there are too many variables involved, too many ways shit can go wrong."

"Better to hurt than get hurt."

"And I thought you weren't a poet."

She lit up another cigarette. Took two puffs and did the same routine, ran water over the tip and tossed it in the trash. She saw me watching, looked at me like she was a mind reader.

She said, "Hate the smoke. The smell brings back memories."

"Good or bad?"

"The same kind that were in your eyes when you were sipping your drink last night."

"You're a regular Miss Cleo."

"No, but I recognize the reflection of myself in others. Saw it in you. You loved somebody." She leaned against the counter, pulled her hair away from her exotic face, hummed along with the classical music. "You're a good-looking man, Driver. So fucking beautiful."

"As beautiful as the man you're trying to forget?"

Her eyes turned sensitive. That memory softened her conniving heart and stole her edge. She regrouped and gave me her one-sided smile. "Before we go any further, you in or out?"

"On the fence."

"You're even agnostic about business decisions."

I told her, "You haven't guaranteed me a cut."

"There are no guarantees. Sometimes it's jackpot, sometimes it's a dry run, a bust."

"Bust or jackpot, I need an advance."

She thought on it. "Let's say I advance you ... mmm ... two thousand."

"Seven."

"Two. Be glad I didn't tell you to walk."

I considered my situation and my lack of options before I said, "In."

"Be sure. No cooling-off period."

I repeated, "In."

She smiled like I had said the magic word. I halfway expected her to sit me down and make me watch an Amway-type videotape about this scamming business, maybe even have people who worked with her pop in and give testimonials about how much money they made and how they loved their jobs. We shook hands, straight business. Her skin was warm.

She looked for trust in my eyes. I did the same with her. Thieves were liars and cheats. There was no honor among thieves. I knew because I lived with the best the South had to offer for two years. Still I nodded my agreement anyway. She held her grip and did the same.

She said, "I'm the boss on this operation. Everyone answers to me. Everything comes through me. If you have a problem working for a woman, let me know that now."

"Long as a paycheck is on that end, no problem on this end."

I let her hand go first. Her thin fingers made an erotic trail across my wide palm, made my Adam's apple dance in my throat. Her eyes moved up and down my frame.

I asked Arizona, "Who do you serve?"

"When you have money, everyone serves you."

15

Arizona rubbed up against me as her sugary walk took her into the bedroom.

The sofa welcomed my weight with an easy give and a mild sigh from the springs.

She came back in the room five minutes later, hair down, face made up, looking like the siren who had played me last night. She had her dark purse on her shoulder and a long leather coat across her arm. Her perfume had a light scent, the kind that could easily go unnoticed.

She said, "Let's go for a ride."

"Where?"

"You want that advance, right?"

She pulled a box filled with garment bags from the other side of the bed. We packed up the fancy outfits, put one in each garment bag. I carried the awkward load. She led the way. I followed. To the elevator. Then to the garage. She hit her remote. The lights on her silver BMW flashed. Doors unlocked. Engine started purring before we made it to the car.

She made a frustrated sound. "Keep hitting the wrong buttons."

"New toy?"

"Something like that."

She fumbled with the remote until the trunk opened, crept up nice and easy.

I loaded the merchandise. New car smell perfumed the air.

I envied her ride in silence. A car told you about a person's character, how they saw themselves, how they wanted the world to see them. Cars weren't just transportation, they were symbols. All about perpetrating and projecting. L.A. people were attached to their rides. Ugly women and mackless men could hop in a ride like this and let the car do the sweet-talking.

The leather seats were like warm butter, smooth and soft to the touch.

We passed by my ride. That back window shattered.

Arizona drove toward Hollywood, went down Ventura, a strip that had a lot of stores like Gap and Baja Grill, a regular Traffic Light Row. She dug in her purse and took out a small black device, pointed it at the intersection and pushed a button. The traffic light changed back to green, just like it had done for her last night when she left Back Biters.

I asked her, "What's that device?"

"It's a MIRT. Mobile Infrared Transmitter."

I was impressed. "How does it work?"

"You point it and it changes red lights to green lights. It's the same technology that ambulances use to get to emergencies faster."

My cellular rang. UNKNOWN CALLER on the ID.

I answered and heard a lot of happy noise in the background, the sounds of people chattering, forks and spoons clanging against plates, soft jazzy music. It sounded like one of those special and discrete Hollywood parties that Rufus and Pasquale went to from time to time.

Lisa said, "Playa, Playa. Watch your back while you're having fun in the valley."

She hung up.

I looked around to see who she had on my tail, searching the headlights for trouble, thinking that I'd have to use the .380 before the night was done, wishing I'd brought the .357 along as well. I tried to sit still but I kept moving, checking the rearview off and on.

Cars were an extension of the driver's personality.

Arizona drove a vehicle built for speed and pleasure.

Lisa drove a vehicle made for battle, the kind used in a war.

16

We landed near La Brea and Melrose, the artsy side of the city lined with vintage shops, the dividing line between L.A. and Hollywood, between the working class and the dreamers. Chili and fresh turkey burgers came to me on the breeze. Pink's, one of L.A.'s oldest hot dog stands, was one block away. My gun was secure in the small of my back.

Arizona was taking her time asking me things. Getting me to tell her a little at a time, like she was in no hurry, not desperate at all. Having fun. She smiled at me a few times, every smile feeling like a soft kiss, the kind of smiles that made the blood drain from my brain to strengthen my loins. She was good. Knew how to use the Power of the Pretty Woman without giving up the pussy.

Arizona valet parked. Handed her keys to a Mexican dressed in black pants, white shirt, and a red vest, said a few words to him in Spanish, then she came and took my hand.

I searched the streets again, then followed Arizona's quick pace toward a small theater. They stopped us at the door, did that like we were terrorists, then got a closer look at Arizona and moved to the side apologetically, let us in without a word.

The billboards and signs posted told me that we were at the play *The Graduate*. The cast's headshots were plastered on the walls. I saw the face of Arizona's friend. The pickpocket's name was Pamela Quinones. She was playing the part of Mrs. Robinson.

I motioned toward the headshot and asked, "Pickpocket working the crowd?"

"This is legit."

We sat in the back. There was a small audience, all Hollywood types. A few of Hollywood's black actors were in the crowd, people who hadn't worked since *The Cosby Show*.

A couple of dramatic scenes went by and they dimmed the lights.

Mrs. Robinson came on stage. Big applause. High heels and a floor-length fur coat. The fur coat slid away from her frame, showed her flesh a little at a time. Red french-cut panties made her long legs look like stilts. Her breasts pushed against her silky bra like they were trying to break free and run home. Wonderful body, long hair, the stage lights all in her favor, lit her up like she was Lauren Bacall in *To Have and Have Not*. Her erotic moves, the way she drank her wine, her drunken sashay, the way she sang, the way she went about seducing the young and confused college graduate on stage had the audience moaning and shifting in their seats.

Arizona whispered, "She got herself done all up."

"Done all up?"

"Tummy tuck. Breasts lifted."

"There's a lot of that going around."

"Like an epidemic."

The pickpocket set the room on fire when she seduced her daughter's boyfriend. She didn't look that old, might've been my age, but the makeup gave her some maturity over her costars. And this was Hollywood, where when it came to having a career on a stage, men aged at a normal rate but women aged in dog years. If she was my age and still working at a theater off La Brea, she probably had to pick as many pockets as she could to have her ends make acquaintance.

Arizona asked, "What do you know about Frank Sinatra?"

"Who?"

"Freeman's woman. Old blue eyes."

"Thought Freeman was the mark."

"He is."

I shrugged. "Just know her name is Folasade Titilayo Coker. She drinks the hell out of vodka. Speaks Italian. Just met her. Maybe I should ask you what you know about her."

"That brat's clinging to Freeman's success."

"What else you know about her?"

"Alcoholic. Loser. Spoiled. Typical rich people problems."

I said, "Didn't know those were rich people problems."

"And she's jealous of his success."

"You get that info online?"

She said, "Straight from Freeman. We talked this evening. He said she wrote a book a few years ago. It tanked."

"That bad?"

"He said she couldn't sell shit to a fly."

"No shit."

"He was trying to figure out how we could hook up. He wanted some."

"Some what?"

"Don't get stupid on me."

"Little Miss Africa came to L.A. and she's not putting out to the million-dollar man?"

"Variety is the spice of life, you know that. He could get that and still want this."

"No doubt."

"He said she's getting to be a problem. Trying to hold him down."

"If she's a problem, why doesn't he kick her to the curb then?"

"Who cares? Driver, you know how men are better than I do. From where I'm sitting all I know is men hate you, mistreat you, but won't ever stop taking you to bed."

"But you can't keep away."

"No, they can't keep away. No matter how misogynistic, no matter how codependent, no matter how low their self-esteem, they always look for comfort in the bosom of a woman."

"Like I said, you can't keep away."

"Not from the intelligent ones in nice suits." Arizona's voice dropped down to a seductive whisper. "Too bad you didn't answer last night."

"Yeah. Too bad."

"Why didn't you kiss me?"

"Business."

"Can we take a break from business?"

"Sure."

She leaned my way. I leaned hers. We kissed, soft tongue, gentle and sweet.

She looked at me, gave me the same eyes she did last night in the parking lot.

We kissed again.

She moaned a little. Got heated up, touched my face with her hand.

I forgot about Panther. Forgot about Lisa. Forgot about Wolf. Forgot about Rufus, Momma, and Reverend Daddy. Forgot about everything that haunted me.

Then we went back to watching the play, her hand on mine.

She was good at her game. Real good. But I had to be better at mine. I gave her the same kind of smile I gave her last night, didn't give any more than that. Money was involved. Women were involved. Both caused the kind of trouble that sent a man to an early grave.

I asked, "You fucking Freeman?"

"So direct."

"You said he wanted some. Are you?"

"That Pikachu-looking brother is a trip. He's hot on my girl."

"Oh. Thought he was hot on you."

"Oh, God. That cockhound is calling us both."

"Playing the odds."

"Right. Thinks we don't talk."

"The player is getting played."

"Fo' sheezy my neezy."

"So you're fucking him?"

"We had phone sex. Well, he got off. I played my part."

"No real fucking?"

"Haven't. Lot of money at stake."

"If it comes down to that?"

"Will if I have to."

"The pickpocket?"

"My girl is down too. We have that understanding."

"Big pimpin'."

"Business."

"Sure. Business."

"Right. Nothing personal. It's business."

"Well, you're the prettier one."

"She has the better body."

"Depends on what you like."

"Get real. You see her ass? If my booty was like that I'd rule the world."

"If I were him I'd go for you."

"If Freeman looked and dressed like you, shit, this would be a pleasant job."

My cellular hummed again. Rufus's number again. I let it roll. Then two more calls came in back-to-back, both from the UNKNOWN CALLER. Later on I'd wished I'd answered those calls. But right now I didn't know what was going down. I ignored the hums, then powered it down and went back to checking out the play, the pickpocket in particular.

On stage the young college graduate's affair with Mrs. Robinson went south. The aging nymph flipped from erotic to vindictive. Old with few choices. Desperate for affection. It was like watching Lisa lose her mind. Maybe I was tired but my eyes started burning and in that heat she started to look like Lisa. My wound came to life, throbbed its own beat, put waves of tension in my neck and back. I would've walked out, but I couldn't do that without causing a disturbance.

I sat there, staring at Mrs. Robinson, hating that character the same way I did Lisa.

The play ended and I expected Arizona to wait for the pickpocket, but we left the theater and hurried to valet. She handed the Mexican who had handled her car a C-note. It was only five dollars to park. She didn't ask for any change. This time no Spanish words.

Arizona made red lights change to green until we got back to Sherman Oaks.

She pulled back into the garage, opened the trunk. The load of designer clothes was gone. Three white envelopes had taken the place of the garment bags. She opened one of the envelopes, the thinnest of the three, counted out three thousand in C-notes, folded that Chicago roll in half, handed it to me, stuffed the other envelopes in her purse like it was no big deal.

I said, "You said two."

"Honest. I like that. Let's just say I tip well."

She asked about Freeman. Wanted to know where they were staying.

I told her they were crashing at Shutters. I think she already knew that, but I didn't put that question out there. It was my turn to do the gamming, so she chilled and let me talk. I told her about security, that Sade had come back to the bar by herself. That must've been when Arizona was on the phone with Freeman. Told her that it didn't seem like him and Sade were on good terms, but the love was there, just didn't know what that love was based on.

She asked, "What do you mean, based on?"

"Different kinds of love. Could be amative."

"Amative?"

"You know, physical, a sexual thang, that kinda love."

"Do men love any other way?"

I knew I'd never win that argument. I changed the subject, asked what else she had going on, just in case this Freeman shit was a bust. She said that one of the things she had done over the years and was good at was counterfeiting credit cards, knew all about a card's magnetic strips.

I asked, "You doing that at the play?"

"We have credit card readers in a few places around the city."

She fired up a smoke. I asked her how that credit card scam worked and she changed again, smiled and turned all pro, started sounding like Professor Grifter.

I said, "I heard equipment for that kinda operation was expensive."

"It is." She dropped her cigarette, let it burn and scent the stale air. "Not hard to get on the open market. Embossing machines cost. Silk-screening equipment doesn't cost as much."

"Thought you were into real estate."

"I'm into more things than you'll ever know. I learned managerial skills from the best."

She was smart, but I'd met smarter people on the other side of The Wall.

I checked my watch again, felt like a clock was over my head counting down, its glow in red neon. It had been a long night and a longer day. Sleep was looking for me and I was avoiding it like the plague. I gave in to a yawn, moved the conversation back to the task at hand.

I asked, "If you can pull down this much cash, why bother with Freeman?"

With a crooked little smile she said, "Because jacking a book has never been done."

"All fun and games for you."

"What can I say? I love my job. Would be nice to do something . . . different . . . creative."

I understood, told her that with a simple nod. "You're a trendsetter."

"Always looking for new opportunities."

"When did you get that idea? To jack a book for bucks?"

"Last summer I saw this thing on the news. I was in North Carolina, working a nice little grift back that way. John Grisham was getting paid seventy-five thousand to come to a library. From the time his plane landed to the time it took off, he was in North Carolina for three hours. Seventy-five thousand. I thought, what if somebody jacked his next book."

"Damn. But you couldn't get to the Grish."

"He didn't look like the type. Then I saw Freeman on C-SPAN, bragging about his big payday. The perfect mark. So full of himself. So arrogant. Did some research online."

"God bless the Internet."

"A grifter's toolbox. Anyway, stumbled across something unrelated. Years ago Toni Morrison's house burned down or something. She lost a manuscript. The article talked about the unpublished manuscript, and of course how millions of dollars in literature had gone up in flames. The part that stuck with me was how, even if she started over, she'd never be able to reproduce what she had, not the way it was. It couldn't be duplicated, was irreplaceable."

"I'm on the same page with you. You jack it, it can't be replaced. So it's worth a mint."

"I went to a few writers' Web pages. Freeman's Web page was somewhere in the middle of the list, shot him an e-mail, he responded within two hours."

"Just like that."

"Surprised me too."

"You send Bobblehead a picture with the e-mail?"

"Of course."

"I'm not gonna ask what kind of picture you sent."

"Nothing you haven't already seen."

We laughed and traded yawns.

We talked a little more. Everything had to happen tomorrow, no later than the next day.

I told her, "Make sure I get the call to drive the new black aesthetic."

She nodded.

I said, "I need fifteen."

She nodded. "We'll do what we can do."

Anger was rising, but I felt better. Cash in my pocket made my load feel lighter.

I ran my hand over her hair, asked, "Gonna invite me up?"

The gate to the garage whined open. Another new BMW pulled

in, just like Arizona's, only it was jet black. The pickpocket was driving. Now her hair was short, in a pixie cut, longhaired wig removed. She saw us talking, nodded at Arizona, drove to the end and parked.

Arizona told me, "Your timing is bad."

"Same goes for you."

She tossed her smoke, flipped her hair. "You should've answered last night. Had the place to myself. She stayed over in Encino with her boyfriend. Her costar in the play."

"Mrs. Robinson likes 'em young."

"Look who's talking."

"I'm tired anyway."

"You look it. Get your rest."

The pickpocket was sashaying our way, her thin heels clicking against the concrete. D&G belt. High-end purse that had a lot of little Gs in the leather. Ralph Lauren shades at night. Leather pants and a white top that exposed the ripples in her flat stomach. Same long coat she wore in the play was keeping her warm. She was talking, laughing. On her cellular.

She pushed a button, muted her phone and told Arizona, "Freeman."

"He called you?"

"Blowing up my phone."

"So he's an ass man."

"Don't hate the butt, mutt."

They both laughed and said a few things to each other in Spanish. Her friend was asking about me, her eyes told me that, so did her body language. Didn't like her. Not at all.

Her eyes told me she felt the same way about me.

The pickpocket went back to getting her mack on with Freeman.

"So, they're running a book event you did on C-SPAN tonight?" The pickpocket rolled her eyes. "Sure I'll stay up and check it out. I bet you did tell them a thing or two."

I wondered where Sade was. Probably in a vodka-induced coma.

Arizona waved and followed the pickpocket to the elevator, four heels clicking in exhausted rhythms, asses moving with Grey Poupon sashays. They vanished on the elevator.

I took the gun away from the small of my back, held it down at my side as I headed to my car and its broken glass. Put the piece in my lap. Turned the heat up high. Drove toward a ruined apartment, glass crumbs falling in the backseat every time I hit uneven pavement.

I walked in my door, stepped across the soaked and bleached carpet, turned on the lights.

2　　　　　　　　　2

2

2　　　　　　　　　　　　　　2

I was three thousand richer.

Twelve thousand away from being able to sleep at night.

17

Crumpled-up dollars made puddles at her feet.

Panther did a few spins and offered her rear to the crowd. More crumpled dollars. Her shiny dress flew off and she was down to her G-string. Her body oiled. She fondled her blond wig and took to the pole, did a gymnastics move and ended up upside down, came down slowly, gyrating, then flipped slow and easy, landed in a Chinese split. She double-timed the beat and did some erotic African moves, lower body rotations that sent out waves of pleasure.

A tanned Asian girl passed by. Six-inch stilettos. Long black hair. Long satin kimono.

She said, "Hey, Driver."

"Hey, China Doll."

She stopped at a table next to me, did a dance for a brother and his woman, mostly for his smiling woman. That was the norm in a spot like this. The ratio of men to women had to be fifty-fifty up in here, all competing for the same soft-legged pretty girls at ten dollars a song.

I walked over to the stage, sprinkled a few dollars. Panther came over, dancing in her thigh-high boots, isolating butt cheeks, first making one move, then the other, then together.

I said, "Thought you weren't working tonight."

"Didn't hear from you."

"You have an attitude with me now?"

"What you think?"

"Need a place to crash."

"And?"

"Can I still come over?"

"For what?"

"What did I do?"

"What you think?"

"Why don't you just tell me and we'll both know."

"I'm working, Driver."

I let that go and headed back over to the bar, grabbed me a Jack on the rocks, watched Panther wag her onion for a moment then turned away, looked at other dancers. It was easier for me to watch other women work. Watched women dancing for women. For men. For couples. Watched the Asian girl take a brother into a back room where special things happened for the right price. Was hard to watch Panther do this. Don't know when I started to mind. Crept up on me. Her life. Didn't seem right and didn't seem like my place to tell her anything different.

My past. Seemed like I saw my past sitting in front of me, swimming in that glass.

Sometimes I stared at my JD and saw her complexion. Didn't matter if I drank from a glass or a paper cup, her face was in every drop. I swallowed and heard her calling my name.

I let that go. Anger sent me back to the problems I had now.

Panther came off stage, passed me by. All attitude. Nothing like the woman I'd been inside this morning, not at all like the woman I'd seen this afternoon. She ended up flirting with the guy standing next to me. A blue suit sporting a hundred-dollar tie and crisp white shirt. Flirting hard and strong. She sat next to him, her hand on his leg, laughing, telling him how fine he was. Then she started dancing for him, swerving her backside up against his crotch.

My right hand started shaking. Needed to hit somebody.

I stopped Sexy Chocolate as she passed, asked her to come perform for me. She nodded toward Panther and shook her head, telling
me no. I grabbed her arm and pulled out a C-note. That changed her
mind. Panther cut her eyes at me, then did the same toward Sexy
Chocolate.

Sexy Chocolate stopped dancing. "Driver, I don't know whassup,
but I ain't involved."

She told me to keep my money, politely stepped off, headed
across the room.

Panther finished her dance, stuffed her ten spot in her garter,
walked away without acknowledging me. China Doll wouldn't come
my way. Same went for Diamond, Mercedes, Spanish Fly, Butter
Pecan, Alize, Milkshake, Chardonnay, Honey Dip, and a few others.

I downed my Jack and headed for the exit.

People with day jobs had started leaving the strip mines about the same
time I walked out. The irresponsible and unemployed stayed until the
last song. Waitresses started leaving around one-thirty. Then Panther
came out. She had on pink sweats, a leather jacket, Adidas bag over
her shoulder. Some guy was walking with her. Big, wide dude. One
of the bouncers. She saw me by her car, said something to him. He
turned around, went back toward the club.

Cool. Jack had calmed my nerves. I didn't feel like hitting nobody
anyway.

She stopped right by me, ran her hand over her hair, let out an ex-
asperated sigh.

"Two minutes, Driver."

"Five."

"You just lost ten seconds."

I nodded. "Want to tell me what's going on?"

She shifted, dropped her bag, leaned her butt against her car.

"Today . . . at lunch . . . got emotional—" She cleared her throat,
waited for a car to drive by us. "Got carried away. Said it."

I sucked my bottom lip. Tired as hell. Didn't need this shit
right now.

"That did it." She nodded. "Told you I love you. You didn't respond. You didn't even acknowledge that I told you I loved you."

"That's why you're acting crazy?"

"I opened up. You blew me off."

"You hung up."

"You had all day to call me back. Told you that and I haven't heard from you."

"Didn't blow you off. Hell, I opened up too."

"You did not."

I snapped, "With all the shit I'm dealing with, did the best I could, dammit."

That shut her up.

Head busted with a 7-Up. A Glock pointed at me. Stalked. Apartment trashed. Clothes either soaked in bleach or ripped to shreds. This bullshit was the last thing I needed.

She took her tone down a bit. "Why didn't you call me to let me know you were okay?"

"Been busy."

"You have a cellular on your hip at all times. What, you couldn't find two seconds?"

I shifted, ran my fingers over that day-old scar behind my ear. I understood women the way most poor people understood the economy.

"I told you, you igg'd it." She let out a wounded chuckle. "Just like you're doing now."

"What was I supposed to say? I mean, it was a statement, right?"

"A statement. Like 'The sky is blue.' "

"Well if you had said that, that would've been different because the sky is gray."

"Not funny."

I sighed.

She said, "Doesn't matter."

"Then why are you so angry?"

"Not angry. Frustrated. Disappointed. Don't matter. Love ain't done nothing for me but get me in no-good relationship after no-good relationship, had me doing immoral and illegal shit for niggas that I knew I shouldn't be doing. Never should've left Atlanta. Never."

"I ain't never asked you for nothing."

"Rrright. Now I'm a damn gun runner."

That hollowed me out. I said, "It matters."

"I cook for you. Sleep with you. And I don't even know you, you know that?"

"You didn't have to get the guns. I asked. You coulda said no."

"I just hate . . . all day . . . regret I said . . . *that. To you.* I don't understand you. What we have is real fucked up. I mean, I admitted I loved you . . . no response . . . your prerogative."

I shifted a bit. Wished I had a shrink to come in, tell me why I couldn't open up. Why when women got this deep I wanted to pack up and run to a river that had shallow emotions.

She stayed where she was, arms folded.

I asked, "What about that dude you were seeing?"

"Married man?"

"Yeah."

"That was a one-night stand that lasted three years too long."

"So you're saying that's over."

"Was over last Christmas. Had a revelation. Got tired of being the cleanup woman."

"Sure about that? I mean, you moved out here to be with him."

"Oh, I'm sure. It got ugly. Real ugly."

"How ugly is real ugly?"

"Restraining-order ugly."

That was the way of relationships. Everything overlapped until something good came along, then all others went on standby until that something good became something permanent.

More women came out, caps and sweats, dressed down, escorted by bouncers.

I said, "You were all over homeboy up in there."

"This is where I work. That's what I do. So don't trip."

"I know."

"I'm a lot of men's fantasy, Driver. Women too."

"You've been with women?"

She said, "You're good at changing the subject when I try to be real with you."

Panther looked at the back window of my car, saw that hole where a window used to be, shook her head, looked at me. "How's your injury? You're looking pretty bad. Head hurting?"

"Aches. Need to change the bandage."

She caught herself, backed down from her feelings, looked away, made a noise that said she was getting cold, but didn't move from where she stood. "You in a serious bind?"

"Yeah. My place is hot."

"How hot?"

"Hella hot. Couple of motherfuckers are playing the terrorist role. Broke in. Trashed it."

"And that's why you need the burners."

"Yeah. I'll give you the story later."

"Tell me now."

"Tired as hell now. Look, my spot is hot."

"Stay with your brother."

"My brother's roommate . . . We don't get along . . . that wouldn't work."

"Sounds like you're burning bridges all over town."

"Look . . . Panther . . . Need a place to crash for a minute."

She leaned away from me, still shaking her head. "So you need me."

"Yeah, I do."

She sighed, her frown so deep. That love she had for me already turning to hate.

I told her, "You're right. Look, I'll call you."

"Don't."

"What?"

"Don't call. Don't call me, Driver."

I nodded, waved her ass off, and headed for my ride, long strides, not looking back.

She called my name, snappy and demanding. Not the way for a woman to talk to a man.

I ignored her.

She called my name again, this time her tone better to my liking.

I turned and faced her.

She said, "Look . . . Driver . . . you can come over."

"That's okay."

"Let's not do this circle dance."

"Didn't you just tell me not to call your ass anymore?"

"Just come over."

I hesitated, stared at her a moment, my frown as deep as hers, then I nodded.

She cursed and shook her head.

Panther yanked up her gym bag and got in her convertible.

I got in my ride.

That was the longest drive I'd made in a long time.

I thought I had time to rest, time to think, but the night would only get worse.

Panther got to her studio before I did. Street parking was limited. I'd parked uphill near Highland, grabbed my last suit from the back of my car, hoofed it down the concrete hill to her place, had that and the heavy backpack with my weapons of mass destruction at my side.

She ran out of her front door, saw me coming, called my name, sounded terrified.

She rushed back inside, turned her light on, cursed and screamed.

I double-timed, that pain kicked in my knee, reminding me that I had gone down on it hard chasing Lisa yesterday. It slowed me down, but adrenaline masked the agony.

When I got to her porch, she was on the floor, holding her eye, sweat suit damp.

I asked, "What happened?"

I grabbed her arm, pulled her to her feet. Her floor was soaked.

"Slipped and hit my eye on the end table."

"You okay?"

"Hell no. That shit hurt. All this damn water on my floor."

Her door had been kicked open. This time they didn't try to be discreet. Like they had rushed. The scent of bleach met me on the streets. We stood and looked at her studio. Her futon cut at a thousand different angles, colorful quilt ruined, a lot of her clothing had been shredded.

Panther held her eye, tensed up. "That bitch Selina broke in here and did this shit."

She cursed, thought her married friend's wife had done all this damage.

I grabbed her arm, slowed her down, said, "Wait, Panther . . ."

Panther pulled away, ran into the bathroom. The shower had been running long enough to flood the living room floor. I didn't have to follow her into the bathroom to know that her clothes were stopping the drain. Her place was small but her walls looked familiar.

2   2   2   2

I cursed and went to the bathroom door. Makeup, clothes, her expensive shoes, all of her work clothes, all of that was piled up in her shower. Five bottles of bleach. Crime of passion.

I told her, "Panther, this ain't about you. This is about me."

"What the fuck you saying?"

"Married woman. The one I was dealing with. She did a B&E at my place."

"What are you saying? She came down here and did this?"

I told her that this was the same thing they had done to my place. I ran outside and looked around. The streets were quiet. Ran back inside and told Panther to grab her bag, what she could, so we could get out of here. She didn't move. I couldn't describe the look she gave me if I tried. A woman had never scowled at me like that, not even my ex-wife had glared at me that way in Memphis. My ex-wife's glare was close, was bone-chilling, but it didn't unnerve me the way Panther's scowl did. This situation was different. Maybe because my ex-wife was handcuffed, on a curb, was no way she could get her claws on me.

Panther held her eye and sloshed through her damp floor, still looking for something to salvage. She found a few things. She was wet from her backside down to her ankles.

A single black dress had been left hanging in her closet.

Funeral clothes. Something for her to wear while she cried over my cold body.

I leaned against the wall, dialed Lisa's cellular. Got her message center.

Lisa knew I was in the valley. Knew when it was cool to break in my apartment. But that was different, I was on the clock. But I hadn't been here, not since I went to work.

But I had slept here in Manhattan Beach, got here late last night, left early this morning.

The lion and jackal followed me down here last night, tracked me like I was an animal.

My mind went back to work. To this morning. The extra red dot on the computer screen. What I had seen when I glanced over Sid Levine's shoulder when I was at work this morning.

I took my cellular again, called the job on the private line. Sid Levine was in, working late or working early, I didn't ask. Was glad he was there burning the midnight oil.

I asked Sid, "Yo', Sid, you in front of the computer?"

"Yeah, Driver." He sounded nervous, my calling had thrown him. "Having probs with some software. Came in to reinstall. What's the deal?"

"Check it out. You have access to the screen with the car info?"

"Scheduling?"

"The GPS thing you were showing me this morning."

"Yeah. I can look at global positioning."

"Where are Wolf's cars right now?"

"What you mean?"

"Where does the GPS tell you the cars are?"

He told me that a limo was heading back in from Hollywood, another driving a customer who had refused to fly since 9/11 out to Palm Springs. He listed several of Wolf's rides.

I asked, "What about Manhattan Beach?"

"No."

"Alright. Thanks."

"Wait. Somebody is down in Manhattan Beach. Near the ocean."

"Which car? What car are they in?"

"Dunno. It's not . . . let me count . . . hold on two seconds . . . well, all of his cars are accounted for. It's like an extra . . . maybe it's a glitch. Been like that all week."

"The glitch moves?"

"Strange. It was in the valley a while ago. Stayed there a while. I went to grab a bite to eat and when I came back it was close to South Central. Now it's in Manhattan Beach."

I'd been tagged. Didn't know when I'd been bugged. She had plenty of opportunities.

I asked, "Does the boss call in and ask where his rides are?"

"Wolf? Nah."

"The wife?"

"Mrs. Wolf? She doesn't have to."

"Why not?"

"She has a handheld tracker."

"A handheld?"

"It's cool. Wolf is tight on the technology, ain't he? The one she has, everything that's on my screen, she can get on a device the size of a Palm Pilot. Cool, huh? Think she has it hooked up at their crib too. That way, if Wolf is away on a trip, she doesn't have to come in."

I clenched my jaw, gritted my teeth. Panther faced me, silent, arms folded. Nothing was salvageable. Couldn't tell if she wanted to shoot me or stab me in the throat with a knife.

Sid Levine said, "Glad you're on the phone. Freeman's people called not too long ago. Didn't know if you already know it but you're dealing with that Freeman guy tomorrow."

I told him good night.

I faced Panther. Too many emotions running through me, no way to latch on to one.

She stared at the damage, chest rising and falling, each breath deeper than the one before.

I said, "Panther . . ."

"Get that bitch on the phone."

"She's not gonna answer."

"Give me an address. I'll call my girls."

"It's not safe. She didn't do this. Her bullyboys, they're crazy."

"Well, I'm crazy too."

She was already heading out the front door, bag over shoulder, keys in hand, her emotional barometer operating in the red zone. Hate had replaced the blood in her veins.

I wanted to go up the hill, tear my car apart and find that GPS, but now wasn't the time.

18

Panther drove her ride like she was Batman, her pissed-off foot heavy on the pedal.

She sped north up Sepulveda to Rosecrans, east to the 405, north to the 10, then east, got off at Crenshaw, headed through the refried bean section, sped toward Hancock Park.

A motorcycle officer came out of nowhere, pulled up behind us. Panther cut her speed, cruised below the limit. He followed us for at least two miles. She changed lanes. He did the same. Never backed off. We stopped at a light. His lips were moving, calling in the plates, maybe just talking to somebody. I swallowed. Panther did the same. We were five minutes from Lisa's home. He hit his siren, put on his flashing lights before we made it to Wilshire.

Panther pulled over.

"Turn off your engine."

That voice came over the P.A. system. Panther obeyed.

I said, "These are her people."

The motorcycle officer didn't engage us in any way.

Panther asked me, her voice cracking, "Who is this bitch?"

"Her old man used to be chief of police. Compton. She was an officer. LAPD. She killed a couple of people on the clock. Wanted me to . . . paid me to kill her husband."

"What?"

"Paid me, but I didn't do it."

"You're joking, right?"

"That's why she has those motherfuckers after me."

I waited for her to ask me what kind of man I was. If she did, I didn't have an answer. Saw a thousand images in my mind, the strongest being that memory of me, Reverend Daddy, and Rufus, all of us in that alley, Rufus's shaky hand pulling the trigger on that gun.

Panther stuttered her words, "How she know we . . . ?"

"Don't know. She told me that if I came her way, I'd be dead before I hit Wilshire."

Panther swallowed hard. Hate became fear. LAPD had a way of making that happen.

Her voice owned some tremble, she asked, "Those guns I gave you . . . in your backpack?"

My jaw clenched, teeth gritted. All that and a hard breath was my answer. Somewhere along the line my ride had been tagged with a GPS. Looked like Panther's had been tagged too. But Sid Levine had only seen one dot moving around in Manhattan Beach. Mine. Had to be mine because Lisa had tracked me all over the city. That was how Lisa knew I was up in the valley. Just don't know when she would've tagged Panther.

I asked Panther, "You have a record?"

"Aggravated assault. Did a few days. Married man's wife came down acting crazy and I had to break her off proper. She filed a restraining order on me after that."

I let her words settle a moment before I said, "I'll claim the burners."

She ran her hands over her wet clothes, thinking. "Driver, you have a felony."

I took a breath, told her, "You got 'em for me."

She inhaled, let it out slow. "My burner is in my backpack too."

"Why do you have a gun?"

"Long story. Look at this shit. My damn eye feels like it's the size of a grapefruit. I'm soaking wet." She wiped her nose with the back of her hand. "Great. Catching a damn cold."

My mind kept doing inventory. Three guns. Over three thousand resting in my pockets. Panther had a bag filled with stripper clothes, her pockets filled with smoky dollar bills.

Two more police cars came out of nowhere, sirens blaring. Expected to see half of LAPD show up for Rodney King, The Sequel. Waited for them to appear like roaches running toward sugar. Flashing lights lit up the night. One police car was in front of us. One behind us.

They killed their sirens but left their lights flashing.

We sat like that for twenty minutes. Panther shivered. Kept wiping her eyes and nose.

The men who were paid to protect and serve just sat there, harassed us with silence.

My cellular rang. Lisa's number on caller-ID. I answered.

She said, "Think twice."

The connection broke on her end.

The motorcycle officer loosened his gun holster, crept up to the window. He tapped the glass. Panther turned the key so she could get power to let the window down.

He looked at me, at her, then asked both of us, "Is there a problem?"

Panther shivered and shook her head, answered, her tone nervous, "No problem, officer."

Her voice had never sounded so Southern. Never imagined her being afraid or anything.

The officer went back to his motorcycle.

The other officers drove away.

Over the P.A. system he told us to have a nice evening.

Panther started her ride, made a U-turn at the first legal spot she found.

The motorcycle officer U-turned too, followed us back to Pico Boulevard.

Then he zoomed by us, went to find new people to harass.

All I could hear was our hearts beating, not in sync.

19

We landed miles away on a rugged strip of Crenshaw Boulevard, a few blocks shy of El Camino College in the city named Torrance. A working woman's alley. Motel row. Good place to hide out with people who didn't want to be known, people who didn't want to be found.

We hav cabl and clean sh ets

The motel's ragged sign had chipped black letters; two in its name missing, the phone number the only thing complete. I took out my cellular, put a finger over my ear to block out the never-ending sound of the sirens in the distance, dialed the front desk, asked the accented lady that answered if they had any vacancies. They did. Asked if they took cash. They did.

I told her I had it, but Panther pushed me a fistful of smoky dollar bills.

I told her, "Look, I'll straighten this out, hit you back for the damage she did."

Her silence told me she didn't want anything from me. Just wanted me out of her car.

I asked, "This good-bye?"

No response.

I grabbed my stuff, went inside and made up a name for a room, John Kerry. The Iranian lady behind the bulletproof Plexiglas hardly looked up, asked me how many hours I needed the spot, then took my forty dollars, counted the money, tossed it in a drawer, handed me a door key.

A thin-legged, heavy-chested white girl with matted black hair was leading a young Spanish man upstairs. He had a potbelly, sported a military haircut. She had an awkward shape, like two straws stuck in a grapefruit, two plums and an orange resting on top of that. Over the top of his dark shades, military man kept peeping to see who was watching him. He saw me and stutter-stepped, regrouped, then picked up his pace. She didn't care who saw or heard her.

She was explaining to her customer, "No booty love. I don't do that or half-and-half."

"What if I pay extra?"

"How much extra?"

Everybody had a price. As she passed her eyes went up and down my frame.

I shook my head, not interested.

Sirens filled the air, a slew of police cars wailing down the boulevard. A ghetto bird was flying about eight blocks away, shining its lights down on the brown- and black-skinned people.

Fifty years back this area used to be Black Hollywood. A few miles over, Central Avenue had jazz clubs on every corner. Nat "King" Cole, Sarah Vaughn, and Josephine Baker walked these streets. *American Idol* couldn't hold a blowtorch to the entertainers on this side of town. Reverend Daddy told me and Rufus that all of this fizzled out after the war. The recession. Riots. Their heaven deteriorated into our hell. Broken neon signs. Pimpville, USA. Now they could drop a nuclear bomb on this part of town and barely do ten bucks in damage.

Thought Panther was bailing on me, but she parked across from the room. I stood where I was, looking at her. She sat there a moment, still scowling at me, before she shook her head and got out.

She hit her alarm and hurried up the walkway, head down my way, dodging broken bottles that used to hold liquid crack, bona fide syringes, and used condoms. She was shivering, black-and-white Adidas gym bag over her right shoulder, her purse over her left.

She followed me without talking, not a word as I used the pass-key and opened the door.

The room looked ghetto-fresh. Stale air was loitering like un-pleasant thoughts. I pulled back the golden covers, checked the sheets. The musty covers looked newer than anything else in this room. The toilet had a paper strip across the seat, traces of a harsh cleanser still floating in the water. A Bible that had another hotel's engraving was on the scratched veneer dresser.

After I closed the shades and cranked on the rattling heat unit, I took the guns out of the backpack, left them in reach on the night-stand. Panther went out the door and came back with a bucket of ice, hit the bathroom and ran a bathtub of hot water. I went in be-hind her. She ignored me. I pulled her wet sweats off her. She was resistant and frowned at me with sharp eyes.

I looked at her eye. Swollen. No serious damage. She cringed and frowned. Bruises like that hurt a lot more than she let on. She was a champ. Hardly squirmed. Soft body with a high tolerance for pain. Made me wonder about her life, how many fights she'd been in.

I said, "Let's run you to the emergency room at Daniel Freeman."

She shook her head, moved my hand away, got in the tub, sank down as low as she could.

She closed her eyes and muted her ears to anything I did or said.

After I washed her down I wrapped one of the paper-thin towels around her and walked her to the bed. Thought about Sade for a moment, how she had demanded top-shelf sheets to lay her ass on. Must be nice. I undressed and took a warm shower. When I finished Panther was under the covers, on her stomach. Wasn't sure if she was asleep. Then I heard her light snores.

I dialed my brother's number. Had to make sure he was okay. No answer.

I paced the floor.

The sounds of a too-squeaky bed with a loose headboard wormed its way through the walls. Moans and bangs. They were above us creating an earthquake. Lasted all of two minutes. Sounded like they were in the final sprint of a long jog. Somebody laughed and walked across the room at a drunken pace. The toilet flushed. Laughter. Footsteps went back across the room. Bed creaked under their weight. Ten minutes later another earthquake.

I turned the television on. Looked for C-SPAN. Surfed up on a rerun from Pasquale's television show. He was in syndication. Big bucks. Watched all the women act like they were swooning over him for two seconds before I shook my head and went back to surfing. Found C-SPAN. Saw they were doing book events, something they'd recorded up in Harlem last summer. Kept the volume down low. Was gonna wait to see what Freeman had to say.

Sade and Freeman. Lounging in a seven-hundred-dollar-a-night suite.

Arizona and the pickpocket. They stayed on my mind, hope to the hopeless.

Three thousand in my pocket. Twelve large away from easing this headache.

Looked at Panther. Her place had been trashed. My sins had followed me. If she had been home when the bullyboys came through, never know how this shit would've gone down.

I dialed Rufus's number one more time. Had to check on him. Would've gone by there but I'd become a black cat and didn't need to cross anybody else's path, not if I didn't have to.

Got the answering machine again.

I got in the bed next to Panther. Didn't touch her. Wanted to stay up but was so tired I had to close my eyes. Put a pillow over my head to smother out the pleasure squeaking down on me. The heater hummed its asthmatic lullaby. Eyelids weighed fifty pounds each. Fought the sandman as long as I could. Sleep found me in two groans and three deep breaths.

A chill covered me, sent me to a cold and unfriendly place where blacks, whites, Asians, and Latinos all wore prison blues and stayed segregated. Remembered this motherfucker coming at me. Testing me. Move. Strike. Move. Move again. My fist pile-driving into his jaw, leaving it broken. Then ending up in the Adjustment Center, lip busted, ear bleeding, fists swollen. Staying in the hole so long I thought I was going crazy.

Heard something and jerked awake. Panther was sitting on the bed, yoga style, watching me. When I pushed up on my elbows, I saw she had her gun resting between her legs.

A broken voice came to me, said, "I'm always attracted to the last kinda guy I need to be attracted to. Caught feelings. That's a big no-no. See where this got me? This is screwed up."

Panther was finally talking, soft and Southern. Her words thick and emotional.

"Dammit, Driver. Been worried about you all day. Called you over and over."

Said the first thing that came to my mind. "Didn't know you carried a gun."

"Of course I have a gun. I've *always* had a gun. My daddy made sure we had guns."

She moved her gun to the nightstand, added it to my collection, rocked, shook her head over and over, touched her wounded eye, pulled a pillow into her lap, stared at the wall.

I asked, "You . . . what you need me to do?"

"Oh, trust me. You've done more than enough. Now I'm naked and homeless."

"Okay, that was a stupid question."

Laughter from upstairs. Footsteps across the room. Toilet flushed.

Panther snapped, "What, you don't know how to return a phone call?"

"Stop nagging."

"I called you all day. Don't you know how to call people back?"

"Stop hitting me with that pillow, Panther."

"I'm so damn mad at you."

"Stop beating , . . chill out with the pillow."

"You're arrogant. Inconsiderate. Mean. Selfish."

"Stop. I'm tired, dammit."

"I was scared for you, missed you a lot today."

"Stop hitting me. Been through enough shit."

I jumped up. She threw the pillow at me. I slapped it down. She threw the other pillow.

I said, "That's your last time hitting me with a pillow."

"Whatever."

I got back on the bed, the hard mattress squeaking under my weight. She leaned up against me. I stroked her hair, touched her face. She moved my hand away from her eye and relaxed her head on my chest. We lay there, deep in thought, comforting each other. She started kissing my fingers. I took her hand, did the same, kissed her fingers and her hand, moved my fingers over her full lips, over the curves in her baby smooth skin, over her petite breasts, down over her small waist to her backside, touched and appreciated the fullness of that Southern gal.

She ran her tongue over her teeth. "Heifer did the same to your place, huh?"

"Yeah. Destroyed damn near everything I own. Bricked my car."

"Well, me and that psycho heifer, we have some personal issues now."

I sat on her words, her attitude, her anger.

Another earthquake started over my head. Somebody was up there long stroking, taking his balls to the wall over and over, killing it like crazy. Imagined somebody as fine as Halle Berry was up there.

Panther went to the bathroom, blew her nose, washed her hands, came back, got under the covers, took a few hard breaths. "Perverts upstairs are doing the damn thing big time."

"You picked this spot."

"Like I was going to go to the Ritz looking like this, all wet and my eye jacked."

Squeaks came from above us and next door at the same time. An orchestra of sin.

Panther asked, "How did Married Woman know we were heading her way?"

I thought about that for a moment. I wondered, "You have a GPS on your car."

"Yeah. OnStar came with it. Tells you everything. When the air bag goes off, has tracking, remote door unlock, can get driving directions, yada, yada, x, y, and z."

"I know, was thinking out loud. You have a GPS." Eyes burned from lack of sleep. I shrugged and gritted my teeth. "Maybe she figured out how to tap into your GPS or something."

"How? I mean, can people do that?"

"Dunno. But she knew we were rolling her way. Almost like . . . she had some sort of . . . maybe she has it set on some sort of perimeter alarm, get close to her crib and it goes off."

"If she can do all that, then she would know where we are right now."

I took a gun and went back to the window. Saw nothing outside. Opened the door and stepped out into the cold. Saw nothing. Coldness was frosting the windows on Panther's ride.

I went back in the room, sat on the bed, put the gun back with its brother and sister.

She said, "Wanna tell me what's going on? I mean everything."

"No."

She pulled at her hair, shook her head, emotions dark and smoldering.

She took a deep breath, back to being serious. "Think you're gonna be safe tonight?"

"Even evil has to sleep."

"What if evil works third shift?"

"True. They could be union."

I heard something, went to the window. Saw a working woman and her meal ticket.

Panther raked her hair from her eyes. "Sorry."

"Why are you apologizing?"

"I mean for what's happening to you. You said your brother was sick . . . now all of this."

Her apartment gets trashed and she worried about me. I sort of smiled. "It's cool."

"You coulda at least called me back."

"You're starting to sound like a broken record."

"I upped and said the L word. That's a big no. Wish I could take it back."

"I'm catching feelings for you too."

"Negro, please."

"Serious. You're cool."

"I tell you I love you and you tell me I'm *cool*. What the heck is that?"

"I said I was catching feelings, dammit."

"*Cool*. Like I'm one of your boys or something."

Panther looked at the ceiling. We listened to the sounds. After a while those noises, the sexual energy that was coming through those walls, that shit made me tingle, made her eyes get tight. We looked at each other. She licked her lips. I did the same. She moved across the room, pulled out the armless chair, sat down, touched her breasts, ran her fingertips around her nipples.

I said, "Don't do that."

"What?"

"Don't put on a show for me. Just be you."

She smiled.

"Driver, baby, you get inside me and I melt. Like I become liquid fire."

She stood up and motioned for me to come to her. I went over and sat down. She kneeled in front of me, traced her fingers over the tattoos on my forearms, moved her breasts over my chest, rubbed her face against mine, my stubble rough against her skin. She did that a short while, her face moving back and forth, then she kissed me. Our first time kissing.

She shivered and whispered, "God."

"What?"

"Been wanting to kiss you . . . wanted to do that for a long time."
We kissed again.

She shivered, whispered, "Slower. Take your time. I'm not going anywhere."

First time in a long time I had been nervous about kissing a woman. Scared that I might not do it right. Kissing her got easier. Think I was better at it than she was. We got into it; then she belched and laughed. It tasted like chicken sandwich, French fries, and apple pie. I laughed too, but held onto the kiss. She put one leg on each side of me, eased us shut, started moving up and down. Kissing changed into moans and nibbles and biting. Together we lost our breath.

She whispered, "You're gonna make me come so good."

Her leg trembled. She came. A soft orgasm that lasted a long time. She held on, gasped over and over. When I thought she was done she shuddered some more. It was the kinda deep-rooted orgasm a woman had that was followed by soft tears. The kind that unnerved a man.

When we were done we stayed like that, me inside her, kissed some more.

She rubbed my bald head, asked me to tell her what was going on. I did.

20

"Mansion. Lamborghini." Panther quieted. "Married Woman promised you a lot."

I nodded.

A few minutes had passed, long enough for the feeling from our orgasms to fade. I told Panther about meeting Lisa, taking the fifteen large, then not going through with the job.

I asked, "Think I'm stupid?"

"No dumber than I am. People like that, they read us. Catch us when our guards are down, emotionally vulnerable. When we're broke for money or hungry for love."

My eyes went to hers. She looked away, embarrassed.

I asked, "What did Married Man—"

The stairs rattled. She stopped icing her eye, picked up a burner and went to the window, peeped out. I stood up, burner at my side. She looked back at me and told me it was nothing.

I repeated my last question, asked about her affair with Married Man.

"Driver, I don't want to get into that. I'll just say in the end I felt like a damn fool because I'd spent over fourteen thousand. Driver. Don't look at me like that, Driver."

"Fourteen thousand? Damn, Panther. Fourteen large?"

"I know, I know. He sweet-talked me out of my life's savings. Stupid. Trying to come back from that loss right now. That was my little nest egg. Gone because . . . all gone."

I dug in my suit pocket. Took out that passkey to Shutters Hotel. The million-dollar asshole and his blue-eyed woman. They were lounging in a beachside spot that cost seven C-notes a night. I was on Hoodrat Lane, a spot cockroaches refused to patronize. Dug in my bag and pulled out Freeman's book, the one Sade had given me as a present to my brother. It was worth its weight in gold.

Panther went back to the bed and sat down. "Question."

I responded, "Yeah?"

"If she—"

"Lisa. Married Woman's name is Lisa."

"If Lisa has these thugs after you, saying they'll kill you, if she has that kinda pull with the LAPD, then why didn't she just get one of her hired boys to kill her husband? Why you?"

"We didn't have a public connection. It would've been untraceable."

"Still, if her ass was so in love with you—"

"Don't hate."

"Whatever. Why not just let her boys do the dirt and let you walk in and sit at the throne? Why get you caught up in the mix like that?"

"Nobody knew about us but us."

"Whatever. Look, Driver. I watch Court TV. I know these things. The first suspect would've been Married Woman. The spouse is always the first suspect. That's why Scott Peterson's trifling ass is gonna fry like a piece of Jimmy Dean sausage."

"California uses lethal injection."

"Glad you're up on those things."

"Even if she was the suspect, like I said, I was untraceable. Like strangers on a train."

"You watch too many Hitchcock movies. You were not strangers on a damn train. You just told me you met her at Yum Yum. Everybody on Crenshaw Boulevard probably saw that."

"That was one time. A long time ago. Nobody would remember that."

"You'd be surprised. To make it worse you went inside the man's house. Drove the man's car. Somebody saw you somewhere and that somebody would've made the connection."

I quieted and paced the floor. Stairs rattled. Peeped out the window. Alexithymia popped in my head. I was as restless as a shark, moving around like I had ADHD.

She said, "You better ask yourself why she picked you."

The mirror stared back at me, showed me that John Henry, railroad-worker build I'd inherited from my maternal granddaddy. My forearms strong, both filled with warrior tats. Six-two. Dark as an open road. A king that could only pass for a suspect in this country.

My blackness was part of the reason they pulled us over down South.

"Bottom line, it was legit." I said that as I sat down on the squeaky bed. Said that to convince myself I wasn't stupid, as naive as Wolf. "She gave me fifteen large. Cash."

"Cash money."

"Cash money."

"Handed you fifteen thousand just like that."

"Yeah."

"Damn. Married Woman must be balling out of control."

"She was. She is."

"How much you got left?"

"None. It was gone inside two weeks."

"You got some kinda habit I need to know about?"

I shook my head. "Used most of it to bury Momma, the rest to help Rufus out."

"Driver . . ."

"What?"

"I came to your mother's funeral. Was worried about you."

I paused and looked at her. "How did you know where it was?"

"You told me it was going to be at Angelus Funeral Home. Kinda called up there and asked a few questions. Didn't know your momma's name, but I figured it out." She moved her hand over her mane, chuckled. "Ended up going to two funerals before I found the right one."

"I didn't see you."

"Well, you were looking pretty bad. Felt for you. I came late. Stayed in the back. Left before everybody got up to view the body. I don't like looking down at dead people."

"So you were there."

"Yeah. Saw you and your brother. He sang a real nice song."

"Yeah. He did. 'Amazing Grace' was her favorite church song."

"Your brother . . . albino?"

I nodded.

She shifted and softened. "You said that he was sick. What's wrong?"

"Let's just say he's sick. Leave it at that. His meds cost a grip."

Panther nodded, then shook her head, shaking off some memory. "One of my girls died a few years ago. Nobody even knew she was sick, not like that. She worked at the club, danced with us. Just stopped coming to work. She lied to everybody, said it was her thyroid. She'd answer my call but never had time to hang out or hook up, always had excuses, always busy. Next thing I knew, got a call she was gone. She didn't even look sick. I mean, she had lost some weight, but she never looked that kinda sick, no sores, not like a walking cadaver or anything. It was so sad. We had to call the guys we knew that she had slept with, tell them that she had—"

"Panther."

"Sorry. Didn't mean to make you uncomfortable. If you don't want to talk about—"

"I don't."

She nodded again, this one meant she understood. "That money you took . . . the fifteen thousand . . . have you tried to pay any of it back to Married Woman?"

Again, I quieted. Alexithymia and ADHD held my hands, led me around the room.

It didn't make sense in my mind, but I was searching for some justification, and all that came to mind were words, weak words, couldn't think of a ten-dollar phrase to elevate what I'd done to a literary level. I cleared my throat and shrugged, told her, "Guess I thought that after what happened, my momma dying, hoped she'd let it go, cut a nigga some slack."

"Sweetie, nobody lets fifteen thousand go."

"I know. But it ain't like it was her money. It was Wolf's money."

"Moot point, Driver. It wasn't your money either."

"I know it wasn't my money, dammit. She dumped cash money right in front of me. I was broke as hell, couldn't get a fucking job, barely had two nickels in my motherfucking pockets. What the fuck would you have done? Shit. Now get off my damn back."

She stared at me, at my sudden burst of anger, her eyes wide, mouth open. Exhaustion had robbed me of sanity and patience. Hands were fists. I felt irrational, like I did when Lisa had made me lose it out on La Cienega, when she had hit me with that 7-Up can, when she had told me that a nice suit couldn't hide the real me. Maybe that illegal money, maybe this legit job I'd taken, maybe all of that was about me trying to get away from the real me. I knew I wanted what Wolf had, wanted a life like his. Where I lived there wasn't a ladder that went up that high.

Panther said, "I'm on your team. Remember what my place looked like?"

Head hurt like a stroke was coming on. Had to sit down where I stood.

Panther's voice followed me, soft and sincere. "Would you rather a woman lie to you and tell you everything is all right, or would you want the truth, no matter how bitter the taste? Let me know what kind of woman you need so I can know what kind of woman I need to be."

My eyes remained tight. Darkness running over my mind. Ran hands over my forehead.

She asked, "How much time she give you?"

"Three days."

"A spiritual number."

"What you talking about?"

"Three. Something biblical about the number three. Father, Son, and Holy Spirit. Jesus rose up in three days. Three is a spiritual number."

"It's not."

"Is."

"Three Stooges. *Three's Company. Three the Hard Way.*"

"Whatever."

Stairs rattled again.

Panther turned the TV off, made the room dark, wrapped a blanket around her naked frame, rushed and peeped out the window again. Nothing. She turned the TV back on.

I sat on my thoughts, the ones that told me I was a failure on both sides of the law. A hired killer who didn't do the job.

She came over and kissed me awhile. Tried to get lost in her tongue.

She said, "First thing we do is get your brother. Then you let that job go."

"Can't."

"Why not?"

"Have to go in at least two more days."

"Forget that job."

I shook my head. "Working on something."

She looked at me, her Southern eyes telling me that she had been born a hustler, would be a hustler until her last breath. Panther shifted around, asked, "What kinda plan you got?"

I told her about Arizona and the pickpocket. About getting the fifteen large.

She said, "A scam artist comes up to you at a bar. What's her angle?"

Then I told her about Freeman. What Arizona had in mind. That I was the inside man.

She nodded. "Again, ask yourself why this heifer picked you."

I leaned against the dresser and thought. Again exhaustion and aggravation made everything opaque. Searched, tried to wade through that mental black ink, but thoughts fell in and vanished like a man in quicksand. No answers. All I could do was wonder. Wondered if there was some connection between Arizona and Lisa. Didn't make any sense for there to be.

Freeman's face appeared on the television. My unibrowed salvation haunted me too. I imagined that the pickpocket and Arizona were in Sherman Oaks watching the same broadcast.

Panther raised a brow, cleared her throat. "Thomas Freeman? I know that guy."

"How you know Freeman?"

"I don't *know him* know him. Went to one of his book signings."

"When was that?"

"Long time back. Years ago. At least three. Maybe four."

Panther was wide awake. Alert. Her time of night. My body wanted to shut down.

I yawned. "Where you meet Mr. Bobblehead?"

"Bobblehead?"

I dug in my bag, took out that bobblehead Freeman had given me as a gratuity for a day's labor, tossed it to Panther. That got a good laugh out of her. Me too. Eased our tension.

She said, "Met 'im at a black bookstore on La Brea."

"Which one?"

"Forgot. Only three people showed up. I wanted to bounce up out of there but I was sitting right in front of him, center stage. Didn't want to be rude. He wasn't as . . . as . . . as . . ."

"Arrogant?"

"Not like he's acting now. He's showing out. It's like he has a different personality."

"How was he back then?"

"Flirty. Tried to get me to go to a late dinner, you know how it goes."

"No, I mean—"

She shushed me, tossed the bobblehead back on the bed, turned up the volume.

Distribution is in white hands . . . gatekeepers and rule makers . . . treachery never stops . . . we get the same stereotypes over and over . . . conspiracy is pissing on our legs telling us it's raining . . .

Panther said, "He sounds like the Al Sharpton of literature."

I repeated my question, "How was he back then?"

Panther waved her hand, kept motioning for me to shut up.

But I guess y'all can't handle the truth, huh? These are the books y'all need to be buying. Let me say it again, for those of you Negroes who came in late, let me repeat myself just in case some of you don't understand what a real book is about. I deal with real—

Freeman went on and on, edges of a repressed Quitman, Mississippi, accent coming and going. The camera pulled back enough to show that the other writers were sitting with tight lips and arms folded, irritated by his rant. Then a shot of the audience. Sade was in the crowd.

I was in a hotel room with a stripper who had been in and out of love with a married man, staring at an African Queen on a thirteen-inch screen, imagining her accent and her smell.

Panther was in a zone, impressed by the million-dollar man.

Everybody loved a winner.

Hollywood better wake up. They should be begging to make a movie out of my books.

She lowered the volume. "When I met him, he was cool, talked a lot about himself, not really humble, but not like that."

"Bling bling changes people."

She made a humming sound, tilted her head. "Don't see how he got successful."

"What you mean?"

"The first one of his books I bought . . . horrible . . . think I threw it in the garbage."

"Heard it was pretty bad."

"The book was full of words like *conversely, thereupon,* and *thus.* Who talks like that?"

"Jesse Jackson."

"Besides Jesse Jackson. Brotherman used those words five times each on the first page. The second book, same thing, got my money back. Couldn't get past the second chapter."

"Didn't know you read."

"I do more than run guns and swing this real estate from a pole, Driver."

The camera panned and showed the briefcase Freeman had on the table next to him.

Panther asked, "What's in the briefcase? Secret to the A-bomb or something?"

Just like whoever was watching C-SPAN, I stared at that intellectual property handcuffed to his side, the seven-figure labor of love he guarded with his life. His Maltese falcon.

Then I told Panther what was in the briefcase; the book he was writing, *Truth Be Told*.

She made an incredulous face. "A million dollars for one of *his* books?"

"Yeah. That's what it said online."

"You know what I'd do if I had that kinda money?"

"Supersize your breasts. Buy a Porsche 356 Carrera Speedster."

"No, Driver." Her voice was soft, vulnerable. "I'd adopt my sister's two kids. Both of them. Maybe even adopt another kid. Some kid who had lost its parents. Give the kid a chance. Pay off Momma's house. I already pay her mortgage. That's what I'd do with that money."

"Cool."

"What would you do with that kinda money, Driver?"

"Supersize your breasts. Buy a Porsche 356."

She showed me both of her traffic fingers.

Panther picked up her damp clothes, looked angry as hell, so much hate for Lisa and her bullyboys in her eyes as she hung everything up in the bathroom. On the way back I handed her the book I had, *Dawning of Ignorance*. She looked at Freeman's picture, flipped it open.

"Driver, that girl you met, they're gonna jack his briefcase?"

"Steal his computer. Ransom it back to him."

"Have to tell you, it sounds stupid. But hey, I'm just a simple girl from Atlanta."

I nodded. "Okay Miss Atlanta, why does it sound that way to you?"

"He has to have it backed up somewhere. Like five or six copies lying around."

"I thought the same thing. But he did an interview this morning, said he didn't show it to anybody. Not even his fiancée. Anyway, the grifter I met, she's been in contact with him, think they might be freaking or something, and she seemed to be sure about it."

Panther raised a brow, made a thinking face. "And they're gonna give you a cut."

"Trying to come up on enough to get out of hot water."

I changed the channel on the television. Stopped on a movie channel. Dean Martin, Frank Sinatra, Sammy Davis, Jr., and the rest of the Rat Pack were in the original *Ocean's Eleven*. Men trying to come up on their fortune by ripping somebody else off. Two white men were talking about how they always had to take what they wanted growing up, always had to fight. My life had always been just as unpretty as theirs. Not a complaint, just a fact.

Panther fell into that movie just like I did. Listened to the schemers scheme.

I told Panther, "After that, I'll be back to zero because I'm quitting that gig."

"Broke and jobless. Now that's attractive. Tell me more, tell me more."

"Broke ain't nothing new. I can always walk around and find some labor. Fuck sitting in a damn car all day getting soft. After I pay Lisa her money, I'll figure out something."

"That's some bullshit."

"What?"

"As far as Married Woman's concerned, you don't owe that heifer a damn dime. Matter of fact that terrorist owes us. And when I see her, it's on. I'm gonna collect like I'm the IRS."

I rubbed my head, let her talk shit awhile. Then we went back to talking about Freeman.

Panther fell silent. She got up and walked the room, paced in the nude, the cornbread and buttermilk walk taking her gifts from above from wall to wall, highlighted hair in a loose ponytail, arms folded under her modest and firm breasts, anger stiffening her tongue, her tongue pushing out her top lip. I watched her. She saw me staring then came and sat by me, kissed my head, touched my hand, opened her mouth to say something, then paused until I looked at her.

"Driver, if that book is worth a million . . . that's a lot of money."

"Uh huh."

"Hypothetically, what if we cut out the middleman and jacked his briefcase?"

My eyes studied the seriousness in hers. She didn't blink.

I told her, "Don't think like that."

"I was joking."

"Don't."

Silence fell over us. The energy between us changed, moved in a bad direction. Money had a way of doing that. I got up, went to the bathroom to get some space, came back, sat down.

My eyes went back to the movie. Smooth criminals, every last one of them.

A couple of thinking minutes went by. The passkey to Shutters stayed on my mind. It would get me to the elevator, and after that the key would be useless. Kick the door down, call in a bomb threat and hope they clear the hotel, I just didn't have any idea what to do after that.

Money changed people. Made people who didn't have it go crazy trying to get it.

We got into the bed, the mattress sagging, the box springs giving and squeaking under our weight, the headboard slapping the wall when we moved too much. If a motel room could talk. It took a minute, but we got in a comfortable position and cuddled up, half-watched the movie, fell into a series of yawns. Moans and squeaks wormed into the room, then a series of earthquakes. All around us beds were squeaking, people were on fire, sending us their heat.

Panther shifted her butt up against me, rubbed her legs against mine, then looked back at me, her eyes dreamy, those nipples erect. I had the desire to join the festival, but I didn't have the energy. An erection would've helped too. I rubbed my hand up and down Panther's skin. Kissed her here and there. She reached back and touched my dick, held that softness in her hand, moved it up and down, made it raise up a bit. She turned around. We kissed. I sucked on her breasts, put my finger between her legs, massaged her nice and slow.

But every time I heard someone walking the stairs, every time I heard a car, I was on my feet. Wasn't the time for romance. Not for me. I grabbed a chair and pulled it up to the window, stared out at a fatherless community that had been destroyed by riots and social neglect.

Panther didn't complain, just grabbed Freeman's book, turned on a light, started reading.

My eyes went to the tube.

Sammy Davis, Jr., was the poor hustling garbage collector. He was standing on a table singing that someday he'd have a chauffeur and a long black limousine, that someday he'd have a penthouse. The black man just had to be the trash man. The poorest and blackest of the lot. Singing he was gonna come up. Yeah, me too, Sammy. Someday. Some-fucking-day me too.

Lisa was lounging in Hancock Park, sleeping on custom bedding and linens, goose-down pillows, being catered damn near every meal, all the accoutrements of the rich.

Freeman and Sade were living in a similar world, all room service and caviar.

My brother didn't have two dimes to rub together and still managed a similar lifestyle.

I was hiding out in South Central, inhaling the stench on Fuck Row. Someday. Some-fucking-day.

Panther turned on her side, then sat up. "Driver, this book is good. Better than the crap I bought. Only on page ten, but it's like . . . like he had some serious writing classes or something."

"Maybe that's why he took three years off, to up his game."

"Think so?"

"Heard actors and actresses do that when their shit ain't work- ing, take time off, study their craft, come back strong. Three years would be enough time to up your game."

"Then he upped it. Better than anything I've read in the last ten years."

She went back to reading Freeman's masterpiece. I needed to clear my mind. I found a crossword puzzle in my bag, found a pen, put on my glasses, let that ease my rugged thoughts.

Across the room, minutes and pages of *Dawning* had gone by be- fore Panther looked up and saw me watching her, crossword in my hand. She had fallen into Freeman's world and seeing me jarred her. She read my face, sat up with her legs folded under her, watched me awhile before she asked, "Why you looking like that? What are you thinking, Driver?"

I glanced at *Ocean's Eleven* again. Sammy, Dean, Frank, Joey, the whole crew was walking single file, credits rolling. They had won, ripped off Vegas. All of them were strutting out into the sunshine, their names on the giant marquee behind them. Crime had paid. Paid well.

I sent my attention back to Panther.

I swallowed. "How much do you think we could get?"

21

Pedro blew up my cellular less than an hour later. It was close to sunrise. The sexual earthquake that had been over my head had finally slowed down. Panther was on her cellular, the burner between her legs like she was on watch, talking to one of her friends.

Pedro told me, "Got that information for you."

I fought the heaviness in my eyes. "What you find out?"

Pedro's sister worked at the Department of Motor Vehicles. I'd memorized the plates on the Expedition the lion and jackal had been in, passed the info on to Pedro yesterday afternoon.

He said, "The vehicle is registered to somebody who stays in L.A. County."

"Local talent."

"Looks that way."

I gave him an update, told him what they had done to Panther's apartment.

I asked, "You feel like taking me for a drive in that expensive Hyundai? Want to see how this talent lives. Might have a conversation or two and you could help me do some talking."

"Me and my baseball bat could use some fun, but man I got the kids."

"Where's the wife?"

"In jail."

"Jail? What the fuck did Marissa do?"

"Things got outta hand on the picket line. They locked strikers up, civil disobedience."

"You serious?"

"I'm proud of Marissa. I really am. The kids understand. They're proud too."

"Tell Marissa I said the same. Proud of her. But I gotta handle my situation over here."

He gave me the address. Had to hold my anger at bay. Wanted to go out and hunt them down, but now wasn't the time. Didn't want Panther involved any more than she already was.

But she was getting up, putting on her damp clothes. She'd burglarized her way into my conversation with Pedro. She picked up her gun, put it in her bag. Grabbed her shoes.

My cellular beeped. Arizona's number came up on caller-ID.

I let Pedro go, clicked over. Arizona came on the line and told me the pickpocket was gone for the night, her needs sent her out on a booty call. She invited me over for the same lesson in sexual healing. I paused, glanced at Panther, told Arizona I'd see her tomorrow.

She said, "Occupied?"

I licked my lips, rubbed my eyes. "Tired."

"I'm really horny. Really want to hook up with you. I'm laying here with the lights off. Touching myself. Would be nice to have you inside of me right now. Getting it from the back."

Her tone was so damn sensual. Saw her naked in my mind, the way she had been with me a few hours ago, that honey-brown skin, long hair and Filipina features, standing on her tiptoes, turning a slow three-sixty. Remembered how she had kissed me. Tasted her tongue.

My eyes went back to Panther, then down to the floor. Exhaled. Didn't want to burn no bridges on either side of the phone line, not before I had my business squared away with Lisa.

Arizona said, "I could come to you."

I kept my voice stiff and distant. "Next time."

"Just thought I'd give you first right of refusal."

"Thanks."

She laughed. "Get your rest. See you tomorrow. I'm depending on you."

I hung up. Stared at my cellular phone to keep from facing Panther. My cellular had zero bars across the top and the LOW BATTERY message was flashing its warning. My cellular was a minute from becoming as useful as a paperweight.

She said, "Whassup?"

"Battery needs to get charged."

I got the charger and searched for an outlet, ending up facing Panther. She looked at me with jealous eyes but didn't say anything. That last call left me in a fucked-up situation. Panther had been supportive and vulnerable. For a moment I saw that look in her eye, the one a woman gets when she wants to know who else was sucking your dick.

I put my cellular on its charger.

She said, "Ready?"

I suited up, grabbed my two guns. Fitted the .380 in the leg strap, the .357 in the shoulder holster. Was nervous. Not about the mission, but about Lisa tracking us. About the police.

I told Panther, "Leave the burners."

"Are you crazy?"

I took my hardware out, undid the leg strap and shoulder harness. "If the po-po stops us again, they might search your ride next time."

"Why didn't they search us then?"

"Think we just got lucky."

She hesitated, then made a face, handed me her burner. I tucked all three in a drawer.

Outside, I spent a few minutes going over Panther's ride. Popped the hood. Looked underneath. Men and women came out while we were in the lot. Playtime was over for the working man. Back home to the family. I searched high and low. Couldn't find a tracker.

* * *

The address Pedro gave me was twenty minutes away, up Crenshaw to MLK Jr. Boulevard, then west to Coliseum Boulevard. We sat there staring at an empty lot.

She said, "This can't be right. This used to be a small church."

"Give me your phone."

I called Pedro. Verified the address. I hung up, gave her the cellular back.

I agreed with Panther, said, "This ain't right."

I looked around at the fading darkness and streetlights. We were in The Jungle, where Denzel Washington had filmed *Training Day*. Smelled some ganja in the air. Second-rate apartments lined the area, but on this one corner, nothing but potholes and an empty lot. Cars passed by. Nobody slowed down, nobody shot at us. No police rolled up on us.

I asked, "You sure this was a church?"

"Yeah. I know this area. I go to church right up the street by Baldwin Hills Mall."

"Where?"

"Maranatha. By the swap meet."

"You go to church?"

"Of course I go to church."

I had a bad feeling. Thought about calling my brother. Panther handed me her phone again. I called my cellular number, checked my messages. Nobody had called.

She said, "We better get back."

"Yeah."

"Try to get some of that oomph . . . oomph . . ."

"Omphaloskepsis."

"Yeah. Get some of that."

I closed my eyes. No sleep for the weary.

"Driver, I know this is a bad time, but this is what I feel."

"Panther, do we have to do this now?"

"We have to do this now."

"Save it."

"I have to be straight up. I'm not seeing or sleeping with anybody else. If you don't feel the same way, just let me know. I'll still be cool with you. I just have to know."

I didn't open my eyes. "What do you want from me, Panther?"

"Respect." She didn't raise her voice, just said that in a level tone. "That's all. I'm not trying to marry you or trap you. I like you and I care about you. I'm trying to get to know you. Maybe spend some time with you. That's all I'm doing. All I want is respect."

She took to the street, Speed Racer with breasts and an ass that wouldn't quit, and hurried us toward our wonderful accommodations on the gritty side of our second-rate Sin City.

I didn't say anything else while she rode back down Crenshaw, not for a couple of minutes. In my silence, I wished I had a shot of JD. Didn't have any but I saw that liquid lover in my mind, its color as beautiful as a memory gone by.

I said, "Marriage is overrated."

She repeated, "Marriage is overrated? Where did that come from?"

My mind moved from my ex-wife to Lisa. On my bitter channel, Lisa was the clearest, had the best reception and focus.

I said, "Was married once. Ever tell you that?"

"No. Divorced?"

"Yeah, I'm divorced."

Don't know why I chose to talk about that. Fear was rising up inside me. When a man was scared he had to talk about something, anything, even if it was driftwood.

Then she simply asked, "What happened?"

"I went to jail." I smiled. "She felt like I chose my brother over her."

I told her that my brother used to have a drug problem. My wife and I were heading to her hometown in Tallapoosa County. We were taking our Explorer on a cross-country trip. Part of the reason I planned the trip was because of Rufus. A cousin knew about a good rehab program for Rufus to get in down in Memphis. We'd crossed into Shelby County when we were pulled over. My wife was sleeping. Rufus was in the backseat. He jumped nervous. Saw it in his pale eyes. Dogs went apeshit before they made it to the Explorer.

Rufus was breaking down. A hundred pounds of marijuana and a shitload of cash were in his footlocker. The police dragged my wife out of our SUV. Left her handcuffed and sitting on the curb, sweating, crying, screaming, confused, her yellow and blue sundress blowing in the summer breeze. Shit went down faster than I could think. They were on me like they owned me. Always after the big black man. I started yelling that everything was mine, just knew I had to protect my brother.

Panther sounded surprised. "You went to jail for your brother?"

"Did two years."

"And your wife didn't stand by you?"

Right then I remembered Memphis, being on the Gray Goose, shackled, trying to stay awake so I could take in all the sights because it was the last thing I was going to see for years.

I said, "She never accepted a phone call. I wrote her a six-page letter. Poured my heart out. She never wrote back. Never came to see me."

My hands closed tight, tried to strangle that memory.

Blood was thicker than platinum, but handcuffs were even thicker.

I'd do it again. I'd go to jail hundred times a hundred for Rufus if I had to.

"That's horrible." Panther's voice finally came to me. "You two have kids?"

"Yeah. No. I mean, had a stepson."

"How old?"

"He should be ten or eleven now."

"Was he . . . was he with you when . . . when . . . ?"

I shook my head, remembered the sheer hurt in my ex-wife's face. The last expression I saw, the one etched in my mind. I hoped nobody else in the world ever had to respond to hurt at that level. Hard to hurt like I did and try and show no emotion for the choice I'd made.

I whispered, "Two roads diverged, but I could not travel both. A man cannot be two travelers, only one. Most choose the fair road, not the one with hills and undergrowth."

"That from a book?"

"Yeah. Something I read when I was in that cage."

Panther's warm fingers grazed my flesh, then her hand lingered on the back of mine. I told her all those things to push her away, but instead she put her hand on mine.

She fell silent.

I was silent too.

Panther got in the bed with her clothes on. I got in behind her.

I kissed her neck. She moaned in a way that let me know she'd wanted that for a while. I sucked her skin. Slow. Pulled her top up, took out her breasts. Massaged and licked one, then the other. She shivered, held the back of my neck. My hand moved between her legs, massaged her pussy through her clothing. Her legs opened and she welcomed me, let my hand slide inside her clothing, let my finger go inside. She was damp, her heat rising. Felt her climbing that stairway. I hardened. She moved slow against my hand until she couldn't move slow anymore. She was there, eyes tight, mouth shaped like the letter O, all ragged breaths.

Her back arched when she began crossing that threshold, a moaner, a wiggler, a screamer.

I kept fingering her, suckling her breast, watched her face cringe and glow.

She came in jerky motions, whining, moaning my name.

Her eyes opened wide. She swallowed.

I pulled her clothes off. Took mine off. Her legs opened, welcomed me.

Day's break eased into the room, squeaks and moans fading with the rising of the sun.

The clock told me it was time to shower, get dressed, head toward LAX.

Panther asked, "You gonna be able to make it on no sleep?"

I didn't answer. I didn't know.

Her cellular rang. It was her mother, calling for their morning conversation. Panther went into Southern-fried daughter mode, all smiles and giggles, restless, moving that cornbread and buttermilk body back and forth. Since she didn't have pajamas and slippers, she put on my suit coat and shoes. My clothes swallowed her. She paced, checking the window every time she heard a noise, her voice sounding like nothing was wrong. Overheard her asking about her sister and her nieces, then they went on talking about her brother being deployed in Iraq, another man living in a combat zone.

My cellular blew up.

Lisa's number showed up. My head wound came back to life, throbbed.

I touched my old Band-Aid, stepped into the bathroom and answered.

She wanted to meet.

22

Lisa's Hummer was in the employee parking garage of the Hilton. She had told me to meet her on the lower level, right outside the entrance for 24-Hour Fitness. Panther had dropped me off across the street at Carl's Jr., then I had walked over.

There were a few people downstairs, blue suits and dark dresses. Some were setting up for some sort of technology convention.

Lisa was standing next to a column, dressed in a black suit, low heels, hair in a bun.

Smiling.

She asked, "How're you coming on getting me my money?"

"I should slap the fuck out of your crazy ass."

"Penalties and interest, Driver."

"That shit wasn't necessary."

"Whatever you said to my husband wasn't necessary."

"Oh, you're the good wife now."

"I hope that's where you and your whore were heading last night, to bring me what you stole from me. And instead of lying up in a cheap hotel with your whore, you'd better get busy trying to get my money."

She knew where I was last night. That stopped me. I'd looked around last night, made sure we weren't being followed. I snapped, "What, you put a GPS on my friend's car?"

Lisa laughed.

I asked, "You got somebody following me?"

Her laughter grew.

My chest rose and fell, out of sync with my throbbing head. A few people came our way, stared at us, walked by without saying a word, got on the elevator.

I sucked in a hard breath, eyes burned from being open all night, head hurt from not eating. Despite all that, I took it down a notch, said, "Here. I have three."

"Three? This some kind of a joke?"

"Working on the rest."

I handed her the money I'd gotten from Arizona. A rubber band held it together.

She held the three large in her right palm, like her hand was a monetary scale.

She sounded like she was in a state of extreme agitation, said, "That's not the deal. You have a problem with integrity, a serious issue honoring your end of the contract on all levels. I said get me half, and you give me three?"

"Will that get your ass to back off for a minute?"

"Penalties and interest accrue all day. Every second of every minute."

It took all I had to not backhand her ass right then. She owed me for the damage she had done to me, the damage she had done to Panther. I wanted to slap her down into the pavement, but all I could do was shake my head, laugh a bit, push my heavy lips up into a sardonic smile.

I asked, "Until I get half, what can I do to make this better?"

A pause rested between us.

She said, almost in a whisper, "Oh. Now you want to fuck me?"

"I didn't say that."

I stayed strong. Felt like I was facing a nigga on the yard. She was just as bad, just as relentless. I told her, my tone hard, "Back off. I'll get you your money."

"That's sounds very Christian. Now you have integrity, a man of your word."

"Save the Flip Wilson routine. I'll get your fucking money."

"You ignored me. Rejected me. Insulted me. Assaulted me. Stole from me. Taunted me every day. You've earned this. How many times did I tell you that I loved you, Playa?"

People looked our way. Didn't know how long they had been feeling our heat.

I took her by her arm, pulled her toward the elevator. People were getting off as we got on. I pushed the button for P6, the lowest level, six floors below surface level, one above hell.

The door closed, left us in a space the size of a coffin.

Lisa jerked away from me, moved to the far side of the elevator. "Don't believe you grabbed me. You don't put your hands on me, not like that."

"You pulled a gun on me."

"I didn't touch you."

"You busted my head with a fucking can."

"And you kicked me out of your apartment, manhandled me, assaulted me, pushed me around like I was one of your two-bit whores, then . . . nothing. Not going to say it."

I held my tongue. Reasoning with her was like giving CPR to a corpse. I don't think the prefrontal cortex of her brain had fully developed. But she had me in a corner. She had sucked me into her game. So maybe my own prefrontal cortex had some developing to do.

The elevator door opened. Stale air greeted us. Level six was the least used, hardly any cars came down this far. Nothing was down here but cold concrete, dust, and our echoes.

I took a few steps out, kept my eyes on Lisa and put some space between us, looked around, made sure this wasn't a setup, saw nobody else.

I asked her, "Why the hell you call me? Why you wanna meet?"

I expected her to keep going off, talking crazy, maybe say something else about last night, about the police hemming me and Panther up on Crenshaw. Or about us riding out and looking for her bully-boys. But Lisa shrugged, her stance softened, voice turned tender, voice lost all of its nastiness.

She spoke in a soft voice. "Just wanted to see you."

"See me? For what?"

She sucked on her bottom lip, shook her head. "You don't get it, do you?"

"Get what?"

"I miss you, Driver. I hate for us to be like this. I really do."

I said, "What, now you want to fuck me?"

"This isn't about sex, Driver. For me this is way deeper. Way, way deeper."

"Why won't you back off? You're taking this too far."

"You're my *sancho*, and I'm your *jeva*. Just your *jeva*. I wanted us to be more."

Silence eased down like a feather, settled between two fornicators. Something within her reached inside me. Something that was undeniable.

She said, "Been . . . been almost six months since we've been together."

"I know. Almost six months since my momma died."

Silence revisited us.

I asked, "Why did you pick me, Lisa?"

"I didn't *pick* you. We met. We had the right energy. I'm old school. We would've been bonded through our crime. I would've been Bonnie to your Clyde. Loyal to you."

"You make it sound like you asked me to wash your car. You asked me to kill for you."

"For us. It was for us."

"Be real, Lisa. The mariticide . . ."

"No big words, please. Not now. I'm not a friggin' crossword puzzle."

"Killing your husband, that was for your benefit."

"Would've reciprocated, killed someone for you, at no charge."

"I'm supposed to believe that."

"Have I ever deceived you? I loved you. Fucked you any way you wanted to get fucked. I sucked your dick the way you liked it sucked. I fucking fucked you the way I'll never fuck my fucking husband. I loved you. I dressed you up. Made sure you were well dressed, well fed."

We paused. Her emotions were like both fire and ice. They ran through me, froze the parts of me that her flames couldn't turn to embers, did that all the way down to my marrow.

I asked, "What do you want now?"

"Don't know. One minute I want to love you, the next I want you to . . . to not exist."

Another moment passed. A moment that was as heavy and graceful as an elephant.

"I'll get your money. Call your boys off, Lisa."

"I'm tired of being fucked over and lied to. Wolf lied to me. What kind of man would get a vasectomy and not tell his wife? Shit like that fucks with a woman's head. I'm forty. I wanted kids." Her voice crackled, flames rose behind her eyes. "Makes a woman mad enough to kill her husband. Or get him killed."

I shifted, took a hard breath, rubbed my eyes.

She asked, "Am I boring you?"

"Look, I'm . . . I'm tired. Tired as hell."

"Now you know how I've felt the last six months. You think I've slept at night?"

"You're stalking me. Breaking in my place."

"That's how I feel every day you walk into Wolf's business. In *my* business. Disrespected. Like you're stalking me. Like I'm being burglarized. Not a good feeling, huh?"

I opened and closed my hands. "Call your boys off."

"You played me for a fool. Every man I've ever met, same thing. I'm tired of motherfuckers taking me for granted and walking over me. Both of those perpetrators I shot and killed, they did the same thing. They looked at me, took me for granted. I showed them."

"Lisa. Call. Your. Boys. Off."

In a soft voice she asked, "Why did you put your dick in me? Why did you make me feel like this then just throw me away? Be honest. I won't hold it against you. I just want to know."

Silence and love turned inside out, heated the air, made it hard to breathe.

She wanted a cut-and-dried answer when that kind of answer was out of season. An old sermon came to my mind, saw Reverend Daddy in the pulpit. His voice came out of my body, sudden and strong, said, "Stolen waters are sweet, and bread eaten in secret is pleasant."

"From a non-believer. How sacrilegious."

My answer didn't matter. Nothing I said was going to make a difference, nothing I said would give her sanity. I was the poster child for every man who had done her any injustice.

"Lisa, I need your help on this. I'll admit I was wrong from the start. Wrong for having an affair, wrong to think I could kill a man. Wrong to take your damn money. Wrong to spend it, no matter what happened to my family. Now back off and I'll get you all of your money."

"*You're not in charge.*" She changed just like that, gave me that police officer's tone, the eyes of a spoiled mayor's kid. "I'm in charge, dammit. I back off when I'm ready to back off."

She turned to walk away. I grabbed her, spun her around. Her hand lashed out, slapped my face three, maybe four times. Like I did fools in days gone by, I wanted to let my fist cannon my frustration into her face. But anger took over and my big hands attacked her little throat before I realized what I was doing. Too far gone to turn back now. Had crossed that line. Couldn't let her go. I choked her. Just like in my daydreams and nightmares. I squeezed harder. Her eyes widened. Never seen anybody look that surprised. Wished we were closer to a concrete column, wanted to bang some sense into her head until blood ran like a river.

She tried to hit me again, her short and toned arms swung at me, fingers clawed at me, then her face filled with panic. Lisa struggled for her purse, wrestled with me and tried to get her hands inside her handbag. I knew what she was reaching for, saw the handle of that Glock as I shook her up, shook her hard enough to loosen her brain, choked her until she couldn't breathe.

Her face turned shades of red. The disbelief in her eyes turned to fear, that fear broken down into small pieces of panic, panic that told her that *sancho–jeva* shit was a done deal, that I was going to kill her before she had a chance to kill me. Her strength faded, arms fell away, gave up trying to get her hand in her bag, gagged, scratched at my hands, weak scratching.

She was on the express train, heading to the other side of West Hell.

I glowered in Lisa's eyes. She was slipping into the shadow of the valley of death. No goodness or mercy following her. I could taketh away. Could be free inside a minute.

She stopped fighting, stared me in my eyes, her eyes glazed over with death.

"Shoot him, Rufus. Be a man and shoot the bastard."

I saw my brother pulling that trigger, heard that click. Rufus did it begrudgingly, but he did it. I let Lisa go all of a sudden, moved my hands like her neck was on fire and I'd been burned, let her go and stumbled away, grunting over and over, hands tingling, eyes wide.

She collapsed against a column, then doubled over, choking and spitting. She wheezed awhile before she could stand up straight. One of her shoes had come off during her struggle to stay alive. She went and picked up her shoe, had a coughing fit, dropped the shoe, picked it up.

I was ready for her to come at me hard. Shoe in one hand, the other hand on her neck, her chest rising and falling, she limped around in a circle like a wounded dog, sweat covering her face. Her hair came undone, fell, framed her anger. She moved hair from her eyes and scowled at me. She moved in circles, favoring the leg with the shoe, that shoe making one leg three inches longer than the other, eyes glazed, disoriented, found her purse, pulled out her Glock.

She bounced death against her leg. She caught her breath, looked around, thinking, maybe remembering that people had just seen us in a heated conversation in the lower lobby, considered her alibi, maybe even imagining how a gun's report would echo like thunder in this hollow chamber, how the sounds might carry up level after level, maybe resound all the way to the lobby, shook her head as if she'd come to some conclusion, then stuffed her Glock back in her bag and limped away, each step backward, pushed the button on the elevator.

We stared at each other until the elevator door opened. She limped on, coughing, gagging, back bent, rubbing at the fingerprints and bruises I'd left staining her neck.

She stared at me, mouth open, that disbelief still in her eyes, like I had been the crazy one in this institution of infidelity. I expected her to get real nasty, to curse and shout out threat after threat, maybe even take a shot at me before she vanished. She looked hurt. Vulnerable.

She spoke simply, her tone political, said, "You just activated the acceleration clause."

The elevator door closed.

My reflection faced me in the steel door, the image of madness.

My hard breathing echoed.

Sancho.

Jeva.

Sweat grew on my face, ran down my neck, stained my crisp white collar.

The wound behind my ear double-timed, throbbed to life, the beat of an African drum.

I snarled, straightened my cuff links and silk tie, did the same with my Italian suit.

Wiped down my shoes. Frowned at the new scuff marks on the heels.

Adjusted my cuff links.

Then I wiped my mouth, faced my reflection again.

I took a step. Stopped. Looked up and around.

Cameras.

Had to be security cameras down here. More than likely security wasn't watching them, too busy eating a ham sandwich and reading the sports section of the *L.A. Times*, but they had tape rolling. Big Brother was always watching, if only with one electronic eye.

I got on the elevator.

Headed through the hotel, expecting security to bum rush me.

Nothing happened.

Left the hotel, took hard steps toward work, fifty-degree air was cooling my dank face.

Walked through the glass doors into the bright yellow lobby of Wolf Classic Limousine.

Lisa was up front, talking to Sid Levine, Margaret Richburg, and a few other people.

Laughing like she was the centerfold for *Better Homes and Gardens*.

But that laugh she had was weak and fragile. Her eyes told me she was rattled.

She had put a colorful scarf over her neck, my handprints hidden.

I walked through her scent, the stench of lies and treachery.

Wolf came into the office as I was getting the keys to the sedan.

We stood, faced each other. A wordless exchange that lasted a good five seconds.

"Good morning, Driver."

"Wolf. Morning."

"You look a little tired."

"I'm cool. Just need some coffee and some Visine."

"I have some Visine on my desk. Help yourself."

"Yeah. Cool. Thanks."

We shook hands like nothing bad had happened between us yesterday. Hypocrites in dark suits. We held our grips. Two warriors. Two men. Two classes. Two worlds. I looked him in his eyes and he did the same with me. He loved Lisa beyond reason. He was looking for that betrayal, wanting to see how deep that river ran. Wondering if his queen had taken a few trips back to the Motherland. The truth was there, unhidden. Getting deeper by the second. Self-preservation in full effect. In that silence it was like we were two prisoners on Lisa's yard.

Wolf looked like a man corroding, six feet of inner angst masked with a rusty smile.

The accumulation of the hurts from this marriage and the one before, maybe many relationships before that. Men hurt. We were people. Couldn't count the number of motherfuckers who cried in jail.

Didn't matter what size, build, or color. Robust men broke down just like the frail ones, shed tears like babies when they finally gave up their ghosts.

Wolf saw my fresh wound, the pain inside me, the past he had brought up when he had mentioned my ex-wife, how she had left me rotting in that cell. I saw the pain, but nothing else in his eyes. Nothing that told me which way his mood was slipping. He was unreadable. All I knew for sure was he was in pain. Any man who touched Lisa lived in agony.

Lisa adjusted the scarf around her neck, followed her husband into the office, each of her steps jittery. Her eyes met mine before she vanished. Hate colored her pupils. Nothing but hate.

Two seconds later she was laughing with her husband.

I remembered what Wolf had told me. That the poet Fontaine had said that every man was three men. Who people thought he was. Who he thought he was. Who he really was.

The same went for women. A lot of us had the enemy living between our sheets.

I headed to the garage, got into one of Wolf's sedans. Became a red dot on his computer screen. Big Brother was watching. Even had people reporting when I borrowed a Pilot pen.

I pumped up the music, had the volume as loud as I could stand it, a DMX tune keeping me alert, jamming me into a new mood, but the same song played over and over in my mind.

You're my sancho. *I'm your* jeva.

This wasn't over. Not close to being over.

Should've killed her ass. Should've killed her while I had the chance. Could've put her head in a FedEx box, left it waiting for the lion and jackal on the front seat of their Expedition.

23

One million wretched thoughts later.

In L.A., distance was measured by time, by how long it took to get somewhere, not by the miles. Santa Monica was fifteen miles away from LAX, but the bumper-to-bumper drive took an hour. An hour of dealing with road rage, arrogant pedestrians who stepped out in front of your ride and frowned like you were an asshole, bad drivers who did a California roll at red lights, motherfuckers who cut you off and flipped you the bird because you obeyed traffic laws.

DMX had been put to sleep. Radio off.

I was in driver mode. Professional. Non-expressive. Like I could be somebody else. Daytime offered me a new persona, the way it allowed Batman to change into Bruce Wayne. But still, even with the suit on, I was the same as Sammy Davis, Jr., in *Ocean's Eleven*. I just needed to make my own ends and walk into the sunshine, smiling while the credits rolled.

There was a lot of movement in front of Shutters Hotel, a lot of chatter spoken in at least six different languages. Cars and taxis blocked the front of the building, the rich and not so famous had valet parking working overtime. Early morning checkout pandemonium.

A different world. No brothers in unbuttoned shirts with their pants hanging on their hipbones. No sisters wearing queen-sized earrings echoing the same gotta-be-gangsta mood.

I followed suit and left my town car with the valet, handed him a few bucks to watch over the ride, and stepped inside. I'd talked to Arizona while I drove this way. Had talked to her and found out what her master plan was. I went to the house phone and asked for Thomas Marcus Freeman's room, called and let him know I was downstairs.

He went off on me, "Why are you calling my room?"

"It's pickup time."

"Don't ever call my room. I come down when I come down."

He hung up, slammed the phone down in my ear.

I cursed that motherfucker. Wondered if I'd have to beat his black ass this morning.

My cellular rang again. Rufus's home number on caller-ID. The number to their main house. I grunted, answered expecting to hear my brother's voice, but it was Pasquale. He never called me. Never. His voice was splintered, laced with anger, like he was coming unglued.

I asked, "What's going on?"

"Somebody broke in my home."

He had my attention. "Trashed your place?"

"I said I was robbed, not invaded by Molly Maid."

"They mess up your walls?"

"Damn right my walls are fucked up. My home is ruined."

"They broke in . . . shit. What all they do?"

Pasquale sounded insane. "What do you think they did? Stole all of my art. My Woodrow Nash sculptures . . . my collection of jazz . . . Lady Midnight, Cool Cat, Bourbon Street, everything is gone. They broke glass, turned over my pedestals . . . you should see these walls."

He made it sound like they had taken a sledgehammer from wall to wall, gutted his mansion. I moved to the side, away from all the high-class people. "Where Rufus at?"

"I don't know. That's why I'm calling you."

I rubbed my temples with my free hand.

I asked, "When was the last time you talked to Rufus?"

"Last night."

"You ain't talked to him since yesterday?"

"Had this . . . disagreement. We fell out. And I left."

"You didn't come home last night?"

"Was on the lot all day."

"Was he home last night?"

"I just got here."

"Does it look like there was a struggle? Any blood anywhere?"

"This is unbelievable."

"When you get there? I mean, how long you been—"

"Five, no more than ten minutes ago."

The lion and jackal had stalked me two nights ago, turned around in Pasquale's driveway.

I asked Pasquale, "Was Rufus there when your place was broken in?"

"Nigga, didn't you hear me say that I just got here? My home has been wrecked. Paintings have been taken. My sculptures are gone."

I snapped, "Stop yelling at me, motherfucker."

"Fuck you."

"Last time, Pasquale."

"Oh, now you can get my damn name right."

He went on and on about how his crib had been looted and ransacked.

I wanted to know if that punk motherfucker had any idea where my brother was.

I told him, "Look. A lot of . . . some . . . hold off before you call the police."

"Are you on crack? Didn't you hear me tell you I've been robbed?"

"Give me a little time. At least an hour. Let me check on something."

"Whassup, nigga? You know something about this bullshit?"

"Look, my place was broken into yesterday."

"Your arrogant, drug-dealing ass . . . this has something to do with your bullshit?"

"All I'm saying is hold off on calling the police for a few hours."

"You think I didn't call the police?"

"Wish you hadn't done that."

"What do you know about this?"

"Cancel that call to the po-po until . . . give me time to check on something."

"Too late for that. You better talk up. LAPD is pulling up in the driveway right now."

"I can't . . . look . . . Pasquale . . ."

He hung up.

I cursed a thousand times. Dialed Rufus's cellular. It went straight to voice mail.

Everything was unfocused and opaque.

Penalties and interest.

Damn. Not much more than a friggin' hour had gone by since I choked Lisa. Didn't know if that was enough time for her to send her bullyboys back out. I knew it was. I knew she did that to prove a point. That this wasn't going to be over until she wanted it over.

Sancho. Jeva.

I opened and closed my hand, still felt Lisa's neck. Regretted I didn't leave her body on that dusty concrete, six levels closer to hell, hated myself for not completing the task.

I went back to the front door, stepped out and took a breath, was about to leave.

Freeman.

Had forgotten all about Thomas Marcus Freeman. His initials were TMF. T followed by MF. That had to stand for *That Mother Fucker*. His momma gave him those initials for a reason.

Stood there and struggled, had to decide which way to go. I headed back inside.

Two workers were monitoring the elevators. Traffic in the lobby was as congested as the 405. Three busloads of Asians had pulled up, most out front with their luggage at their side. Outside of that crowd, at least a hundred more people were down here, most checking out.

Freeman got off the elevator. Leather jacket. Jeans. Dark shoes. Right hand stroking his goatee like he was deep in thought. His briefcase wasn't shackled to his wrist. I swallowed. Opportunity was exploding in my mind. That million-dollar prize had to be in his room.

I put on my earpiece. Dialed another number. She answered.

I adjusted my glasses and whispered, "He just came downstairs."

"You okay?"

"I'm cool."

"You're pacing a lot. You look uneasy."

"I'm fine. Freeman's coming this way."

Her rushed voice came through my earpiece crisp and clear. "Briefcase?"

"Not handcuffed to his wrist."

"His woman?"

I paused, waited to see who else got off the elevator. "That bird is still in the nest."

"Oh, boy."

"Maybe she had too much vodka. She was hitting it pretty hard yesterday."

"Hold on."

The bar was a few feet away, closed, but Jack Daniel's still stood tall and whispered my name soft and sweet, asked me to come make love to a pint, one shot at a time, all back to back, each shot glass lined up like they were customers and I was the best ride at Disneyland.

She came back to the phone, said, "I just called his room. She didn't answer."

"She could be sleeping."

"This changes things in a bad way."

I squinted away some tiredness, needed some comfort. "Calling it off for now?"

"Can't break in the room unless we know where she is."

I asked, "You know what suite he's kicking it in?"

"Bet you a thousand I can find out before he gets in your car."

"Before he gets inside the sedan?"

"And I have no idea right now."

"I'll bet you two large."

"We have a bet."

I nodded and broke the connection. I moved over by the fireplace. People were reading the morning paper and sipping coffee on the cushy furniture. Freeman saw me. I didn't go to that motherfucker. Just waited where he could see me. He came over and asked me if Sade had come down yet. Didn't give a brother a good morning, just looked up and talked down to me.

I owned no smiles this morning. I opened and closed my hands, this time pimpsmacking and choking him until his neck snapped and wobbled back and forth like one of those cheap-ass bobbleheads, told the motherfucker, "Guess she comes down when she wants to come down."

He frowned his way over to the house phone.

"Driver?"

I heard my name and turned around. Sade was coming out of the restaurant, almost up on me. She was more beautiful today than she was yesterday. Maybe because she was smiling. Her Ghirardelli complexion and Frank Sinatra eyes made an exhausted brother stare a little too hard. She had on jeans and boots, a red sweatshirt with the word MANUMIT across the front. Manumit was the same word that I'd seen on her luggage tag in bold red letters.

We spoke with brief smiles, our eyes, and nods of our heads.

She said, "You've come to collect us."

I nodded again. Blue eyes. Long legs and short torso. Her long hair in a single braid.

She said, "I was reading the local paper and enjoying the view. The waters are so beautiful. The sunrise was wonderful this morning. Saw it from the room. Wish my room faced the ocean so I could watch the ocean waves. If it did, and I had a stock of McVitie's, maybe could watch *Trisha* on the telly whenever my heart desired, I'd never leave this place."

"Sounds like you've fallen in love."

"I fall in love too easily, I suppose. For all the wrong reasons."

We both sat on her words. My eyes were on hers. Money. I bet her passion had to do with Freeman's money. Money was power, the ultimate aphrodisiac. Compared to her beauty, Freeman was a beast. He had enough cabbage to fill up her pot. Men hooked up with the most beautiful woman they could afford. Women hooked up with the richest man they could find.

I told her, "I called your room."

She looked surprised, her blue eyes brightened up. Her right hand went to her left, toyed with that sparkling engagement ring. She bumbled, "You called . . . when did you call?"

"Mr. Black Aesthetic wasn't too happy about me calling your room."

Her mouth was open, no words, a slight smile, then she shifted like she was about to say something, then shifted again like she changed her mind. The smile lessened.

I motioned toward Freeman, told her he had an APB out on her.

She sighed, did one of those dismissive hand moves, this one aimed at her man.

Our eyes went across the room, to Mr. Black Aesthetic. Freeman took out his cellular. He shook his head and a frown furrowed his unibrow as he punched in a number. Sade chuckled when her cellular phone rang. She rolled her eyes and took it out of her purse, clicked it on.

She answered like a whip, "I'm right behind you. On your left. Your *other* left."

Freeman turned and turned until he saw Sade standing next to me.

Sade hung up. He closed his phone and marched over. "Where were you?"

"At a table facing the ocean having a bagel and orange juice, waiting on you."

He shook his head. Ocean air thickened between them.

He asked, "What's up with that sweatshirt?"

"It's cold."

"You know what I mean."

"Good morning to you too."

"Why are you wearing that sweatshirt?"

"Wanted to be casual. West Coast people are so laid back. Everyone wears jeans and T-shirts out here. If I had a pair of trainers I'd wear them, but I didn't bring any trainers."

"Don't start acting up, Folasade."

"Because it's *my* sweatshirt, Marcus."

"What about the agreement?"

"It's just a friggin' sweatshirt."

"Do I need to call my attorney and have him handle this?"

"Consider the repercussions from such a phone call. Start a battle and end up in a war."

She adjusted her purse with a rebellious movement, did the same with the leather coat she had draped over her arm, started to walk away, straight-backed, the stroll of a charm-school girl.

Sade headed for the door. Freeman followed her. I brought up the rear, a little bit confused. Sounded like she was his business manager. Either that or she was big-time pimping, a serious macktress who had put her man in check. Either way Freeman was her paycheck.

If this worked out, Freeman would be my paycheck too.

Without looking at me, Sade told me, "Driver, I need Starbucks."

Her tone had changed, lost all friendliness, like the kindness had been sucked out of her.

Freeman shook his head. "This is why I tour by myself. You don't respect my time."

"And I still need Starbucks."

We had to maneuver around the tourists and their oversized luggage. A svelte Asian woman with red hair hurried up the walkway. She had her purse and bottled water in one hand, one of those cardboard holders from Starbucks in her other hand, balancing four cups in the holder the way a waitress carried a tray at a nightclub, like she was a pro at multitasking.

Freeman was too busy running his mouth to notice the woman. He ran right into her, knocked her to the ground, her Starbucks spilled all over her and Freeman. Nothing she had was hot, everything some sort of apple cider, the kind of drinks you gave to children at breakfast.

Sade stepped back from the mess, lips moving up into a smile, a chuckle on her lips.

Freeman ranted that he had to go back upstairs and change.

The Asian woman went right behind him, ranting, just like Freeman. When she got to security she was so busy talking and apologizing to Black Aesthetic that nobody stopped her.

The Asian woman got on the elevator with Freeman, frowning,
wiping herself down.

The elevator doors started to close.

The Asian woman glanced my way.

Sade went as far as the fireplace, then stopped at a spot away
from the people, a hermit back in her shell, arms folded, eyes to the
ground, a look of apprehension painted on her face.

My cellular rang.

I answered.

She said, "Looks like you're gonna owe me two thousand."

"Looks like."

"Now he has to go back to his room. She'll get off on the same
floor, walk the same way, see what room he goes in. Then he leaves
with you. Was that slick or was that slick?"

"How she gonna pull a B&E?"

"We have something figured out."

"She gonna seduce him?"

She laughed.

We hung up.

That sweatshirt issue was no big deal, but it stuck with me. He
hadn't known what she was wearing, didn't know she had on a
sweatshirt. Sounded like he wanted her to dress like Jackie Onassis
or Coco Chanel, because he was the superstar and she was the dime-
piece on his arm representing him. Still, something wasn't right about
their attitudes about that. Then the broad smile that Sade gave me
when I'd told her I'd called her room, that stuck with me too.

I waited a minute then went over to the house phone. I asked
the operator to connect me to Folasade Coker's room. That was the
name I'd seen on her luggage tag. The phone rang until the hotel answering machine came on. I hung up and called the operator again,
asked them to connect me to Thomas Marcus Freeman's room. He
answered on the second ring.

I hung up.

Again I asked the operator to connect me to Folasade Coker's room. Again no answer.

My eyes went to Freeman's blue-eyed woman. Her skin, her hair in that long braid, those long legs and short torso, her keen features. Classy. The kind of woman most men wished for.

I called Rufus again. This time it rang four times before his message center came on.

Twenty nerve-wracking minutes passed. I was pacing, but not as bad as before.

Freeman got off the elevator.

He had on black jeans, white shirt, black leather coat. Still no briefcase.

No sign of the Asian girl either.

Sade looked at her watch and snapped, "Well that took forever."

"Was on the phone." Freeman cleared his throat. "Agent called again."

"Brilliant." Sade *tsk*ed and rolled her eyes. "What's the issue now?"

"Said editor is still asking for pages. Publisher wants a chapter to post on the website."

"*No,*" she snapped. "That is rubbish. No sample chapters. Stick to your contract."

Freeman said, "Look, Folasade—"

"Don't Folasade me, Marcus."

"*Truth Be Told* is behind. I can't baby-sit you. Stay sober. Lay off the mini-bar."

"Whatever. Zip it. Look, I have to whip and use the bathroom now."

Sade headed across the room, asked a worker where the ladies room was, then hurried in that direction. I stood next to Freeman, neither of us acknowledging each other. In slavery days, masters never had to address or acknowledge slaves. Freeman rode in the back. I was the driver.

My cellular blew up again.

It was Rufus. He sounded bad, like he was in intense pain, his anger worse than Pasquale's. His voice was fractured. I stepped to the side and told him to slow down, couldn't understand what he was telling me. He told me some of what went down. My head exploded. Head wound cranked up to about an eight. That injury was alive, breathing on its own.

When I stepped outside to talk in private, I saw them. They were following their regular pattern. The Expedition that was pimped out with forty thousand bucks worth of ghetto rims. They were on the opposite side of the street. Motherfuckers were doing their taunting routine.

I eased the phone down to my side, took a few steps their way, stopped in the middle of the roundabout, sidestepped tourists and luggage, foreign languages being spoken all around.

Two eyes locked on four.

I became that bear. Wished they would get in arm's reach so I could be their friend.

They nodded my way, then pulled away, cigarette smoke pluming from their ride.

They headed away from the ocean, vanished up Pico Boulevard.

It wasn't over.

Seconds later a car followed them. Panther was at the wheel. The dancer who cried when she watched documentaries on Rita Hayworth, the woman who took medication for depression. Cynthia Smalls. Panther. She sent money to her mother in Georgia. Wanted to take care of her sister's two kids, maybe even another. Her brother was on foreign land defending a country that would never love him, not the way black men like him should be loved.

I went to the sedan. Did that because I saw a slip of paper under the window. It was another newspaper article. Man found dead back East. Duct-taped and drowned in the ocean.

I tried to call Panther on her cellular. Got no answer.

Hoped Panther knew what she was doing. Didn't need to wash a woman's death away from my hands, not with my own tears. Didn't need any more ghosts flying around in my mind.

24

I had to chauffeur Freeman to Howard Hughes Center. West Los Angeles. Off the 405 at Howard Hughes Parkway. From Santa Monica it was a traffic-filled ride. I drove, waited for my cellular to blow up, and listened to Freeman and Sade go at it like an old married couple.

Sade said, "Let's get a few things out in the open, Marcus."

"Not now."

"Yes, now. I'm really tired of your groupies. The way they disrespect me in my face. If I wanted to go through this sort of thing I would've dated an NBA player. Then I would have expected this sort of lifestyle. Ever since this book has come out . . . everything has changed."

"You've changed, Folasade. You're more jealous every day."

"I'm jealous? Ha! You should hear yourself talking. Your interviews, what's this *Chester Himes and Ralph Ellison level* nonsense, Marcus? Rubbish. This *on the walls of Barnes & Noble* crap is flapdoodle. You're jealous of everyone. What are you trying to do?"

"Controversy shakes it up, sells books. Look at those white boys, Wolfe and Updike. All the press they got. And Richard Ford and Colson Whitehead, you see that?"

"It's sad, that's what it is."

"No, it's real. Mad, stupid *New York Times* press. They'll be screaming 'a fight, a fight, between a nigga and a white' and sell a ton of books. That's what it's all about. The bottom line is the numbers. I need to come out and stir it up like that, push the sales through the roof."

"That's horrible, Marcus. All about numbers? If you feel that way, it's horrible."

"Have you ever been able to sell a single book, Folasade? Show me your numbers."

Sade shut down, scooted away. I caught her in the rearview, body language tight, pointing away from Freeman, eyes out the window, an expression filled with disgust and pain.

The freeway was under my tires, passing by at seventy miles per hour, the same pace as their conversation, the same velocity as my own anxious thoughts and worries over Panther.

"Fine, Marcus. Since you insist on being rude. You should hear the wicked and evil things your so-called fans say about you. I do because I'm in the back of the room, unnoticed."

"Look at the numbers," he retorted. "They love Thomas Marcus Freeman."

"Marcus, I love you. I wouldn't be here if I didn't. Don't kid yourself about the other people. It's the book. The words. The poetry of that resounds the . . . the . . . the truth about their own situations, their own lives. They don't know you. They have no idea who you are."

He chuckled. "You're the expert on Thomas Marcus Freeman, right?"

"Please, don't start referring to yourself in third person."

"Answer the question. Are you the expert on Thomas Marcus Freeman?"

"I'm your lover. I'm your fiancée. I'm your friend. I tell you this for your own good. At the airport, while you were doing that interview, I overheard one of your fans say that your ignorance and low self-esteem springs from your tongue every time you open your mouth."

"What do you know about the book business?"

"I'm only the messenger."

"About having to hustle? What do you know about that? Tell me, Folasade."

The more they argued, the more she sounded both African and British. Freeman's anger yanked him back to his Quitman, Mississippi, roots, his accent and words getting more Southern.

"I know you should get together with Kobe and do an infomercial on infidelity."

"I'm not messing around, Sade."

"Have you graduated to the point where you and Collymore can do an ad for dogging?"

"Nobody is dogging."

"Should I contact your publicist and arrange that? Or have you become her Beckham?"

Freeman spoke in a soft voice, said, "I love you, Folasade. Only you."

"Don't patronize me."

He whispered, *"Sisimi. Mo fe e."*

"Stop. I'm not playing with you, Marcus. Stop it."

First there was more silence between them, then giggles from her and whispering sounds from him. The leather seats sighed, made some tender noises as Sade scooted closer to Freeman.

"I know what you need, Sade."

"Give me romance, Marcus." She whined. "Stimulate my mind first."

"We need a vacation."

"We do need a holiday, Marcus. This . . . this book . . . it's . . . it's killing us both."

"Maybe we can go to Zurich in March."

"That would be nice." Her voice softened. "I know this beautiful resort in St. Moritz."

"Maybe we can go snowmobiling. You know how you like snowmobiling."

She laughed a naughty laugh. Then came the wet sounds of deep kissing.

"When are we getting married, Folasade?"

"My head hurts, Marcus. Can we please get Starbucks?"

"Driver, Starbucks."

I nodded without looking back. "A Starbucks is right across from the bookstore."

Sade said, "Brilliant. That's lovely."

Her eyes came to mine in the rearview. Then we both looked away.

Like I was being paid to do, I kept driving. Eyes and ears.

Freeeeeee-Man! Freeeeeee-Man!

Reps from Borders Books and Music met Freeman curbside, all smiles and handshakes, each one waving a Freeman bobblehead. Moses on the mountaintop waving the rules. They came to the car so they could escort him through his legion of loyal fans. Women were flashing digital cameras, the high-tech women taking pictures with their cellular phones, some extending their cellular phones and begging him to talk with their momma or cousin or best friend.

Freeeeeee-Man! Freeeeeee-Man!

Others were fanning themselves and yelling out his name like he was their first cousin resurrected. Freeman leaned forward and waved, serious like he was the Democratic nominee.

Sade saw that crowd and moved back into a corner, shut down.

Freeman told her, "Me, Sade. They come to see Thomas Marcus Freeman. Read the banner. Listen to the name they're calling. Driver, you want to let me out or what?"

I went around and opened his door. Freeman got out of the car, went on without her, never looked back. No kiss good-bye so she could feel special in front of the crowd. I didn't know a lot about women, but I did know they liked to feel special. I looked in at Sade.

I swallowed, asked Sade, "Did you want to get out?"

"Let the sheep follow their Moses into the bookshop so I can have some room to walk."

My clock was ticking. Needed Sade out of the car. My weary eyes went to the crowd.

I closed her door, headed back to the driver's side, got back in, still cursing in my mind.

The pickpocket was already here. She had shoulder-length dread-locks this time. That Mrs. Robinson smile all over her face, the kind that made a man feel heat in his loins. A blouse that was tight, short enough to pimp out her abdominal six-pack. Tight jeans over a tight ass. I understood what Arizona meant about having an ass like that and ruling the world. No wonder Freeman had called her first. Arizona looked more like a woman you'd take home to Momma. She was long-term parking. The pickpocket had the kind of ass a man wanted to saddle up and ride off into the sunset. Or up and down Sunset. She wore heels, sexy pointed-toe shoes that helped pimp out her rotund ass that much more. Shoes were rust-colored, just like her leather jacket, a jacket that she wore wide open. Forty-plus with the body of a twenty-year-old.

Freeman's stoic image and name were up all over the joint. Thirty-foot banners. Bold letters. Reds, golds, and greens. Like it was a movie premiere at Mann's Chinese Theatre.

THOMAS MARCUS *FREEMAN*

AUTHOR OF

POOL TABLES AND POLITICS

AND

ALL THAT GLITTERS

AND

truth is stronger than lies

READS AND SIGNS HIS

#1 *NEW YORK TIMES* BESTSELLER

DAWNING OF IGNORANCE

25

I didn't know what was going on at the time.

Had no idea what was going on back at Shutters.

Later on I'd find out the way everything went down.

The Asian woman got out on Freeman's floor, soaked in Starbucks. Watched Freeman storm into his room. Saw the maid's cart down the hallway, went down and peeped to make sure the maid was on the floor. An older Spanish woman. Too busy cleaning up someone else's mess to look up. Then the Asian woman went and stood near the elevator. When Freeman came back out, she passed him in the hallway again, let him rush and get on the vertical carriage. Then she took out the bottled water she had in her bag. She undressed. Head to toe. Got butt naked. Wearing her birthday suit was no big deal to her. She worked in that uniform three, sometimes five nights a week at Strokers. Worked naked in six-inch stilettos, music bumping while she was swinging from a pole, breasts and vagina on display, smoky dollars raining at her feet.

After she undressed at Shutters, she stuffed her clothing in a plastic bag and hid them in the trash container by the elevator. She took her bottled water, opened it, and poured the overpriced purified water made by Coca-Cola all over herself. Next she took out a bottle of shower gel, soaped herself up head to toe, used a bath sponge and got a decent lather going. She let her hair down, let it shadow her features so the cameras—if there were cameras and if those cameras were on—wouldn't get a good shot of her face. Then she ran down the hallway all wet and smelling good, breasts bouncing like two kids on a trampoline, and rushed to the Spanish maid, embarrassed and hysterical, the bath sponge throwing soap and water every which-away, bad acting at its best, but good enough to shock the maid and make her say things in Spanish and genuflect. The Asian woman told the Spanish maid that she thought she heard somebody knocking at the door while she was showering, went to the door, didn't see anybody, took a step out, then the door closed hard, hit her foot, she jumped out of the way to keep her pedicure from being messed up, and she got locked out.

A naked Asian woman running up and down the hallway at a swank hotel.

Then, of course, just like any normal person in California, she threatened to sue the hotel. Her toe might be broken. And her pedicure, well, they owed her a free night because of that.

The maid didn't question her story. Maybe she'd seen stranger things. She just wrapped the con woman in a towel as fast as she could and let her in the room so fast it wasn't funny.

Two minutes after Freeman had gone, the Asian woman was inside his room.

Elvis had entered the building like a motherfucker.

The silver briefcase was on the unmade bed, locked and heavy.

She showered the gel off her body, rushed through Freeman's personal things without drying off, piled up everything she wanted to take. She pulled Freeman's suitcase out of the closet and put everything she had gathered inside. She pulled out a pair of gray sweats that Freeman had packed, put them on, then wiped down everything she had touched. Made sure none of her hair was left behind. She grabbed the suitcase and wheeled it out the door like it was no big deal. Her hair was still down, shadowing her face, head down, eyes on the ground.

The silver briefcase was tucked inside the luggage.

She tossed her used towels into the maid's cart.

At the elevator, she opened the trash container, got her clothes, put her sandals back on.

She went downstairs, passed by the security that was guarding the elevators without making any eye contact, pretty much blended with all the other moneymakers in the lobby.

She went through the crowd, straight out the front door, headed for the roundabout unseen and unnoticed, went to the window for valet parking and gave them her ticket.

Valet pulled her car around, smiled, and loaded her bag in her trunk for her.

As they opened her car door, she gave the worker a two-dollar tip.

She drove away. Smiling.

As Sade would say, brilliant.

Back at Borders Books and Music.

I was resting fifteen miles from Shutters Hotel, on Howard Hughes Parkway, parked in front of the bookstore, watching Freeman get admired, waiting for Sade to get out of the sedan.

Sade sat in the backseat, staring at that banner. Staring and not saying a word.

Sade said, "The titles of the first three are larger . . . much larger than *Dawning*."

Her stiff body language told me she wasn't moving, just staring up at Freeman's praise.

She said more words, dots and accents in the air, then said, "Unbelievable."

Felt like I was supposed to talk back. Didn't know what to say. Just wanted her to get out. I checked my watch, looked up at the banner, said, "Hadn't heard about the *truth* book."

"Was his best book. It went as fast as it came. That was right around Nine-Eleven-Oh-One. Almost a year to the day after we met. We were both taking the same writing class. Had a conversation and got on pretty well. One thing led to another. Seemed like serendipity."

Lights. Camera. Action. Today L.A. was Freeman's city. Over

five hundred excited people were waiting for him, ninety percent of them anxious women, more of his loyal fans rushing in like they were going to see the resurrection of Jerry Garcia at a Grateful Dead concert.

She said, "His book never made it out of the boxes. Died on the vine."

My cellular wasn't ringing. Checked my watch. Needed to hear from Panther. If Lisa had a GPS on her ride then she knew Panther was riding her boys tough. She wouldn't get too close, just close enough to let them motherfuckers know that two could play this game. Let them know that I was after their asses too. Just like Panther had said about Lisa, I had some personal shit with the bully-boys. Every time I thought about them I wanted to pull out one of these burners and send some heat to the closest one. Shoot him once to hear him scream. Shoot him again to shut his ass up. Then do the same to his friend. What order I got them in didn't matter.

"I asked my mum what she would say if I brought home a chap they didn't approve of. She said, 'Well, as we Yoruba always say, why smell what you won't eat?' "

"I'm sorry. What was that?"

Sade was rambling, letting out the thoughts that were cluttering her mind. My mind was cluttered as well, was back at Shutters on the Asian woman who had made her way upstairs to try and do a B&E and on Panther tracking the lion and jackal.

Sade sighed hard, dug around in her purse, repeated what she had just said.

I cleared my throat, stopped bouncing my leg, said, "I have no idea what that means."

"My people, they are always using proverbs and stuff." She laughed. "Mum's point is if I know that they wouldn't approve of a guy, why would I date him? So basically, why smell something that you already know you won't eat."

I said, "Your peeps don't approve of the Black Aesthetic."

"They do not." Stress weakened her voice. "No, my *peeps* don't approve of Marcus."

"Why not? He's successful."

"Because he's . . . Marcus is . . . at times . . . our ideologies . . . we're from different cultures."

"Because he's African-American?"

"To be honest, I prefer the term Black over African-American because 'African-American' is misleading." She had pulled a tiny bottle out of her purse. She'd hit the mini-bar. She struggled, then twisted it open. Sipped her colorless and odorless liquor. Sighed. "A white person who was born in Africa, then moved to America would be an African-American. Charlize Theron, the actress in that movie *Monster*, is South African; that makes her African-American."

Sade sipped again, made a soft and sensual sound, like she had what she needed to adjust her attitude, control her angst, calm her nerves. Or maybe that bottle was the only paradise she had in her life right now. Or she had found out that at the bottom of every bottle lived the truth. Just like me, she took a hit and made a sound, the sweet sound of an addict who finally got a fix.

She went on, "They would qualify for financial aid, all of the benefits and entitlements of a black person. And they will get the jobs and pay privileges afforded to whites."

I cleared my throat again. More people were coming this way, the ones who always showed up CP-time. A few had bobbleheads. So many cameras were flashing that it looked like an electrical storm was in full effect. The pickpocket had worked through the crowd, had got next to Freeman. She pulled his attention away from a few other women, kissed him on his lips and they hugged. She gave him the kind of contact that could make a man lose his wallet.

Sade saw that exchange, closed her eyes, said words filled with accent marks and dots.

The pickpocket left the bookstore, her cellular up to her ear, a wicked smile on her face. My heart sped up. Sweat tried to flower on my collar. That meant she had completed her mission and Freeman was one wallet lighter. Her sashay took her east toward the parking garage, then she vanished into its entrance, her pace calm and cool. A seasoned rip-off artist.

My cellular rang. Arizona. My eyes went to Freeman's big sign. The million-dollar man.

Two rings went by before I clicked my phone on, didn't say anything right away.

Arizona's voice was all business. "Hit me when they're heading back to their hotel room."

"Now what?"

"Guess we go from door to door, see which one the key opens. Shouldn't take long. Only eleven suites in their hotel, won't take long at all. It's a walk in the park from here. Fun, huh?"

"Yeah. Fun."

She said, "You look good enough to put in a JCPenney window."

"Thanks."

"Glad you didn't let me down. I was depending on you."

I swallowed a lump of deceit and treachery.

She whispered, "Missed you last night. Had to self-service again."

"Yeah. Same here."

"When this is done maybe we can celebrate."

"Cool."

We hung up.

The streetlights changed all of a sudden. Arizona's silver BMW whipped out of the exit for underground parking, took to the streets with speed and smoothness. She passed by me, grinning, that high-end chariot moving anxious and even, the pickpocket at her side, all business. I caught a glimpse of them. The pickpocket's mane was back in a pixie cut. Locks removed.

Arizona didn't know she had been double-crossed.

I licked my lips, checked my watch. Needed Panther to ring my goddamn number.

Sade interrupted my thoughts, asked me, "Where are you from?"

"Here. L.A. Born right here." I paused, Arizona gone from my sight. "What about you?"

"Nigeria." Sade hummed. "Driver, I love your Black-American accent. It's wonderful."

I clicked on my professional smile and told Sade, "Your accent is pretty sweet too."

"Thank you. I'm British-Nigerian. I grew up in South London, Brixton Hills."

"I hear some of the Motherland in your accent too."

"My parents are Nigerian. That's the Yoruba in me."

"Yoruba. That's a religion, right?"

"Yes and no. In Brazil. Really big there." She perked up a bit. "In Nigeria, there are gods worshipped that are particular to Yoruba people—you heard of the Orisha?"

"Not at all."

"Never mind. Well, in my home, Yoruba is not a religion. My mother says that it's some stuff some Americans made up to give people some 'back to Africa incentive' . . . no offense."

"None taken."

"A lot of my family, especially my grandparents, gets insulted when people say that Yoruba is a religion. It's a language and a tribe." She chuckled again. "And they hate it when you use the word tribe because of the negative connotations of backwardness attached to it. European groups are never called tribes, but African ones are."

It looked like she was about to end her mini-lecture and get out, but another book-carrying crowd whisked around the corner. Sade retreated, moved around a bit, then opened her purse. She took out another small bottle. This time she had a hard time twisting the top.

I offered, "Let me help with that."

I broke the seal. She thanked me. Took the bottle. Sipped. Made sensual sounds.

She stared at the banner. Twisted her lips. Eyes misted up. She kept sipping, fell deeper and deeper into her own thoughts. Then the bottle was dry. She had reached her truth.

She asked, "Ever been across the pond?"

"Pond?"

"Ocean."

"Nah. Far east as I made it was . . . made it as far as Memphis, Tennessee."

"You must travel."

"Keep telling myself that." Camp Hill, Alabama, came to my mind in a flash, that memory swimming around like a ghost. I blinked that ghost away, paused, then I saw her face, the image of my ex-wife, heard her screams and cries, then needed to hold a hit of Jack, stare at its complexion. I shook that memory off, checked my watch again. "What's Nigeria like?"

"Oh, God. Until I moved to the States I spent most of my time in London, Brixton actually, but home, Nigeria, is nice, warm, palm trees and coconut trees. But it is also very class-conscious. London has this North London and South London thing going. People never cross the river and go from south to north. Nigeria has its own thing too. You know, with an educated upper class, and a non-educated upper, both might be wealthy, but they still snob each other."

"That class thing sounds a lot like Black L.A. to me. Y'all have a Crenshaw Boulevard?"

She laughed a little. "*Y'all*. Americans slay me with that word. *Y'all*. Marcus's people are the kings and queens of *y'all*. *Y'all* do this. *Y'all* do that. *Y'all* come back."

I adjusted my rearview, looked at her, played along. "Heard you were a writer too."

Her laughter died an abrupt death. "Where did you hear that?"

"Dunno. Think I overheard somebody talking yesterday."

"Yeah, I . . . I self-published a book."

"Self-published, what does that mean?"

"Means I did it myself."

"You didn't get a big tour and bobbleheads?"

"No big tour. No merchandising whatsoever." Her misty eyes and turned-down lips went up to the signs praising Freeman. She took out another bottle, stared at it, thinking, then put it back in her purse. She mumbled, "No publisher championed me or financed my tour."

"That self-publishing thing, that cost a lot? I mean, was that hard to do?"

She mumbled some more, "No enthusiastic crowds. No huge banners. No limousines."

"You're not promoting too?"

She blinked out of her stupor. "No. Those days are behind me."

"Too bad. I'd like one of your bobbleheads."

That got a brief smile and an uncomfortable laugh out of her.

I said, "Maybe I'll run inside after I park and pick up one of your books."

That was my subtle hint for her to get out and go.

All she did was shift and shift and shift, shake her head nonstop, sink deeper into the backseat. "When I was out there, my book never made it to a bookshop of this magnitude."

I repeated, "After I park, I'll run inside and buy one so I can get your John Hancock."

A moment passed before she answered. "It's out of print."

"Out of print? What does that mean?"

"You won't find one."

"After I park, can I run in and ask them to order me one?"

"Out of print means just that, out of print. It no longer exists."

I asked, "Can I buy one from you?"

She gave me a polite smile. "I don't have any."

"How much it cost to self-publish your book? Couple hundred bucks?"

"Cost me ten thousand dollars."

"You spent ten large on doing a book, didn't sell any, and you don't have one left?"

"I destroyed them."

"All of them?"

"Had a bonfire party with every last one."

"Why would you do that?"

She laughed a plastic laugh. "What, are you interviewing me?"

I laughed too, mine made of the same recyclable material. Something wasn't adding up.

I switched gears, thought about the kind of women I was involved with, everyone from Panther to Lisa, then looked back at the

African Queen, posted up a smile, said, "I'm just . . . I find you . . . cool . . . fascinating. Most beautiful women aren't that smart, not like you. Not the women I know. Freeman is lucky. You're beautiful and intelligent, if you don't mind my saying that."

She smiled a little, this smile girlier. Almost blushed. Not used to compliments.

I said, "Didn't mean to bother you about the book thing. I'm still pretty new to the job. Six months in. Never picked up a writer before. So I guess it was like this when you were out there doing the book-hustle thing. But you make it sound like your experience was pretty bad."

"Horrible. I stood in a mall all day like some sort of a homeless person, at a table, begging strangers to buy my book. You think you do a book about something important, something not laced with flapdoodle and sex, and people will show up and embrace your efforts."

"They don't?"

"Please. They pick your book up, put it right back down, then have the nerve to ask for somebody else's book, right in your face. They choose hot and steamy over anything intelligent. You spend all day staring at a blank sheet of paper and they come and shit on your hard work."

Silence flooded the car.

She went on, "I had delusions of grandeur. For all it's worth, I might as well have driven down the road throwing money out the window."

"Sounds rough."

"It was a labor of love greeted with mass rejection. Humbling to say the least."

"Sorry to hear that."

She ran her tongue over her top lip, her blue eyes back on that banner. "Everyone loves *his* book. Everyone is *his* number-one fan."

She leaned forward like she was getting ready to leave, then sat back again. She sighed, rocked like an addict, trying to decide if she was going to give in and let that little bottle win.

I asked, "What was your book about?"

She laughed again, but her eyes told me that I had asked one question too many. Impatience hardened her face. "Talk about something else. I hear about books all day long."

I looked down at the word on her sweatshirt. MANUMIT. Her eyes followed mine.

I asked, "What does manumit mean?"

She paused, then told me, "To release from slavery."

A wave of agitation came and reminded me that sleep hadn't been my friend for the last two days. Rubbed my eyes. Took another breath. This job was my prison, this car my cell.

Sade said, "I'm ready to get out."

I hurried out of the car, tiredness weighing down my body, adjusted my suit and took long strides, but had to slow down because of that pain in my knee. Head wound hurt too. I cursed Lisa to hell and limped a few steps. By the time I made it around Sade was standing curbside.

I closed the car door for her, asked, "How long will this book signing last?"

She took a hard breath, the spirits scented my face. "Hours. Marcus lives for praise and pandemonium, loves the sound of his own voice so much he talks to himself in his sleep. Will go on and on as long as one person in his dream is listening."

"Listen, I have to move the car, but I'll be no more than five minutes away."

"Brilliant. What's around here? Any bars open?"

"Still early. Looks like you have your own private stock."

She gave me a thin, apologetic smile.

I said, "If I was off the clock, I'd grab a glass and join you, first round on me."

Her smile changed again, widened. "That would be lovely. Join me?"

"Wish I could. I'd get up on a bottle of Jack."

"Then do. Perhaps we can be discreet and add some flavor to something from Starbucks."

"Maybe some other time."

Playful disappointment painted her face.

I said, "When I'm off the clock, if you're available, maybe we can hook up at the bar."

She smiled again, this one not as wide, but winsome all the same.

"Now, Driver, besides Starbucks, what else is there to do in this plaza?"

"Movie theater upstairs." I looked around, tried to remember what else was over here. "Few places to eat. Rubio Baja Grill. If you want to shop there's a Nordstrom Rack."

"There's a Nordies upstairs?"

"Yeah. An outlet."

"Starbucks and discount shoes. That's lovely."

I handed her another business card, my cellular number circled in red ink.

She smiled. "I kept the one you gave me yesterday."

Sade lingered like she didn't want to go, didn't know what to do with herself.

She said, "Thanks."

"For what?"

"Calling me beautiful. It was appreciated. Been a while."

I nodded at her, my face in a half smile. She was quality. A diamond.

"Almost rang your limousine service last night." She kept talking. "Was going to see if I could request you, have you tour me around when the traffic was more favorable."

"Hate to disappoint you, but L.A. traffic is never favorable."

"So I heard. Wanted to get out and see that Crenshaw Boulevard I keep hearing so much about. The waters were wonderful, the food magnificent, but the hotel seemed so sterile."

"Crenshaw? You look more Rodeo Drive than Crenshaw Boulevard."

"I wanted to get away from everything pretentious and be around some good music and real people, not obsessed book readers or cardboard cutouts and caricatures from *Baywatch*."

A thunderous applause shut her up. Flashing cameras. Freeman was on.

Sade put her shades on and waved good-bye with her fingers, then lowered her head, tightened her shoulders, maneuvered around a crowd of latecomers, women who damn near ran her down, all of those women racing toward the store, cameras, books, and bobbleheads in hand.

Sade seemed so small. They bumped her like she was invisible, like she was a ghost passing through someone else's world. No apologies. The swarm moved on and hurried inside the store. Sade recovered, headed for the escalator, her straight-back charm-school sway shaken and disturbed. Looked like she stopped and took a breath, shook her head, profane dots and accent marks filling the air. I caught her profile as she ascended to another level, her face struggling to relax as she moved away from the pandemonium. She turned around and faced me.

Manumit.

I raced the sedan downstairs. Rufus was down there waiting for me.

He told me that he'd hide out one level down, told me to turn right and look for a U-Haul. That white and orange rental was easy to spot. Same for Rufus. His pale skin and gray eyes made him look like a colorless cat. Easy to find in a crowd of people, black, white, or otherwise. Over six feet tall. Messenger bag hanging over his shoulder. Dada jeans. Daredevil sweatshirt. Timberland boots. Honeyblond locks. Soft-shouldered stance. I hit my bright lights, screeched into handicap parking. His hips brought him my way, first with the hurried walk of a Vegas showgirl, then he squared up his shoulders and strengthened his body language, went into an almost unhurried gangsta stroll, mimicked the way Reverend Daddy walked.

Memphis ran through a fog that blanketed my mind.

I got out of the car, moving like quicksand was up to my waist.

Slammed the door and my anger echoed like thunder. Took my glasses off. Rubbed my eyes. Faced my doppelganger.

When Rufus got closer I saw that his Daredevil sweatshirt was ripped, boots scuffed, scratches on his neck. His face had the most damage. His thick locks were pulled back into a ponytail. He'd taken a hard blow, hard enough to swell his left jaw up like a blowfish. Not as bad as Ali looked after he had that rumble in the jungle with Joe Frazier, but it looked like he'd been in a battle for his life.

26

Back in the day Reverend Daddy had an old boxing bag rigged up in the garage. The bag was black, had duct tape wrapped around the center where it had taken the most blows. He put it up there when we were boys. Made us cut grass, trim hedges, and hit that bag until we couldn't hit it anymore. He said that evil was out in the streets training every day. We had to do the same. Think that bag might've been rigged up before we were born, from back in the day when Reverend Daddy used to get his workout on. In between sermons he broke a few jaws back in his day. His right hook wasn't a secret. Made sure we knew how to deliver the same pain.

That was years ago.

Rufus had dug deep into his bag and called on those skills today.

I didn't know my brother could do that, didn't know he had that kinda animal inside him. He couldn't kick ass like I could, was closer to being a pacifist than an aggressive man, couldn't take a blow or deliver a punch the way I did, but he had done his best.

He'd been the last man standing in what he called hand-to-hand combat.

Reverend Daddy would've heard Rufus's story, been happy, might've smiled. Might've been prouder than he was the day Rufus pointed a gun at Ulysses's head and pulled the trigger.

Maybe. Maybe not. Reverend Daddy was in the ground so I'd never know, not for sure.

To be honest, somehow I doubt that Reverend Daddy would've been proud of his youngest son. Think I was just hoping for that happy ending. Maybe just missing those days.

Rufus hated those memories. I loved them.

Still Rufus had dug into the bag and used what Reverend Daddy had taught us.

Momma taught us in a different way. It didn't end at lifting chickens from Boys Market. She schooled us on the art of self-preservation, the kind that was born with the death of Reverend Daddy and the birth of desperation. Within a year after Reverend Daddy was gone, we knew how to steal clothes from The Broadway, take what we had stolen back in a gift box, get full credit plus tax. Rufus would steal mail, cash checks, use credit cards, the whole nine.

Then came the drugs. The streets taught him how to make a dollar out of fifteen cents.

Here we sat. Brothers. Sons of a preacher man. Sons of a thieving woman.

Two men doing what they had to do to stay alive another day.

We were in underground parking, leaning against Wolf's sedan, watching cars go by, watching people head for the stairway that led to the plaza. Rufus was doing most of the gamming. I stood there, head hurting, hungry, my hands deep in my pants pockets.

Rufus babbled on, "I wanted to go to San Francisco and get married. That was the plan."

"Rufus."

"You saw the luggage. You saw the plane tickets. So I know I'm not tripping."

"Both you fools tripping."

He went on, "We've known each other thirteen years. That's long enough to know what you want. I mean, we had made plans, packed, had plane tickets, hotel reservations—"

"Rufus—"

"We could get our marriage license in hand, even if it doesn't mean anything outside of San Francisco." He opened and closed his swollen hand, groaned. "It's symbolic. I know that what that piece of paper means is unclear, so far as the government is concerned."

I snapped, "Rufus."

He shut up.

Somebody passed by in a convertible, music blasting. Dave Matthews's song filled the garage, the acoustics making it echo like we were in a hollow room. Dave moved on with his blues, told the world that when we dug his grave make it shallow so he could feel the rain.

Rufus rubbed his eyes and mumbled, "Four hundred couples a day can get processed."

"Look, I've got enough shit going on. Just open the U-Haul."

"I told Pasquale that we can't let them put limitations on our relationships. NAACP won't stand up for us. Clinton went bitch and came up with that 'Don't ask don't tell' mess. Bush won't do nothing that doesn't involve killing somebody. We have to stand up for us."

"Open the truck."

He paused at the back of the U-Haul, keys in hand. He put the key up to the padlock, then winced with the pain from his injury. He pulled the keys back, told me, "I did this for you."

"Open. The. Motherfucking. Truck."

He fumbled with the keys. The U-Haul truck was a bona fide twelve-footer.

Rufus turned the latch. Pulled hard. Metal against metal, the door sang as it went up.

I held onto the side of the truck and pulled myself inside. Half of the U-Haul was packed with boxes, all the packages roped down and held in place. Rufus followed me, grunting and moaning. I opened a few containers. Sculptures by Woodrow Nash. Not ordinary sculptures, but Afrocentric art that looked like real African people, every feature in detail; some were busts, others were detailed sculptures about the size of a real person. There were paintings by that dead guy David Lawrence. Large, abstract paintings by Denea Marcel. Rufus had horrific photos of a Sierra Leone amputee soccer team. Photo of an AIDS village in China. That shit was depressing.

I told Rufus, "You took the man's track and field trophies."

"And both of his NAACP Image Awards."

"Who's this on this picture with him? His son?"

"His nephew. His five-year-old nephew."

I stopped looking through the boxes, turned and looked at him, shaking my head.

There had been no lion and jackal invading his den. Just him and Pasquale fighting over whatever people like them fought about. Pasquale left after their rumble in the jungle. Then Rufus turned vindictive, leased a U-Haul, and ganked Pasquale for what he really cared about.

Rufus was staring off in space, talking. "I always end up with jerks who like having me as a trophy. Look at the strange bird I caught . . . this albino mutt with the red eyes and long hair . . . hold on, watch this . . . he can spell 'euthanasia,' bake biscuits, and give a blow—"

"Rufus."

"Sorry." He tugged at his locks. "Got emotional. Forgot who I was talking to."

"How the fight get started between you and that idiot?"

"Last week we went to a poetry reading at the PAFF, it was cool. Then we went to one at Shabazz. Man, I thought I was at a Black Panther Party meeting. It was awful. Just such anger in their poems. Talking about the 'blue-eyed devil.' After each poem, I didn't know whether to run out in the streets and slap a white woman, or pump my fist in the air and yell out 'Power to the people.' I guess I really didn't know they were like that. I think I'm cool on spoken word. But that was more like spoken rage. I expected the FBI to come in and arrest everybody. I'll just stick with poetry readings. There is a definite difference. I'm sure they could tell I was looking uncomfortable. Made me want to smear shoe polish on my pale skin. Anyway, we had an argument about what was real poetry and that too-late-for-the-train pseudo Black Panther racist noise we had been listening to. But we made up and—"

"*Rufus.* Cut to the chase."

"I'm getting there."

"Get there. Look, who hit who first?"

"You know how I ramble when I get upset."

"Who. Hit. Who. First?"

He moved and grunted like he felt raw. "What difference does it make?"

I looked at the stolen goods again. High-end art and boss sculptures. A pirate's treasure.

I whistled. "Rufus, you have about, what, ten thousand dollars worth of shit."

"You don't know art. More like eighty. Wholesale. I can fence it all."

"Damn."

"We can pay that psycho her money. Momma would turn over in her grave if she knew you took that skank's money to put her in the ground. All this drama. You shoulda kept on sleeping with Lisa. All she wanted was some chocolate thunder because the pink stick ain't—"

"Shut the fuck up, Rufus."

"No, you shut the fuck up. Put all that noise in an oven and bake it at three-fifty."

"Don't make me kick your ass."

"Your black ass."

"Lightbulb."

"Sambo."

"Casper."

"Dressing like P. Diddy and got money like Fred Sanford."

I said, "You're broker than Medicare."

"At least I'm trying to help you."

"Don't believe you did this. Next you'll be selling body parts at UCLA."

"Look, I'm worried." Rufus shook his head. "She pulled a gun on you."

"Rufus—"

"And you gave me part of that skank's money. I owe you, dammit. Owe you my life."

That stopped me. So much fear and love for me was in his voice. I opened and closed my hands. Imagined my fingerprints glowing on Lisa's neck. Should've killed her.

"Pasquale called the police," I told him. "Take the man his stuff back and try and—"

"To hell with Pasquale."

"Last time I'm gonna say this. Take the man his property back."

I walked to the end of the truck, eased down so I didn't stress my knee. Rufus jumped out like he was Spider-Man, all energetic and kid-like, landed on both feet and stumbled, almost fell over. He had good knees, but his body was weak. Don't see how he had won a fight.

He yanked the back of the truck down. It banged hard. He locked up his goods.

I asked, "Who hit who first?"

"Don't you sound like Reverend Bastard."

"Watch your mouth."

"Put that in the oven with the rest of it. Bake until crisp around the edges."

Part of me wanted to cannon my fist into his chest. But he sounded like his so-called superpower had him having one of those hypermnesia episodes, reliving all the things Reverend Daddy had done to try and turn him into the kind of man he wanted his youngest son to become.

Rufus's swollen lip quivered, sounded like those memories, all the times Reverend Daddy had forced him to fight, to bed women, to put a gun to a man's head and pull the trigger—he sounded like each one of those moments was etched indelibly in his soul.

My memories took me back to that day we were in that alley, the day we stood over that beaten and battered man. I asked Rufus, "Would you have killed Ulysses?"

"Ulysses? Good Lord. Why the hell you bringing that old news up?"

"It's been on my mind. You pulled the trigger over and over . . . like it was easy to do."

"It was hard. Then it got easy. Real easy. Wanted to blow his brains out."

"What made it get easy?"

He paused, eyes glazed over. "I imagined that Ulysses was Reverend Bastard."

That lowered my head and pushed my heart up to my throat.

He said, "Every time you bring up Reverend Bastard's name it feels like I need to soak in Calamine lotion. So do us both a favor and don't bring him up. That's all I'll ever ask of you."

We took a walk upstairs, him limping, my knee trying to go south. When we got to street level, I took a hard breath and pushed the conversation back to what he was dealing with now.

I told him, "Why don't you run over to King-Drew Medical Center?"

"King-Drew? Please. Give me my dignity. I'd rather die in the streets."

Again I asked, "Who . . . who . . . Pasquale hit you or . . . who threw the first blow?"

He groaned, limped on, asked, "You get my book signed?"

"Rufus. Who?"

He took a breath. Irritated. "Won't matter. Maybe to Judge Judy, but not to LAPD."

He folded and unfolded his arms, put a stray lock back in place, adjusted his bag.

Things had changed since I dropped Freeman off. Somewhere between ten and twelve protestors had shown up, all carrying signs. FREEMAN IS A SELLOUT! FREEMAN IS THE CHARLES BARKLEY OF LITERATURE. Others had signs that admonished the new black aesthetic for not being four miles away on the black side of town at a black bookstore.

We walked by the mini-mob.

Rufus asked me, "Did that woman just tear the head off a doll?"

"That was a bobblehead."

The bookstore was still packed. A few women were leaving, signed books in hand. No sign of Sade. Rufus caught a table inside Starbucks. I ordered us two Venti-sized liquid cracks.

I sat down, my mind changing direction, now on Panther. Then my brother laughed.

I asked, "What's funny?"

"I beat Hollywood's ass. Spends half the night at Gold's Gym and I whooped his ass."

Any other day I would've been on the ground laughing hard enough to break a rib.

Any other day.

Then Rufus looked sad. Not proud of what had happened between him and his friend. Had the same expression a man had after a falling out with his wife. Proud and sad all at once. Proud for standing up, then sad for things getting out of control. That look of love in limbo.

My eyes went to that huge banner praising Freeman. Then to the flock of loyal fans. Then to the protestors who were walking back and forth in front of the store.

I told Rufus, "Yeah. Got you that signed book. It's in the sedan."

"I got halfway through his new book and . . ." He made a face, then sipped his brew.

I sipped mine. "And what?"

"Almost every page was a déjà vu. I must've read it before."

I shrugged.

He said, "I double-checked the bookcase. Pasquale makes me keep all of my books listed by author and in alphabetical order. I didn't have *Dawning of Ignorance*. But I know I read it."

People stared at us. Latecomers and worshippers of CP-time rushed by, Freeman's latest book in one, if not both, of their hands. Most of those stares were directed at Rufus. Albino. Swollen face. Soft shoulders. They hurried on, celebrity worship and shopping on their minds.

Rufus said, "They must think we're a couple."

I shifted, shook my head.

"The metrosexual and the homosexual. We could do a treatment for a sitcom."

I ignored his joke. A discarded *New York Times* was on the table next to us. I grabbed it. Front page had a story about a Humvee that had run over a land mine in Iraq. Thought about Panther's brother for a second. War was far from over. Skimmed that article. Soldier killed and the family felt slighted by the military. Not even a phone call. Soldier had an eleven-month-old infant daughter. Wife hadn't seen her husband in seven months.

I went to the crossword puzzle, took out that Pilot pen I had in my pocket.

"To incite by argument or advice." EXHORT. "Liable to be brought to account."

Rufus put his hand on the paper. "Don't leave me. Don't run away. Not right now."

I put the paper down, left that dimension and the last answer hanging in the air.

Rufus didn't want me to escape.

Me and my brother sipped our high-octane liquid crack like time was on our side.

Me and my brother.

I forgot about my world. Forgot about Freeman and Panther and Arizona and Lisa. Forgot about million-dollar books and destroyed apartments and guns being pulled on me. Just thought about the medicines Rufus kept in his cabinet. I never talked to him about what he was going through, just had looked it up on the Internet. Read about CD4 cells and plasma viral loads. Didn't really comprehend what all they said. Just knew that there were four kinds of medicines used, medicines with words like nucleoside and transcriptase and inhibitors.

On the outside we looked like night and day. Yin and yang. From build to hair we've always looked different. But Rufus was like me. Same DNA. Nothing like Lancaster in that old black-and-white movie. We were brothers. Refusing to chill out and wait for death to come.

Reverend Daddy had said, "Hate unites people. It's almost like we need somebody to hate in order to pull together. When we stop hating, we all seem lost, like we have no direction."

In between the women he put his healing hands on, Reverend Daddy was preaching about how hate of the white man and oppression united black people. How the ignorance and fear that spawned hate had bonded so many others. How without a clear and common enemy people seemed to fall apart. I'd seen how hating terrorists had united the country, how their hate of things this country had done had united them against us.

I didn't hate homosexuals, didn't give a shit about what went on between men in jail, in West Hollywood, or on the steps of city hall in San Francisco, just hated that my brother was part of that special interest group. Hated he was queer. Hated that I'd never have any nieces or nephews to ride on my shoulders or play piggyback with. Hated hearing people call him a faggot when we were growing up. Hated hearing about that fucking disease. I hated knowing that my little brother's medicine cabinet was filled with experimental shit, and I hated he could die a horrible death. Hated my cushy job. Hated working for the man whose wife I'd been fucking. Hated Lisa. Hated I was at the bottom of the pool looking up and couldn't see the surface. The suit, the cuff links, the glasses I wore so I could fit in with the rest of the world, had just as much disdain for that shit as I did most everything else. To be honest, in this moment, I hated so much.

And I hated that I hated it all.

I reached up, touched my head wound, did that because that hate from Lisa throbbed again, level three this time. I asked Rufus, "You been taking all your meds, right?"

"Where did that come from?"

"Answer me. You up on the meds or what?"

"Seems like that's all I do. Lord knows I take more cocktails and pills than I eat food."

Again I rubbed my burning and weary eyes. "You got insurance, right?"

"I told you. When I go, put me in a Viking, bake me until crisp, e-mail all my friends."

"You're sick, Rufus. In the head, you're sick."

"Have to have a sense of humor or I'll be boo-hooing twenty-four-seven."

We sipped.

I told Rufus, "Your boy called me talking crazy. Said he called the police."

"That's punk. Then I'll file charges on him too. I'll call KTLA and KCOP and have a reporter meet me at the emergency room. See how Mister Hollywood likes that. Should get him some good press. Let's see if Pasquale could handle being on *Extra*. Or seeing me on *Extra* outing his ass. Got Star Jones' boo some nice press. Pasquale ain't telling the police nothing."

"Rufus. TMI."

"He's always fronting like he's high-class. He grew up in boring, cold, below-zero temperature, no-entertainment-having, politically incorrect, hick-town Flint, Michigan. He used to tell me the best time his family had was when they left town. Now he's Mister Hollywood. Puh-lease. If you get close enough you can still smell the government cheese on his breath."

"I'll take your word."

Sade came down the escalator. She didn't see me in the tinted window. She had two bags in her hands, had done some damage in the shoe department at Nordstrom Rack.

Rufus asked, "Who is that?"

"Freeman's woman."

"Her shoes are fierce."

"Bet."

"Manumit." Rufus read her sweatshirt, sipped. "I've seen that before."

He asked me her name. I told him the name from her luggage. Folasade Titilayo Coker.

He said, "Name sounds familiar too."

"Nigerian. Folasade is kinda original, I guess."

"I meant her middle name."

"Thought you didn't forget nothing."

"When I'm upset, that's like kryptonite to my superpower."

"So it only works when you're calm."

"For the most part."

I chuckled, tore the crossword out of the newspaper, stuffed it in my pocket. Rufus stood up first, stretched, made a pained face. I looked at him. He gave me a look that told me not to worry about him, not now. We grabbed our java and headed back to the parking structure.

My cellular rang. It was Panther. Her voice was rattled. She was speeding back this way. She told me that she had followed the lion and jackal from Shutters. Told me they had come back out this way, landed around the corner at the Coffee Company, ate and read the newspaper like regular people, then the lion dropped the jackal off at Slauson and Vermont.

She asked me, "You know what's down that way?"

That was my shopworn part of town, where I grew up. Palm trees rose high over people who depended on public transportation. More than a few survived on public assistance. Wasn't far from where Boys Market used to be. Every business on that corner was etched in my mind.

I said, "Banks. Check-cashing places. Lots of small shops."

Sade paused and looked up at Freeman's banner before she peeped at the crowd. She saw the protestors, turned around and got back on the escalator, headed back upstairs.

Panther told me, "The bony one hurried and went inside El Pollo Loco."

She was talking about the jackal.

I asked, "The other motherfucker?"

She told me she shadowed the Expedition. Let a few cars stay in between them, like they did in the movies. First those high-end spinners turned around, took Slauson back toward the 110. Then the Expedition sped up, made sudden turns. Lefts and rights that went nowhere. She trailed the ride down side streets, rolled deeper into South Central. The SUV slowed down. Stopped in the middle of a ragged avenue. Panther pulled over. Waited. Minutes went by.

The lion got out of his SUV. Stood in the middle of the streets, mad-dogging Panther.

He pointed at her, two fingers extended like a gun.

He knew.

He'd picked up her scent.

She turned around and headed in the opposite direction, tires spinning fast.

I'd made it back downstairs by then, Rufus at my side. I leaned against the sedan, rubbed my eyes for the nth time, said, "Fuckin' GPS shit. Damn."

"I don't know about that, Driver. Look, I was thinking, unless you told her, no way for her to know my car, not before last night. I mean, it's not like I see you all the time, you know."

Something wasn't right. If they had been watching the tracker, they would've known we went hunting for them last night, would've been on guard at sunrise. It bothered me that Lisa didn't mention it this morning. She knew when I was at Back Biters. Knew when I was pulling up in front of my apartment. Knew I had gone to Rufus's crib on the hill. Knew I was with Panther until sunrise. Even knew I'd been at a hotel on Fuck Row last night. She had brought up my every move, had done that for a while, like she had a bird's-eye view of the chessboard representing my life. But I don't think she had any idea I'd gone after her bullyboys.

I asked Panther, "Then what you do?"

"At first I was making lefts and rights, getting on and off the 110, making sure he didn't try to turn it around and follow me. I doubt he would because it was broad daylight."

"Kennedy was shot in broad daylight."

"So was Reagan. What's your point?"

I asked, "Sure he didn't trail you?"

"I'm sure."

"If the bullyboy had a tracker he wouldn't need to follow you."

"True. But he would've known I was following him hella sooner."

"You're pretty good at following. Where you learn that?"

"Dating skills. All women learn to do that at some point."

She told me what she saw when she went back to El Pollo Loco. The jackal was still there. So busy broiling chickens that he didn't look up and see Panther walk through the joint.

A horn blew and I jumped. I turned around and saw Panther. She had been talking to me while she rode my way. Guess she thought sneaking up on me was cute.

What she had done was stupid. But she was young. Had to remind myself that.

We both hung up. I walked to her ride. Her top was down. She got out and hugged me. Her body was trembling, still shook up from whatever look the lion had given her.

She reminded me, "You owe me two from this morning."

"Your girl B&E Freeman's room?"

"That your brother?"

"Yeah. Rufus. Come here."

I introduced him. He waved and fell into the background.

Panther asked, "What happened to him?"

"Long story. What happened at the hotel?"

"Don't blow me off, Driver. What happened to your brother?"

"Domestic bullshit."

"Nothing to do with Married Woman?"

"His and his . . . I mean him and his friend got into it."

"Looks bad. I've seen worse, but it looks like he needs some medical attention."

"Yeah. But he don't want go to King-Drew."

" 'Cause he wants to live. Guess he's a stalwart soul, just like you, huh?"

"Stalwart?"

"I know a few ten-dollar words. Atlanta's school system ain't that bad."

That was when Panther told me that her girl, China Doll, had grabbed Freeman's briefcase. Between trying to hunt down the lion and the jackal, dealing with them and trying to gank Freeman for his intellectual property, we'd been doing our own multitasking.

She popped her trunk. When it opened Freeman's briefcase was staring at me.

My heart did flips. I was excited and scared all at once. I was staring at my own manumit. Maybe more than a little manumit. I rubbed my fingers over it and almost smiled.

I asked, "You open it?"

"It's locked up like Fort Knox."

"Can you pick it?"

"Gonna have to do more than pick it. You'll need at least a crow bar."

I chuckled. "Damn. A million-dollar prize."

Rufus asked in that wounded voice, "What's a million-dollar prize?"

I shushed him with a stern hand movement.

I wanted to transfer the briefcase to the sedan, but Sade was upstairs stress-shopping, had a load of new clothes and shoes. Might have to open the trunk while they were looking.

Panther asked, "What next?"

When she asked me that, everything got heavy. I'd done crimes, stolen, fought, but I'd never been a true grifter. Had never been that clever. Right now I was a ship without a sail. One false move and it could all fall apart, we'd all be living in a cage getting three squares a day.

I said, "Have to figure it out."

"How're you feeling?"

"Overwhelmed."

She hugged me, held on.

She whispered, "Wish I could take the stress away. Maybe later, if all goes well, we can get a nice room in Hermosa Beach, light some candles. Would love to cook you dinner—spaghetti, salad, and French bread. Take a really nice bath together. Rub you down. Give you the best damn blow job. Have your toes curling for days. Just a thought that crossed my mind."

I hugged her back, held on. She pulled me to her heart, a leaf clinging to a tree.

She said, "We don't have a lot of time. We have the upper hand. Need to keep the ball rolling. I think we should call from a pay phone and leave a message at his hotel room."

I paused. Arizona. She'd know. Had to work this out. Needed to bypass trouble. Nothing clear came to mind. Just the fact that I had slipped in and one-upped Arizona after she'd sucked my tongue and dropped three large in my hands, good faith money for the faithless.

Arizona was using the power of the pretty woman combined with the promise of the pussy to get me to feed her what I knew so she could rip off Freeman. Didn't trust her. She could get the goods, vanish like smoke in the wind. Had to make sure I didn't get fucked over.

No honor among thieves. Never has been, never will be.

I told Panther, "Soon as I dump Freeman and his woman I'll hit you on the cellular."

Another thought came to me. Arizona said that she had access to other things, could get banking information and find out how much cabbage Freeman had in his pot.

I needed that to make this scheme work. Couldn't go in there like Ray Charles.

"One more minor thing," Panther said. "We need to get our apartments tightened up."

"Damn. Need to get what's left of my car from off the streets too."

She said, "And we have to kick down China Doll four large for the B&E."

"She didn't know what was in the case?"

"Had no idea and couldn't care less. She's all about getting her cut."

"Keep it that way."

She said, "Told you."

"Told me what?"

"To tell me what kind of woman you wanted me to be and I could be that woman."

She kissed me and got back in her convertible. Drove away.

I wondered what kind of woman she'd been for Married Man.

What all she had done for him. About the pills she had in her medicine cabinet. Wondered who she really was.

Rufus came over and nudged me. "Panther. Cute name. One of your girlfriends?"

"I think so. Yeah."

"Sounds like you have some scandalous mess going on."

My brother was eavesdropping his ass off, judging my life, face swollen like a blowfish.

I ignored that query, asked Rufus, "How bad you hurting?"

He stood up straight. A stab of pain hit him. He was hurting pretty bad. I took a step toward him and it felt like pain jumped off him and stuck to my knee. I hit the remote to the sedan. The trunk clicked open. I pulled out the gym bag Panther had given me. What I handed him rattled him. He looked inside and what he saw brought back the memories. He'd grown up in a world where fists and guns were a way of life. He'd been forced to point a gun at a man.

I told Rufus to keep the hardware at his side until all of this blew over.

I told him, my voice strong and gruff, "Anybody steps up to you, pretend whatever you have to pretend, even if you have to imagine it's Reverend Daddy, just don't hesitate."

"Okay, Lone Ranger." His voice trembled. "Tonto thinks it's time to call in the cavalry."

"Not over a woman."

"Newsflash. A bitch with a gun ain't no woman. You better ax somebody."

"Ask."

"Ass-kick. Ass-k. Ask."

My cellular rang again.

This time it was Arizona.

She said, "Congratulations."

27

The sun was going down. Daylight hadn't been my friend. But ever since Lisa had started acting like Baby Bin Laden, every sunset had brought me a new kinda trouble. Tonight wouldn't be any different. I was back at Shutters Hotel, on the edge of the roundabout. Freeman and Sade had been let out and they were heading inside.

All the way back from the book signing Sade was quiet. Wordless. Freeman was on his cellular. He kept going like the Energizer Bunny. Made me want to kick the batteries out.

The Hispanic bellman walked behind Freeman and Sade, carrying Sade's Nordstrom bags. Sade walked that well-bred charm-school walk, one foot directly in front of the other, turned on the balls of her feet. Freeman was hyped. A unibrowed midget who was ten feet tall.

Something else was tugging at the back of my mind. I called Sid Levine back at the office, asked him about the blips again.

Sid said, "Funny you asked about that glitch. You got me curious last time I talked to you. I mean that glitch moved all over the city. On the freeway, headed toward Hollywood—"

"Hancock Park area?" I asked.

"Hold on. Call coming in."

A woman hurried over to Freeman, stopped in front of him, got his attention. Another fan. Sade moved on by him, pulled out her passkey and got on the elevator. By the time her elevator had vanished two more women had joined the first one. They were smiling and gamming Freeman's head off, pulling out pieces of paper for him to sign. Tourists. Locals don't do that. Out here if you're not Denzel or Julia Roberts you ain't all that. Freeman was probably the closest thing they'd seen to a real celebrity since they got to Cali.

I left the car with valet, headed inside, was almost at the bar before Wolf's resident computer guru, Sid Levine, came back on the line.

Sid said, "Sorry about that. Prince is coming to town. Everybody's trying to get a limo."

"Hancock Park."

"What?"

"The glitch."

"Oh, yeah. It headed toward Hollywood and—"

"Did it head toward Hancock Park last night?"

"Hold on. Phone again."

I grabbed a seat at the bar, sent a smile toward Daniela the Bartender. She came over, put down a napkin, and I ordered a ginger ale. A few seconds later my drink was in front of me; so was that crossword puzzle I had put in my pocket.

"Hasty." First letter F. Fifth letter I. Eighth letter T. Nine letters total. Had no idea.

I was holding on, bouncing my foot, letting the mental challenge calm me down.

By the time I got settled Sade had come back down, was getting off the elevator. Freeman was still jabbering. Sade moved by him like she didn't know him and made a beeline for the bar. He saw her and didn't acknowledge her. She saw me and smiled. She did just like she had done yesterday, put her pretty little purse in a seat next to me, then squatted a seat down.

I looked back toward Freeman.

I lowered my cellular, told Sade, "Freeman's hot."

"He's about to go upstairs and get the bobbleheads."

"Cool. He gives them away."

"Oh, please. He gives them away for a twenty-dollar donation."

Palms damp, I stared back at Freeman. Anxiety was kicking my ass from all angles.

At the elevator Freeman took out his wallet and brandished his passkey.

That pissed me the fuck off.

A minute went by before Sid came back on the line. By then Sade had her legs crossed, was three sips deep into her chocolate martini, sipping her salvation and going full throttle in a conversation with Daniela the Bartender, all words being spoken in Italian.

I made like I was deep in my crossword, challenging my brain.

"Hasty." Nine letters total. FESTINATE was the answer. That had been bugging me.

It took a minute of jabbering to get Sid Levine back on track, back to the glitch.

He told me, "Come to think of it, the glitch did move in that direction, stopped, went south for a little while, then I think it stopped moving somewhere in South Central."

Manhattan Beach toward Hancock Park then to South Central. That was the route that Panther had driven me last night. When she wanted to speed her need for revenge to Lisa's front door. Hancock Park was on this side of Hollywood, so it would've looked like the dot was moving toward the land of waiters, waitresses, and broken dreams. Sid told me the dot went to South Central. That was when we had regrouped and found that cheap hotel on Fuck Row.

I asked, "You tell Wolf?"

"He didn't care. As long as all of his property was accounted for, the glitch didn't bother him too much. He's been . . . dunno . . . he ain't been all there lately. Distracted. Out of it."

I yawned, then shook off my exhaustion. "The glitch roll back toward L.A. after that?"

"The glitch? Nope. Stayed in South Central until this morning."

"Until this morning?"

"Yeah."

"It didn't move toward Leimert Park, the Crenshaw District . . . ?"

"Not on my shift. I got up a few times, but I didn't see it move. I was here messing around until almost two in the morning. Came back in around nine. Maybe eight-something."

We'd gone out hunting for a lion and a jackal after that stop in South Central. Maybe the tracker wasn't on Panther's car. If it was on my car it would still be down in Manhattan Beach. Head hurt. Needed sleep. Couldn't think. But I tried. The only thing that made sense was that it had to be a signal on the ride of whoever she had trailing me, and they had to be damn good.

Then everything shifted. There was some drama going on at the front desk. Winds were stirring, the start of a hurricane. A manager was on the phone, freaking out, like somebody was cursing at her and she was trying to calm them down. She hung up and made another call.

I stayed on point and asked Sid, "Where was the glitch when you came in this morning?"

"Came out here."

"What you mean?"

Sade's cellular phone rang. She looked at the number, made a face, and put the phone back down. Her expression told me it was Freeman and she wasn't in the mood. She sipped her martini. Sipped it like it was water after days in the desert, did that with integrity and control.

Sid told me, "When I came in the glitch was moving toward LAX."

"Uh huh. Went to the airport?"

"That's what I thought. But when I went and got coffee and came back, it was in our parking lot, with the rest of the fleet, at least it looked that way."

"You go and look to see who it was?"

"Was too busy. Got caught up watching Alicia Keys, Sessions at AOL and—"

"Is the glitch still there?"

"Alicia Keys. She is so damn—"

"The glitch."

"—beautiful and talented. Her, Missy, Tamia, and Beyoncé in concert? Awww, man."

"Sid. The glitch."

"Oh. The glitch moved a few times."

"Where is it now?"

"Hold on. Have to pull that screen back up. Damn pop-ups. I'll have to go out and surf Google for a better pop-up blocker."

Sade's cellular rang again. She looked at it again. Made a stop-bothering-me face.

Hotel staff was rushing for the elevator with a member of hotel security.

Sid came back, told me, "Santa Monica."

I said, "I'm in Santa Monica."

"Yeah. You had the Freeman thing. Oh, yeah. I see the signal from the car you're in. Dag. If I'm looking at this right, you should be able to see whoever it is from where you are."

"How far is it from where I am?"

"Wait, let me change the screen and look at latitude and longitude. Push this button . . . get yours . . . and . . . get that one . . ." He paused, then got all excited. "Dag. Check this shit out."

"What?"

"It's on top of you. This is wild. Same friggin' longitude and latitude."

My insides jumped. I looked around. Lots of cars were outside. Whoever it was could be right outside the front door, on the other side of the roundabout. Lots of people were in the dining area grubbing and at the bar getting their drink on. Even more people were out on the beach. Right now everybody looked like a suspect. Even old white women carrying poodles.

I looked down at my shoes. My tie. My cuff links.

I looked up at the sky.

Impossible.

I asked, "How accurate are those things?"

"My guess would be no more than fifty yards off. Seventy-five max."

I walked out and looked, tense and ready. Too many cars to count. Could be anybody.

Then I thought about last night, about us going to hunt the lion and jackal.

Lisa didn't know.

It didn't show up on the GPS screen.

What didn't make sense made sense. Realization hit me hard and strong.

Lisa was vindictive, that went without question. Cunning. The kind of woman who ran a background check on every man she met, did that before she bedded him. The same way politicians bugged their adversaries' offices, she bugged her lovers. When I thought about it I realized that Big Sister had been tracking my every move damn near since our first kiss.

My bones felt white hot, vision dark, eyes red, could hardly get a breath.

Sade's cellular rang again. This time she answered with a whip, "What, Marcus? Why are you calling me a thousand times a minute?"

She listened. Her eyebrows furrowed.

"Broken into?"

Her mouth dropped open.

Then she was on her feet, rushing toward the elevator.

I told Sid Levine I'd holla at him later, maybe when I got back to the office.

He said, "Driver."

"What up?"

"I figured it out. The glitch."

"Did you?"

"Yeah. I know what's going on."

"What's going on, Sid?"

Sid Levine paused for dramatic effect.

"What's going on, Sid?"

"Wolf is following his wife around. Like they do in the movies. I think she's cheating on him and he's tracking her. Smart, huh?"

"Yeah. Smart."

I hung up, knowing.

* * *

I expected squad cars to pull up in front of the hotel, guns drawn for the killing. Expected the media to flock in, expected helicopters to start circling overhead like vultures.

Nothing happened. The hotel staff looked hyped, something was going on in the background, on Freeman's floor, but they kept up a good show at the front desk.

I went to the house phone. Asked for Folasade Coker's room. Already had made up a reason to call. Could tell her she had left her drink, ask if she was coming back. Maybe even tell her that we could get together for that drink as soon as I turned the sedan in. No answer. Asked for Thomas Marcus Freeman. The line was busy. Folasade Coker again. No answer.

The passkey I'd lifted from Sade was sleeping in my pocket. All I had to do was brandish that key, take the elevator up to the fifth floor, and look down the hallway to see what was going down. But a foolish move like that was why a lot of men ended up living in a cage.

Fear crawled up my back, moved around my neck, whispered in my ear.

I rushed for the front door, then changed my mind. Walked back to the bar. Ordered a shot of JD. We'd been apart too long. Gazed at that golden amber liquid. A man's salvation and liquid courage. Made love to my friend in a way I had never done before. It was a quickie, not long and tender and methodical and pleasing. I downed that shot and headed for the sedan.

Fear didn't leave, but the bitch stopped whispering.

By the time I made it back to the plantation Sid Levine was gone. I passed by Margaret Richburg in the garage. She was leaving, had a pickup at LAX that was going to Palmdale.

Lisa wasn't in the office. That was good.

But Wolf was waiting for me. Not good. He called me into his office. Shut the door.

I'd choked his wife halfway to hell. I was using his business to commit a crime.

I looked behind me. Still no police. Heard no sirens.

But they didn't always turn on their sirens, sometimes they just stormed a room.

Wolf stood on one side of his desk. I stood on the other. He didn't ask me to sit down.

Today he was Donald Trump with a long ponytail, Nordic features, a James Dean stance.

Tension clouded the room and thickened the air. He moved a little. I did the same. No words between us. Just stares. Felt like we were in a remake. *Gunfight at the O.K. Corral.*

This day, this moment was inevitable. All that was done in the dark came to light.

Wolf told me, "I want to apologize for the other day."

"Man, don't even—"

"Hear me out, Driver."

"Sounds like you're pulling rank."

"If I have to. If I need to. This isn't easy for me, so bear with me."

I told him, "You were right. About my marriage."

"What I said wasn't necessary."

"It's cool. The first marriage is always like the first pancake. Always fucked up."

Wolf nodded. No time for jokes to cover his uneasiness. He'd been wrestling with this all day, I could tell. Sitting here waiting for me to get off so this confrontation could happen.

"Driver, hear me out. I've lost a lot of sleep over this. I can't do this anymore."

I settled where I stood, discomfort surrounding me with an Arctic chill. That hit of JD had only settled my nerves, wasn't enough to send me toward Don't Give a Shit, USA.

This man had been my friend for half a year. Had never done wrong by me.

Wolf was shifting, clenching his jaw, finding it impossible to look at me. I was doing the same. We wanted this done so we could get the fuck away from each other.

Wolf said, "It's not your fault what's going on in my marriage."

"Maybe it is, Wolf."

His lips created a smile. "Whatever is going on was going on before you were around."

I nodded.

"I love that woman, Driver. Love her beyond reason."

"I know. She knows it too."

We both took deep breaths.

He said, "Like I said, I wanted to apologize."

"I want to apologize myself."

He nodded.

I asked, "Want to meet at Back Biters tomorrow? We can talk it out. Man to man."

He shook his head. "I'm taking the Cessna to Vegas tonight. My daughter has a part in a play at school. Plays the part of a tree in a forest. I have to be there. Have to keep my promise."

"Thought you and the wife were taking off for a few days."

"Can't break a promise to a kid. They're the ones who love you no matter what."

"The wife's not going with you?"

"No. It's easier dealing with them separately. Easier and hard. It's like I have two separate lives. Running this business is easier than managing a wife and ex-wife. Not to mention my parental obligations, which I have no problem with. My children are my heart."

"I understand."

We stood there, eyes on each other, motionless. Still dancing around the truth.

I told him, "Thanks for the chance. But I want to give you my two weeks notice."

"I accept it."

Nothing was said for a moment.

"You knew about me and Lisa."

"I knew."

"How? You have her followed . . . what?"

"The way you two regard each other. I could tell. The office knows."

"How long have you known?"

"A long while. Before the night you came here."

I nodded.

I asked, "Why did you want me to work here?"

He paused, then said, "Friends close."

The phrase was friends close, *enemies closer*.

I understood the method to this madness. I'd never been his friend. Friendship had a foundation made of honesty. Ours was built on laughter and lies. If he had me under his thumb he could monitor my comings and goings. Giving me work benefited me, but it also gave him comfort in knowing where I was most days, knew I couldn't be with his wife during those hours.

He asked, "How long did it go on?"

"Few months. Not while I was working here. Ended the night I came here."

He struggled. "Were you in my home?"

I nodded. "Yeah."

My simple word struck him like a meteor slamming into the dark side of the moon. I'd tried, but I'd never hit a man that hard with my fist. Words had more power than the hands.

His home. His car. His wife. I'd been in them all.

He shook his head. In angst on the surface, most of the damage on the inside.

I told him, "She paid me to kill you."

With all the words I know, I couldn't describe the look on his face. Maybe it was the pained expression a man had when denial was being scrubbed away with a Brillo pad of truth.

He asked me how much, a man wanting to know what dollar amount had been put on his life. I told him she had given me fifteen large, half of a thirty-large payday.

He repeated, "Thirty thousand."

I nodded. "Gave me fifteen up front."

A moment went by. He understood how deep this was.

Those meteors never stopped slamming down on him.

He asked, "Why didn't you?"

I'd stolen. I'd beaten down more men that I could remember. I'd violated more than half of the laws some people believed Moses brought back down that hill and gave to the people.

I was born a sinner and had fallen from grace more times than I could remember.

My eyes went to the pictures of his children, to the images of his parents.

I answered, "I'm not a murderer."

We all had our lines in the sand, even if they didn't run deep.

I waited for him to go off, demand some explanation of the madness that had been going on around him. He was a rational man. Too rational for his own good. Looked like a million thoughts heated up his mind. Sweat popped up on his nose, could almost smell its acid.

He said, "You're not a murderer."

"No."

"But you . . . you took the money, came to kill me."

"Yeah, I did."

We stood there, his expression never changing for the better, the pain never lessening.

He said, "Before you walked in, I knew . . . knew death was coming."

"And you waited. You sat here and waited."

"I waited. Then you came inside. Like you were struggling with yourself."

"My mother had just died. Told you that."

He asked, "If your mother hadn't died that evening?"

I felt heaviness in my chest, like my soul had been encased in a cement tomb and dropped in the ocean.

He asked, "Did you love Lisa?"

"Thought I did." Felt like my mouth was filled with cotton. "Thought I could."

"What was it?"

"Need."

In my mind she had promised me heaven, clouds filled with naked angels. But if the soft stir of a butterfly's wings could cause a violent storm a world away, Lisa could kill us all.

I stood there scared for him, ashamed for myself. I should've felt a sense of relief, but there was none. Wolf was a good man. Like another brother. I'd been the Cain in his life.

Back to silence.

He said, "On that two weeks' notice, I accept it."

We shook hands, tight and strong. Warriors at the end of a battle. Two flawed, morally impure men who just wanted life to work out in a good way.

He said, "We're all murderers, Driver. We all kill what we love."

The memory of my ex-wife came to me hard and strong, then I pushed it away.

But he wasn't talking about how I had killed what I had loved.

He said that like he was confessing that his lie about being able to have children and his one-time infidelity had killed the love between Lisa and him, but whatever she had done hadn't put a damper on what he felt for her. He blamed himself. His lies had given her a pass card.

I reached in my suit pocket, took out the Pilot pen I had borrowed from his desk. I handed it back to him. He took the pen, nodded, rolled it over and over in his hand.

I said, "Your snitch won't have to worry about me lifting your pens."

"There is no snitch."

"Who told you I had your pen?"

"My children. My relatives. My family. They watch over me. They see everything."

He motioned at the wall, somewhere over the pictures of his ancestors.

My eyes went to that same wall. I said, "Camera?"

He nodded.

I asked, "Lisa knows about that hidden camera?"

"Was her idea. One of her connections gave us a good price."

We stared at each other, two men who had been bitten by the same snake.

With that knowledge, I left his office.

28

Panther was waiting for me over at Carl's Jr. She drove me back down to Manhattan Beach. All the way she talked about getting back at Lisa for what she'd done to her apartment and clothes. All the way I told Panther to be patient, to wait a little while longer.

I told her about the commotion at Shutters.

Panther said, "China Doll had an attack of the sticky fingers in Freeman's room."

"What all she take?"

"All she could. I told her to just get the briefcase. Her rougish butt."

"Don't think that matters too much right now. What's done is done."

"Regrets?"

"I'm accumulating regrets every time I breathe."

My car was right where I left it. Had a parking ticket to go along with the dirt and bricked-out window. Panther popped her trunk. I took Freeman's briefcase from her ride and put it inside my trunk. Stared at it for a moment. Tried the lock. Decided not to break it open.

I told her, "Don't go back to your place."

"Why not?"

"Won't be safe. Get a room. Call me."

She asked, "Where you rolling?"

"Have to see a man about a horse."

"I'm going."

"No."

"Yes."

"You gonna have to trust me."

"That's a million-dollar prize, Driver."

I nodded.

She said, "I should go with you."

I shook my head. "They might follow me."

She asked, "You know how they're doing it?"

I told her.

She bit her lip.

I pulled her to me. Kissed her. Looked in her brown eyes and saw that she didn't trust me, not on the level I needed her to. Money put that kinda barrier between people. I couldn't ask her to trust me. I didn't know what I was going to do. Didn't know what I would have to do.

We kissed and kissed and kissed.

She said, "When this is done, maybe we can go to the museums, jazz cafés, hook up and do all the touristy sightseeing stuff. Haven't really done any of that since I've been out here."

"Sure."

"Picnics?"

"Cool."

"Promise?"

"Promise."

"Cross your heart and hope to die, stick a needle in your eye?"

"Yeah. All that."

She smiled at all of my lies. She was a smart woman, read my face, knew it was all a front. We were talking about tomorrow because we didn't think there would be one, not for me.

Lisa had destroyed all Panther's clothing, left her that one black dress. A dress to wear when she watched them give me back to Mother Earth. A dress for my pending funeralization.

I touched her face, said, "One of us is gonna have to come up on some furniture."

"All we need is a bed and a nice sturdy chair."

"Cool."

"And someplace for me to cook."

We kissed again. If I could've packed up and moved inside that kiss, I would've.

I got inside my car, took a long look at her. And I stared long and hard. It was like when a man was on the bus heading to prison. He stared at things long and hard, tried to absorb and memorize them, etch them in his mind. I was absorbing, remembering, etching.

I rolled down the window and asked Panther, "You working tonight?"

She shrugged, wiped her eyes with the back of her hands. Her face had reddened, heated up by her insides. Her fearful tears were about to come on, but she was holding them back.

She asked, "What you need me to do?"

I told her, "Don't go to work. I don't want you anyplace they can find you. Do like I told you and get a room. Go to San Bernardino if you have to. I'll call you in a little while."

"Take me with you."

"No."

"Driver—"

"No."

She nodded.

I asked, "You know any good clubs near Hollywood?"

"A few. Club 360 is tight. That hot spot is on Highland and Willoughby. Why?"

"Get that room. I'll call you if I can."

"What do you mean if you can?"

We looked at each other. Her sadness was about to erupt. What saved us was her cellular phone. It rang. It was her mother calling. She answered, still staring at me.

I drove away, took to the madness in L.A. traffic once again, Club 360 on my mind.

A newspaper clipping was on my seat. Read it while I drove. Police had reported to the scene of a car on fire in Lake Terrace. When they put it out they found a body in the trunk.

I tossed that threat to the wind.

My cellular rang. It was Lisa. My number one *jeva*.

I answered talking, told her, "Wolf knows everything."

She didn't say anything.

I said, "Lisa, and I know that his family keeps their eyes on him. I know. Smart move."

Nothing on her end.

I said, "You there?"

"Look in the mirror. Look in the eyes of a dead man."

My *jeva* hung up.

His family keeps their eyes on him. She knew what that meant.

I loosened my tie, let my window down, put my hand in the wind, let my fingers dance while I drove from Manhattan Beach to the edges of Hollywood, made a stop on Willoughby, drove in circles, checking to see if they had picked up my scent, then moved on.

La Brea and Melrose.

Bright lights were shining. Mrs. Robinson was on stage, in diva mode, once again in her fur coat, high heels, and thong. Once again that ass, tummy tuck, and upgraded breasts were seducing her young costar. She sang, she moved those hips, she seduced, had the room three degrees hotter than hell.

Arizona came to the doorway, motioned at me. She had on leather pants, high heels, makeup done, hair down, long and wavy. Her finesse peppered the air.

She said, "You double-crossed me."

"You don't sound surprised."

She gave me a one-sided smile. "Where is the Maltese Falcon?"

"Talk first."

She pushed her lips up, looked like she was trying to figure out what to do with my tense mood, how to play me away from my anger. She knew I needed her to make this happen.

Right now I had more desperation than anger. That was her saving grace.

Arizona said, "If I told you there was a truck down the street and it had a million dollars inside, and we were going to rip it off at noon tomorrow, tell me, would you wait until noon, or try and get the jump on me, be there at sunrise and claim that million-dollar prize for yourself?"

"Smart woman."

Her expression was slick, cunning. "Let's walk."

"Sure. Let's put one foot in front of the other and take a stroll."

She handed me her leather jacket. I held it while she slipped it on. Valet ran up as soon as we stepped out the door. The worker was anxious to please. She spoke to him in Spanish. I don't know what she said, but he looked at me, then looked away. She lit up a cigarette. Cloves scented the air, mixed with the exhaust from bumper-to-bumper traffic. The light was taking too long. She took out her MIRT and made the light change in our favor. She walked like she kept a bottle of time in her pocket. By the time we crossed La Brea she'd tossed her smoke to the concrete. Over at Pink's we stood in the long line, mixed with everybody from regular Joes to dignitaries and grabbed two turkey burgers, fries, and sodas. Arizona found a table and we sat down. I sat down with my back to the wall, had to be able to see who walked in.

They were out there. I felt it.

"Nice night," Arizona said.

"Get to the business."

"You're pissed off."

"I don't like being played."

"No one does, Driver. No one does."

We took bites of our burgers. Tasted like heaven. Seemed like I hadn't eaten in days.

She asked me, "What gave me away?"

"Freeman still had his passkey. When we got back to the hotel Freeman still had his passkey. Pickpocket never lifted his wallet. I don't think she intended to get it. It was a show."

"If you had dropped them off and left, you never would've known."

"But I didn't drop them off and leave. I hung around."

Again she smiled, this one like she was happy to know where her scheme fell apart. She said, "I'm still learning. Seems like something always falls through the cracks. That's the thing about this business, in every operation something always goes wrong."

"So, it was all a show."

She looked down at my ankle. "Pull your pant leg down."

I looked down and saw why it had bunched up, pulled it down, looked around.

Arizona smiled at me. "It's cool. Everybody is too busy eating to notice your little wardrobe malfunction. Straighten your collar too."

I nodded and looked around, then back at her.

She went back to our conversation, asked, "What was a show?"

"LAX. Come clean. How many wallets did your girl lift at the airport?"

She sipped her soda, chewed a fry. "When you picked up Freeman? One. Just yours."

"The stash of wallets you showed me at the pickpocket's apartment?"

"Wallets she had lifted here and there, but not that day. Not at LAX."

"A million limo drivers in L.A. Why me?"

"In this business you have to pick your mark. Have to pick your team. Have to read everybody. Find out what people need or want, play their emotions. I learned from the best."

"Is that right?"

"Pussy and money, Driver."

"What about 'em?"

"The man who taught me all I know, he told me that the promise of either draws men in."

"Pussy and money."

"With you it was about the money. After I had picked the limo service, I pulled bank statements for a few people. You had the profile. Newest employee. No real job for a long time before that one. Bank account was low. Pay not that good, just enough to cover your bills."

"That's everybody in L.A."

"You were one paycheck away from being homeless."

"Give me a break. Motherfuckers in Malibu are one paycheck from being homeless."

"True. But you had a prison record that didn't exactly leave you upwardly mobile."

I told her, "A man's heart and soul, what he's about ain't in a damn computer. You couldn't pull up my ethics on a credit report or a bank statement. Or on a prison record."

"Or how good you were going to look. Saw you at Back Biters and . . . and . . . damn."

"Don't start with that you-love-men-in-nice-suits-and-chocolate bullshit."

She laughed.

I said, "So you walked in Back Biters and dangled a carrot."

"Your profile. Low bank account. Felony. Easier to get a criminal to do a crime."

"Bullshit. Most niggas would rather die than go back to jail. It ain't Club Med. It's a cage. And when you get out that cage comes with you, stays in your mind twenty-four-seven."

"When you get angry you slip, your speech changes, gets gruff, sounds so street."

"Then don't piss me the fuck off. Hate to show you how street I can get."

Her expression was smooth and easy, never intimidated by my size or irritation.

Without sounding apologetic she said, "I digress."

"That getting a criminal to do a crime, straight bullshit."

"Most times, not all the time. But you have to remember that I'm the craftswoman at this table. You're the working stiff pulling a nine-to-five. A legit man might be too hard to sway, and if he sways he's too unpredictable. They might have a moral attack or something."

"The felony. My record. That was what drew you to me."

"Of course. That and your bank account needed some revitalization."

I took a breath.

She said, "Be real. A felon doesn't get a lot of chances to make this much money."

"Martha Stewart."

"You know what I meant."

I said, "So, you'd never planned on breaking into Freeman's room."

"It was still a big improvisation. Yeah, I planned on getting the computer. That's original and could be profitable. But I had to get you to do that for me, boo."

"You could've done it yourself."

"Oh, no. I'm not a thief. Not that kind."

"Uh huh."

"That hotel has too much security. A smart grifter never shows her face. My girl knows that too. She's rising up in Hollywood, so she wouldn't take any chances on getting busted."

"You could've rented a room on the same floor. Worked it like that."

She shook her head. "Never show your face."

"I'll jot that down in my criminal notepad."

We ate some more, each bite tasting better than the one before. The night air became cooler. L.A. was always like that at night. The bitch always sent you to bed with a chill.

I asked, "How did you know I'd steal it?"

"Didn't. Just fed you enough information. You didn't know me. Didn't trust me."

"Still don't."

"I know. And I don't trust you. So that keeps us in a good position."

"I hit Freeman. I straight up double-crossed you."

"I would've done the same. Like I told you, a million dollars on a truck."

I told her, "I'm not buying all of that bullshit. Somebody put you on to me."

"Kill the conspiracy theory. It was random."

"Like searching for a four-leaf clover on a sidewalk."

"Nice analogy. Can I use that?"

"Stop the bullshit. Yesterday you said you protected your sources. Today it's random."

She gave another one of those cute and criminal smiles.

I asked, "You pulled Freeman's bank info?"

She reached inside her purse, handed me a golden envelope. Making red lights change to green. Pulling a man's bank information. I was impressed and nervous with what she could do.

Freeman had six thousand in his savings. Around three hundred in his checking.

I said, "To be a baller, he's conservative."

"Look here. He bounced quite a few checks in the past year."

"Damn. He sure did. On his old Quitman, Mississippi, bank account."

"He needs a better accountant."

"This is just checking and savings. Checking gets no interest and savings is so low it might as well be no interest. He has to have his real money somewhere else."

"I expected him to be like the typical Nuevo baller, big money in useless accounts."

I said, "Doubt if he hooked up with a woman like Folasade because he's stupid."

"Well, I wouldn't sleep with my nest egg under my pillow. I'd diversify my investments, buy property. Any disposable income would be in a high-interest account."

"He got a seven-figure deal, so this is his chump change. He probably has more accounts than he can count. What else did you come up with?"

"My contact is still on it. You done eating?"

"Yeah. Shoulda picked up a bottle of JD to wash this down."

I tossed our garbage. We headed back toward the theater. She fired up another cigarette while we strolled, stood at the corner and

smoked more than half before she tossed it. Once again she made
the light change in our favor. Pushed a button, made the world stop
for her.

I asked, "Besides using the lot to fence hot goods, what's your
connection to the play?"

"What makes you think there is one?"

"The way the valet and doorman looked at you. Like you're a
queen."

"I tip well."

"They looked at you like that before you tipped."

"We have some money invested."

"Legit money?"

"Yeah. Me and Mrs. Robinson."

"Your personal pickpocket."

She laughed.

I said, "Saw her headshot on the wall. Pamela Quinones."

"The one and only. That's my partner. I'd prefer to do it alone.
That way there is no split. All the guts and all the glory. But she's cool.
We've been hanging tough for two years now. Rent scams. Vending
machine scams. God, we've done more shit than I can remember."

"Quinones. Spanish?"

"Part Puerto Rican. A mutt, just like me."

"Lovers?"

She laughed, shook her head, but didn't answer with any words.

I said, "That's how she got the lead. Invested in her own play,
hired herself as the star."

"It was either that or do like Angelyne—buy herself a pink Cor-
vette and lease a billboard on the Sunset Strip. You have to show-
case. You do what you have to do in this town."

"Tummy tuck. Breasts enhanced."

"Teeth capped. You name it and they do it in the name of
Hollywood."

"What about you?"

"No upgrades."

I checked my watch. It was getting to be that time of night, the time when trouble woke up and took to the streets. Lisa's bullyboys should be on the prowl by now.

I was ready to get it over with, but I wasn't going to rush.

I asked Arizona, "How's the play going?"

"Losing money. This production has turned out to be a money pit."

"Why don't you shut it down?"

"Not yet. It's a great way to clean up some dirty money."

"You're doing a lot. Got your hands in a lot of pots."

"I want to work my way up the ladder and be Queen Scamz one day."

"Credit cards. Ripping off the Internet. Sounds more like organized crime."

"A fool is born every minute and there's enough business for everybody."

"Ambitious."

"Would love for you to tag along. For personal reasons if nothing else."

She tiptoed and kissed me. Her tongue got reacquainted with mine.

I thought about Panther.

Arizona said, "When I was naked in front of you, I wanted you to take it."

"That's what got Kobe in the situation he's in now."

"Baby, this ain't Denver." She laughed. "Was so wet for you."

We kissed again.

She whispered, "Imagined your tongue moving inside me . . . just . . . like . . . that."

I wasn't into her, not like I was the night we met. Was playing the role. I was doing like Panther did at her job. In the back of my mind I saw how she let men touch her, how she teased them with her real estate in order to get over. Ten dollars a song. Slow dance to heaven.

Arizona pulled away, held my hand, looked me in the eyes, her eyes dreamy, that cunning smile back on her lips, and asked me, "That package you have . . . ?"

"Back to the money."

"Yeah."

"Told you I don't like being played."

She asked, "What are we going to do about Freeman?"

"The ball is already rolling." I let her hand go. "I want a bigger cut."

"Define a bigger cut."

I said, "My crew gets fifty. Your team gets the same."

"You're insane. No deal."

"Fifty percent."

She laughed, still gloating from the work she had done.

I didn't laugh. I told her, "So you get a dime, I get two nickels."

"And if I get nothing?"

"I get half of that."

She twisted her lips. "Fifty percent. Geesh."

"My crew bumped it. Now it's between you and Freeman."

She ran her tongue over her bottom lip.

Time danced around us while I waited for her decision.

She said, "Guess we should look at the merchandise. Right, partner?"

I told her, "I'll get the briefcase."

Her lips went back up into that slick smile. "I already have it."

"I'm not surprised."

"Bummer."

"Expected your valet guy to go through my car. I'm guessing that's what you told him in Spanish. Figured that was why you wanted to take a stroll over to Pink's, to buy some time."

"You're thinking like a con man. I like that."

I said, "One more thing."

"Uh huh?"

"Let's say I buy the bullshit you sold me about picking me at random, about looking at all the employees at Wolf's company. That meant you could find me at work. Or home. But how did you know I'd be at Back Biters? That's not on my résumé or in my credit report."

She chuckled, didn't give up any answer. Kept that answer to herself.

I followed her around the corner. Her car was there. Another one of her workers was waiting for her. More Spanish words and he used the remote to open the trunk. Her trunk was filled with more high-end clothes, all sorts of designer dresses and shoes. Freeman's silver briefcase was resting on top of it all. She checked the locks, then said more Spanish words. Her worker ran off, came back with a black bag, pulled out tools that would make any lock useless.

She asked, "In a hurry?"

I wasn't. Nothing but trouble and death were waiting for me.

"Let's inspect the merchandise."

I nodded. Didn't expect Arizona to let me raise up without an inspection. Didn't want to leave before I knew what I had given her. I hadn't opened it, not because of the lock, could've broke that myself, but I was scared of what might be inside. Or what might not be inside. Scared that what China Doll had grabbed might not be the real prize, but a briefcase loaded with those damn bobbleheads. The lock popped. I held my breath. Expected it to fly up and see a hundred little Freemans running for freedom, heads wobbling, images of the new black aesthetic with two books held high, the Moses of the book world.

The briefcase was sturdy and professional, designed especially for a laptop, lined with black protective foam. Had separate compartments for the power cord and other accessories.

Snuggled inside that foam was a computer. Silver. A Sony VAIO.

I had expected it to have a radioactive glow like the Holy Grail did in one of those *Indiana Jones* movies, or its contents lighting up the room like that briefcase did in the movie *Paycheck*. It didn't glow. Doubt if it was the latest VAIO Sony had to offer.

Arizona powered it up. I didn't think it would come on. It did. I expected to need a password. I didn't. The screensaver was a picture of Freeman and Sade. Both had I-love-you smiles. Had to be a couple of years old. No ring was on her finger. She looked happy.

I noticed that the briefcase looked thicker than the compartment.

"Looks like Freeman's briefcase has a false bottom."

Arizona smiled, shut off the computer, and closed the briefcase. She didn't check to see what was hidden underneath Freeman's million-dollar book.

I nodded.

She did the same.

"One more thing."

"Sure."

I handed her a business card. Told her to turn it over. A name and an address were on the other side, written in black ink, my own handwriting, block style so it would be readable.

I told her, "If for any reason I'm not around, that's who I want you to give my cut to."

"If you're not around?"

I nodded.

She said, "You trust me?"

"Don't think I have a choice."

"I know they busted your head. Things that bad?"

My head wound didn't hurt anymore. I asked, "Can you do that?"

She read the card. "Rufus—"

"My brother. Anything happens to me, wanna make sure . . . can you do that?"

I'd already left Rufus a message, told him to kick some cash down to Panther, left her number. Told him to remember and honor what we had said about not wasting money on funerals. And I told him to remember the rules of the streets; no police.

A big red clock was over my head, ticking down.

Momma. Reverend Daddy. Thought about both of them.

Hoped Rufus and Pasquale . . . hoped they worked that shit out some kinda way. I didn't have time to call. Should've gotten over my own issues and called my brother. Hated that I acted like Reverend Daddy with him all the damn time. But that was all I knew, all I understood.

Arizona smiled, this one not that of a grifter. Her walls came down and everything about her became softer. She looked like a lost little girl who was trying too hard to be a conniving woman. Her smile was real. Held sincerity and worry. In that moment I saw some innocence, corners of who she used to be before life tripped her up and she landed on this side of the fence.

Then it was gone. That tenderness lasted as long as a candle's flame in a hurricane.

She said, "Sure."

She reached over, patted my hand, touched my flesh like she wanted to feel its warmth.

Feel the warmth before it went cold. Touch this skin before it changed back to dirt.

Rufus wouldn't be involved, would be out of harm's way. Panther wouldn't be involved. Nobody I cared about would be caught up in this game, not any more than they already were.

That was that.

I told her, "They're out there looking for me."

"What are you going to do?"

"It'll never end. I have to do what I have to do."

"Be careful."

"Just live up to your end of the bargain."

She said something in Spanish and the valet nodded, ran off, came back with my ride.

Arizona reached inside her purse and took out her blade. She made it dance open, then made it dance back into its shelter, then offered it to me.

I thought about it, but shook my head, a thankful smile on my weary face.

Think I understood how Lancaster felt in that movie. Tired. Just plain old tired.

She told me, "He's dead. The man who taught me all I know, he's dead."

"I kinda figured that."

"I know you're a big and strong man, but be careful."

She put her blade back in her purse, headed back inside the theater. She didn't look back this time. Think it was too hard for her to. Death had been a part of her world, probably had been the trauma that made her who she was right now. She vanished into the theater. I heard a huge applause. The stage show was ending, curtain was coming down, the pretending was over.

I got in my car and started driving, out of habit my tired eyes went to the rearview.

Cold air came in through the broken rear window.

Felt strange not having my glasses on.

Felt stranger not having my cellular at my side.

That phone had been on my hip for months.

Lisa had given me Italian suits.

And she had given me that cellular phone.

It was a high-tech phone with a GPS inside. The same kinda phone some parents gave their children so they could keep geographical tabs on them. Twelve thousand miles over my head a satellite had been tracking me, making me a blip on her screen. She might've been able to pull that information up on her cellular phone. Lisa had been able to follow me for months.

Brilliant. Her flapdoodle had been nothing short of being brilliant.

Still felt like I was being followed.

Like death was behind me.

That was good.

29

Willoughby and Highland.

Still on the edges of Hollywood, not too far from the Sunset Strip.

Before I rolled to meet with Arizona I had dumped the cellular outside Club 360.

That was as far as I wanted them to track me.

The hunted had flipped the script and become the hunter.

They would pick the time, but I would pick the place this shit jumped off.

Sid Levine had said the range on the GPS was about a hundred yards. I parked a few blocks away, closer to Hollywood Boulevard, took my time walking over from there.

I was outside a supposedly twenty-one-and-over club, a rave joint that stayed open after hours, a club that played techno, had access to the customer's drug of choice, and charged megabucks to get on the other side of the velvet rope. Looked like it might've been free up until a certain time, maybe had a discount on admission for the early birds—the long line told me that.

Music bumped out of the open doors, loud enough to shake a few leaves off the trees and draw the people in. Women were bareback, showing off their legs and erogenous zones, tugging their Lycra skirts back down below their panty lines, most of them shivering with their arms folded over their erect nipples. A cool breeze brought the hint of some strong and potent marijuana. Kids. Their parents were probably at home holding their third double martinis, wondering how their kids got so fucked up.

The lion appeared, think he had been down in this area prowling for a while. This time he wasn't rolling in that Expedition, didn't have forty large in rims spinning underneath his chassis. That damn near caught me off guard. He was in a 1964 Deuce-and-a-Quarter—an Electra 225, that 425 motor humming. Bland colored, no bling anywhere. A dull ride that didn't stand out like the bling-on-wheels cruising the boulevard. Something that would've thrown me. They'd gotten me used to seeing the pimpin' Expedition and switched up.

Even if I hadn't seen his profile when he passed by, I'd've recognized the shape of his O.J.-sized head when a car's headlights hit him from the back. Didn't have to see his tiny teeth or that smooshed nose. His shadow was ugly to the bone. I wondered how his momma felt, how her eyes bugged when the doctor pulled that out of her and laid it across her breasts. Bet she passed out. Bet his daddy screamed for them to put it back in the oven until it was done.

He was a few feet from where I had dumped the phone. Lisa's locator was on point, better than Sid Levine had said it was. I shook my head at how easy it was for her to track me.

Her bullyboy slowed down and double-parked that gas-guzzling boat in the shadows.

I shook my left leg, corrected that wardrobe malfunction again.

The lion pulled out and cruised the block twice before he found a spot facing the club. He was on his cellular. He kept missing me because I was tucked across the street, almost a block down between two gum trees. He whipped into a space and turned off his lights. But the fool kept his foot on his brakes, so his taillights were lit up like it was the season for giving.

Then once again he pulled away from the curb.

I didn't move. Stayed rooted on sidewalk that smelled like old urine and fresh fertilizer.

The jackal was out there somewhere. That made me jittery because

I didn't know if he was trailing the lion, maybe rolling in another car, or if he was in the Hummer with Lisa.

I stayed sandwiched between the trees.

I wouldn't have heard him over the noise from the club. He would've been on top of me before I had any idea that he was keeping low, moving military style, creeping up behind me.

But his cellular rang, the tune "Play That Funky Music, White Boy" gave him away.

When I jumped around, the jackal was standing a few feet from me, dressed in his throwback gear, Minneapolis Lakers. Face hard to the bone. Slanted eyes. Pock-faced, thin man etched in penitentiary muscles. Markings up his neck to his throat. He'd been doing the same thing, keeping to the shadows, stalking for me.

My suit coat was already off, left it in the car.

My sleeves were rolled up, my warrior tattoos on display.

I was back on the yard.

His hands were empty. No shank in sight.

No words were needed. We knew how this went.

The motherfucker charged at me, raised his leg when he jumped up in the air, caught me off guard, planted a karate kick in my gut, made me lose my wind and stumble back toward traffic. A car zooming by at forty miles an hour almost clipped me. I got my balance, shoved the pain aside, and went after him full throttle.

The motherfucker was bouncing around in steel-toed boots like they were ballet slippers.

I gruffed, raised my hands, faked like I was about to rush his ass. He came at me with another kick, caught me in my ribs. He was so fast I didn't see that steel toe coming up, just saw it going back before I felt the pain. I stumbled, damn knee went south, and I fell against a car.

My jaw tightened. He came toward me while I struggled to get balanced.

He threw another kick, his foot coming at me hard and strong.

I caught his leg this time. It hurt like hell because his round kick hit my rib cage like a hammer. I'd left my arms up, sacrificed my ribs and gave him that as a target. He was quick but I brought my forearm down hard and caught his foot between my rib cage and arm, struggled with him and fought my own pain, held his leg like it was in a vise grip. Trapped. His eyes widened. He tried to flip the other leg around and heel kick me, but I dragged him backward, stole his balance while I recovered mine, then drew my leg back to Ohio and treated him to a strong kick in the groin. My hard shoes bull's-eyed the fleshy part between his legs.

I had to let his leg go and deal with my own pain.

He didn't go down, just stumbled back. I went after him the desperate way Sugar Ray went after Tommy Hearns in their first battle, like I was a warrior behind on all the scorecards, went after him hard, threw blow after blow, missed most but managed to land a hard hook to his temple. That should've taken him out, but it just staggered him. Then I landed an uppercut. Those two blows used to take much larger men off their feet, make them fly. I had been hit harder and didn't hurt, not like this, not in a way that had me scared. I was pissed off at myself for being this out of shape. Driving people around for the last six months had left me soft.

I threw another uppercut, then a left hook that sprung my wrist.

Both of my hands were hurting. Hitting a man hurts the fists like hell.

He came at me again, his own pain slowing him down to a speed I could damn near handle. He threw a couple of wild punches, haymakers that missed the target, then another kick. Slower. The kick was much slower. Slow enough for me to catch that leg again.

He cursed me and my mother.

Then I did it again, kicked him in his love sacs, let the square toe of my shoe lift and separate his family jewels, did that two more times, bull's-eyed the same spot. He wheezed with each blow, exhaled hard, eyes tried to pop out, then he crumpled and fell where he stood. He pulled his knees together, moaned some kind of a prayer. Blood and spit rivered from his mouth.

He held his nuts and struggled while I stood over him, wheezing my-damn-self.

I told him, "Don't get up. Get up, you're really gonna get hurt."

"Fuck you."

"Let it go, man. Let. This. Shit. Go."

"Fuck you."

Then he got on his elbow and reached under his shirt. The fight had been fair so far, but a street fight was all about winning. I didn't have time to conjure up a weapon. I jumped on top of him, rolled around, socked him in his head, threw elbows and demonic blows, tried to beat him to whatever he was struggling to grapple from his waistline. Blood stained his face and he wouldn't give in. I felt the handle he was struggling to get a decent grip on. I held it down, jammed my fingers in his eyes, then did a Mike Tyson move and bit the tip of his nose as hard as I could. Tried to make my teeth meet. He screamed like an old woman. I bit him again. He kicked and his scream came out ragged and deranged. He had to choose between his nose and his gun. He followed the pain and let go of the burner. A snub-nosed .38. The screams didn't end. I'd never heard a man shriek so loud, his song out of key with that horrible techno music.

A few people looked our way, saw nothing but parked cars and shadows, then went back to trying to get to the other side of that velvet rope. No sign of the Deuce-and-a-Quarter.

The music had covered most of his wails.

I was sweating strong, breathing hard. My arms ached, hadn't pumped any real iron in too long, skin burned, felt scratched up from where he had dug his claws into my skin.

I got a grip on his burner, threw the snub nose up high and hard. It landed on the roof.

He told me, "You. A. Dead. Man."

He was bloodied, beaten, and still threatening my life.

"Play That Funky Music, White Boy" came on again, his cellular blinking in neon colors. He'd dropped the phone. It had landed close to him. Bullyboy was calling. Jackal scampered toward that song. I stomped down on his knee, heel first. Gave him something to sing about.

He howled out his own chorus, a low out-of-breath howl that went into the pavement.

I leaned against the wall, tried to catch my breath.

He grabbed his leg and gurgled, his mouth filled with saliva. The way we were situated, nobody could see us in the shadows. I turned and walked away, chest heaving, only made it a few steps, stopped to rest, catch my breath, my bad knee still giving me grief, but not as much.

"Dead." He moaned, and sent me an evil smile. "You. Dead. Motherfucker."

"Shut. The. Fuck. Up. Nigga."

"Be a shame if your brother had an accident tonight. Be a shame if they found him in that house all burned up because he was caught on fire."

My rage took over, put fire behind my eyes. I balanced myself on the brick wall, raised my foot, tried to bring my knee up to my chest, then brought my foot down on the side of his head. Went Klingon on his ass until he shut up and went into his private siesta. Rage wouldn't let me ease up. Kept trying to stomp him into the concrete until I thought I heard his neck snap.

I staggered away, my shirt torn to shreds, halfway on, halfway off my body. I yanked that rag off me. Stood with my top bare. Exhausted, eyes wide, sweat raining from my head.

He'd issued one threat too many. He didn't know me. I didn't own a mansion. Or a Cessna. Didn't have the keys to a Lamborghini. Wasn't a soft-ass limo driver.

I was Reverend Daddy's oldest son. I was East Side. Had done time like a man, and beat down many men since I was born. I was my brother's keeper.

Nobody threatened my family. Nobody threatened my brother. Nobody.

That music bumped loud in the background, loud enough to

drown out the last two minutes of fights and moans on this side of the street. The world went loud, but the space between me and my enemy was as quiet as Inglewood Cemetery at sunrise.

I couldn't tell if he was breathing, saw no rise and fall in his chest.

If death came tonight, I wasn't going to ride through those burning gates alone.

"Play That Funky Music, White Boy" played again. I stomped the phone to pieces.

A red dot moved across my chest, my eyes settled on its rise and fall. The beam moved up across my nose, did that to make sure it had my full attention, then went back to my heart.

Lisa had come up on me, moved through the shadows, the night breeze kicking up like she had demanded the commotion, like she was Storm, winds whipping her white linen dress left and right. Angelic head to toe. She had an Egyptian shawl wrapped around her head, looking all dolled-up like she did the night I'd seen her at Back Biters. Her stone face made her look evil enough for me to have doubts about trying to bum-rush her. Couldn't run now if I tried.

I caught my breath the best I could, my eyes on the source of the red dot.

I asked, "I see. You got. Your Glock."

She said, "Not the Glock. It's a new toy I picked up at a trade show."

"Heard. About. That. Toy."

"Got it at the Taser International Booth."

"Right." I opened and closed my aching hands. "Las. Vegas. With. Wolf."

She pulled her scarf away from her head and neck, winced, made a sound like that simple move hurt her down to the bone. She wanted me to see the red and purple bruises, all the marks and fingerprints I had left behind. My fury had marked up her skin, left her hurting pretty bad.

She asked, "Ever been blasted with fifty thousand volts?"

"Not. Lately."

"Like being hit by a hundred lightning bolts. I volunteered at the show. Got zapped."

"Don't. Do. This. Lisa."

"Pretty cool. Compressed nitrogen gas shoots electrode-tipped wires out at a hundred miles an hour. The prongs harpoon in your skin. You couldn't shake it loose if you tried."

"Lisa."

"I can zap you two hundred times. No gunshot. No echo."

"Don't. Lisa."

"With that loud music across the street, hell, I can watch you dance all night."

She lowered her stun gun, moved it down, pointed it at the ground. Old emotions had taken root. She didn't have the Glock at her side. She didn't want me dead, not here, not now.

People talked when they didn't want to kill. People joked when they didn't want to die.

I told her, "You had set me. Up."

Her shoulders softened, the flame in her eyes lowered. "Are you okay?"

"From the get go. Your boys. Would've killed me before. The next sunrise."

She knew what I was talking about. The camera in Wolf's office told me the truth about her intentions. She knew about it. Anything I had done would've been caught on tape.

She stayed ten, maybe fifteen feet away from me, no doubt the length of the copper wires in that gun. If she backed up, the barbed prongs wouldn't reach me.

I moved a foot away. She followed.

I moved toward her. She backed up.

"What did you want, Lisa?"

"To be loved by someone. I loved you, Driver. I really did."

I coughed, got my wind. "We had no connection. Police would've found the tape. Out-of-work felon down on his luck. Or out-of-work black man robs rich white man on Christmas Eve. Take your pick. End of story. End of my story. Would've . . . would've closed the loop."

She sounded so tender. "You think I would do the things I did for you if I didn't love you? That tape would've been for my own protection, not for the police. My insurance."

I straightened up the best I could, looked down at the battered and twisted jackal.

It bothered me. What I had done bothered me.

The bloodied body of the jackal didn't faze Lisa, didn't disturb her at all.

She said, "Ask yourself why you're not already dead. I could've had this done the day after you reneged on our agreement, could've made a phone call the moment I walked in and saw you working at my business. Didn't."

"Why didn't you?"

"Part of me wanted you there. A big part of me hoped . . . I had hopes, Driver. What I feel for you is deeper than you'll know. I never lied to you. I love you and I hate you for using me like that. The way you just ignored me. Why did you pick that stripper over me?"

I didn't answer. She had her own version of what was going on.

"I told you I wanted you to give me babies. You said you loved me."

The music kicked up across the street. Headlights hit us. Her bullyboy came out a couple of blocks down, was coming this way, creeping down the block, looking for us.

"I pull up in the parking lot at Back Biters and I find you all over some young ass, tight-eyed half-breed. You were standing in the middle of the lot kissing her." Lisa paused, cringed like she was trying to focus. Looked like too many conversations were going on inside her head. Her voice splintered. "Why did you push me, reject me, and go see that stripper whore?"

Still no answer. I wanted to ask her if this three-day shit was because of Arizona, or Panther, but I think it was all of the above. The green-eyed chickens had come home to roost.

"Playa, Playa, Playa."

"Stop. Calling me. That."

"Playa. Playa."

The Deuce passed by, still on the other side of the block.

"I threatened to tell Wolf. You came to work. I pulled a gun on you. You came to work. I destroyed everything you owned. You came to work. I did the same with your whore. You. Came. To. Work. Why didn't you leave? You had nothing to pack. Why didn't you just leave?"

I could've told her that Reverend Daddy never taught us how to run, taught us to hold our ground and fight. But I didn't have the breath to waste on words that would make no difference.

Lisa's eyes went to her bullyboy, the one I'd left sleeping on the ground.

He wasn't moving. Might as well put two pennies over his eyes.

I said, "End it here. Walk. Away."

"I think about you all the time, Driver. Thoughts of us and what was, what wasn't. I knew what I wanted. Now I need to figure out who I am without you next to me. It's hard. Never done anything this hard in my life. I guess we had the right love at the wrong time. Maybe me loving you was too much for you. And you not loving me wasn't enough for me."

"Lisa. Just. Walk away."

"Can't, Boo. We've gone too far to back it up now."

Her cellular was in her other hand. She lowered the stun gun long enough to hit her speed dial. She raised the phone to her face. Hesitated, stared in my eyes before she said, "Found him. Across the street from the club. Just make a U-turn."

She hung up. Lowered her cellular. Her tongue moved over her lips in a tense motion.

Headlights came right up on us, then turned off, sent us back to darkness.

Lisa took a step toward me. "I'm going to . . . I'm going to miss you, Driver."

She raised the stunner, put that red dot on my body. Every part of me ached, but my adrenaline was pumping. Had to get at her. Tried. But she pulled the trigger. Before I could bob or dodge to my left, the barbed prongs had harpooned my skin. Felt like a high-voltage power line had been routed through my body. Fifty thousand volts. I growled, refused to fall.

It hurt too much to scream.

She pulled the trigger again, sent electricity in bursts, searing pain that made my muscles contract uncontrollably. Disrupted the messages to my brain and took me to my knees. Muscle control was gone, body went hysterical. Confusion and disorientation crawled all over me.

Darkness tried to swallow me up. Every sound was a hundred miles away.

"He's a tough one, Lisa."

"Arrogant."

"As hell."

"See what he did to your friend."

"Damn. His nose is jacked up. Shit. His neck is broke."

"That jerk. Told his dumb ass to call us if he found Driver first."

"Do I get his cut? I mean it don't look like he's gonna be needing it."

"Hurry before somebody comes over here. Put him in the backseat."

"No room in the backseat. Trunk. Grab his feet."

"He's still combative."

Voluntary muscles wouldn't cooperate, but still I fought to get up off my knees. In my mind I *was* getting up. I was swinging. In reality, I hadn't moved an inch. They stood over me and I couldn't do a damn thing. Lisa pressed that trigger again, opened up my nerves, took me flat to the ground. I crashed hard. I struggled in my mind, but my body wasn't fighting.

I fell into a warm pool of darkness.

I changed everything. The last time Lisa was at my apartment, I made it go in a different way. I saw her come in the room again. This time I kissed her. She took her blouse off. Unsnapped her bra. Her nipples were strong, dark as midnight. Her hands went down to her waist. Unbuttoned and unzipped her skirt. It whispered its way down her legs, hit the carpet without a sound. She stepped away from her pool of clothing. Just like Arizona had done.

My chest rose and fell. I stared at Lisa, at her softness. Licked my lips.

If I did this, all would be well. No damage to Panther's life. Rufus would be safe.

She turned around and walked toward my bedroom, one hand over her head, the other on her waist, her pear-shaped frame moving with slow and easy sway, with feminine pride.

Music came on. Lights went off.

Her silhouette moved across the room, got on top of my bed.

I took my glasses off, took off my tie, eased toward the bedroom, taking my time.

"Get naked, Driver. Hurry."

"What's the rush?"

"Wolf will be looking for me."

I took off my suit, all my clothes, dropped them where I was.

"Be honest, Driver. You want me in your bed every night."

I nodded, gave in and admitted my strong desire for her. Her lips were full and wet.

"Come here. I want to take you in my mouth."

I let her feed. Then I got in the bed with her, touched her between her thighs; her sex was like Seattle in April. Ran my fingers over her backside and the curve in her hips, her small waist.

Her body was Panther's body.

Lisa said, "Do me every way you can imagine."

Whatever you want.

"Beat your chest, sex me the way I deserve to be sexed, do it nonstop."

Whatever it takes.

"Get your manumit. Come get your manumit."

Then she laughed. Her voice turned British and African, like Folasade.

Her knees moved away from each other, showed me her gloom.

She said, "One moment I want to kill you, then . . . then . . . I want to feel you inside me."

I gave her everything she wanted.

She groaned. "This. Was. All. You. Had. To. Do."

Over and over I entered my friend's wife like this pussy was mine for the taking.

My friend. No. My former friend.

Lisa owned a barbaric expression, that desperate look that came when the orgasm felt so good. She tumbled into that ecstasy, held the sheets like she was trying to break her fall. She trembled, her back arched. I fucked her hard, showed no mercy, yanked her back into me over and over. A thousand waves passed through her. She kept jerking. Like I was stunning her.

My big hands went around her little neck. I choked her as hard as I could. No matter how hard I choked her, all she did was smile. Smiled and sang and came over and over.

Little by little, I came to. Half a sense at a time. My eyes felt like they were swollen, glued shut. They opened and I saw nothing, an endless blackness deeper than death.

Everything came back to life. Everything hurt from my head wound to my ankles.

I was in the fetal position. The small space I was in was cramped. Felt like I had been beaten and tossed in the Adjustment Center. There was a lot of bouncing, like I was riding a coffin down a bumpy road. Then my hearing came back. Loud music. Couldn't move my hands. Or my feet. Something over my head. Could hardly breathe.

Other cars roared.

More bumps. Each one hurt to go over. She was taking me down Route 666.

Lisa said, *"He's moving."*

"Just the car shifting him around. That motherfucker out."

I was in the trunk of that Deuce. Large trunk. Bad suspension.

The smell, the way the engine roared, and the way it rode told me that. They needed shocks and the brakes squealed like they were fifty thousand miles overdue for new pads. The stench of spilled oil and dust and battery acid thickened and poisoned the little musty air I could get.

"Maybe I should check on him."

"Lisa, relax. He ain't going nowhere."

The car stopped. Somebody pulled up next to us, music loud enough to send the vibrations through me. The music moved ahead of my prison, bumping hard and fading fast.

Chest rising and falling, air thin, I tried not to panic, but that claustrophobic feeling had me terrified. Had to think. In The Hole. I was back in The Hole, a place where seconds moved like hours. Every vehicle that passed, its noise was on the left. We didn't pass anybody, not that I could tell. I was on my right side. My own sweat became a river that flooded my right ear. All I knew was that the car I was in kept to the slow lane, maybe doing the speed limit, maybe a little over, had bad shocks, needed a new muffler, and was trying not to draw any attention.

Sweat puddled in my eyes. I struggled, kicked. Wrists were tied in front of me. Something was wrapped tight around my knees, cut off my circulation. Lisa didn't tie me up. I wasn't hog-tied LAPD style. I kicked my feet. What covered my mouth muffled my yelling.

"Lisa, I'm going to pull over so you can zap his ass again."

"Not yet. Have to be careful. Don't want his heart to give out."

"What difference does that make? It's gonna give out anyway."

"Not yet."

"Can I zap him a few times?"

"No."

"Don't go soft on me. We doing this or what?"

"We're doing this. I have to get on with my life."

Cars and SUVs whistled by. No eighteen-wheelers. With all the stop and go, we weren't on the freeway. Freeway was all stop or all go, lots of lane changing, more cars passing by.

The sound of city traffic faded.

"Lisa, you know I'm all about the business."

"What now?"

"Make sure I get homeboy's cut."

"All you worry about is money."

"If I had money I wouldn't worry about it."

"I got it right here."

"Kids in private school. That shit costs a grip."

"How's your mother?"

"Lisa, you know, you really should call Auntie from time to time. She's getting up there. Since you hooked up with white boy you ain't been hanging out with the family too much."

Thought I heard an airplane taking off. All flights took off going west, then turned and found their bearings. We were heading west. That meant we were heading toward the ocean.

Then my weight shifted toward the front of the trunk. They were going downhill.

"Lose the headlights."

"Headlights lost."

All I could smell taste feel was my own fear.

These would be the last voices I heard.

"Lisa, mind if I smoke?"

"You firing up a joint?"

"Nah. Smokes I picked up when I did a job in Canada."

"Looks like a blunt."

"Du Maurier. French."

The car rode a moment, slowed down, squealed to an easy stop. My heartbeat sped up. Sweat rained. The stench from his cancer stick made it that much harder to breathe. The car was dilapidated. The backseat had to be ragged enough for smoke and sounds to come through.

My feet were as numb as my hands. Pain muted by whatever they had tied me with. I breathed with the pain, chest expanding like a woman in labor, short puffs through my nose.

"You're going to drown him?"

"Unless you want me to get some gas. Brought some just in case."

"No. I'm not down with that. Just . . . no fire. Water is fine."

"We'll take him to the water."

"How long will it take?"

"As long as you want it to. Told you that, Lisa. We can toss him in, watch him struggle, or we can do it right off. Your money, your call. Why that face? Problem with that?"

"Just . . . no. I don't have a problem."

"He's beat down, but your boy ain't no joke. All I have to do is tie him up with some duct tape, take him out, drop him in the ocean. Three minutes later gurgle gurgle and we're heading toward Jerry's Deli. Unless you want to make it last a while. We can play with him."

"Just . . . Just . . . Just get it over with."

I imagined.

Imagined Rufus sprinting across the beach, sand kicking up behind him, his colorful locks flying behind him like Superman's cape, that gun I had given him extended, scowling like he was the Punisher from the comic books, barrel blazing, bullets flying, taking out the lion.

"You getting out?"

She paused. "No."

Or Arizona appearing out of nowhere, naked like she was the night I searched her, her streamlined beauty, long hair, and golden skin catching the lion off guard long enough for her cunning smile to disarm him, then to use her switchblade to cut him every way but loose.

The lion said, "Give me the stun gun."

"For what?"

Imagined Freeman showing up and throwing books like missiles, those bobbleheads charging and attacking the lion and Lisa, taking them down, tying them up like Gulliver.

"I'mma zap him a few times, soften him up."

Panther. Imagined her running across the beach in boy shorts and thigh-high boots, her long hair flying behind her, tears in her eyes, wailing like a banshee, gun extended like she was on her way to be the lead in *Kill Bill*.

None of that was gonna happen.

After a long hesitation, Lisa told the lion, *"I'll get out too. I'll see this through."*

"You don't have to, Lisa."

"I have to."

I got my leg to move. Struggled and got my swollen hands to my ankle. Panther's gift was still there. They hadn't seen the ankle strap. Too busy trying to rush me inside this Deuce to search me. My fingers found the .380. Heartbeat was drumming between my ears.

I was blind. A gun in my hand and living in Stevie Wonder's world, a world devoid of a sense that I needed right now, a world not to be taken for granted.

The car door opened, heard them get out of the car, all of their words muffled. But they kept talking. I focused on that. Their words. Their sounds. That was all I could do.

Each breath that came out of me was hard and uncertain, my last breath over and over.

I did something that I hadn't done in years. I prayed.

That's what I had been doing all along.

Not imagining. Praying.

A key went into the lock. The lock clicked. The trunk creaked open. It felt like the world had opened up too. Cool air flooded this tomb. Salty air filled up my damp pores.

Couldn't play possum and wait because they might zap me again. Hands aching, I squeezed the trigger. First I aimed at their voices, then I shot at their screams.

Pop. Pop. Pop. Pop.

Felt like I had missed. I raged, tried to get up, tried to hear where they were.

Pop. Pop. Pop. Pop.

Lisa screamed again, wailed like a Gaelic female spirit. My death had arrived.

Then a hundred lightning bolts went through my body.

30

Reverend Daddy used to take me and Rufus to the movies. Momma was into movies like *Claudine*. Reverend Daddy was crazy about *Dirty Harry*.

In movies, gunshots echoed like cannons. In reality, most just sounded like pops. A quick noise that, in a land of car alarms and back-firing trucks, made people crank up the volume on their televisions so they could hear what color scheme they were talking about on HGTV.

I tumbled out of the trunk of the Deuce. Suffered awhile. Expected more lightning to race through my body and deep fry my soul. I was frantic, yanked the prongs out of my flesh. Struggled and did the same with the dark covering over my head, pulled it hard. Hands were swollen, hurt so bad I could barely get loose. I held on to the bumper, made it to my feet. Leg cramped and that stab of pain hit me hard, sent me backward, threw me into the sand.

They were watching me cling to life. I knew they were.

This was their entertainment for the night.

Pain grew.

Had to sit there spitting sand out of my mouth, with sand all over my face, sand caked on my sweaty skin. Wait for them to have their fun.

They didn't say anything. But I knew they were there, circling me. Darkness became lighter, but only by a few degrees. I tried to shake the sting out of my eyes, but too much sweating had left me almost blind.

Focus, boy. Focus.

I mumbled, "Yessir."

The moonlight showed me that the .380 was next to me, sinking in the sand.

I grabbed that smoking gun, juggled it until I got my swollen finger back on the trigger, and growled out my warning, pointed the gun wherever I heard noise.

Ocean.

Seagulls cried.

Heard a noise.

I jumped, pulled the trigger.

The .380 was empty.

A car or two hummed in the distance.

No homes were in this area, none that I could see. So I wasn't in Venice or Santa Monica. No homes etched in the side of the hills, so I wasn't up by Malibu. They'd taken me down to an industrial strip, a remote spot where no one would be around in the thick of the night. Where no one could hear me scream. My mind told me I had to be somewhere between Marina Del Rey and Long Beach. Then my mind told me I was wrong. Could've been down in Orange County, somewhere on that strip of PCH that went into Dana Point.

I blinked over and over until I managed a little vision. The world was like a television with bad reception. It gave me a blurry vision of the lion, dressed in jeans and a black jacket, his hands in gloves, that big, square head under a black skullcap.

He was on the ground, on his side, sand dusting his body. He stared at me with one eye. His right eye. A bullet hole was where his left eye used to be. The stun gun was next to that cave in his head, a cavern created by a hollow point. The prongs were extended. He was the one who had shot me. Maybe we shot each other at the same time.

Looked like his fingers were moving, like he was typing a farewell e-mail to his children.

Then he stopped typing. Guess he had hit the send button.

My legs had been tied with Lisa's Egyptian shawl, the knot was pretty good. I got free, stumbled away from him. Bile rose in my throat. My reaction to all the abuse my body had taken rose up and came out of me in a harsh lurch. Freezing water rushed up to my shoes. We were on the edges of America. The bitter water spread, chilled my entire body. I gave that bile to the Pacific. Cold sweat came out of every pore. Another ocean wave came in, hit me, and I went down to my knees. Another wave rushed up my back, and splashed up on my face.

I crawled away from the water, then got back to my feet.

The night air covered me, felt like a strong breeze was coming in from the Himalayas.

She was out there. Lisa had a Glock and she was out there.

Anxiety never ceased.

I limped toward the car. Expected to hear the engine roar to life, and watch the car pull away.

It didn't.

Lisa's purse was in the sand, resting on the other side of the lion.

I kept limping, kept looking, kept listening, kept waiting.

Her Glock was there too.

Wanted to pick it up, tried to bend, but it hurt too much.

I kept limping.

Down the way, I saw a white flag flying in the sand.

I kept limping that way.

Followed small footsteps that had left their impression in the sand.

The space between the footsteps became less and less.

Less and less.

Inside some of those last impressions was blood.

That white flag was Lisa's beautiful dress. She had run, looked like she was headed away, trying to outrun her own pain, looked like she didn't know where she was going. Just running. A hole was in her abdomen. Death had caught her before she could get away.

31

Those prongs had fishhooked me and broken my skin, had stolen traces of my DNA.

My DNA could be drying up in the back of that Deuce.

My DNA and prints were already in the criminal justice system. Couldn't leave any traces of me behind. Wanted to call for help. Hand went down to my side. No cellular. I looked out and saw darkness. The exit was up an asphalt driveway. The main road was at least a hundred yards away. Wouldn't've been able to walk far, not up that incline in my condition. That hill would become a mountain. A hundred yards would be like a marathon. There was only one way for me to get out of there. I hobbled back, took the keys to the Deuce off the lion's body. I took the stun gun. The scarf they had tied me with. Got in the car, kicked up some sand.

I slowed when I passed by Lisa. Slowed down and stared.

White dress dancing in the wind.

I sat there, heart aching as much as the rest of me, wishing a lot of things. None of those wishes would come true. Father Time marched in one direction. I had to do the same.

I gave it some gas. Motor stuttered a bit before it roared. Something shifted in the backseat. I looked back. A can of gas and a roll of duct tap. My heartbeat tripled again. The backseat was damaged.

Had a hole in the right side, a hollow tunnel. That was why I could hear them talking.

I put the Deuce in gear and rattled out to the streets, drove slow, looking for landmarks and street signs, saw that I was down at Dockweiler State Beach, right off Imperial Highway. The black beach was what we called it. Headlights went by. Nobody slowed down or stopped.

Imperial Highway took me up by LAX and put me on the 105. The 105 to the 110, the 110 to the 10, the 10 to La Brea, La Brea to Edgewood to Highland to the gritty streets in Hollywood. Didn't know if I was doing the right thing, but I drove that Deuce back into the mouth of Hollywood, my mind spinning. Had taken as much freeway as I could, didn't want to take a chance on the streets. Didn't know if the hoopty I was in was hot. Didn't know if the registration was current. Didn't want to chance the police stopping behind me at a light, running the tags. Didn't want to stop at a pay phone and ask anybody to come get me. Johnny Law could pull up then. I ignored the pain the best I could and drove. I was a driver. I knew the city. Knew that bitch like she was my own woman. Loved Los Angeles enough to die for her. Hated her enough to kill her. It was a long and painful drive. Surreal. Like I was on acid, riding through a Salvador Dali painting. I don't know art but I know he had some weird shit. Hollywood was forever away, but I made it back to the land of broken dreams.

My car was still there. No ticket on the window this time.

I waited until no headlights were near me and left the Deuce sitting on one of Hollywood Boulevard's side streets. I reached in the backseat and got that gas can, poured gas all over anything I had touched and where I had been held hostage. I tossed a match as I limped away, dusting as much sand off me as I could. I hurried around the corner and got in my ride without anybody seeing me, flames rising behind me, my DNA being incinerated.

The wealth of pain came back as soon as I got in my ride.

I wiped sand from my face, put my soggy shoe on the pedal, and drove as fast as I could.

I couldn't drive far. Just wanted to drive far enough away to dissociate myself from that Deuce. Ended up going two blocks over to Club 360. I put my suit coat on and went toward the crowd. Club was still bumping, but a lot of people were outside. I had expected that would be a crime scene too. Thought that by now the jackal would have been wrapped up and carted away.

No one was on that side of the street.

The crowd was so fucked up, so busy laughing and leaning on each other they didn't give a shit about me digging in the bushes and coming out with that cellular. With the filth and sand all over my skin they probably thought I was one of L.A.'s homeless. Street people were always ignored. I needed that phone. Had to call for some help. Panther answered on the first ring.

I caught my breath, held the pain at bay, and asked, "Where you at?"

"Why it take so long for you to call?"

"Relax."

"You okay?"

"I think so. Yeah. I'm okay."

"You don't sound okay."

"Not now. Where you at?"

"When I called your brother . . . we were worried. I'm at his crib."

"How things between him and his friend?"

"Okay, I guess."

"They fighting?"

"Pasquale's mad, but he's not tripping."

"Good. That's. Good."

I told her where to meet me, hung up, walked my agony across the street.

The jackal was still there. He looked like one of L.A.'s homeless, a man down and out on his luck and taking a break from life's struggle by napping on the concrete.

I had planned to take the .380, plant it in his right hand, make sure it had his prints.

I had wiped down the stun gun, had thought about sticking those

prongs in his flesh. Pushing them deep enough to get covered with
his DNA.

I didn't.

That would've been too complicated. A fool's move.

I took the .380 and stun gun with me.

I drove on Highland until it changed into Edgewood, then went
south on La Brea, stopped in the parking lot of the Starbucks that
was on the east side of the street, just north of San Vincente. Panther
pulled up right when I did. Rufus was in the car with her.

Both had worry etched in their faces, borderline tears in their
eyes. Whatever they saw when they saw me was more than enough
to put a new level of horror in their expressions, stole their breaths,
did the same to all questions. Everything but my suit coat was soaking wet. Sand all over my body, bruises in my skin. Hands swollen.
Walking like grandpa. That was what they could see. If those prongs
had done any internal damage, I didn't know. Couldn't tell.

Rufus and Panther got out of her car. I called for Panther to get
back in her ride, told Rufus to come to me. I left the driver side door
open, hobbled around the rear of the car, got in the passenger side. Rufus was inside and behind the wheel before I got my door closed.

In a gruff voice that sounded like Reverend Daddy, I told Rufus,
"Drive."

He drove. Panther followed. They didn't drive fast, kept it normal. La Brea was a main artery, plenty of red lights, always had nonstop traffic. Looked like we'd run up on a crowd that was coming
from Roscoe's or Mixed Nuts Comedy Club.

Something shifted when Rufus changed lanes, slid from under the
seat on my side.

Rufus's eyes went to the noise. He saw the .380 and the stun gun.

He looked at me and froze up.

I repeated, "Drive, man. Drive the damn car."

Then I jumped. Reached behind my ear, touched my head wound.
I had so many new pains that that old one had been sidelined. Was

afraid that it had opened up, that I had dripped blood from Dockweiler to Hollywood. My hand came back wet, but with sweat. No blood.

We were sitting at the light at La Brea and Washington when Rufus stopped tapping on the steering wheel and asked, "Ever hear the joke about Texas Mating Spiders?"

"Rufus—"

"A preacher watched his daughter playing in the garden. He smiled as he reflected on how sweet and innocent his little girl was."

"Rufus."

"Suddenly she just stopped and stared at the ground. He went over to her and noticed she was looking at two spiders mating. 'Daddy, what are those two spiders doing?' "

"Rufus."

"I'm nervous, dammit. All this bull with that psycho is going on, you vanish, come back looking like hell warmed over, left that message with me . . . I called your girlfriend . . . you have more guns than Charlton Heston . . . look at my hand . . . see my fuckin' nerves are shot, dammit."

"Okay. Okay. The spiders."

He took a deep breath, ran his hand over his locks, moved his hair away from his swollen jaw. " 'They're mating,' her father replied. 'What do you call the spider on top, Daddy?' she asked. 'That's a Daddy Longlegs,' her father answered. 'So, the other one is Mommy Longlegs?' the little girl asked. 'No,' her father replied. 'Both of them are Daddy Longlegs.' The little girl thought for a moment, then took her foot and stomped them flat and said, 'Well, it might be okay in California or New York but we're not having any of that shit in Texas.' "

Silence.

I asked, "You done?"

"First time I heard it, thought it was funny."

The police pulled up next to us. A black-and-white. I looked over at them. The driver looked at me. I nodded. He did the same, chuckled, then went back to talking on his cell phone.

Silence.

The light changed. Rufus drove, hands gripping the wheel, knuckles bruised like mine. In the car behind us, Panther had an eye that was swollen from when she'd fallen and bumped her face. We'd become a parade of the walking wounded.

He asked, "Somebody . . . you . . . those guns . . . how bad did it get?"

"Less you know the better."

Seemed like police cars were all over La Brea, moving in all directions.

Rufus asked, "Will you be needing an alibi?"

"That would help a lot better than a joke."

"I told you I was nervous. I tell it better when I'm not nervous."

"I'mma need some clothes. And shelter for a few hours. Shelter with people around."

"Don't worry. *Mi casa, su casa.*"

"What about your boy?"

"Oh, please. Right now Pasquale is in the doghouse. He'll do anything I ask him to."

"I'm hurting to death over here."

Pasquale's guest house was bigger than my apartment. I'd never spent the night at their crib before. Had never been comfortable over there. Rufus brought me some fresh towels, a pair of oversized sweats, Vicodin, and a bottle of JD. My last suit was stuffed in a garbage bag. Rufus was going to drive a few blocks away and toss it all. I showered all the sand and murder off my skin, as much as I could, then collapsed on the bed and turned on the flat-screen. The volume was low, but I couldn't hear. Panther had taken the vacuum to the carpet, sucked up the sand that I had tracked in, then she took some cleansers and did the same in the bathroom.

My body was exhausted but I was scared to let sleep find me. Scared of what images might find me in my dreams. I waited for the news. Scared to see that too, but had to know.

Panther sat next to me. I was glad she was here.

We kissed for a while. I kissed her like I was lucky to be alive. I kissed her neck. Her legs opened and she welcomed me. She laid back and I was on top of her, her hand reaching for me, rushing me inside her, and I was moving slow, listening to her moan for Jesus and his father.

She got on top. Worked me something good.

My ex-wife didn't matter anymore.

Lisa didn't matter, not in that moment, not in this way.

Sunrise found me in front of the television.

After watching reports of more troops being slaughtered in Iraq, then about Jesse Jackson coming to Inglewood to protest the opening of a Wal-Mart supercenter the size of seventeen football fields, the wretched story I was waiting for hit the local news stations.

Panther was cuddled up next to me, holding me without smothering me. Touching me without clinging. She hadn't slept a second either. The news about Iraq had her chewing her lip, shaking her head, and bouncing her leg.

BREAKING NEWS—DOCKWEILER STATE BEACH

I closed my eyes, had another one of those philosophical moments where I hoped the life and things around me were just a product of my own mind.

I opened my eyes.

Squad cars. Medical examiner. His and her hearses. News vans from every local television station. Morning traffic, congested because of all the commotion. Photographers. Looky-loos in sandals or running shoes. People hanging around the perimeter, binoculars and digital cameras in hand, ready to shoot the scene and upload it to some perverted Web page.

Remoras in search of their next shark.

Rufus tapped on the door. Panther covered herself before I told him to come in.

Rufus told me, "Found it."

"Found what?"

He tossed me a book. Paperback. Small. Colorful cover. No pic-ture on the back. It was written by F. Titilayo Coker. *Manumit Yet to Come.*

Then he tossed me his copy of *Dawning of Ignorance.*

Rufus said, "Told you I had hypermnesia. Talk about a déjà vu."

I put the books to the side and shushed him.

Our eyes went to the television.

That could've been me, my body covered by a secondhand white sheet.

The noontime report had more details, was updated and told about a thirty-nine-year-old African-American male and a forty-year-old African-American female being found dead on the sands of Dock-weiler State Beach in Playa Del Rey at sunrise. The bodies were found sixty yards away from each other. Both had been shot.

Playa Del Rey.

Playa.

Lisa had taken me to Playa.

A gun was found on the scene. That was Lisa's Glock.

The news peeps said the police had bodies but no details. No wit-nesses. Names were being held pending notification of relatives. Full investigation. Full-blown crime scene. Helicopters. Crime scene in-vestigators. Yellow tape all over the place. More officers than I'd ever seen in one spot had swooped in, had their lights flashing up and down the highway.

Rufus came back to the guesthouse, looked at my wounds again, his swollen face trying to read me to see if that news had anything to do with my injuries. I remained stone-faced, emotions being held down. Then he sat down in one of the chairs, crossed his legs, folded his arms, and watched the flat-screen television with us.

An old man with a metal detector had been up at the crack of dawn, walking Dockweiler State Beach like he did most mornings, working out his arthritis while he looked for a lost pirate's treasure. He'd stumbled across a dead black man on the beach. Before he could scream out, an early morning jogger and her dog ran up on a dead black woman, bruises on her neck, her white dress stained in red, parts of that dress still waving, moving like she was still running.

The jogger and the old man were on their cellular phones dialing 911 at the same time.

The news said that robbery was ruled out. Ruled out because they had found forty thousand dollars in Lisa's purse. They didn't say her name. We knew who it was.

Forty thousand.

The price of love.

The price of hate.

Forty thousand.

She hated me more than she did her husband.

I had to get up, had to walk out of that room. I went outside, sat by the pool. I heard something and turned around. Saw Pasquale inside the house, in the kitchen, his lip busted and right eye swollen. He nodded at me. I waved and nodded, my way of telling the brother I appreciated his hospitality. He waved back, nodded the same way, with that gangsta expression all over his face. Could tell he was uneasy, embarrassed. Rufus passed by and went into the kitchen. Rufus and his friend were talking. My brother poured some fluids into a container, shook them up, and poured the mixture into two glasses. He drank one. Pasquale drank the other. They went on with their business. I did the same and went back to my own thoughts.

I thought about Wolf.

He was in Vegas with his kids. He had his alibi. My guess was that his daughter didn't have a part in a play. He left because he knew things were going to be bad. Left and spent time with his two children, playing with them while waiting for a phone call. He knew there would be a phone call. Just didn't know what kind of call it would be.

His last words to me had been "We all kill what we love."

That was his warning to me. He knew how Lisa felt about me.

Knew what she was going to do last night. Maybe he wanted to get those things off his chest because he knew.

I was sad for him. Sad for myself. Sad for the man Lisa had made me become.

I had put three people in the ground.

Panther came out, a robe wrapped around her heavenly frame, and sat next to me. She could pass for sweet sixteen. No makeup, none of the accoutrements from her night job. She looked so innocent. I wanted to ask her how she ended up on a stage dancing for money.

She said, "You okay?"

"The meds you have in your cabinet—"

"Helps me keep my emotional barometer . . . it needs to be calibrated at times."

"How often you . . . ?"

"Every day. I take 'em every day."

"They help?"

"I'm not crazy, if that's what you're asking. A lot of women suffer from depression."

"Why is that?"

"Because of men."

I asked, "They help?"

"They help. I'm still here. They help."

"And you take 'em everyday?"

"Supposed to."

"Got any extras?"

Her mouth opened, no words came for a minute.

She said, "I can get you some."

"Thanks."

"What else you need?"

My eyes went to those books that Rufus had left behind. One written by Freeman. One penned by Coker. Page ten in one was the same as page ten in the other.

I told Panther, "I need to go for a ride."

"Take my car. Your window needs to get fixed."

Her buttermilk-and-cornbread sashay took her across the flag-stone walkway, back inside the guesthouse. She came back and handed me her keys without asking another question.

She said, "Another news report was on. Said they found a man dead in Hollywood."

"They say it was related to Lisa?"

"That was all they said. Then they went to sports."

I looked at my hands again. Kept looking at them like they were smoking guns.

I said, "I killed three people last night."

She sat down, her leg bouncing.

"I want you to know that. Want you to know who I am, what I've done. Want you to know about my ex-wife, my brother. Want you to know all that. But most of all, want you to know that you're dealing with a murderer. I killed a man with my hands, shot two people."

"I gave you the guns, Driver."

She said that like she had pulled the trigger. I gave her silence.

"Were they gonna kill you, Driver?"

"Yeah. They were gonna . . . yeah."

Silence.

"All I care about is they didn't. I don't look good in black, not when my eyes are filled with tears. I don't like looking down on dead people. Don't know what I would've done."

I nodded.

She asked, "What do we need to do now?"

Silence.

She said, "They stalked you. Threatened you. Beat you. Driver, they terrorized you."

"Not the same."

"I know it's not like the Bush-shit they're going through overseas, but you were in a war. Plain and simple. You did what people try to do in a war. You stayed alive."

I stared at my hands again. Wrist was sprung, might've had a hairline fracture.

She said, "You're not a murderer."

Her hand rubbed over mine.

She asked, "Is it over?"

I shook my head.

Around ten unused bricks were by the patio. I went and picked up three.

We headed back inside the guesthouse.

Evening came.

The sun went down like it always did. Traffic was bad. Smog was thick. Kids rolled by bumping their sounds. Nothing had changed in the world.

The television was still on. Same news report had been playing off and on. Now Lisa's name and picture were up on the screen. They flashed a picture of her in her police uniform. A picture of her with her father, back when he was terrorizing the city of Compton.

Then they posted a picture of Kenny Washington. His smooshed nose and square head took up the screen. They said he was Lisa's cousin. A man with a criminal record as long as Sepulveda Boulevard. People were speculating that it was a hit on Kenny and Lisa happened to be with him. Wrong place, wrong time. News people speculated, not the police. The police had been on the scene, could tell how they were shot, had done a *CSI* down there.

I grabbed the backpack Panther had given me. I took the stun gun out, went to the bathroom, cleaned the prongs. Then I put it back in the backpack. Put the three bricks in the bag too. I picked up those books, *Manumit* and *Dawning*, put them inside a paper grocery bag.

Our eyes went back to the BREAKING NEWS.

They replayed old footage of them taking the bodies away.

Tried to hold it back, but a low moan came from my body.

Panther reached over, wiped a few tears from my face.

She pulled her hair back, put on some sweats. She had bought herself a few things yesterday. She walked me to the gate. The guesthouse had its own entrance.

I told her I'd be back before long. I wanted to check on my crib, see what I had to do to get it back right, run a few errands, go check on things that I didn't want her mixed up in.

She said, "Ask your brother if we can stay here until we get our cribs hooked up."

"If we get a Shop-Vac and some heavy-duty trash bags, I can have your place cleaned up by tomorrow afternoon. Can hit mine tomorrow evening."

"But, baby, dag. His shit is phat. I want to get a bikini and get in that heated pool. And that sauna. And the steam room. And the tub has jets. I mean, damn. You see that kitchen? He has Viking appliances. *Viking.* Man, if I could cook a Sunday dinner over here . . . dag. I feel bad because I don't even like that whack sitcom he's on, but this crib . . . phat as all get out."

I almost smiled. She sounded her age. That was good.

She motioned at the backpack, asked me, "Mind if I ask where you're going?"

"To finish this. And I have to make what wrong I can right."

I thought about it, gave her her keys back. Would chance it in my own car.

Sunset. I took a trip to Santa Monica. Parked in the mall like everybody else. Mixed with the crowd and headed down the hill to the pier. Walked by kids bundled up to get on the Ferris wheel and roller coaster. I made my way beyond all that to where the fishermen hung out, went to the railing. I dropped the backpack at my feet and looked out at the ocean.

When I didn't think anybody was looking I kicked that backpack. I had turned around and started walking back toward Santa Monica Place before I heard it splash. The incoming tide swallowed most of its sound, added it to the rest of the ocean's secrets.

The high-tech cellular phone I had, I broke that in half while I walked.

Down at my old job, a red dot faded from a computer screen.

32

Shutters was five minutes away.

I parked on the streets this time.

Freeman was leaving the hotel as I walked toward the round-about. Leaving with his head down, shoulders hunched, lines in his forehead, mouth fixed in anger. He looked up at me, that frown and unibrow cutting deep. Then he had that look of recognition. I could tell he didn't know where he knew me from. His desperate and depressed stroll took him around me.

No sedan. No Italian suit. Black man in Old Navy sweats. I was nobody special.

Saw the workers motion toward Freeman, all were talking in Spanish. If I understood the original language of *Wenot*, the original settlers in *Yang-ya*, I'd've known that they were talking about how his room had been broken into and his million-dollar book had been stolen, about how by the time the police had arrived something had happened and Freeman sent them all away without filing a report, said he had made a mistake. Whatever news had been on about Freeman's fiasco had been a blip, a blip that I had missed because I was too busy killing a man with my hands, too busy trying to stay alive.

When I thought I was about to die, I had prayed. That feeling was still with me.

Sade was at the bar, chocolate martini at her side. Her keen features, her makeup, her hair down, rolling over her shoulders. She looked real good. Beautiful woman. Nice brown pants over her long legs, sheer blouse. Could see the outline of her bra, the shape of her breasts.

I sat a barstool away from her. A copy of *The Voice: Britain's BEST Black Paper* was in front of her, her eyes tuned into an article about cops beating a race rap in a brutal beating case. She didn't notice me, not at first. Daniela wasn't on duty. Sade had no one to talk to.

She saw me and smiled like it was her birthday. After a day like today, with Freeman's million-dollar baby getting ripped off, I'd expected her to be swimming in her own tears.

She said, "Splendid. Was hoping I'd hear from you. I rang you once or twice."

"Saw Freeman walking out. Where's he going?"

"All the way back to Quitman, Mississippi, for all I care."

"Your man is here and you called me."

"Wanted to take you up on that offer, buy you a drink."

"I need one. That's one reason I came."

She was finishing up her chocolate martini and ordering another. She asked, "What are you having?"

I ordered the usual.

The televisions were on. Lisa's face was all over the news. Showed her with her father, years ago. Showed her and Wolf's wedding picture.

Sade said, "Tragic. She looked so young and beautiful. They said a lot of money was found on the beach. Something like forty thousand. The man she was with, heinous individual based on the news accounts. Her relative to boot. She mixed in something horrible, it seems."

I turned away from the TV. "Can I ask you a question? About you and Freeman."

"Let me guess. Hmmm. Why am I getting married to a self-absorbed, egomaniacal, greedy, publicity-seeking son-of-a-bitch?"

She chuckled.

I said, "You're slurring."

"I love vodka. It doesn't take anything away from you. It's not a tyrant. Never pompous."

"Sounds like you're celebrating while Freeman is mourning."

"Join me."

"Heard Freeman's room was broken into while we were at Howard Hughes."

"What of it?"

"Any idea who did it?"

"Marcus has so many enemies, there are so many people that would love to get their hands on that book to bring him down. It could fetch a pretty penny on the black market."

"How many drinks have you had?"

She shrugged. "Who knows?"

"Maybe you should slow down."

"Tonight I'm getting rat-faced. And that means I'm going to be vulnerable."

Her eyes met mine for a moment, testing me.

I said, "My brother has hypermnesia."

"What's that exactly?"

"His superpower. He remembers almost everything."

The books were at my side. I put *Dawning* on the counter.

She smiled.

I put *Manumit* on the counter, left them side by side.

She stopped smiling. A wave of soberness washed over her face.

She said, "Maybe we should go to my suite. We can talk in private."

"I'm not here to start any . . . flapdoodle."

"Money? You want money for this discovery?"

"Not money."

"Then what is your purpose?"

I pulled the books off the counter, put them in my lap.

Didn't really know why I was here. Maybe it was because I had dishonored most of the Decalogue and I needed some redemption, no matter how small. Part of me wanted to undo something I'd done to make myself feel better. Death was a done deal, couldn't undo that. This was all I had on my plate that could be fixed. Killing had left me in a state of alexithymia.

"What if I stole the briefcase?"

"Did you?"

"What if I had it taken from his room?"

"Then you'd be brilliant."

"I know you have separate rooms. I just don't know what this was all about. Maybe it's not about money. If you married him you'd have his money, at least access."

"God, no. I have my own money. Always have."

She paused, then gave me a charm-school smile.

I asked, "What was in that briefcase?"

"If you stole it, as you claim, then you would know."

"The computer."

"Bravo."

"What else? Was it just the book . . . or . . . what?"

She adjusted herself, leaned in closer. "Underneath that computer was my manumit."

"You lost me."

She held that I-have-a-secret smile, sipped her martini.

She said, "They don't have a clue that Marcus based his persona on Tom Cruise."

"His persona? What do you mean?"

"Marcus changed his lame image, became over-the-top after he saw the movie *Magnolia*. Started emulating the 'Seduce and Destroy' guy Tom Cruise played in the movie."

"Thought he was doing Sharpton."

"Tom Cruise."

I shrugged. "Never saw the movie."

"A terrified boy hiding inside of someone pretending to be a misogynistic, heartless leader. What a farce. Tom Cruise all the way. A very bad version of Tom Cruise at that."

"Obviously."

She shook her head over and over. "Now he believes the hype."

"A man doesn't get ahead in this world by holding his tongue and sitting on his hands."

"Same goes for a woman." She sipped. "Same goes for a woman."

She sipped her martini again, looked around the room. My eyes went to the television. Cameras were out in front of Wolf's home in Hancock Park. Would see that home in my dreams until I couldn't dream anymore. Saw Wolf's two little children in the crowd, but I didn't see Wolf. I saw Lisa's relatives in the mix. Everybody was so solemn. Los Angeles was waiting.

Sade asked me, "Are you familiar with T.S. Eliot? Or his wife, Vivienne Haigh-Wood?"

I rubbed my eyes, told her, "Not at all."

"I just remembered a poem about their relationship, read it a while ago. Theirs was a rocky marriage that ended up with him committing her to a mental institution."

"Lot of that going around."

"It is argued that she was his muse, even sometimes editor, and possibly the mastermind behind his genius. But she also had a mental imbalance that made her do neurotic things."

"Uh huh."

"He didn't give her any credit for anything. She recovered and wrote about how he abandoned her. About how lonely she became."

She paused, went into her thoughts.

I watched the television. Hoped my mug shot didn't flash up on the screen.

I said, "You love 'im. Freeman, you love 'im, right?"

"My blue eyes and dark skin, I'm the perfect reflection of the paradox of who he is. Supposedly so freaking Afrocentric and concerned about issues involving black Americans and the elevation of the mind, but really he's the ultimate study in narcissism."

I held my ground. Maybe I wanted to tell her how deadly this game was that she was playing. She didn't see it as a game, but she was playing chess, trying to checkmate him in the dark. Blood was on my hands because of a game. Blood that would never wash away.

She said, "I *love* writing. I *love* telling stories. *Love* making a difference. He's all about the dollar. All about being a celebrity. Wants to be Hollywood-bound so bad it kills me."

I kept holding that ground.

She shook her head. "He has all the fame. All the *asaewos* photograph him."

"What does *asaewos* mean?"

"*Bitches*. Rude, inconsiderate bitches." Her eyes went blank. "Marcus loves attention. I've lived with him for three years. I'm the soon-to-be wife of the man who sleeps with the bitches who love his books because it boosts his ego, does something for his low self-esteem."

I stared at my glass. "So, you're going to marry him."

She chuckled. "Bobbleheads. T-shirts. And this. And that. He's a bloody one-man marketing machine who is trying to make the world believe he serves a valuable purpose."

"You don't think so?"

"Hype. Straight Hollywood hype. So much sound and fury, signifying nothing."

"Then why you pick him?"

"Well, it ain't because he has a thirteen-inch dick, I can tell you that for sure."

I let her words go by without comment. Didn't want to stop her flow. Alcohol was both a truth serum and a tongue loosener. That vodka she was sipping made this a lot easier for me.

She said, "I used to see something in him. Saw what was lacking in me."

I nodded.

She went on, "He couldn't write a damn postcard, let alone a book."

She stood up, wobbled a little bit, eyes out of focus.

She gave me a nervous smile, asked, "Shall we move this to my suite?"

I shook my head. "You and Freeman have separate rooms. Same floor?"

"We have separate rooms on separate floors. And separate lives from here on out."

"No marriage?"

She shook her head. "He's not worthy."

I sipped my JD. Saw it clearer now. The dynamics. How Sade had stayed away from Freeman. At the airport. At the book signings. How she had her own room on a different floor. She kept herself in plain sight and away from the scene of the crime at the same time. If I hadn't been too busy looking for a lion and a jackal I might've noticed this from jump street.

She had been close to Freeman, all eyes and ears, the true inside man on this scam.

I said, "You knew they were gonna steal it here. In L.A."

"She didn't say exactly when, but I knew it was going to be here. She had four days."

"Who set this up?"

"Received an e-mail one day. It had one word in it."

"Manumit."

"Exactly. Then I met with a woman while we were in Dallas. She never said her name."

I described Arizona.

Sade nodded.

I said, "That was her. At the airport. We know that, so stop bull-shitting."

Sade smiled.

I said, "You set him up for the hit."

"You make it sound like an assassination."

"You're killing his career."

"I'm reclaiming mine. That's what she told me I should do."

"Who told you that?"

"My mother. She told me to do whatever I had to do to reclaim what was mine."

Sade gave in, came back and took the seat next to me, an expression of surrender painting her face. I waited. Let her take a few hits of her chocolate martini. The words were dancing around her lips, trying to come out and play. Each sip opened that door a little wider. She reached the bottom of her glass, got down to where the truth lived. Sade ran her hand over her hair, her motion so tipsy, and those words that were trying to get out were set free.

She said, "His book, the *truth is stronger* one, was released on September 10, 2001."

"The day before Nine-Eleven?"

"The next morning, while he was at the airport waiting to go on tour, the world changed, shut down. No way to fly anywhere. No way to get any television or radio coverage. Died on the vine. *Truth* was decent. For his level of writing, it was decent. That was because I edited it, brought it up the best I could. After the numerous changes I put in, the final piece was a mere simulacrum of the original manuscript. He resented me for that. Told me he did not need my help. But the manuscript he turned in after *Truth Be Told* was . . . was simply horrible. Publisher rejected it. Threatened to file a lawsuit to get their money back. Marcus was falling apart."

"Long story short, the pressure was on and he used your book."

"Yes. I went against what I believed in, signed that contract and created a monster."

Crossword puzzle words lined up in my mind. I said, "Plagiarism."

She shook her head and whispered, "T.S. Eliot and Vivienne Haigh-Wood."

I wasn't going to argue. I'd let her believe whatever she wanted to believe.

I sipped my drink, thought about how Freeman had blasted Jayson Blair. If I wasn't hurting, I would've laughed. That Mother Fucker had pulled a Milli Vanilli on the book world.

I said, "I guess, when you think about it, nobody ever really knows who writes a book."

She nodded. "All they see is the name on the cover."

I checked my watch, then rubbed my chest, put my fingers on the spots that had been harpooned. Those wounds would heal and leave me two scars. I'd add those to the rest.

Sade sipped her drink. A new chocolate martini had replaced the old one just that fast.

I asked, "Who gets the money from these books?"

"Oh, I get the lion's share. I'm not insane. It's my work. Eighty percent of the profits, extraordinary monetary compensation for my labor of love."

"Eighty percent. How does that work?"

"His attorney drew up a contract between us, then my attorney reviewed it, talked about the ramifications in detail before I allowed him to use my intellectual property. The contract reads like a gag order. I'm not supposed to tell anyone, not even my mother."

"And you're not supposed to wear that *Manumit* sweatshirt."

"That pissed him off good, didn't it?"

"Yeah. Three cheers for Alfalfa."

I sipped. She did the same.

I asked, "What else was in the briefcase? Was it just the book?"

"No."

"What?" I barked at her. "All this shit I've been through, hit me with some knowledge."

Now she was afraid of me. I saw that. The Italian suit was gone, so was that person. I pulled up the sleeves on my sweatshirt, pulled them up enough for her to see the warrior tattoos on my forearms. Her eyes went to those markings, then her attitude adjusted a little more.

"The contract I signed. He kept it chained to his wrist. Kept me chained to his wrist."

"A legal contract between you and him."

"Our literary marriage."

"That's what this was really all about."

"Getting that back was . . . was . . ."

"Your manumit."

"Yes. I got it back. It's been shredded. And those shreds have been burned."

She went deep into Quiet Land. So did I. We enjoyed that silent ride for a moment. I didn't allow my eyes to go back to that television screen. Wanted to tackle one sin at a time. Reverend Daddy said that all sins were equal. Didn't feel that way, not at all.

She told me, "I want you to seduce me."

"Why?"

"Because . . . I deserve to be seduced . . . because . . . I . . . I . . . I mean, why not? He does it with . . . with . . . them. They want him for no reason other than his photo is on a book. All over the country he does it with them. He has perpetrated a farce and they throw themselves at him."

"You don't know that."

She laughed a laugh that asked me not to insult her.

I asked, "How much did you pay to get this thing handled?"

"I didn't pay a single cent. Ha. Marcus paid. Two hundred thousand. Over one hundred British pounds. It cost him every dime he had taken in the name of my blood, sweat, and tears."

"How did they know how much to ask for?"

She smiled a telling smile, one that told me who gave Arizona the banking information.

I said, "So, you're bankrupting the man?"

She smiled. "He has to pay. He has to spend every fucking dime he's made on my labor of love. Every dime. He was on the phone transferring money as soon as they asked for it."

She laughed, ran her fingers through her hair in a beautiful, erotic motion.

I asked, "He paid already?"

"He wants that book. Doesn't want to lose his fame. Doesn't want that kind of scandal."

"So, it's over?"

"God, no. It's only beginning."

"What happens now?"

"I have twenty copies of *Manumit*. Twenty copies of *Dawning*. I mail them to twenty different places. First class. No return address. Marcus's bloody publishing company. His bloody editor, his publicist, they are all on that list. *New York Times, Publishers Weekly,* and *Essence. Washington Post.* Many others. All get a note from 'Ms. Avid Reader' who is 'outraged by this farce.' And the note lists the other places that have been notified."

"Then what? You destroy him? You become famous."

"That's not the goal. But maybe. Who knows? *Oprah. Regis and Kelly. Trisha.*"

"And you publish the book you're holding out . . . what?"

"Under my own name. As it should be." She took another sip of her drink. "My child will have my name, not that of some surrogate writer."

"You wrote all of his books?"

"You're repeating yourself."

"It's the Jack. Bad habit of his. Jack likes to be clear on things."

"No. Just the one that made him famous." She moved her hair from her eyes. "He wrote the horrible ones. The ones that have the large fonts on all the signs, the ones no one cares for."

"He'll figure this shit out. You know that, right? Soon as you publish the book."

"Marcus never saw the real book. I refused to let him see the work until it was complete. That way he couldn't e-mail it to his publisher or agent or whoever. So they couldn't claim my child as being his. He didn't get his hands on the computer until I made it here."

"If you're so unhappy, and it's not about the money, why don't you just leave? You could've sent those books out at any time."

"I did leave. Left a long time ago."

I wanted to ask a lot of questions, but my eyes went back to that BREAKING NEWS.

Sade closed her eyes and started singing, *"Bashero mi mo fe e."* Dots and accent marks of joy filling up the room. Her drunken happiness told me why she had stuck around. She wanted to be on the front row so she could watch Freeman fall like Saddam's statue.

She stood up, stumbled on the pretty stilts she was wearing.

"I'm drunk, Driver. It's getting late. I'd better go."

"Let me put you on the elevator."

Again she asked, "Join me tonight?"

"The elevator is as far as I'll go."

She shook her head, disappointed. "I can manage on my own."

"Sade—"

"One last thing."

"What?"

So much tension was in her forehead, in her blue eyes. "You know what writing does?"

"Have no idea."

"It says *I was here. I existed. I was important. I made a difference.*" Her eyes were wide, words seeping out on a long, woeful moan. "I don't exist. I'm not important. I'm not making a difference."

She took out her passkey.

I asked, "You gonna be okay?"

She answered with a pained smile. "Twelve-letter word. Commensalism. I'd attached myself to a shark and didn't know how to let go. I'm free. I'm free, Driver."

I watched her make her way to the elevator. She got on. Then she was gone.

My attention went back to the bar. The news conference started. I held my JD tight and asked the bartender to turn up the volume. I imagined everyone down at Back Biters was glued to the same thing, Pedro leaning over that bar, shaking his head.

A family representative was at the podium. He said that Wolf had received the horrific news while he was visiting his children in Las Vegas. Lisa had planned on going to Las Vegas with her husband, but changed her plans at the last minute citing a family emergency. The representative said that Mr. Wolf was devastated to get this tragic news, as could be expected, but with the love of his family and the community, he'd pull through this crisis. The entire family was shocked that something like that could happen to someone so wonderful, a woman whose family was a pillar of Compton's and Los Angeles's African-American community.

They closed in on Wolf, his heartbroken face taking up the entire

screen. I saw it in his face. He wasn't going to turn me in. I knew because when he stepped to the podium and thanked the community
for its love, in the end he told them, "There are no suspects."

No suspects. No spooks would be sitting outside my door.

My hands loosened around my glass. A boulder the size of Texas
rolled off my back.

Wolf's face vanished from the screen. And out of my life.

Friendship was over. That hurt me deep, hurt more than any of
the pain I already had.

I went to the pay phone and called Panther. She was watching the
news conference.

She asked, "Where are you?"

"On the way back."

"You can't keep doing me like this."

"I love you, Panther."

She paused. "Wow."

"Look, what kind of man do you need me to be? Think about
that."

"Driver, you're about to make me cry."

"Earl."

"What?"

"My first name is Earl."

"I know that."

"Call me Earl."

"You want me to call you by your first name?"

"Yeah. Fuck that Driver bullshit."

"So, you're gonna start calling me Cynthia?"

"Yeah."

"Yuck. Earl and Cynthia. God, we have some old, corny names."

"Don't bother me none."

"Where are you, *Earl*?"

"On the way back, *Cynthia*."

She laughed. "I called some people about cleaning up our
apartments."

"Cool."

"And I cooked. Rufus asked Pasquale and he said it was cool, let me use the kitchen."

"Where are they?"

"Outside by the pool. Think they're playing bones."

We hung up. I was anxious to get away from this place. The books I'd had, *Manumit* and *Dawning*, didn't have them anymore. Had left them at the bar. Didn't matter. Not to me.

I left Shutters the same way I had come in, unseen and unnoticed.

Ten white-and-gold boxes of See's Candies were neatly stacked on the passenger seat of my car. It was easy to get inside my car. I didn't have a rear window.

My sobriquet name was on the top box written on a plain white card.

Red letters.

Feminine handwriting.

Driver. I love chocolate.

Driver. Hoped I would never see that name again.

I opened the top box. Chocolates. Two layers. It was uneven. I pulled up the top layer. Money was underneath. Hundred-dollar bills. I dumped the chocolate. Looked like at least ten thousand dollars in hundred-dollar bills. I swallowed. Then my eyes went to the other gifts. I opened another one. It held the same distribution in dead presidents. My eyes went to the other eight. Had to be one hundred large. Fifty percent of what angering Sade had cost Freeman.

I looked around. Didn't see anybody. Didn't see her silver BMW.

She had just left my ride. The warmth in my seat and the scent of cloves told me that.

The traffic light in front of me danced from red to green to red to green.

Did that a few times, then it stopped. I waited. The stoplight show never started back up.

Arizona was gone to wherever people like her go at the dimming of the day. Imagined her speeding away, top down on her ultimate road machine, hair dancing in the breeze. Bet she had one of those cigarettes up to her mouth, taking smooth inhales, that cunning smile painting her face as she exhaled the scent of cloves to the wind.

She was a hustler.

I was a working man.

I nodded toward the darkness, toward that mystery, knowing I'd cross paths with her again.

Until then I could work on buying my own redemption.

I drove away hoping Cynthia liked chocolates.

ACKNOWLEDGMENTS

Sara Camilli, my wonderful agent, thanks. Here we are at book ten.

My new editor, Brian Tart, and his copilot, Julie Doughty, much love to you and all the peeps at Dutton/NAL. Thanks for being so wonderful and patient with me on this one. Thanks for the support in a major way.

To the people in publicity, Kathleen Schmidt, Lisa Johnson, Betsy DeJesu, thanks.

Omonigho Ufomata, thanks for allowing me to come into your world and ask you question after question. The parts of Folasade that are positive and correct I owe to you. If I made any errors, that was all on me. Hope I represented that fictional woman in a wonderful way.

Thanks to the peeps who read this and its many changes: Amy D. Mason, Dana Wimberly, Anthony Lyons, Jenai Chin, Emil Johnson, Lolita Files, Yvette Hayward, Olivia Ridgell, Sibylla Nash, and Tiffany Pace. Okay everybody, group hug. Mmmmmmmmmmm. Not so tight. Again. Mmmmmmmmmm. Better.

And Tish Tosh wanted to see her name in my book. She didn't do anything. she was just feeling left out, hating on everybody, wanted to see her sobriquet in print. Here ya go, Tish Tosh, o ye queen of the runners. Watch out, I might catch up with ya before you get to the top of Valley Ridge . . . soon as I find a cab. Now go buy my book. And read it. There will be a quiz.

ejd
05–06–04

Read on for a preview of
Eric Jerome Dickey's novel

GENEVIEVE

Available from New American Library

1

She rests on top of my body, naked, wrapped around my leg, her head on my chest. Her skin is still hot, set fire by too many orgasms to count. I've never been with a woman who came so hard, so often. My tongue tastes like her secrets. Her lavender aroma lives on my flesh. She stirs. My leg is sticky where her vagina rests on me. My come drains from her, adds to her wetness. I stroke her breasts, fingers pulling at her nipple, and she purrs. Her hand holds my penis with a never-ending longing, holds my flaccidity as if she wishes it were hers to keep.

My cellular vibrates, hums like her favorite carnal toy, dances on the dresser.

We both jump, startled away from our private world.

Her cellular glows and sings an urban beat, a hip-hop ring tone. Usher. My confession.

We don't reach out to answer, just hold each other's guilt and wait for peace to return.

We grip our silence as if speaking were the bigger sin.

We kiss. Touch. Her kisses are intense. I whisper, "We should leave."

"Little bit longer, baby?"

"They'll look for us."

She sucks my tongue, bites me with passion. "Please?"

Her tongue finds its way down my chest. Her mouth covers my penis.

Oh, God. Oh, God. Oh, God.

My fingers stroke her hair, hand encourages her rhythm. She looks up and smiles at me, rubs that rigid part of me against her face, glows as if it has healing powers. Her mouth covers me again. She hums. Sounds starved. Heat. Sweet, sweet heat. The wet sounds arouse me.

I moan, let my hand gather her hair into a fist, keep encouraging her motions, her head moving so smoothly. Every nerve comes alive. I writhe toward an undeserved heaven. My flaccidity hardens. I look down at her. She smiles, proud of the power she has over me inside of this moment. Kisses me and my insanity escalates. She pulls me to where she needs me.

Her legs open and I climb on her. The lips of her vagina whisper my name.

She takes me inside her and there is a shift in consciousness as we integrate in sin. She moves and I fall into her anxious rhythm, her undercurrents. Her words are soft, her moans are soft, and her skin is soft. They all create a spark. And that spark becomes a raging fire.

I put her ankles around my neck, hold her ass, pull her into me a thousand times. She looks down to witness our connection, then stares into my eyes. My measured strokes go deeper, create madness. She grabs my ass, shudders, tells me she wants me faster, deeper.

Her arms flay side to side. She yanks the sheets, finds a pillow to cover her mouth, give that softness her wild sounds. Her legs shake. I yank the pillow away so I can see her face. Have to watch her. Her eyes close tight. She tremors and grabs her breasts, squeezes them so tight. Her legs spread like wings. Under my every stroke she flies and cries like an eagle.

I turn her over, position myself between the bed and the wall, use that wall to give me power. She can't move. Can only take what I give. She's there. She's coming strong and often.

Oh, how she quakes.

Oh, how her expressions morph into a beautiful ugliness.

The room sounds like an exorcism in progress.

In between my grunts and moans, I call out to her, say rude and demanding things.

She whispers things to arouse me even more, growls, touches herself, then licks her own fingers, touches herself, then feeds me her juices, grabs my ass, tells me to fuck her, fuck her hard, whines and moans and squeals and tells me how hard I am, how strong I am, how good I'm fucking her, how deep I'm going, demands my steady thrusting to never stop, goes insane and tells me I can come anywhere I want to, that she will take it in any orifice or drink it like wine.

I turn her over, take her to the center of the bed, suck her breasts while she reaches for my hardness, rushes me back inside her, those hips of hers thrusting upward, taking me with her own measured strokes. I'm not moving, just holding my position, trying not to come, struggling not to go insane. We have breathless kisses, devour and bite each other, so gone, and I'm somewhere else, someone else.

Time stops.

My senses are focused on her.

I lose control of myself.

There is no fear. There is no guilt.

She loses her breath, tenses up, back arches, and she sings my name in three octaves.

She comes. She comes. She comes.

Then we rest. Sweat dripping from our flesh, we fall away from each other and we rest. Minutes pass before I can collect my breath and move. I can barely turn my head to look at her.

She moans. "I think I just had an out-of-body experience."

We look at each other's worn expression; then we laugh.

She asks, "Ready to go again?"

"You're insatiable."

"I've never been like this with anyone."

"Never?"

"Never."

She puts her face in my lap, hums, then sings part of a love song I don't recognize.

She whispers, her voice sounding disturbed, "God, what have you done to me?"

I don't answer. I could ask her the same, and my question would go unanswered as well.

"You make me tingle." Her voice remains a song. "Make me horny. Think of you and I get wet. You're very intense. The way a lover should be. I find you damn sexy and tender."

Her hand traces my flesh; then I feel her tongue on my skin, licking my sweat. She takes me in her mouth again, does that like she owns me. In her mind I am hers. She nurtures me. I arch, I jerk, get the jitters, but flaccidity remains. That doesn't discourage her, doesn't wane her madness. She is determined to raise the dead, determined for this not to end.

My phone vibrates again.

Her cellular sings again. Usher, still confessing.

She is not mine.

She is my wife's sister.

This is our affair.

2

How does an affair begin?

I think that mine, like most, started unintentionally. I'm not malicious; that is not in my nature—hurting someone I love, that is.

My wife. Genevieve.

She is thirty-two. Has been turning thirty-two over and over for the last five years.

Her name has been Genevieve since she turned twenty-one, the day she marched to court and rid herself of the name her mother had given her. In her eyes her birth name was too urban. Too Alabama. A reminder that her ancestors had been slaves and that her family still lived in chains, some physically, some metaphorically, some in the psychological sense.

She is not one of *them*. Not cut from the cloth of people who name their children after cars and perfumes and possessions they cannot afford, or have a home filled with bastard children, each of those bastard children named after drugs the parents were addicted to at the time. She is not one of the people who took a simple name and bastardized its simplistic spelling to the point that it looked ridiculous on paper and sounded ludicrous as it rolled off the tongue, then pretended the name was that of an unknown king or queen, its origin rooted in Mother Africa.

She is Genevieve.

Genevieve.

She loves her name because to her ear, when spoken correctly, Genevieve sounds intellectual. Not Gen. Not Vee. Not any other variation. She will only respond to her name in total, Genevieve. And she is particular about that. She frowns on the Americanized pronunciation, "JEH-neh-veev." She prefers the elegant-in-tone French version, "ZHAWN-vee-EHV." She will answer to both, but only the French version is accompanied with a smile.

She is a precise woman. She is not five-foot-one; she is five-foot-one-and-one-quarter. I suppose, to a woman, a quarter of an inch could be the difference between pleasure and a night of frustration.

She has come up from poverty and, once again I state, has declared herself an intellectual. Not one that has stumbled out of the womb and continues to stumble through life without meaning or purpose. Not one of the problem children Bill Cosby rants about. She has endless goals. My wife is a planner. A degreed woman who knows what she will be doing for the next twenty years. She has it mapped out, literally.

She says that when she was a teenager, she mapped her escape from a small town called Odenville, from her past, drew a road to her future.

She did that the day her father murdered her mother. Cut her throat. She told me that her mother was a woman who had many lovers. Her father was a man who grew tired of being ridiculed in his small town. A man who lost it, then called the police, and sat waiting for them to come take him away, tears in his eyes, his dead wife in his arms being rocked and sung to, his every word telling her how much he loved her, how she had made him do something bad.

No matter how I have tried, Genevieve refuses to let me into her past. That leaves me feeling shut out in that part of her life. She only gives me part of herself. Thus, my needs are beyond those of the loins. My need is to feel complete. To not have this glass wall between us.

Genevieve's desires are flowcharted, every move thought out like a chess player willing to sacrifice her queen in order to slay her opponent's king. Every move from Odenville to undergrad at Spellman to grad school at UCLA to PhD from Pepperdine University in Malibu, everything that she has accomplished or plans to accomplish is on light green poster-sized engineering grid paper, laminated and framed, hung at eye level on the west wall of her office, facing due east. Like a prayer. Her ambitions hang on the wall facing east for another reason as well. That way her map to total domination of the free world will be brought to life and highlighted with every sunrise.

The light of my life, the fire in my loins.

LaKeisha Shauna Smith no longer.

Now Genevieve Forbes.

When we married, she kept her last name, the one she had decided would be hers from the first time she picked up a magazine with that title, the new one that sang of richness and power and old money, the name she crowned herself with.

Genevieve.

Not Gen. Not Vee. Not "JEH-nee-veev."

Genevieve. "ZHAWN-vee-EHV."

Write her name in soft italics; cross the ocean and learn to speak it in its native language.

Let it roll off the tongue. Allow it to melt like warm butter.

Genevieve.

I love her because she is an intellectual. Brilliance is an aphrodisiac. I despise her for the same reason.

3

"Tell her Willie done passed."

"Willie? Who is he?"

"Willie Esther Savage, her grandmomma."

It starts with a phone call. The caller ID shows area code 256, one that I was not familiar with at the time. It was a call coming in from the Birmingham area, the Pittsburgh of the South. The voice on the other end sounded like that of an old man who took his Jim Beam over ice, his tone Southern and rooted in both poverty and ancestral slavery, a raspy-voiced smoker who had—based on the way he punctuated every other word with a cough—seen his better years: I'm not a doctor, but a deaf man could hear emphysema and bronchitis dancing around inside his frame. When I had answered he had asked for Shauna Smith, a name I was not used to hearing. I told him he had the wrong number. Before I could hang up, he changed and asked for Jennifer. Then tried again, asked for Jenny Vee. Struggled with that name, my guess being that was the closest he could get to the pronunciation of Genevieve. He did not know her as Genevieve.

Cough. "The name she was borned with was LaKeisha Shauna Smith."

He has my attention. "Yes."

"I think she calls herself Jenny Vee something-another now she done moved away."

I say, "I think you mean Genevieve, not Jenny Vee."

He pauses, then answers, "I reckon so."

My chest tightens as I lean back from my desk, away from the notes I'm looking over, notes regarding the breakdown of the infected enzymes in semen and drugs we've developed, and my eyes go to the clock. It's after eight, close to the time she usually gets in. Genevieve is off work, leaves at five on the dot, but today is Tuesday. Tuesday and Thursday are her Pilates days. Wednesday is an African dance class in Leimert Park; then from time to time she walks across the street and watches poetry at World Stage. She writes poetry but is not one to perform her work. Those are the evenings she gives herself time to do something in the name of self.

I lean forward and ask, "May I ask who is calling?"

Cough. "What was that?"

"Who is this? Who are you?"

Cough. Cough. "Grandpa Fred. Mister Fred Smith Junior. I'm her granddaddy on her daddy side. Need to get her the word her grandmomma on her momma side done passed early this morning. Willie Esther was gone before the cry of the crow."

"She . . . died?"

"Willie Esther lived to see eighty-three last fall."

My lips move in awkwardness. "Sorry to hear that."

"We calling all the family we can find right now." Another rattling cough. Sounded like his lungs were coming undone. "She passed early this morning. Held on as long as she could after that last stroke, but she done been called to glory. We calling everybody and we didn't want to not call LaKeisha Shauna Smith and let her know when the funeral gon' be."

I correct him. "Genevieve."

"Death don't give a rat's ass about nobody name. All Death care about is coming to collect his due, and Death always collect his due. We all gon' die. With open arms, or kicking and screaming, come time, we all meet Death, we all make that trip to the other side."

"Yes, we all will."

"Yessir, I look out my window and see Death's doing every day."

He speaks of death with ease, matter-of-factly, as if it were just a part of life.

I get up from my glass-top desk, roll my chair back so I can stretch my back. My hamstrings stick to the chair's leather. I have on a gray T-shirt and wrinkled shorts, what I wear most of the time I am at home. I look out the window and see our small backyard, which has a pool, bamboo trees that give us privacy, the gazebo that houses our Jacuzzi. Then I glance due east and see parts of downtown L.A. glittering miles away, its smog and lights in the distance. In that same glass I see my gangly reflection. Hair a little too long. As usual I need to shave.

I say, "May I have Genevieve call you?"

There is another pause. The kind that comes when a person's mind is spinning, questions rising. I imagine that old man, his back bent, skin leathery and wrinkled, a road map to days gone by, sitting in a worn and frayed chair, cane at his side, thick glasses on, his free hand dragging back and forth over the stubbles and rough texture in his pockmarked face, maybe shifting his stained false teeth side to side, contemplating me and my accent that rings of education and twenty-five years of living in California, my disrespectful urban way that doesn't add sir to the end of a sentence.

He asks, "Who this I'm talking to?"

"Her husband."

Cough. "What her last name now?"

"Forbes."

Cough. "You Mister Forbes?"

"No. Genevieve kept her last name."

"Woman who keeps her last name don't intend on keeping the man she marries."

That is his litmus test for a healthy marriage. Intentional or not, it stings.

"You talk real proper. Where you from?"

"Born in . . . I grew up in Fresno, California."

"You sound the way they talk on television out there."

I chuckle at his Southern drawl and say, "Okay."

"When she done married?"

"She done married . . . uh . . . she done married two years ago."

"You don't say." Cough. "What kinna work you do?"

"I'm a research analyst."

"You do what kinda searching?"

"No, research."

"What kinna work is that?"

"I'm a research analyst. I study and analyze cancers, neurodegen-erative diseases, and now I'm working on AIDS research training in the form of neurology."

When I finish rambling, he says one word: "Cancer?"

"I'll have her call you. Let me write down your number."

"She know the number. Same number we done had since nineteen-sixty."

Grandpa Fred falls into a coughing fit.

The phone goes dead on his end.

My heart worries for Genevieve's loss. I look at my wedding ring. Her loss is my loss. This phone call has left me the bearer of bad news, a task I do not want.

The phone screams in my ear, lets me know that it is time I hang up.

His call leaves me feeling prickly, the smell of both mystery and death in the air.

Genevieve has spoken of tragedies in her family, reluctantly. Of her murdered mother and incarcerated father. Only mentioned them once. Never gave any details.

I remember my mother. I remember her dying. Remember living with my grandparents. Remember feeling lost and alone. Remember not being able to attach to anyone for the fear of death separating us and leaving me emotionally stranded.

I remember losing unconditional love.

Now I search for the remedy to my inner pain, bask in pleasure to dull its sting.

* * *

Grandpa Fred's voice fades as I put my work to the side and look at the television. *The Lover*, the adaptation of Marguerite Duras's novel, is on Showtime. What I see makes me pause. She is beautiful and naked, in one of her erotic scenes with her North China Lover, on top of him, her face sweaty, in the throes of passion. She relishes him as he does her.

I envy them, the sensuality they have for each other, their love.

On the television, the lovers love on, endless pleasure and exploration. She is a teenager, still in boarding school, young and inexperienced. He is in his thirties, a playboy, a master lover. Both characters are nameless. Names, those labels do not matter in the end.

I try to get back to my work, but I cannot.

I smile in appreciation and continue to sigh in envy.

But in the end, the erotic moments are not why I watch.

It's what is said at the end.

That is what I wait for, the words I wait to hear at the dimming of their day.

I watch to see how she answers the phone, now her body aged and worn, and his voice is on the other end, listen to hear how he tells her that despite them parting ways, despite their separate marriages, despite the grandchildren, despite all the irreplaceable years that have gone by on the breath of time, he loves her still, loves her now as he did then, and will always love her.

That is when my face gets hot, when my throat tightens.

That is what I want. That is all I want. Love eternal.

They loved each other to a depth that they could not comprehend.

Yet their affair was doomed.

All love is doomed.